# Second Chance

## *A Romance Novel*

*Meg Tandy*

authorHOUSE®

*AuthorHouse™ LLC*
*1663 Liberty Drive*
*Bloomington, IN 47403*
*www.authorhouse.com*
*Phone: 1-800-839-8640*



*Published by AuthorHouse 03/03/2014*

*ISBN: 978-1-4918-4106-8 (sc)*
*ISBN: 978-1-4918-4105-1 (hc)*
*ISBN: 978-1-4918-4107-5 (e)*

*Library of Congress Control Number: 2013922191*

*This book is printed on acid-free paper.*

*TO NORMAN*

*Tho' lost to sight, to mem'ry dear*
*Thou ever wilt remain;*
*One only hope my heart can cheer,*
*The hope to meet again.*

*—George Linley*

# CHAPTER ONE

In a New York state of mind, Liz Brady sat relaxing in a rattan armchair, optimistic, unflappable and nurturing an adventurous spirit that promised relief from the same old, same old routine that she had escaped from in New York, as if it were possible for a fifty-year-old woman to ever escape the blahs of lonely widowhood. She browsed through a magazine and waited patiently for Jon Reese, the manager of the tennis center in Hamilton, Bermuda. She didn't mind waiting.

A door slammed and attracted her attention. A man stood at the entrance door of the clubhouse, sunglasses and a visor obscuring a full view of his face. Liz made a quick assessment of him. He wasn't tall, about five foot ten. A tight-fitting tennis shirt defined his lean torso, and muscular biceps swelled from his shirtsleeves. Very well put together and sexy, she thought. Then she remembered, she'd been there and done that, and now sex was an exclusively distinct memory of her husband and definitely not on her agenda.

He spied Liz and approached her. "Hi, you here for a ten o'clock match?"

"Uh . . . , I'm not sure. I left a message with Jon yesterday and booked a court for ten. He was supposed to call me back and confirm, but I haven't heard from him. Is it ten already?"

"Almost. Elizabeth Brady?" He asked.

"Yes, Liz Brady."

"You're our fourth. I spoke with Jon this morning. He gave me your name. We're on Court Three."

She rose from her chair and walked to the check-in desk. "It would be in the logbook," she said.

He followed her to the desk, stood beside her and invaded her personal space. She inhaled a pleasant aftershave citrus scent as he looked over her shoulder. Her finger moved across the ten a.m. entries. Her name was written on the log, but no name or court assignment was entered alongside it.

He tapped Liz on the shoulder.

"I've asked Jon not to use my name. Privacy issues."

"Oh?" She turned around and looked at him and wondered, why hadn't Jon scrawled something that indicated a match had been arranged for her?

"The name's Harry, Harry Bergman." He said as he removed his sunglasses and stuffed them in his shirt pocket. Liz stepped back. She recognized the name as well as his face when he removed the glasses. She clearly understood what privacy issues meant. He offered his hand.

Harry smiled. "Good to meet you." Liz felt a smoothness in his touch as he held her hand longer than she thought appropriate for a casual introduction.

"My pleasure," she said and looked away from him. Obviously, it wasn't a pleasure for her because she scowled when she shook his hand.

In the past, Jon had respected her wishes for anonymity. First names were exchanged; she played a game, said her thanks and goodbyes and resumed her personal agenda. Comfortable with the uncomplicated arrangements Jon made for her during her three-day visits to Hamilton, the present match-up was not to her liking.

The possibility of publicity cast a shadow on her otherwise sunny disposition. Employed as a freelance paralegal and bound by a confidentiality agreement, associating with a prominent politician could be construed as a conflict of interest at her job. To make matters worse, his moral character was in question because of his reputation as a womanizer.

She wanted to refuse gracefully and tried stalling with an inane question. "Doubles?" The question was a feeble attempt at delay. It must be doubles, she thought. He said I was the fourth.

Liz gazed at his midnight blue eyes. No wonder the gossip pages of the newspapers exploited his reputation. He exuded an unaffected sex appeal, in his walk, his voice and his smile. Undoubtedly, women were attracted to his good looks and demeanor. The handsome man standing before her was not at all the staid, formidable political figure he projected in television newscasts.

"Yes. My friends are on the court. I thought you might be waiting in here. Ready?"

She grimaced. "I guess so."

Just as Liz and Harry began to walk toward the courts, Jon entered the clubhouse and approached them. A tawny-skinned, slightly pot-bellied, teddy bear of a man in his sixties, Jon boasted a short trim beard and a full head of hair, both a colorless stone gray.

"Hello, Liz. Hi, Harry. I see you've met. I am sorry I wasn't here to properly introduce you. I had to attend to some emergency maintenance on the courts."

"No problem, Jon," Harry said.

Liz usually hugged Jon when they met, even though, being Bermudian, he didn't welcome displays of affection and maintained his reserve and formal manner. But at the moment she didn't want to hug him anyway, and she intended to rebuke him privately.

"Shall we?" Harry asked.

"Uh, huh. Excuse me for a minute."

"See you there. Court Three." Harry headed for the courts.

Jon faced her and met her eyes. "You're looking fit little lady, as usual. Sorry, I tried to confirm this morning, but I think the phones on board weren't operating."

"Jon, I'm very sorry, but this isn't going to work. I can't play with him."

"Why? What's wrong?"

"You've got to get someone else."

"What's the problem, Liz?"

"It's too risky."

"Risky?"

"Yes, risky. I can see the newspaper blurb now:

> *District Attorney's paralegal plays tennis with bachelor Mayor while vacationing in Bermuda.*

"I can't subject myself to that kind of unfavorable publicity. It would jeopardize my job."

# CHAPTER TWO

Jon stood motionless.

"Liz, what are you talking about? Please, Liz, let's discuss this. You know I can't get anybody at such short notice. Maybe we can sort it out."

Liz was intent on leaving the center. She gathered her tennis bag and fumbled in her jacket pockets for the key to her moped.

"I don't see how, Jon. Not only would my job be at risk, but my reputation. The man is a notorious philanderer. He's always in the New York gossip columns, photographed at a fundraiser or some such event with a socialite on his arm, not that I would qualify as one of his bimbos."

Jon extended his arms, animated in a begging gesture. "Liz, you're eight hundred miles from New York. No one in Bermuda cares who you play tennis with. Besides, when he's here, he's always with family—his daughters. Very conservative and reserved. Actually, we know him as a pillar of the community, very generous with donations and business advice."

"Please forgive me. I can't. Maybe I am overreacting, but I can't."

"Please, Liz. I know you prefer not to play with the rich and famous, but if you could indulge me this one time, I'd be grateful. I mean, it's not as if there's anyone on the courts spying on you."

Jon's argument made sense to her. She was being unreasonable, maybe paranoid. "I guess I do forget, this *is* Bermuda. The paparazzi aren't lurking around every corner as they are in New York."

"He's very supportive of the tennis center, and I feel obligated to accommodate him when he requests a game. You could save me a lot of embarrassment."

Liz relented and sighed in defeat. "Okay, okay. You win. I'll take a chance. But only because I owe you. You've been so very good about arranging matches for me, at least up until now."

Jon exhaled in relief. "Thanks, Liz. I really appreciate it. Oh, I almost forgot. You're playing with a local resident. He insists he's not a mayor when he's vacationing here."

"He's already told me, about not wanting to use his name. How ironic that we both have privacy issues. I'll give it a try." She lifted her hand in a half wave and scurried to the courts.

"Hi," she called out as she entered Court Three. The players stopped their warm-up play and approached the center of the court.

A hunk-type handsome man extended his hand to Liz. "Hi, I'm Andy." Liz guessed he was in his early fifties. A plumage of black, gray-streaked hair crowned his head. His large brown eyes were intense. He was tall, his physique firm and muscular. He had all the attributes of a commercial spokesperson for fitness equipment.

"This is my wife Cody." Andy smiled.

"Hello. How are you on this fine Bermuda day?"

Cody was a conspicuously beautiful woman. Her lean and curvaceous body moved in the quiet rhythm of a Vogue model.

"Good, thank you. I'm Liz. Pleasure to meet you." They shook hands. Liz was impressed. She thought Andy and Cody were quite the beautiful couple, indelibly linked like a President and the First Lady.

"Hi! Do you have a preference? Forehand?" Harry asked.

"Yes, if that's okay with you? If I have a weapon, it's my forehand."

"Well, we'll need some weapons against these two."

After the first game, the players paused to change courts. Harry wiped his face and forehead with a towel. Liz glanced at the tennis shorts that clung to his body and accentuated his muscular thighs. The current length of tennis shorts worn by the pros fell to the tops of their knees. Apparently, wearing a much-abbreviated version of the professional style, Harry preferred to show off his sturdy legs.

Harry asked between a gulp of water, "Where are you staying?'

"Cruise ship."

"Come here often?"

Harry uttered the cliché as if he were chatting up a woman at a singles bar. Was it an impulsive remark or his idea of a joke? Maybe she was too negatively biased and couldn't consider the remark to be innocent as it might have been. And then again, maybe chatting up a woman came naturally to him as part of small talk, the propositional jargon reserved for later in privacy.

"As often as I can." Liz smiled. "I'm always looking for a partner when I'm in Bermuda."

"Good. So am I. I mean—looking for a partner."

The innuendo rattled Liz's sense of propriety. She blurted out the wrong words loaded with the wrong meaning and perhaps gave Harry the impression she was available for something other than tennis, not that she thought for a moment that he would hit on her. She wasn't his type of woman. She ignored his response, pretended naiveté and gave him the benefit of doubt.

"Shall I serve first?" She asked.

"Sure." Harry tossed two balls to her in the deuce court. Liz served an ace to Cody and won the first point. She served the next point wide to Andy's forehand, which was completely out of his reach. Andy just stood there, motionless and muttered, "Show off."

After Liz served Cody yet another ace, Harry smiled and reached to smack the palm of her hand in a high-five. "Good job." He said.

Liz volleyed Andy's return of serve for a winner, and they won their first game. Harry hadn't hit a ball. They walked side by side as they changed courts.

"Wow, great game. Looks as if you don't need me. Are you going to let me play, too?"

"That depends on how well you play."

"Oh? I have a very decent game. On and off the court."

Liz glared at him, "I'll pass on the off-court game. No offense."

"None taken."

She caught several quick glances of him eyeing her body, and when their eyes met, he looked away. She didn't object to his scrutiny. After all, she had been observing him, as well.

Liz was in position in the deuce court, ready to receive Andy's serve. From her periphery vision, she spied a man on the adjacent court, her attention focused on the wide lens protruding from a camera which appeared to be targeted on her. Impulsively, she leapt over the barrier to the adjacent court and struck the man on his arm with her racquet.

"What do you think you're doing?" She yelled at him and grabbed at his arm that held the camera. "You can't take pictures of us."

"Hey, lady, stop it. Get off me." He cried out.

Harry jumped over the barrier and interrupted the fracas that was taking place between Liz and the photographer.

"What's going on here?" Harry yelled.

Liz released the photographer's arm and the camera fell to the ground.

"What the hell's wrong with you?" The photographer addressed Liz.

Harry positioned himself between the photographer and Liz. "Enough! Just calm down."

At first, Liz ignored Harry, adrenaline still careening through her veins. Then, she looked at him.

"You just shut up. You may not object to your picture in *Star Magazine*, but I do."

She picked up the camera from the ground.

"Excuse me?" Harry said.

Harry was baffled as to what her comment meant. He stood there stunned and speechless.

"Lady," the photographer piped in, I'm not taking your picture." He reached over and grabbed the camera out of Liz's hand.

"Really, tell me another lie I won't believe."

"Look." The photographer positioned the camera in front of Liz's eyes and clicked on photo after photo. After about fifteen photos passed through the viewer, he said, "I'm taking pictures of the facilities. I'm from the Chamber of Commerce. We're producing a tourist brochure for visitors."

"Oh." Liz cowered. She blushed in embarrassment. Her eyes veered toward Harry. Somewhat amused by the whole scene, Harry laughed quietly.

"Are you satisfied?" The photographer asked.

Liz turned to the photographer who was inspecting his camera for damage.

"I'm so very sorry. I hope I haven't broken anything."

"Lucky for you lady, no harm done," he said as he packed the camera in its case. "If you ask me, I think you need some anger management counseling." He sneered and walked off the court.

# CHAPTER THREE

"All's well that ends well." Harry said.

"I'm very sorry. I made a terrible mistake." Liz shook her head and focused on the ground, not wanting to meet Harry's eyes.

"No problem. A simple misunderstanding."

Harry leaned forward, searching for eye contact. "Hey, it's over. Forget it. Let's just get on with our game."

Andy and Cody stood at the barrier between the courts, waiting to resume the match. "Everything all right?" Andy asked.

Liz sighed, her shoulders slouched. She still had her racquet in her hand, drooping at her side and no longer a weapon.

"We're good," Harry cried out.

Harry put his arm around her shoulder in attempt to offer solace to what he surmised was an embarrassed and glum Liz. He tilted his head and looked up at Liz. "You okay?"

"Not really," she said. "I owe you an apology. I've totally ruined our game."

"You heard him, *no harm done*. Hey, come on, cheer up. We'll hit the ball around and in no time, you'll be as good as new."

The assault incident quickly fell by the wayside and the tennis game resumed. Liz and Harry played like seasoned partners who read each other's game and anticipated each other's position on the court. An easygoing cooperation had developed between them, and although Andy and Cody were diehard club players, Liz and Harry won the match handily.

Despite his reputation and her prejudgments, Liz enjoyed the game and looked forward to perhaps playing with him again; however, she thought that probably wouldn't happen because she knew Jon wouldn't choose her for another match with him after she made such a fuss about the present arrangement.

Harry casually patted Liz on the ass as they approached the net for the after-tennis handshakes. "Good job. You go girl." Although somewhat taken aback by the gesture, Liz smiled. "Thanks for the game. It was lots of fun. And thank you for being so understanding."

"My pleasure. We're going back to the house for lunch. Would you like to join us? Maybe we can arrange a game for tomorrow?"

Liz didn't respond immediately and hesitated. Once again, the publicity issue loomed before her. She had a question that preyed on her mind ever since she met him. "Does the press follow you to Bermuda?" She asked.

Harry leaned forward and placed his racquet in its cover. He looked up at her with a puzzled look on his face.

"Oh, that's what you meant with that remark about *Star Magazine*. No, not that I know of. Do you know something I don't know?"

"Well, it's nothing personal, but some of my clients would not appreciate a picture of me and the Mayor on page six of the *Post*. Or for that matter, plastered on the cover of some tabloid."

"Oh!" Harry tilted his head back, looked directly at her and snickered.

"Not likely. Don't think the *Post* is interested in who I play tennis with. Doubtful they'd travel to Bermuda for that story."

"Well, I guess—it would be okay. Yes, thank you. Lunch would be nice."

"Great. I promise, no pictures. We're very private when we're on vacation."

Liz smiled.

Cody and Andy loitered nearby and assembled their tennis gear. Aware of publicity problems, Andy grinned in reaction to Harry's remarks.

"The car's over here." Harry said.

A man stood beside the open car door like a massive bronze statue from a town square. Six feet four inches, he towered over everyone. "Liz, meet Thomas." Thomas nodded and said in a typically, friendly Bermudian accent, "Hello, good to meet you Miss." His voluminous basso voice matched his stature.

Harry motioned for Liz to enter the car. She slid across the seat and admired the soft, burgundy leather upholstery. Glasses, liquor, and all the amenities of a bar were entrenched on the side doors; trays folded in the front seats. The interior of the vehicle reeked of luxury and obviously had been customized to limousine status.

It had been quite some time since she had ridden in a car of such substance.

Cody slipped gracefully across the seat and sat next to Liz. Andy collapsed beside Cody, and Harry sat in the front seat and chatted with Thomas. Momentarily, Harry turned around and addressed Andy and Cody, "Martine is at the house."

Cody leaned over, touched Liz on the arm and explained to Liz, "Martine's a master chef and owner of Chez Mere, a five-star restaurant in Hamilton. When Harry stays in Bermuda, Martine sometimes cooks for him. We're in for a treat."

"How nice," Liz muttered and mulled over the present circumstances. Wonderful, I'm about to be wined and dined in five-star style, and I feel like a shabby, wet dishrag. My face is red hot, and I'm still sweating profusely.

Well, we're all in the same condition, she consoled herself. I do have a spare shirt in my tennis bag, and maybe I can make a quick change. I won't feel comfortable eating lunch while I'm still dripping from every corner of my body. But there's no need to be concerned, she thought, about what you look like. The invitation is just a casual, appreciative thank-you gesture for coming out to form a doubles match. Nothing more, she assured herself.

But she did feel concerned and uncomfortable, not only about her appearance, but the undercurrent thoughts flowing in her mind. What was she doing, having lunch with a billionaire mayor and his friends at his home in Bermuda?

# CHAPTER FOUR

Socializing with the wealthy was not in Liz's realm of comfort, even though she had been exposed to the fast-lane lifestyle of her husband and his investment banking career, it had never been her *joie de vivre*.

Liz had loathed her husband's business associates, none of whom she considered to be his friends. She judged his so-called friends to be shallow and ego mongers. Infidelity was a matter of fact and loyalty non-existent, to say nothing of their lack of integrity. The abundance of money—the six-figure salaries they earned—didn't accrue as a permanent asset to a portfolio, but were here today and gone tomorrow and only a means for flagrant self-indulgence.

Fortunately for Liz, socializing with her husband's pals was limited to business functions. He was the love of her life so she compromised and fitted in for his sake, but she was very glad to be relieved of the lifestyle of instant gratification when she became widowed.

Harry turned around and asked, "So, Liz, Jon seems to know you. Been to Bermuda before?"

"Oh, yes, many times. I take a cruise every year, usually in October. I like to get away from the stress of Manhattan. Jon has arranged matches for me for a couple of years."

"You live in Manhattan?"

"Uh, huh. All my life. I have an apartment in Murray Hill. I am the exception to the rule though—a native New Yorker. Everybody in New York seems to come from someplace else."

"Me, too." Harry said. "A native New Yorker. Andy, also. We were both raised in Brooklyn. However, the lovely, enchanting Cody was born and bred in the affluent suburbs of New York, before we knew there were such places as suburbs."

Cody chimed in, "Harry, are you going to throw my family history at me again as if I'm some sort of outsider?"

Harry met Cody's eyes. "Outsider? We're the outsiders. You're the one who's invited to the social events of the season. What would we do without you? You're the real thing, as they say, *authentic.* Compared to you, Andy and I are mere fodder from the league of money-making, self-made men."

He winked at Cody. "Even if you are a bona fide WASP, I love you anyway. You're so classy. What's not to love?" He turned around.

Andy grinned and laughed quietly. "Liz, don't listen to their nonsense. They've been squabbling in class-conscious warfare for twenty years. It's meaningless."

Liz recognized that Harry and Andy didn't belong to the Wall Street ilk of investment bankers. They were from the school of truly wealthy, self-made men—billionaires, playing tennis on public courts. Why weren't they playing at any one of the numerous country clubs in Bermuda? Why didn't Harry's behavior validate her perception of womanizers—the guys who blatantly ogled, bandied sexist remarks and suffered from male braggadocio?

Harry turned halfway around in his seat again. "How long are you staying?"

"'Til Saturday. Ship leaves at noon. You?"

"I go back Sunday. I'm ecstatic I'm able to squeeze out a whole week. I love it here. Get to lay back and think my own thoughts for a change." Harry turned and resumed his view through the front windshield.

"Okay, the big question," Andy said. "Knowing how demanding the job is, are you going to run for another term? You know, make it a habit to think your own thoughts, permanently. Get a life."

"You know me. If I think I'm needed, I'll run again. I love the job. Apart from the fact that those guys downtown can't balance their checkbooks, much less a budget, what else is there, besides parting with my money, to give back what's been given to me?"

"Yeah, but maybe it's time to take a break, get a little selfish."

"I am selfish. I'm doing what I want. It's very satisfying, contributing something more than money."

Harry turned around again and looked at Liz.

"You didn't hear that part about running again, right? Not for public consumption, if you know what I mean."

"Running for another term? Another privacy issue?" she asked.

"Uh, huh."

"My lips are sealed."

She found Harry's eyes engaging. When he smiled, a glint of mirth in his eyes reflected a Peck's bad boy and a devil-may-care attitude, keen on adventure and spontaneity. That was part of his sex appeal—that bit of mystery that confirmed in her mind that there was more to him than meets the eye. She told herself she wasn't attracted to him, but merely being sociable.

Liz knew she certainly wasn't the glamorous socialite Harry was often photographed with, and aside from the fact that she had no interest in seeking male companionship, she felt comfortable in his presence—rather safe—and an unlikely candidate for seduction.

She enjoyed the reassurance of her own little world that she had constructed since widowhood. Everything was under control, prescribed and predictable: her job, her family, her friends and her health. There was no room in her world for spontaneity. She had survived nursing a terminally ill husband, his death and the consequent depression that followed. The tragic experiences were behind her, and she was secure and happy with the insulated life she crafted for herself.

But she did crave something more, not like a skydiving adventure, but something to add a zing to the same old, same old. Maybe she needed to take a few baby steps outside the box. Wasn't that why, although the weather was ninety degrees and the tourists were still rampant, she convinced herself to take her yearly cruise in August instead of October? It was time for a few changes. Wasn't that what vacations were for? Not just the simple relief from the daily humdrum or stress, but an opportunity to experience something new and different or possibly recreate a part of oneself.

# CHAPTER FIVE

The car pulled up before a huge, glossy black wrought iron gate mounted on two granite columns. Thomas punched in the security code on an apparatus attached to one of the columns and drove up the small, circular driveway to the front of the house. Meticulously landscaped shrubs and flowers adorned the grounds; the blue stucco house towered above the adjacent pastel-colored homes and blended in with the picture-postcard Bermuda sky.

Thomas opened the car doors and led the entourage to a gate and a path that swerved to the rear of the house. Several steps ran to a large patio and ended at the entrance of glass enclosed paneled doors that unfolded like an accordion unto an interior bar and lounge.

"Make yourself at home." Harry said to Liz. He picked up the remote to the sound system and asked, "What's your pleasure, guys—adagios, easy listening, 70's hits?"

"Something mellow and soothing." Cody said.

Two large mauve armchairs adjoined with mahogany tables were situated opposite a modern gray leather sofa. An elongated coffee table, easily accessible from the seating arrangements, was centered in the area. An elaborate sound system was installed on the wall, each compartment holding an electronic device. Beneath the system, a wide screen television was installed on a swivel base that probably created a view from every angle of the lounge.

Harry called out from across the room, "Thomas, we could use some drinks."

Liz was mesmerized. What a splendid living arrangement, formal yet warm and cozy. It spoke of luxury and leisure—a place to read the Sunday newspaper, or drink a beer with a pal, a place to relax. Although the room was decorated like a well-appointed resort hotel lobby, it had a casual air and apparently was the living room of the house, functionally assembled and suitable for a feature in *House Beautiful*.

Thomas propped up pillows, adjusted the thermostat and closed shutters that deflected the glare of the sun. Opposed to his formidable physical presence, Thomas blithely sashayed from one task to another like a talented actor on stage, not entertaining, but performing all the acts of seeing to everyone's comfort. Liz had the initial impression that Thomas was the chauffeur, but realized, in fact, that he wore many hats: bartender, caretaker and security guard, whatever was needed. Now he served drinks.

Thomas stood behind the bar. "What would you like to drink, ladies?"

Cody responded, "A pina colada, please."

"The same for me," Liz said.

"I'll have my usual, Thomas."

Andy snagged a beer from the refrigerator behind the bar and simultaneously engaged Thomas in a conversation about last week's local cricket match.

Thomas mixed a martini and announced from behind the bar, "Martine expects lunch will be ready in half an hour."

Harry took Liz by the arm and guided her to the patio. "There are bathing suits in the cabana next to the pool if you'd like a swim before lunch. You've got to see the view from the terrace. It's magnificent, if I say so myself."

"Oh, it is. Very beautiful."

Liz pulled nervously at her tennis shirt. "I would really like to change into something dry. Is there a bathroom I could use?"

Harry offered his hand and led her inside the house and down a corridor to the back of the bar.

"This one's closest. There's no lock on the door, but it's perfectly private." He pointed to a device, like the apparatus on airplanes that read *occupied* once the door was closed. "The door stopper at the back keeps the door open to control the *unoccupied* track when no one is in there."

"Wouldn't a lock be easier?" Liz still felt concerned about publicity and joked to ease her frame of mind. "Any cameras?"

Harry leaned in front of her to demonstrate the door's use. Liz became aware of being very near him as she inhaled his familiar scent of citrus cologne and goose bumps formed on her arms. She didn't know if the shiver she felt was from her wet tennis shirt or her eye contact with his blue eyes. Blood rushed to her cheeks and her face reddened.

Harry laughed, "You do have a problem with pictures. No, no cameras. Maddy, my housekeeper, not once but three times, locked herself in there. The last time it was two hours before Thomas found her asleep in the armchair. Even though she had only suffered a nap, I needed a way to keep the door from locking. It may be complicated, but it solved the problem."

"Oh, I see," Liz said. Harry moved to the side and she entered the bathroom. "Thanks." She exhaled a nervous deep breath and felt her cheeks flaring again in a telltale blush. I'm too old for this, she thought. Maybe it's the hot flashes of menopause.

When Liz returned to the lounge, she noticed everyone had also made a quick change to dry clothing. Cody wore a fashionable bathing suit and a see-through cover-up. She stretched out in an armchair, and Thomas placed a pina colada on the table next to her. The men settled in the nearby sofa. Liz sat in an armchair opposite the sofa. Thomas handed her a drink.

She smiled. "Thank you."

Andy spoke first and directed a question to Liz. "Do you play tennis in Manhattan? We're members at Wykagil, in Westchester. It's a short drive from our apartment."

"Oh, I've played there. I dated a member of that club many years ago. Har-tru courts, if I remember. The club sponsored a few Nancy Lopez golf tournaments. And there was this couple—the Malleys—who invited us every year to their notorious Super Bowl party. Supposedly, a great golf course. I don't play golf. My friend was a scratch golfer."

"I know the Malleys," Cody said. "A very successful real estate broker. Couldn't forget his wife. Every year she donated the same makeover at Elizabeth Arden to the annual Boys' and Girls' Club raffle. But we were never invited to their parties. We don't socialize at the club."

Cody appeared to have all the trimmings of being raised in a wealthy family: personality, poise and confidence, minus the aloofness and arrogance that sometimes accompanied the privileged class.

"I've been a member at Manhattan Plaza for over twenty years," Liz said. "They arrange matches for singles and doubles, whichever you prefer. If you'd like to play there sometime, I can arrange a court."

Liz offered the invitation, and then, in the same breath, hoped she hadn't begged an invitation to their club.

"It's very convenient if you live in Manhattan and if you want a last-minute game."

Liz was curious why they played at the public courts in Bermuda. "I should have thought you'd have a local club membership in Bermuda. For golf as well."

"We both do." Harry said. "Sometimes the private club is more public. There always seems to be a hotshot player or coach in the background, searching for a sponsor instead of a game. It can be intrusive. We manage the golf match-ups all right, but the tennis arrangements have not fared well. Jon, on the other hand, is the epitome of discretion."

The privacy issue open, Andy asked jokingly, "Are you a descendant of that tribe in New Guinea, who lose their souls if their pictures are taken? Or maybe there's a price on your head? What's the problem about a picture with Harry?"

Liz laughed and then explained. No, no, nothing like that. I work as an independent contractor for attorneys who are involved with—let's say—sensitive legal documents that aren't for public consumption: a divorce settlement, a paternity suit, whatever. The paperwork isn't produced in the normal channels because of publicity risks.

"The basis of my employment is maintaining the utmost confidentiality. I've actually signed a legal agreement in some instances. One of my clients in particular would not appreciate even the slightest connection to the Mayor's Office, even if it were only social. It might be judged as a conflict of interest. So, I'm obligated to avoid any publicity. I know it's a stretch of the imagination, but the public does have a vivid imagination. And I probably overreacted about pictures."

"I see," Andy said.

"Well, it's quite normal to avoid the press under those circumstances." Harry agreed. "A legal agreement definitely puts you at risk."

# CHAPTER SIX

Martine entered the lounge quietly, nodded to Andy and Cody and beckoned the group to the dining area in an unidentifiable accent. "Please be seated, and we'll begin."

"Liz, this is Martine," Harry said as he pulled a chair away from the table and motioned for Liz to sit. She nodded at Martine, "Hello. Good to meet you."

"My pleasure, Miss."

Martine was casually dressed in native Bermuda shorts and a designer floral shirt, but Liz thought he should be dressed in a tuxedo to complement the aura of his suave demeanor. He was a handsome man of about thirty-five, his skin smooth and tanned and his body slight and fragile. Except for the miniscule crow's feet at the sides of his slanting Asian-looking eyes, he hadn't a wrinkle on his face.

The conversation languished while everyone ate. Martine had not only prepared a delicious meal of grilled shrimp appetizers, a mixed green salad, and a main course of yellowfin tuna with sautéed spinach, but served the food with the proprietary *savoir faire* of a master waiter, imparting an impressive dining experience.

When everyone finished eating, Martine approached the table. "I must take my leave now. It's been a pleasure."

"Thanks, Martine. Superb, as anticipated. Join us for coffee?" Harry asked.

"I would very much like to indulge myself with some coffee and conversation. I am a very social fellow, but, as you well know, I have a restaurant to manage, so I must say my goodbyes." Martine exuded five-star quality; he not only sounded formal, he was formal and added an elegance to a memorable lunch.

Harry stood up and said, "Goodbye, Martine. Can't thank you enough." He and Martine hugged each other in a brotherly embrace.

"Good afternoon, and a good day to you all." Martine waved to everyone and left.

Thomas cleared the table and returned to the bar to brew coffee; everyone strolled back into the lounge.

"So, Liz," Andy said, "you're an anomaly, a native New Yorker. How come I don't hear a New York accent? You sound Midwestern, like Michigan or Ohio."

Liz had heard the remark, *You don't sound like New York* so many times, she was used to explaining. "My mother was from the South, my father an immigrant, from Sweden. Both my parents had heavy accents. Worse, I grew up in a neighborhood where de's and dem's were the norm. I think was about twelve when I decided I didn't want to sound like that, so I practiced my speech, differentiating the "p's" from the "b's", the "t's" from the "d's." I was an honor student and wanted to fit in and speak like my classmates.

"Bye the bye, Andy, you don't sound like Brooklyn." She said.

"I'm the product of a Catholic School education—and later, the Jesuits. Harry's Ivy League and also the son of an English teacher."

Thomas served coffee.

"I take it your husband doesn't play." Andy probed as to Liz's marital status.

"I'm a widow. It's been three years."

"Oh, sorry. Tough to lose a spouse. Still hurting?"

"No. I'm done with the grief, although it took longer than the year the doctor estimated. It never goes away completely."

"Harry's been there, lost his wife."

"It was much tougher on my girls than me." Harry said.

It had been over seven years since his wife died and subsequently his two teenage daughters, Rebecca and Sarah, seventeen and fifteen, lived with their grandmother, Nana Molly and her brother, Uncle Ted. Liz already knew he had two daughters, having seen the Mayor with them at the U.S. Open Tennis Tournament when the television cameras were scanning the crowd for celebrities.

"I see my daughters at least once a week for lunch or dinner, and then for the family dinner at my mother's on Sunday. I speak with them almost every day, but the job has definitely curtailed sharing activities with their dad."

Liz was surprised Harry volunteered his personal life so openly. Somehow, that part of his life had not been reported in the newspapers. Evidently, family life was off limits to the press.

"They're growing up too fast, growing away too fast. They're teenagers. They have their own lives, which doesn't include taking vacations with Dad anymore. We used to come to Bermuda for a weekend every other month. Now, it's been a year, a year and a half, since they've been here."

Harry leaned back and crossed his ankles. His eyes wandered around the room as he talked about his daughters. "I've been replaced with school, friends, concerts, whatever. They're perfectly happy and I'm stressed every time we have a conversation. Though, I've got to admit Andy and Cody have been a great help to me the last few years, reading between the lines of what teenagers say or mean as opposed to how they act."

Cody interjected, "You're really very lucky, Harry. They tell you everything. They even confide what you don't want to hear."

"Yeah, I really didn't need to hear about Rebecca's run in with that boy at that concert." Harry described a recent incident already known to Andy and Cody. Rebecca had confided to her father a boy at a concert had tried to grope her. "She hauled her handbag at him and yelled at him to *Piss off you pig. No problem, Dad, he took off like a thief.* Rebecca thought it was all very funny, and she was so proud to tell me how she flogged the guy, as she called it. I'm probably overprotective."

"Do you have any children, Liz?"

"No. I have a nephew though, who's been pretty much my son since we lost his parents."

A short time in his company totally altered her opinion of Harry. The personal Harry was revealed to Liz, not a tycoon, not a philanderer, not a mayor, but an indulgent, loving father. Occasionally, she felt his eyes on her and when their eyes met, he looked away. She wasn't sure if she was attracted to him or feeling compassion for the fatherliness he expressed. Maybe the pina colada and wine also influenced her judgment.

Liz glanced at her watch. She remembered she had a four o'clock hair dressing appointment, and it was already three-fifteen. She finished her coffee and stood up.

"Please excuse me, I have an appointment at four and I must leave. Thank you for having me. It was a wonderful lunch. A really great afternoon."

"I'm so glad we met." Cody said. "It was simply so delightful to be in the company of a woman who plays better tennis than Harry and isn't constantly drooling all over him. I hope we see you again."

"Thank you. It was a pleasure meeting you.

Harry rose from his seat. "Thomas, can you give Liz a lift back to the tennis center? She needs to pick up her moped."

Harry walked her to the front door. He asked as he reached for the doorknob, "Can you play tomorrow? Around ten?"

"Sure. Love to. Ten sounds good."

"Great. Then, we'll pick you up a little before ten."

"Oh, I can take a taxi to the courts. There's no need—"

"We're all going to the same place. We'll pick you up. At the dock."

"Okay. Fine, see you then. And thanks again."

Thomas waited for her at the driveway and stood at the open car door. She didn't think she fit the part, but she felt like a princess who had been treated like royalty.

# CHAPTER SEVEN

An after-dinner martini in one hand and a remote in the other, Harry searched the stereo system for some easy listening background music. He called out from the bar, "Andy, what are you doing in there? "You're holding up our gin game."

Andy stepped out of the office and yelled down the hallway, "Reading a fax. Be with you in a bit."

"Fax? What fax?" Harry glanced at Cody who was snuggled up on the sofa reading. She looked up from her book, "He's been in your office since after dinner. Don't have a clue what he's up to." She resumed reading.

Harry placed his drink on the bar, walked down the hallway and entered the office. He peered over Andy's shoulder and spied the letterhead, *ManningSearch*, and *Private and Confidential* stamped in red print across a paragraph of disclaimer information on the center of the page. A few pages had accumulated on the incoming tray of the fax machine.

Harry grabbed the cover page from Andy's hand, read a few lines and shouted at him at a decibel level that could have cracked glass. "What the hell did you do?"

Cody heard his outburst and ran down the hallway reacting as if an accident had occurred.

Harry's anger flared like a summer brush fire. He yelled at Cody, "Stay out of here." He slammed the door shut.

"Why did you do this? You used my code to get a report?" Harry didn't know what offended him more, Andy using the investigative agency for personal reasons or Andy using his confidential code without telling him. It was one and same thing, Andy violated his trust.

Harry's face flushed to a blood red and his voice bounced off the walls. "The purpose of that agency is for business, business only. You know that. What did you do?"

"Calm down, Harry. The information will never be disclosed or for that matter used against her. There's no problem, no chance of anything going public."

"Thanks. I'm glad you're the expert in law and confident I won't be sued. But that's not exactly the issue I'm concerned about. I trusted you with that code. You violated my trust and her privacy."

Harry stood in front of Andy, face-to-face, nose-to-nose. "Yeah, yeah, I know. I broke the rules. Sorry, but I had reasons." Andy's hands fidgeted with the fax pages in his hand, attempting to put them in order.

Harry shouted at him: "Reasons? Presumptions maybe, but no reasons. Absolutely no facts to substantiate what you've done. You're paranoid. Fucking paranoid! When did you do this? We only had lunch a few hours ago."

Andy leaned his head sideways, pointed his index finger at Harry and bellowed: "Because of your fucking history, that's why. Because I'm not letting that goddamn zipper in your pants get you in trouble again."

The shouting match between them ended as quickly as it began. Harry sat down. Andy's voice returned to a normal decibel level. "I emailed from the tennis court. Sit down. And listen."

Harry wanted to punch him. It wasn't the first time he restrained a rash whim to belt his best friend and put him in his place. Those were the instances when he and Andy clashed bitterly, when he couldn't persuade Andy that he saw everything in black or white. There were no gray areas for Andy. Everything was either right or wrong. It was the same old Andy impulsively acting out his version of tell-it-like-it-is, or that's-the-way-it-is, and as usual Andy behaved as if he had to fix it.

"Damnit, Andy. Why didn't you ask me?"

"I knew you wouldn't approve. You just don't get it! When people fear the thought of having their picture in the paper, it's generally because someone is looking for them, like the police. Or they're scammers, or maybe criminals."

Harry knew Andy's shortcomings. He had an all-abiding love of beer and sports, and a propensity for sarcasm and swearing, all of which Harry accepted without judgment or criticism, but he could never accept the pragmatic Andy, the Andy who never gave anyone the benefit of the doubt. Nonetheless, best friends didn't come close to describing the relationship that developed between them over the years. Andy was his confidant, the friend who offered him solace and kept him from falling off the edge in times of crisis. They loved each and were brothers in every sense of the word.

Andy exploded with a rationale in an attempt to justify his action: "One blackmail attempt, two lawsuits over alleged paternity, a few incidents of almost being caught in the wrong place at the wrong time. Pushing the envelope is always okay with you. You never feel threatened."

"That's not new news. There's always a threat. I'm very aware that I'm an ongoing target—a billionaire—and sometimes I forget the risks, but I'm not going to stop living because there's a standing invitation to take me to court. I handle it. You should, too."

Andy sat down. "Don't give me the risk-taker argument. Save that one for the business. I'm not the judge of how many or what sort of women you want. You know that. The bottom line is you don't take precautions. I do! It's as simple as that."

Harry rubbed his neck with his hand and held the fax in his other hand. His anger subsided, he looked directly at Andy.

"Okay! But it's not necessary. It's not what you're thinking. First of all, I'm not interested. She's a lady with some class and a good backhand. That's all! Second, she explained to you and everyone very clearly why she was being careful about publicity. Investigating her is rather an extreme measure, don't you think? God, I don't even know this woman."

"Aha! That's the point, isn't it? You don't even know her. Yet, you pat her on the ass. Yes, Cody and I both saw that. You invite her to lunch, give her the charm treatment: *Would you like to have a swim? Isn't the view beautiful?*" Andy mocked Harry, flashing his eyes and mimicking a fake smile.

"Your eyes are all over her when she's not looking at you. And you're not interested? That's a crock and you know it. You can lie to yourself, but not to me. I've seen it all before."

"So, what? And if I am interested, that justifies an investigation? What the hell do you think you're doing? Protecting me?" As if he could counter Andy's argument, Harry said, "Aside from the fact that I've never shared my bed with a woman here."

"That was then, when your daughters were around. This is now. Besides, there's always a first time."

Just as Harry began the crushing process, Andy snatched the cover page from his hand.

"Harry, I can see it in your eyes. Anyway, *where* is not the issue. If you want to know, which you ought to want to know, she's clean, clean as a baby's bum. Practically antiseptic, in fact. But you don't need to know that, do you? You don't need to be safe."

Andy picked up a few more pages from the machine and aligned them with the cover page he had grabbed from Harry. He read aloud in a monotone the salient factual information in the report:

> *Elizabeth Brady, nee Bergstrom. White, Caucasian, forty-nine years of age, blonde hair, blue eyes, one hundred ten pounds. Resides at 137 East 36th Street for the past four years, previously at . . . . Deceased husband, Phillip Brady (1946-1998), widowed.*

"We know that."

> *Employment with several large law firms as follows . . . . Currently, working free-lance as an independent contractor.*

"Aha, a client list—which includes none other than the illustrious Peter Handley from the District Attorney's Office. And, including one of his notorious assistants, Josh Starkey.

"No wonder she doesn't want her picture taken with you, if she's working for Handley on confidential matters. A bit too close for comfort, if you ask me."

Andy continued reading at a hurried pace:

> *IRS returns. Total net worth approximately . . . . Chase CDs, money market account, . . . , mortgage with Wells Fargo of about $45,000 on a co-op purchased in 1995. Metropolitan Opera subscription. Memberships: Opera Guild, Manhattan Plaza Racquet Club, . . . .*

"From what I'm reading, buddy, she's not exactly your type of woman. Very conservative and stable. Not what you're used to."

"What's that supposed to mean?"

"Well, you remember, for instance, the aerialist—what was her name—Louise? The one with the great body. After you told her you couldn't get her a job with Cirque de Soleil, she organized her own photo shoot. Thought the publicity with you would help her career."

"That lasted all of three weeks."

"Sure. And the psychiatrist? She had more baggage than you could pack for a world tour. Three kids and supposedly separated from the husband, except they still shared the same bed and the same address. Adultery wasn't her only crime. She had no qualms about lifting a blank check from your attaché and depositing it to her bank account. You were lucky you had a friend at Chase."

"That's ancient history, Andy."

"There's more. Shall I go on?"

"You make it sound as if my associations with women have all been reckless, one-night stands. That's not the case and you know it. I'm too trusting, and I'll admit I've been careless at times, but in the end no harm was done."

Andy returned to reading the report in his matter-of-fact tone. "This is new, a medical profile. I didn't know Manning disclosed medical information."

Harry wasn't listening anymore. He was distracted in thoughts about what Andy had determined. At least Andy got one thing right. He was attracted to Liz and had been denying it. He hadn't admitted to himself that she appealed to him. Unexpectedly, he recalled his momentary fantasies of the afternoon, holding her trim, tanned body and imagining his hands caressing her breasts and nuzzling his lips on her long, sensuous neck. Why hadn't his usual pattern surfaced in an outspoken solicitation requiring either a *yes* or *no*?

Andy continued his dissertation:

> *Medical coverage with Aetna . . . , various therapeutic procedures: dental implants 1998, sclerotherapy 1998, . . . . A list of specialists at Columbia Presbyterian, NYU Medical Center . . . .*

"Etcetera, etcetera. What the hell is sclerotherapy?"

"Enough! You've made your point. Mission accomplished. Feel good? What's done is done. I can't change that. I'm still pissed. Don't ask me to thank you. Thank you is reserved for a kindness. That report is certainly not a kindness to her or to me. I need a drink."

When Harry returned to the lounge, his martini wasn't on the bar where he left it. "I put it in the refrigerator." Cody said. "Thought you would need a palatable drink after your tirade."

"Thanks, Cody. Sorry I yelled at you." He recovered his drink from the refrigerator, grabbed a bottle of beer and strode down the corridor to the office.

Harry leaned against the doorframe. Andy stopped reading and looked up at him.

"Are we still talking? Forgive me?" Andy asked.

"Peace offering," Harry murmured and offered the beer to Andy.

They looked at each other eye-to-eye, simultaneously broke into grins and hugged each other.

# CHAPTER EIGHT

The next day when the tennis foursome indulged in the customary after-the-game-handshakes, Harry held onto Liz's hand and said, "Martine has asked us all for dinner tonight at his restaurant, Chez Mare. Seven-thirty. I hope you can make it."

"Oh, how nice. Yes, I'd love to."

Harry hadn't actually asked her for a date but invited her again as if she were the needed fourth in a doubles match, except maybe it was a date after all since Harry very well could have accepted the invitation for himself and his friends, but he made the decision to include her. In any event, the invitation was a welcome alternative to attending the formal Captain's Dinner unescorted and surrounded by strangers on the ship.

"Shall we pick you up, say, about seven-fifteen?"

"You know, there's so much traffic on Front Street in the evening, why don't I just meet you there? Chez Mare is only a short walk from the ship, and you'd have a lot of grief trying to double park at the dock in the evening."

"Yeah, you're right. Okay. Well, we'll see you at seven-thirty then. You know the restaurant?"

"Yes. See you then."

Thomas drove Liz to the dock. When she boarded the ship, she headed directly for the spa. The invitation was special and not in the realm of the same old, same old night out and clearly justified a makeover. Harry had only seen her in tennis clothes, without makeup and her hair stuffed under a cap, and she was determined to transform that image and attract Harry's attention to her feminine attributes.

The ship's beauty salon overflowed with cackling females. She noticed some attendants dividing their services to several clients, hastening from one station to another, and it appeared that the prospect of a last-minute appointment was hopeless.

Liz approached the receptionist, "Is there any chance of a wash and blow dry? I can see it's very busy, probably because of the

Captain's Dinner tonight, but I'll make it worthwhile, monetarily—I mean—if you could squeeze me in."

"What exactly do you need?"

"Wash and style, eyebrows, a facial, if possible. Whatever time will allow. I'd be very grateful."

"Have a seat. I'll see what I can do."

Liz splurged a fifty-dollar tip in addition to the actual cost for services and endured an afternoon in the midst of a noisy assembly of gossipy women. The irritating atmosphere was worth it, and even if it wasn't a date, she anticipated a refreshing diversion and an exceptional evening—dining at a five star restaurant—especially if it was anything like yesterday's lunch.

The afternoon flew by in preparations for the evening. She decided the special dress she bought for the ship's formal night was an appropriate selection and worthy of a special occasion. The many charity events she had attended with her husband had schooled her in flaunting an aura of the belle of the ball, and she pranced off the ship groomed for a solo performance.

The short walk to the restaurant dispelled the butterflies that played havoc with her stomach, and by the time she arrived at the restaurant, her nervousness was expended. She was calm and confident and stood waiting at the maitre d's desk, surveying the room in search of Harry.

At her left from where she stood, dim lights were strewn over a few scattered cocktail tables in a comfortable lounge. The terrace below was barely visible although she could see a wrought iron railing and a partial view of the bay. At her right, the dining room across from the terrace was muted in pastel colors. Patrons were nestled in private niches; a quartet of musicians played music as mellow and well-appointed as the furnishings and the clientele.

"Good evening." The maitre d' approached Liz. He wore an exquisite white suit, attesting to the formal aura of the restaurant. He was dressed like a patron rather than an employee in service.

"Good evening," she said.

"I believe you would be Ms. Brady?"

"Yes, I'm Ms. Brady."

"Your friends are having cocktails on the terrace. They're expecting you. Please follow me. What would you like to drink?"

"A vodka martini, no olives. Thank you."

The maitre d' escorted her through the lounge and to the few steps that led to the terrace. All eyes were on her as she made her entrance with the aplomb of an Academy Award actress who was being directed to the red carpet. She didn't aspire to being on stage and generally avoided being the center of attraction, but circumstances at the moment were not of her choosing. Nevertheless, she rose to the occasion with a broad smile and greeted everyone. "Hi, good to see you again."

She stepped down to the terrace. The provocative red dress she wore flared from her waist, flurried around her hips and accentuated her sinuous body. A short matching jacket clung at her cleavage. She noticed Harry's eyes focused on the dipping line to her breasts. His lips were moving, but no words were forthcoming. After a few silent, breathtaking pauses, he finally mumbled, "Very elegant."

Harry extended his hand to her and led her forward. "Whatever you were shooting for, you've hit the bull's eye. I just hope I'm the target."

"You look lovely." Cody said.

"Thank you."

Cody adorned her simple black dress with conservative diamond jewelry, a perfect accessory, which created an ingenious simplicity. Liz supposed anything Cody wore would enhance her stunning body.

"Your dress is beautiful, especially with that necklace," Liz said.

"Thank you."

Andy was well-fashioned in a cream-colored suit, blue shirt and tie. Harry's white dinner jacket looked as if it was styled and fitted by a Savile Row tailor. The sky blue colored trousers and matching shirt he wore enhanced his blue eyes.

"Well, it seems we all clean up very handsomely once we're out of tennis clothes. Bermuda does that though, doesn't it—mandates you dress for dinner?" Liz said.

"My dear, you are dressed for seduction, not dinner. Is seduction mandated?" Harry asked.

Liz smiled. Torn between flattery and embarrassment, she was uncomfortable with his remark. She responded impulsively, out of character for her, and leaned forward and whispered in his ear,

"Maybe that can be arranged." She needed to say something quickly to conceal her uneasiness.

The maitre d' offered her a martini. She strolled to the nearby terrace railing and commented on the uniqueness of the restaurant, "Great atmosphere, the lounge, the terrace, romantic music and another beautiful view of the bay."

"The terrace was Harry's idea." Andy said. "Martine asked him to sit in with the architect, and they planned the renovations together. It used to be a shabby four-bedroom house. Martine knows about cooking and restaurants, not about gutting and renovating a building. Granted, he was the one with the vision for the restaurant. Now, it's a five-star."

Harry joined her at the railing.

"Do you own this place?" She asked.

"No, I'm not in the restaurant business. I lent Martine the start-up money many years ago. He worked for me at that time, managing the dining at the house when I used to entertain clients. Everybody loved him and was especially appreciative of his good-natured disposition and the way he pampered everyone and made them feel special. So, when he approached me for a loan, I didn't hesitate. We're good friends and I wouldn't refuse him anything. He deserved a shot. He's repaid me and then some. He's never forgotten and always calls and offers his talents gratis. The restaurant is his success, his success alone, and I'm happy for him."

Andy gave Cody a nod, the palm of his hand extended toward the dance floor. "Excuse us, guys. We're trying out the dance floor, see if it still squeaks." Andy and Cody left them alone.

Harry stood beside her and leaned sideways on the railing. He viewed her profile. "I think there's a conspiracy afoot to give us some time alone."

She felt his eyes on her, avoided looking at him and focused on the view, although a slight tremor in her hand on the railing revealed her edginess.

Harry turned around and faced her directly. His lively blue eyes peered up at her, "Have I embarrassed you?"

"Yes.—Yes, I think so."

"Sorry, that wasn't my intent. I simply wanted you to know how stunning you look this evening. I didn't mean to be rude."

Harry took her hand from the railing. She felt his soft touch as he brought his lips to her fingers and ever-so-lightly kissed them, and then turned her fingers over and kissed the palm of her hand. His eyebrows rose in arches as he looked up, met her eyes and said, "Forgive me?"

"Nothing to forgive. It's just—it's been some time since I felt as if I were being undressed in public."

"Maybe we should go private then?"

"You're doing it again."

He smiled. "Sorry. I promise to be nice."

It was clear to Liz what path he was on. She felt the rushes of desire, and the softness of his lips on her fingers lingered as did the kiss on her hand.

A silence settled between them. It was unbearable for her. She scolded herself silently. A grown woman, afraid? Afraid of what? To admit you're attracted to him, that he lit a fire that's been smoldering and practically in ashes, that you desperately want him to touch you. For the last two days, you've been fantasizing how it would feel to be held and kissed by him. And, now, you're discouraging him from going where you know you want him to go. Why can't you just relax?

"I don't want you to be *that nice*," Liz blurted out.

"You're confusing me."

She meant to encourage him. Obviously, he was not confused but elated as a broad smile emerged on his face.

Harry straightened up from his leaning position, took her glass from her hand and placed their drinks on a nearby table. He grasped her hand.

"We're going to dance. At the moment, I have an inordinate desire to hold you in my arms, as well as to engage in some other various and sundry physical contact, but I'll settle for a dance." He guided her to the dance floor that adjoined the dining room.

As soon as they embraced on the dance floor, the uneasiness Liz felt disappeared like the heat of a summer's day dispelled by a cooling breeze. He clutched her waist, released her and spun her back into his arms. She fell into the rhythm of the music and moved gracefully as he released her from his arms and then drew her back to his body again, embracing and holding her. After each twirl, she eagerly awaited the return of his arms to her body.

"You're quite the accomplished dancer. I can tell you've done this before."

"Thank you, Ms. Brady. Uh, huh. Yes, learned to dance in college. Didn't have much luck with the ladies then."

He spun her away, slowly and smoothly, and back in his arms again. "Andy convinced me dancing was the shortest route to the girls' dorm."

"Looking for a dorm tonight?"

Harry didn't answer immediately and continued to whirl her about the dance floor. He guided her to the edge of the terrace steps, dancing in small steps and holding her in an embrace. He stopped and gently folded her arms around her back, pressing her to his chest. He brushed his lips across her cheek, lingering there until she closed her eyes and met his lips. When their eyes opened and locked, she swooned in short breaths, her body tingling and vibrating.

Harry whispered in her ear, "Only if you're going there with me."

Her arms fell to her side and then flowed to his shoulders in an embrace. Their lips floundered and settled in another amorous kiss.

Andy had been scurrying around the restaurant looking for them and finally spied them on the terrace unfolding from an embrace. He called out from the lounge, "We're waiting on you two. The table's ready."

Harry and Liz sat at the table, gazing and smiling at each other. He reached for her hand and held it as he sipped his martini. One dance, an extended kiss and they had acknowledged their attraction. They were of one mind abiding in agreement to relax and loiter in lust.

Andy, holding a menu in his hand, waved at them from across the table. "C'mon, guys, we're hungry. Enough with the foreplay, please."

"You're being presumptuous, Andy," Harry said.

Cody giggled and shook her head. She drew her arm up and signaled for the waiter to take their order. She pointed to Harry and Liz. "Whatever the special is, they're having it. I'm having whatever he orders," placing her fingers on her husband's chest. "We're trying to make a ten o'clock show at the Princess, so we would be obliged if you could accommodate our timetable. Please tell Martine, we're sorry to be in a rush."

Liz leaned over and whispered in Harry's ear, "Yes." She leaned on his shoulder and looked in his eyes for a reaction. The second martini had seized her inhibitions, and she looked up at him, bold and footloose, and smiled.

"Uh, huh," he muttered an acknowledgment.

"I guess you two are not planning to join us for the show after dinner?" Andy said. "Good, because fornication is not permitted in the public rooms at the Princess. If you like though, I'd be happy to book you a room when we get there." The two beers Andy drank had loosened his tongue. He apologized. "Sorry, for the language, ladies, but I'm very hungry and we're wasting time."

Cody coaxed her husband into placation.

"Stop fretting. What's so terrible about missing ten minutes of the show. It doesn't matter. Relax."

Once Andy was chided and dinner was served, he refrained from further disagreeable remarks. They ate slowly, forsaking conversation in favor of the gourmet food. Finally, everyone relaxed and succumbed to the excellent service and romantic ambiance.

When the bus boys were clearing the table, Harry said, "Andy, take the car. It's a long haul to Southampton and you won't make a ten o'clock show if you take a taxi. Thomas can wait for you. Besides, you might have trouble getting a taxi back."

Andy nodded. "Good idea, thanks. See you later. Enjoy your evening."

"Night." Cody said as she slid her waist under Andy's arm.

Harry smiled. "Bye."

He turned and faced Liz, "Coffee? Another dance? We've the rest of the evening to ourselves."

"Yes. I'd love some coffee."

# CHAPTER NINE

Once Liz and Harry were inside the house gate, they paused. Harry embraced her, holding her body against the gate tower, he kissed her forcefully. Liz undid a button of his shirt and her fingers slid inside the opening and across his chest, touching his tight muscles and fingering his dense and silky chest hair. Her heart pounded and the heat of her body simmered beneath her skin. The after-dinner agenda for the evening had already been determined.

He put his arm around her waist and led her to the patio entrance. The lounge was dim with only a nightlight. The house was silent, only the sounds of muffled kisses filled the air. Harry stopped Liz halfway up the staircase and positioned her against the banister. He nestled his lips in the crevice of her neck and nipped at her ear lobes, his short breaths sweeping across her breasts and further igniting her sensating body.

She undid the clasp of his trousers, reached down and caressed him in his already aroused condition. Her desire heightened with each touch, and she restrained her inclination to grip and squeeze him with the savage need that burned from within her.

Harry grabbed her hand and quickly led her to the bedroom. On the way, he dropped into an armchair, sat her on his lap and invaded her mouth with his tongue, groping her breasts from beneath her bra. Liz undid his remaining shirt buttons. He unzipped her dress.

"Bed?" he asked.

"Uh, huh." Liz could have cared less about where the act would take place, only that it would take place. For too long her desire had been occasioned in sparks that quickly disappeared, but now she was elated a flame fired so intensely and burned uncontrollably.

In what seemed like one swift magician's gesture, Harry dropped his jacket, shirt, trousers and underwear on the path to the bed. Liz freed herself from her dress and fell on the bed in her bra and panties. He dropped down next to her naked and unfastened her bra. Her breasts unfolded before him and his lips gently drifted to her nipples. He pulled her pants from her waist.

In a frenzy, Liz threw her arms around him and kicked off the remainder of her underwear. His fingers touched her loins and tenderly probed inside her, enrapturing her with his slow and soft strokes. She grasped his erection at her thigh, folded her fingers around his tautness and reveled in its thickness. She directed him to where she wanted him to be, inside her.

"Please," she begged.

"Slowly. I don't want to disappoint you. I'm on the edge."

Harry complied and moved her hands away. He held his erection and gently pressed her mons, again and again. He penetrated her slightly and gained a little more access each time he pushed himself inside her. Her sighs defined her physical need and became more and more audible with each thrust inside her body. Her eyes half closed, she spied him biting his lip, aware that that the pleasure he ministered to her was intensifying his desire.

At last, he entered her fully. Her warm wetness oozed, caressed and enveloped him. She felt the tightness of flesh upon flesh. He thrust himself in and out as she brought her hips up to meet him and forced his body to respond to the rapid rhythm she initiated. She couldn't linger any longer, her inner recesses plunging into pounding beats. He overflowed inside her, relentlessly throbbing. He was unwilling to withdraw as he felt her involuntary spasms continuing to jolt her and her arms captivatingly clutching him.

He fell off her and they lay next to each other, breathlessly savoring the euphoria. He leaned across her body and sighed, "Quite wonderful!"

Liz smiled at him. "Hmm, yes. Awesome!"

They laughed lightly, closed their eyes and dozed into sleep, drained and naked in each other's arms.

Liz startled him when she awoke and untangled her body from his arms. He reached over and lightly pressed his lips to her cheek. Reluctant to leave the warmth and sweet scent of his body, she felt tempted to embrace him, but instead she rose from the bed and gathered her underwear from the floor.

"What's up?" He asked.

"I have to get dressed and go back. There's a curfew. I think it's twelve o'clock, for getting back on board the ship. I need to use the bathroom."

Liz returned to him naked. He was naked as well and lay on his back, his torso half covered in rumpled sheets. He got up and put on a terry cloth robe, pulled another one from a bathroom hook and wrapped it around her and embraced her at the same time.

"You're not going back," he said. You're supposed to be next to me on my pillow in the morning. It's already eleven-thirty. You won't make that curfew." He clasped her waist and hugged her. "My dear, you are now my prisoner."

"Uh, huh. Well, I'd love for you to be my warden, but it's not as if I brought an overnight bag, with sleepwear and clothes for tomorrow. I can't walk around in the morning in a cocktail dress. Do you see my shoes?"

"C'mere." Harry put his hand in hers and led her through an enormous L-shaped bathroom which connected to his bathroom, both bathrooms ubiquitously marbled and equipped with double sinks and showers, bidets, mirrors everywhere, like the *Taj Mahal Hotel*'s his and hers bathrooms, and then through to Rebecca's room.

"Rebecca uses this room when she's here. She has everything you possibly could need. I'm sure your sexy body will fit into something. Actually, she's taller, but about your size."

"Harry, you can't raid your daughter's bedroom. And I certainly can't."

"Yes, I can. She's my daughter. Since she doesn't know what she has crammed in those drawers and closets, trust me, she won't feel violated. She would probably beg to accommodate you if she were here."

Harry paused and looked around the room. "If it will make you feel any better, I'll phone her in the morning for her approval."

Compared with Harry's decidedly masculine bedroom of clean, stark lines and reminiscent Burberry colors, the lavish furnishings in Rebecca's room reeked of femininity, decorated in floral blues and whites on fruitwood finishes.

"You're kidding. I can hear the conversation now, *Rebecca, honey, I had sex with this woman last night and she needed some clothes in the morning. I hope you don't mind, I gave her a few of your things to wear.* Get real."

"You take the closets. I'll take the drawers," Harry insisted. He was in earnest.

"In fact, it's occurred to me, prisoner," he said as he opened one of the drawers, "Thomas can take you to the ship tomorrow and bring your luggage here, and you can spend the rest of the week with me."

He turned toward her, embraced her and kissed her on the cheek and then her lips. "Doesn't incarceration sound inviting? Admit it, I'd be much better company than a shipload of boring tourists. We'll take the plane back to New York early Sunday afternoon. Say, yes."

It was an invitation to recapture feelings that had long been denied to her. She was eager to sustain her renewed desire for sex. Although she thought it an impulsive offer, she didn't hesitate to accept, not wanting to leave him tonight or tomorrow. She wanted to feel that passion again, so powerful it liberated her from all reason. She was on vacation from reason, her emotions still free-falling, and she didn't want to land on solid, reasonable ground just yet.

Liz really didn't know him and Harry really didn't know her. She didn't trust that their one encounter, however wonderfully consummated, could sustain a few days of living with each other.

Liz unfolded herself from his arms and looked at Harry eye-to-eye. "Yes, but on one condition. If you get bored—or just change your mind—you promise to tell me. I wouldn't want you to just tolerate the situation. Okay?" She asked.

"Deal! The same goes for you. If you want to leave, you'll tell me. You won't just disappear. Settled?"

"Deal!" She said.

Liz stepped up to a closet, humming a tune of her own creation. She drew back the sliding door and surveyed the contents. Harry was right. The closet overflowed with shorts, jeans, dresses, some garments with tags still on them.

She looked over her shoulder at Harry who noisily negotiated with a drawer that brimmed over with underwear, tee shirts, socks and various other teenage paraphernalia. Rebecca apparently hadn't an inkling of organizational skills.

Harry pulled a tank bathing suit from the drawer, "Looks like it will fit."

"That's a bathing suit."

"Really? The kind you wear when you go swimming? On a moonlit night. Like tonight? Like now?"

"What a great idea! Yes. Let's."

# CHAPTER TEN

The water was up to Harry's neck. "C'mon in," he said, "the water's warm." Liz jumped in the pool alongside him, displacing the rippling water and drenching Harry's face.

"Oops, I can't stand." She said. "It's too high."

Harry swept the water off his face with his hands and laughed. He swam to the deep end of the pool, and Liz paddled to the nearest ledge. She lay on top of the water, her arms spread on both sides of the ledge. She watched him glide over the water like a graceful sea animal swimming in its natural habitat.

"Show off." She said.

When he got to the end of the pool, he called out, "No swimming?"

"I don't swim except very badly. I just like to loll around. Don't mind me, just go ahead and do your thing."

She floated to the low side of the pool, threw her arms back again and leaned on the ledge. She kicked, splashed and enjoyed the gently flowing water that hugged her legs. The sky was a dense blue and she gazed up at a tissue of a cloud that passed in front of the moon. A brilliant yellow, the moon was full, and its light beamed on the surrounding trees and shrubs. She was filled with the peace and harmony of the surroundings.

After a few laps, Harry swam to Liz at the other end of the pool. Out of breath, he gasped as he wiped the water from his eyes. "Great night for a swim."

She stood up in the water and faced him. "Yes. Beautiful out here."

"You look absolutely delicious in a bathing suit. And, as I remember, without a bathing suit." His hands settled on her shoulders. Awaiting his touch, she tugged at his bathing suit and playfully pulled him close to her. She wanted him nude and unencumbered. Impulsively, she slid his swim trunks down his legs, and without thinking her hands found him. She curled her fingers around him and stroked him gently. He grasped her face in his hands, kissed her softly and held her close while his erection took place. When he released her from his embrace, he stripped off her bathing suit and flung it across the water.

They stood gazing at each other's body and broke into a simultaneous, soft laughter. He placed the palms of her hands on his ass, took hold of himself and supplely moved his erection around her pubis lips, slightly touching her inside, again and again. He already knew how to tantalize her. They gasped in short breaths. The water dispersed calmly about them in lightly splashing waves.

"Tell me when," he whispered.

"Now."

Harry obeyed, entered her and slowly pushed himself inside, gaining a little more access with each stroke. He positioned her against the pool edge and pressed her hands against the soft flesh of his ass. She pulled him forward and met his thrusts that eased through her wet passageway until he was entirely inside. An assortment of moans and whimpers erupted in the air as his strokes gradually accelerated and the rippling water circled them in a splashing, rapid current.

"Harry, please."

"Sure?"

"Uh, huh," was all she could manage to utter. She was on the edge of delirium, her brain on a journey of forgetting everything except his penetration of her body. He continued to plunge at her against the side of the pool, faster and faster, until momentarily they both were seized with le petit mort and cried out together in gratification. Her knees buckled, and she hung onto him as her body sank into the water.

"I can't walk." Liz said.

"Not doing very well myself."

Harry drew her up to his chest, and they stumbled out of the pool. He draped a terry robe over her nude, dripping body and climbed into his robe. They huddled on a poolside chaise. Faint tears straggled down her cheek. He pressed his lips on her face, overcoming a few teardrops that fell on her cheek.

"No crying." He said. His hands stroked her wet hair and pushed aside the dripping blond ringlets on her forehead. Succumbing to fatigue, they cradled in each other's arms and fell asleep.

It was after midnight when Andy and Cody found them wrapped in each other's arms and terry cloth robes. They had been very quiet; nevertheless, Harry awoke. He got up, put his finger to his lips, signaling not to wake Liz and followed Andy and Cody from the patio into the bar.

Harry sat down, a pensive look on his face, almost frowning. Andy searched for a beer in the refrigerator and asked, "Drink?"

"Yeah, toss me a water."

"I'm tired, good night." Cody said as she headed for the stairway to the guest room.

"Night, Cody."

"Be up in a flash," Andy said.

"So, I presume, from the bathing suits floating in the pool, you had a good evening. Apparently, Liz is staying. Why are you looking so down as if you're deliberating next year's budget?"

"I've asked her to stay. Go back with me on Sunday. But the report. It's been nagging at me all evening. I've got to tell her."

Barefoot and sleep still in her eyes, Liz ambled in from the patio. She heard Harry's last few words and approached the bar.

"Tell me what?" She asked.

"Sweet dreams, you two." Andy swallowed another swig of beer and placed the bottle on the bar. "See you in the morning," he said and made a quick exit.

# CHAPTER ELEVEN

"Ready for bed?" Harry asked.

"Yeah. Tired. What did you want to tell me?"

"I'll tell you later. Do you want a drink?"

"No. Maybe just a taste of your water."

"Let's get you something to sleep in."

Liz trailed behind Harry as they climbed the stairs to the bedroom. They had been on this mission before. "I don't need anything to sleep in." She dropped her robe on the floor and slid nude under the covers. Harry tossed her a pajama top from the bureau drawer, climbed into his pajamas and joined her in bed.

Liz rose from the pillow, knelt on the bed and put on the pajama top and adjusted the sleeves.

"Perfect. You wanted to tell me something?"

"Harry ignored her question, crushed his pillow and lay his head down. It can wait 'til tomorrow."

"No, it can't."

Now that she was fully awake, she imagined all sorts of truths Harry might have withheld. He had a heart problem, or some other health issue—he'd been exposed to herpes and should have used a condom. Her imagination ran wild, like an out-of-control car careening down a steep hill without any brakes.

"It's nothing."

"If you don't tell me, I won't be able to sleep."

Liz faced Harry's back. His head was immersed in his pillow.

"If it's nothing, tell me, then I can go to sleep."

Harry finally relented and muttered, "Andy did a background check on you."

"He did what? What are saying? You investigated me?"

"It sounds a lot worse than it is."

Liz jumped off the bed and yelled at him. "How dare you? How could you do such a thing?"

She grabbed the nearest object, a pillow from the bed, and threw it at his head.

Harry rolled over and sat up in full attention.

"Liz, let me explain."

"Explain? I got it. You had me checked out before you slept with me?"

"No, that's not so."

"What am I, a criminal? A prostitute?"

"Liz, I didn't ask him to get a report. Andy suspected—"

"I guess that's your usual procedure. You could have simply asked me if I had herpes, or used a condom."

His words did not impact her brain. She suffered from selective hearing and didn't hear what he said. The more he spoke, the louder she yelled until her voice evolved to full-fledged, relentless shouting. She thumped back and forth across the bedroom like a wounded, crazed animal.

"It was nothing like that." He said.

"Oh, I know what it was like. I was there. Oh, you were ever-so-charming. Sweeping me off my feet. And all the time you were thinking I was a thief, or diseased. If you wanted to know something, why didn't you just ask?"

"You don't understand. Will you please listen?"

"No. I will not listen. I've heard everything I want to hear. That's it for me. I'm going."

Finally, the shouting stopped and a dead silence prevailed, nonetheless, a silence that spoke of guilt and humiliation.

Liz snatched her underwear from the chair and let the pajama top drop to the floor. She felt ashamed not because he stared at her in the nude, but because she had been so foolish and allowed him to exploit her vulnerability. She groped about the room and looked for her clothes, desperate to dress and leave.

Harry sat on the bed, his knees drawn to his chest, and watched her. She fumbled with her undergarments and tried to assemble her bra. Suddenly, tears flooded her face.

He got up and approached her, but she warded him off, pushed her outstretched arms to his chest and created a distance and a battleground between them.

"Where are my shoes?"

He grasped her bare shoulders and held her. He looked directly in her eyes. "Damnit, you're going to listen to me. Do I need to slap you?"

Tears careened down her face. Drained of energy, like a marathon runner at the finish line, her head fell on his chest. Her hands covered her face and she began to weep uncontrollably.

"Oh, God." Harry's anger immediately deferred to her sobs. He held her tightly and rocked her back and forth. "I'm sorry. It was a mistake. I'm truly sorry. Please, Liz, stop crying."

Liz continued to sob. Harry's hands traveled across and around her back and slowly massaged her trembling body, soothing her as her sobs waned to whimpers.

"I never meant to hurt you. No one meant to hurt you. Andy was trying to protect me. Protect me from myself. From my past. It wasn't you. It was me."

Harry led her to the bed and sat her down. Her head fell forward and drooped toward her waist. "Promise me you won't move."

He scurried into the bathroom and returned with a glass of water.

"Take this." He dropped a pill into the palm of her hand.

She looked up at him with reddened, tearful eyes.

"What is it?"

"Something to calm you. Lie down. Try to sleep."

Liz slithered under the covers, limp and numb, but free of the hysteria that had possessed her. Harry unclasped her bra and removed her panties. He rubbed her back as she lay on her side, whimpering and sniffling. He crawled in beside her, wrapped his arms around her and cuddled her in a spoon position until she fell asleep.

• • •

Harry lay next to her and idly observed her rhythmic breathing. She was calm, restored in sleep. He stared at the ceiling and the image of Liz crying reminded him of his clutching, sobbing daughters when their mother died. He had been their only comfort. He felt Liz's pain and although she was a sophisticated and grown woman, nonetheless she needed his arms around her. She needed to be held, hugged and comforted.

At the thought of his wife, his past returned to the present and revisited him with the guilt that strangled and knotted his heart and mind throughout his wife's illness, still haunting him like a relentless ghost who continued to deliver punishment for his past transgressions. Finally, he drifted into a fitful state of slumber, tossing and turning and desperately trying to dispel the thought of Liz trembling and sobbing in his arms.

# CHAPTER TWELVE

Harry greeted Maddy, his housekeeper. "Morning, Please fix me a tray. Just coffee, for upstairs."

Andy and Cody sat in the breakfast room, lolling in their robes, drinking coffee, reading the newspaper, and enjoying the sun-filled backyard view of foliage and flowers. Harry fetched a coffee and joined them. He sat next to Cody and across the table from Andy.

"Morning. Sleep well?" Andy asked.

"I've had better nights. Okay, when I finally got to sleep. Andy, we are clear, right? We're never doing that again, no matter how much protecting you think I need."

"Huh? Uh, oh, you must have told her. Didn't go over too well?"

Harry caught a glimpse of Cody. She sneered at her husband. "You get the award for Cad of the Year." Cody muttered.

"Cody knows about the report." Andy addressed Harry. "She wanted to know why you looked so glum last night and prodded me until I confessed. She hasn't been talking to me much since then. Says I'm a dumb ass who doesn't deserve civility."

Andy sipped his coffee. "So, what happened? She lock you out of your own bedroom?"

"No, nothing like that. Just a little anger. A bit of hysteria. Some weeping. And I mean weeping. How does a little body like hers shed so much water? I was lucky though. The only thing she got her hands on to throw at me was a pillow. Can't remember when I felt like such a heel. Even beats stranding Marylou at the hotel without paying the bill."

"Damn well you should feel like a heel," Cody interrupted. "Both of you, snooping into her private life. You're incorrigible. I know, you can give me all the reasons why you're right, but it's still unforgivable."

"I gave her a Xanax. She fell asleep like a whimpering baby."

Maddy appeared at the table, a tray in her hands. She asked, "Do you want me to bring it upstairs?"

"Thanks, I'll take it Maddy. See you guys later for breakfast."

Liz was still asleep. Harry sat on the bed and watched her for a few moments. He kissed her on the cheek, and her eyes half opened. A slight smile emerged from her face.

"Morning. Brought you some coffee."

Liz sat up and drew the covers up to her shoulders.

"Feel better?" He asked.

"Harry, I'm so sorry. I behaved like a total brat last night." She took the coffee. "Thanks."

"More like a tiger. Thought I had a temper." He paused. I'm the one who's sorry. It was so unfair. Maybe I shouldn't have told you. I could have saved us some grief."

"No, I understand. I do. I understand the need to do that. I mean, you've a job with public responsibility and you need to exercise care about who you sleep with. But I didn't put it together right away. It came at me too quickly. I felt so violated."

Liz sipped her coffee. "I do go off the deep end sometimes. Menopause doesn't help. Just when I think I'm over it, I find I still may be in the throes." Her lips trembled and her eyes squinted as she looked down into her coffee.

"Hey, don't you go crying on me again. C'mon. It's over. We'll get you something to wear and have some breakfast. Hungry? I need a shower. When I come out of the shower, you're going to be the happy, sexy woman I danced with last night."

Harry pulled clothes from a drawer and a closet and dropped them on the chair across from the bed. "We'll forget all about it, like a bad dream." He leaned over and kissed her on the cheek, not waiting for her reaction and headed for the bathroom.

"Okay." She said. But she couldn't forget about it. She wanted to free herself from thinking about what caused her to be so riled and to feel so betrayed. It was her own fault. Casual sex wasn't her usual behavior, not since the very few one-night stands of her youth. If she had returned to the ship, she would have preserved the self-respect that had been stripped from her like autumn leaves from a tree.

No, she thought. It wasn't my fault. It was Harry. He betrayed the tacit agreement between lovers—the honesty of being mutually vulnerable. There hadn't been a level playing field because he knew all about her and he hadn't been at risk. Still, he didn't initiate the report. Andy did. She should forgive him. But it didn't matter at the moment whether she forgave him or not, because in spite of Harry's innocence, yet she harbored an impulse to slap him across his face.

"Your turn," he said as he emerged from the bathroom, bare-chested and a towel strapped around his waist.

She sat on the bed in his pajama top. Harry sat beside her about to hug her when she suddenly dropped to her knees and positioned herself between his legs. Her lips grabbed him, her tongue sliding up and down his silky skin. She enveloped him like a vise.

"Liz, don't," he murmured. He pushed her away slightly, but she would not relinquish her hold on him as he swelled to an erection and she held him savagely in her mouth, restraining an urge to bite down on his flesh.

"Please, Liz. No." Liz ignored his pleas. She was on a mission. Finally, he relaxed and succumbed to euphoria. In what sounded more like a groan of pain rather than satisfaction, he emitted fluids. His hand was on her head, his eyes were closed, and he fell back on the bed. When he opened his eyes, he pulled her up from her knees and stared at her, "Why did you do that?"

"I felt like it." She said.

"But you can't have been satisfied."

"But I was. Not that I can explain."

"Try me."

"Oh, I don't know. I really can't put it into words. It just happened." She couldn't articulate what was not clear to her, although she felt satisfied—satisfied that she wielded control and overpowered him, and he had yielded.

The intercom buzzed and Harry responded, "We'll be down in a few minutes. Go ahead and start without us."

He turned and looked at her. "They're waiting on us for breakfast. Think you can find something to wear?"

"Yeah. I need a shower. I'll be quick."

• • •

He watched her scamper to the bathroom as he fell back on the bed, irked and thoughtful. He had wanted to prod her for another answer, but the moment wasn't appropriate. She *just felt like it*? What sort of an answer was that?

Ordinarily he wasn't concerned if the woman he had intercourse with achieved gratification. An orgasm was her responsibility, and if she claimed it, all the better, and if she didn't, that was her choice. He had been with too many women who serviced him as if he were party to a business agreement, and sex was a payoff they owed him. Liz didn't owe him anything.

He had only been with Liz twice, but it had been totally different from what he was accustomed to in his usual sexual encounters. They traveled together to the same end, tenderly touching, kissing, and fondling each other. He reveled in the newly performed preliminaries that not only enhanced his arousal, but also stirred his emotions. That's not what had just happened, and he wanted to know why he felt a twinge of guilt.

He got up, put on his underwear, pulled a golf shirt over his head and poured his legs into trousers. He was bothered that he really hadn't made a choice. He felt more like a victim than a participant. Sharing the arousal as well as the orgasm with a woman was a pleasure he hadn't experienced often, and if and when he had, he didn't remember with whom. But he knew he wouldn't forget the excitement and satisfaction of sex with Liz.

He missed something in that sexual episode, however delirious it had been. She had been there, but relinquished gratification for her own reasons, however mysterious her reasons were to him.

# CHAPTER THIRTEEN

Andy rose abruptly from his chair when Liz and Harry entered the breakfast room. He placed his arm around Liz's waist and addressed Harry, "Kidnapping her for a moment," he said as he steered her to the corridor next to the kitchen where they were out of sight.

Andy's huge brown eyes were intently fixed on hers, "Harry told me about the crying. You should know, it wasn't his idea and he didn't even know about it. I didn't mean to hurt you. I had my reasons. They seem dumb now, but they were well-meaning at the time.

"Forgive me? Please. Cody won't talk to me until I apologize. Cody hasn't read the report. She just knows that I'm responsible."

"No need to apologize, Andy. There's nothing to forgive. Really. I understand why. As for last night, all the crying, I may have overreacted."

Andy leaned over and kissed Liz on the forehead. "Thank you, sweetie."

Harry intruded and directed Liz to the kitchen. "Everything okay?"

"Uh, huh," Andy said as he returned to the breakfast room.

"This is Ms. Brady, Maddy. She's spending a few days with us." Maddy was cooking an omelet and turned away from the stove. "Hello, Mr. Harry." Her eyes opened wide and twinkled at the sight of Liz. "Nice to meet you, Ms. Brady."

"Good to meet you, too."

Maddy had been Harry's housekeeper for twelve years and part of his adopted family, as was Thomas. Her husband had maintained Harry's car and when he died in an accident, Maddy needed a job to support herself and her five-year old son. She was forever grateful to Harry. He gave her a job and rescued her from the economic despair of widowhood.

Although Maddy had gained a few extra pounds approaching her fiftieth year, she was as adept and agile as Thomas. Additionally, the natural glow of her complexion and the light in her black eyes confirmed the cheerful disposition that enhanced Harry's home as if her efficient housekeeping skills weren't ample and already greatly appreciated.

When they finished breakfast, Andy and Cody strolled to the patio, prepared for sunbathing and swimming. Andy waved a goodbye. "See you later for tennis."

Harry insisted upon accompanying Liz and Thomas to the ship. "Don't think they're going to allow you on board." Liz said.

She was right. Harry and Thomas waited near the car while she packed. It wasn't very long before she appeared and exited down the runway, rolling her luggage behind her. Thomas ran up to help her. Harry leaned against the car, basking in the sunshine and finishing a conversation on his cell phone.

"That was my daughter Rebecca. She said I should tell you to help yourself to whatever you need. I told her I had invited you to stay the night, offered her your room and clothing because it was too late to return to the ship. So, you have been granted permission to raid her premises. Feel better now?"

"I don't doubt she knows that you were in bed with someone last night. Did you really want to let her know that? I hope you didn't think you had to make that call because of me."

Liz was humbled that Harry had called his daughter for permission. Obviously, he enjoyed a very open relationship with his daughters, especially if he shared the overnight guest story. Liz surmised Rebecca must have read between the lines and Harry knew she would.

"And you told her because I was reluctant to use her things? I feel guilty."

"Don't feel responsible. I didn't tell her that I slept with you, just that you were borrowing some of her clothes. Of course, there's an inference. Actually, I spoke with my mother and told her you're spending the week with me. She'll tell my daughters in an appropriate way. I don't withhold the truth from them.

"Anyway, I couldn't run around the questions about where or who I was with for the next few days without lying. Eventually, I couldn't keep track of the lies and that would lead to discovery unless I recruited Andy, Cody, and everyone into weaving a web of lies with me. I hate lies. They don't work for me."

Thomas finished loading the luggage. When they were seated in the car, Harry said, "Not that I tell my daughters more than they need to know. Anyway, Rebecca thinks you should have dinner with us Sunday evening. Sunday is our usual family night."

They arrived at the tennis courts and played two sets of tennis with Andy and Cody. When they returned to the house, Harry ushered Liz into Rebecca's room. "Something I want you to see."

Thomas and Maddy had unpacked her luggage, hung and folded her clothes in closets and drawers, which they left open so she would know where everything had been neatly stowed away. Even her cosmetics and pills had been arranged in bathroom drawers. Evidently, Rebecca's belongings had been relocated to another guest room.

Liz was surprised and speechless. "I . . . I don't know what to say. It's so very thoughtful." She recalled how comforting his arms were around her the night before, when he held her until she fell asleep. She felt spoiled and pampered.

"Thank you. For making me feel at home."

"My pleasure. That was the idea, to make you feel at home." Harry embraced her with a smile, his blue eyes tearing at her demeanor. "But don't think for a moment that you're sleeping in here."

# CHAPTER FOURTEEN

The afternoon was subdued in the glow of a Bermuda sun. A soothing piano tinkled from the outdoor speakers and enhanced the lazy, relaxed atmosphere. Thomas served lunch on the patio. Afterwards, Cody stretched out on a poolside chaise and attended to her tan. Andy sat at a table reading *Sports Illustrated,* and Harry and Liz lay next to each other on chaises under a patio umbrella. If a bomb dropped, no one would have flinched.

Harry leaned across to her chaise and stroked her smooth, silky skin.

"You know, you ruined me this morning. I'm still wondering what that was all about."

"Just an impulse."

"You don't impress me as an *impulsive* woman."

"Well, you certainly know more about me than I do about you."

"The report?"

"Yes."

"That deals with facts, nothing more. Doesn't profile behavior." He said.

"However," Liz said, "it does *reflect* one's behavior."

Harry sat up.

"Somewhat. But, for instance, it doesn't explain how you managed to maintain such an attractive body." His fingers playfully dawdled around her body—her thighs, her breasts and her stomach.

"How did you do that? You're supposed to have some love handles, or a muffin-bit around the midsection."

"Do what?"

"Stay so fit? You've the body of a teenager. You look like the gals in the exercise videos."

He stopped touching her body.

"The women I've been around who go to the gym always have an issue of some kind, one that can't be remedied, no matter what they try. Heavy thighs, growing hips, cellulite. So, what's your secret, Ms. Brady? Pilates? Sex?"

She didn't know if he was simply complimenting her or really interested in an answer. "Not sex. Haven't been there for some time. Not sure I know what you mean."

"You're in great shape."

"Thank you. I try. I work out at least twice a week."

"And a quarterly visit to Canyon Ranch?"

"No. I guess, you'd say it was an overhaul. I fell into a major depression when my husband died. His illness and death left me in a mess, physically and mentally. I wallowed in grief. I had a weight problem, insomnia, chest pains. I suffered from fatigue, restless leg syndrome. You name it, I had it. Saw an army of doctors. I was hopeless."

"I know what it's like. When my wife died, I felt as if my ego was ambushed, but I had to focus on my daughters' problems, not mine. You were grieving?"

"Yes, totally depressed. And when you're in that state, you don't know it, the degrees of it and how it's affecting you. Maybe the beginnings of menopause also. To make a long story short, I thought I was being treated for a sinus problem or a deviated septum, but the doctor suggested a face lift. He must have read between the lines and recognized I was depressed. He changed my life. My fresh, new face motivated me to nurture my health. I felt alive again, although I did become obsessive."

"Obsessive? About what?"

"About what I looked like. Not only my face, but my body. I saw a therapist, a nutritionist, then Jenny Craig and the gym three times a week. A personal trainer for six months. Overkill."

Liz shrugged. "Once I got rolling, I couldn't stop. I was in excess, trying to fix everything, from spider veins to moles. It was as if . . . as if I traded a remedy for another illness.

"I didn't know the process would heal me inside, but it did. That was a few years ago. I think I'm back in balance, not so nutsy about a wart or a grey hair. I still work out—for health reasons, not for vanity."

"Well you've certainly reaped the rewards. You're very attractive for your age. You must know that."

Then he asked the question she had been expecting him to ask since they met, if not today, tomorrow or the next day.

"How come there isn't a man in your life?"

"How do you know there isn't? That wouldn't be in the report, would it?"

"Well, is there—I mean—a boyfriend? Don't mean to pry, but since you're on vacation alone. You said you were on your own."

He probed a sensitive subject. She had no desire for a male companion in her life and disliked being asked why.

"No. No boyfriend. There was only my husband and no one since."

"Not interested? Seems a shame, you've got so much to offer. You're attractive, very sexy, confident."

"Thanks, but not every woman wants a man in her life. I guess I've had the love of my life. It was quite enough for a lifetime." She didn't want to suggest her chosen predisposition was to be alone, which was the case, yet her answer revealed it all the same.

# CHAPTER FIFTEEN

Liz awoke to birds chirping and sunshine bursting through the window. She showered, stood in doorway of the bathroom in Harry's robe and watched him open his eyes. He propped himself up on his pillow and looked up at her.

"Morning. First one up phones Maddy for coffee."

He buzzed the kitchen downstairs. "Good morning, Maddy. Coffee, for two. Upstairs. Thanks."

"I can't order your housekeeper."

"Yes, you can. It's very simple. Maddy wouldn't challenge you. At the moment, you're the mistress of the house. She's probably in shock since I've never entertained a woman here, so I expect she's already decided we're getting married, because we couldn't be, even for a few days, cohabitating in sin. If you're getting married, it's not a sin."

"You're making fun of her. Guess I'd better get some clothes on."

"No, stay just as you are. I try to spare Maddy her feelings. I'm fond of her and very much appreciate her work ethic and disposition, but she's my employee, and there's no way I'm altering my behavior on behalf of her puritanism. And not yours either. I'm taking a shower. Don't be intimidated."

"Okay."

He's so damn pushy, she thought. And so damn sure of himself and what he wants. He doesn't request, or suggest, he just orders. She muttered to herself how Harry verbally pranced through commands: *Yes, you can. No, stay as you are. Don't be intimidated.*

It was presumptuous of him to think she was intimidated just because she wanted to be dressed when Maddy came to the bedroom. She didn't think it appropriate to be lolling around in front of his housekeeper with only a robe covering her body. Her personal modesty dictated that she be dressed, not that Maddy might have already judged her unfavorably for having slept in his bed. She wanted to tell him that, but decided not to. After all, it was his house, his housekeeper, and she was only a guest.

Generally, she didn't mind his somewhat overbearing personality for he always seemed to have her comfort in mind. She surrendered willingly, knowing she enjoyed his attentions and pampering.

Liz uttered the good morning and thank you pleasantries to Maddy, retrieved the tray of coffee and placed it on the table next to the window. She sat down, poured milk and sugar in her coffee and peered out the window. Her eyes caught a brilliant red cardinal loitering and chirping at the birdfeeder just below the window. It bobbed at the seed, disappeared and reappeared, and blithely behaved as nature intended.

"Ah, I see you've met our free-loading lodger." Harry emerged from the bathroom, a towel strapped around his waist. "We call him *The Chirp.* He's our resident cardinal and nests in that tree across the yard. We supply the feed and he and his mate belt out the warbling. Usually incessant chirping. Can't get passed daybreak without hearing them."

Harry sat across the table from her. His wet hair dripped slightly on his bare chest. He looked out the window, "She's even louder than he is." He added milk and sugar to his coffee and drank.

"He didn't lift a wing to get so beautiful." Liz said. "He just goes about his business—eating, singing, mating. No problems, no thinking, only happening." That's what she thought they were like when they engaged in the act, flowing and happening with each other. Does the cardinal lust and was lust a gift of nature, or merely the incentive to procreate? Of course, mankind was the only species to enjoy sex, she thought, so surely, there was more lust in the world than there were children.

Liz was fascinated with the cardinal. She felt Harry's eyes on her, turned and noticed a grin on his face as he watched her admiring the bird. "Do you know what you want, Ms. Brady?" He gulped more coffee.

"At the moment? I think so. I want to be that bird. Free! No thoughts, no troubles, no world. Feeding and flying. Just being."

"That can be arranged."

"Oh? You have a magic wand and can whisk me off to my fantasy paradise?"

"Well, no. That's not exactly what I had in mind. But it's quite what I want, to take you to that place where there is no reasoning, no thinking, just feeling."

Harry stood up, undid his towel and let it fall from his waist, "I want to kiss your lips, your nose, your ears and whatever part of your body I come upon." He took her hand and drew her up to him, sliding her robe off her shoulders. His hands traveled from her shoulders to her waist, "To get you aroused and see the desire and pleasure in your eyes."

They lay down on the bed and faced each other. He kissed her neck, lodged his tongue in her mouth and caressed her breasts. She inhaled the sweet scent of the almond soap that mingled with the clean scent of his body. He held her hips. They lay side by side staring in each other's eyes. He entered her, retreated, entered her sleek passage again and responded to her when she whispered, "More" His motion propelled her hands to pull his body toward her and intensified her excitement.

"Harry," she moaned and muttered ah's and ooh's of satisfaction. Her cheeks flushed in a pinkish glow that mirrored the hue of her nipples. Her eyes rhythmically blinked and the expression on her face signaled him that she threatened to peak.

"I'm there." She whispered.

"Uh, huh. Whenever you say."

She didn't have time to say when. She let go in a wave of ecstasy and cried out in an euphoric release. Tightly enclosed at the very core of her vibrations, he erupted with her in a rapturous outflow. He kissed her, fell away from her flat on his back, his heart still hammering in his chest. "Didn't think it could get better." He slowly slipped from his high.

Her heart still pounding, she exhaled in a gasp. "I do make a lot of noise though, don't I?"

"Make all the noise you want. It's an added attraction. Not that I need more attraction. You're every woman I've ever wanted and never had."

"I take it that's a compliment, a good thing? We're very compatible. In bed."

Harry kissed her on the cheek, fetched their robes and tossed one on her body and wrapped himself in another. "Yes, a good thing, but that's not what I meant. I hate that word." He said.

"What word?"

"*Compatible.* I spend the better part of every day urging people to be compatible—adjust, change their minds, see another point of view and hopefully eliminate the conflict."

"You mean as the Mayor? Do you hate your job?"

"No. Absolutely love my job. And I'm good at it, getting people to agree, to make adjustments and compromise. I know, it's a contradiction in my thinking and probably my special neurosis."

He stepped toward the bathroom, his back to her. "What I'll never understand in this lifetime is, why can't we want whatever it is, just as it is, without changing it, or altering it? Be at least a little more like *The Chirp*, just being, instead of adjusting, or changing." He paused, turned and looked in her eyes, "I want you exactly as you are. We don't have a difference of opinion or a conflict. We're not compatible, we're outrageously perfect together."

"In bed."

"Yes. Something wrong with that?"

"No. I'm rather enjoying myself. I've had the best sex in the last three days than I've had in years, before and after my husband."

"Really? That's what I mean, enjoying it, just as it is."

"Uh, huh."

"I need another shower. Shower with me?" he asked.

She grinned and followed him.

# CHAPTER SIXTEEN

They arrived in the breakfast room to find Maddy had spread the table with all manner of breakfast food—waffles, strawberries, orange juice. Liz and Harry sat down at the two place settings across from Cody and Andy.

"Morning. How's everyone today?" Harry asked.

Cody sipped her orange juice. "Early evening did wonders for me. Although himself was reading a spy novel in bed and wouldn't turn the light off. I'm putting in an official request for a separate bedroom on our next visit."

"That'll be the day you'll be able to fall asleep on a sofa." Andy said.

Harry poured coffee into Liz's cup. He looked at Cody and then Andy. He smiled at Liz and said, "They never agree."

"I wasn't appropriating a sofa for myself. There are other guest rooms, and I know Harry would accommodate me."

Harry looked at Cody. "Keep me out of this."

"You know I can't sleep if you're not in bed beside me, and if you can't sleep, I can't sleep." Andy said.

Harry turned to Liz, "Don't pay any attention. It's their usual bantering and it'll go on and on. It's meaningless. They're happily married. They've agreed to disagree." He winked at her.

"Now, who has the problem?" Cody said.

"I don't have a problem. If you can't sleep with the light on, you should wear eye patches." Andy said.

"Sure, that's a solution for you, but not for me."

Andy ignored her. He looked at Harry and changed the subject.

"Harry, is Liz going to remove those shackles she put on you yesterday so we can play some golf?"

"Why don't you?" Liz asked. "I could go shopping."

Cody interjected, "Great idea, Liz. Shopping, my passion! Look, you guys go do your thing, and we'll go spend your money. Amenable?" The women nodded in agreement.

"Do you want to meet for lunch?" Harry asked.

Liz and Cody looked at each other and chimed together, "Noooo."

"You can't play nine holes and meet us for lunch." Cody said. "It's nine o'clock already. By the time you eat breakfast, dress and drive to the club, it'll be after ten-thirty. You're not available for lunch."

"Okay, I get it. Don't want us around. Cody, you have to promise me not to tell any tales out of school." Harry said.

Cody squinted and grimaced. "What's that supposed to mean?"

"You know, personal stuff. Girl talk. That sort of thing."

"Are you *asking* me not to talk about you? How would you know?"

"Because I know women. They love to chat."

"You mean gossip, Harry. How dare you speak of Liz and me that way, as if we're common gossipers. I'm appalled. I trust you will understand our conversations shall be of the utmost important and uplifting topics, of course, exercising the usual restraint of discussing the men in our lives."

Cody had the floor and wasn't relinquishing it. "Apart from the fact that you know I am a faithful guardian of your past, what could I possibly say that would influence Liz anyway?"

"Cut. You win." Harry's hands were raised in front of him as if to ward off bullets being shot at him.

"Sorry. I defer to your loyalty. You do love me, and I know you wouldn't dare utter a negative word about me."

• • •

"At Bluck's." Cody said. Thomas dropped Cody and Liz off at Front Street. "Thanks again, Thomas."

"I hope you'll indulge me for a few minutes, Liz. I need to replace some glassware. Then we can browse wherever, have some lunch. Okay?"

"Sure."

Glassware? Not what she would call glassware. The shop was a veritable crystal palace. The lights bounced off the shimmering pieces like fireflies, blinding her so that she could not focus on any single item of crystal on display.

They waited at a counter while the salesperson searched the stock room for the pattern Cody requested. Cody tapped her fingers on the counter. She rummaged through her handbag and pulled out a credit card, and then rhythmically tapped the card on the counter, "Think she's taking a tea break?" She asked.

"It's Bermuda. They're very slow, but very thorough." Liz tried to temper Cody's impatience. "After all this time, I hope she doesn't tell you the pattern you want is not in stock."

Just as Cody strutted in the direction of a customer service desk to seek out a manager, she bumped into her salesperson who was carrying several boxes.

"I am sorry to have kept you waiting, but I needed to examine the glasses carefully before I brought them out, especially since we're shipping them to New York."

Cody paid with her credit card, and she and Liz scurried out of the shop as if they had just been released from jail.

"At last, that's done. Anything you want to shop for?" Cody asked.

"I thought I'd like to buy Harry a present. I had a tie in mind, a pale blue paisley, to replace that bland white one he wore the other night. What do you think?"

"I know just the shop. Around the corner, on Reid Street. Why is it men choose such awful ties? What's worse is they don't know the error of their ways. If he's lucky he has a wife, and she does the choosing. Did you know you can separate the unmarried from the married men in a room by their ties?"

"You've done some research?"

"I'd call it first-hand polling from the days when I was in the market for a man, although the results are probably the same today as they were years ago."

Aston and Gunn was a somewhat upscale shop, and Liz trusted Cody's judgment that it was the place to buy a tie for Harry. They recruited at least three separate salespersons to look for paisley ties and spent more time searching for a tie than buying the crystal.

Cody, an inveterate shopper, picked up a tie, found a blue shirt displayed on a mannequin and propped it up against the dummy. "No, that doesn't work." She chose another tie and tracked down a salesperson who wore a blue shirt and then placed the tie against his neck and muttered, "Ugh, no good."

Finally, Liz found almost what she had visualized—a grey, blue and white paisley motif. "Cody, I think this is it." She thought it would make a subtle fashion statement paired with the blue shirt and white jacket he wore at Chez Mere. Cody agreed.

It pleased Liz to buy a gift for a man who noticeably had everything. If he didn't fancy the tie, she thought he would at least appreciate the thank-you gesture. She wanted to say thank you for the marvelous vacation, especially the way he spoiled her. Being spoiled was a new experience for her.

# CHAPTER SEVENTEEN

"Lunch?"

"Ready if you are. Cody, You won't tell him?"

"Of course not. I wouldn't spoil the surprise." They were on Front Street again. Cody headed straight down the street, intent on her direction. "How about my favorite pub in Hamilton? There's a sweet little outdoor veranda upstairs and very decent food."

"Suits me." Liz said.

Aside from still feeling like the guest, Liz willingly let Cody take full rein for lunch arrangements. She liked Cody and especially valued the quality that Cody wouldn't allow a man to walk all over her. Cody hadn't any qualms about reprimanding both Andy and Harry for obtaining the investigative report. She also took Harry to task when he accused her of gossiping. Clearly, Cody didn't have an assertion problem when it came to men.

Cody and Liz quickly struck up a rapport. Their personalities matched, both of them were cheerfully well-disposed with a lively sense of humor and a live-and-let-live attitude.

"I will warn you, he's going to be very surprised." Cody said. "So be prepared for some, how shall I say, *embarrassment*. He's used to giving the gifts, not receiving them."

They followed the hostess upstairs and sat at a generous table for two. The hostess took their drink order. Cody read the menu and made suggestions. Liz listened, but she couldn't focus on ordering food. *He was used to giving the gifts* echoed and wavered in her mind, hinting that she was being treated like a *bought* woman and not the princess. The thought passed in and out of her mind like sandpipers on the beach scurrying forward and backward to avoid the incoming waves. She had to know and resolve the issue of princess versus mistress.

"Cody, can I ask you something? But I don't want you to answer if you feel you're violating Harry's trust—telling tales out of school, as he called it. I don't want to—"

"Sweetie," Cody interrupted, "I wouldn't tell you anything that would reveal any confidences between Harry and I. I'm glad if I can help. Can't say I've ever been enchanted with the women he's taken up with. It seems they always have ulterior motives in the works, expecting something more from him than him, and obviously you're not from that school, not that it's my place to judge. Don't mind what he said this morning. Ask away."

"Well, when I went upstairs to get my handbag, he stuffed some money in my hand. I guessed it to be more than a thousand dollars, in hundred dollar bills. Whatever. I didn't count. I told him I didn't need any money, and I couldn't accept it. I kept saying I don't do that.

"He got very fussy and annoyed. And repeated again and again. *What do you mean, you don't do that? You need money to go shopping.* I've only seen him angry once. And he got all red in the face, angrier and angrier. Meanwhile, this money is being tossed back and forth, from my shirt pocket to the bureau drawer, back to my pants pockets. He just wouldn't accept no for an answer. I'm not proud. It's just not me. I felt like—I don't know. I can't accept money from men."

"Like a mistress? Cody leaned back and exhaled with a deep sigh. "God help him."

The waitress placed their drinks on the table.

"I left the money on his bureau. I thought he gave in, but when I paid for the tie, the money fell out of a compartment in my handbag. He must have shoved it in my bag when I went to the bathroom. I don't understand. He's so charming most of the time. Although I have noticed he likes to be in control. Stubborn? Is he stubborn? How do I get him to understand, I don't accept money from men. It's just not me."

Cody sipped her pina colada. "Liz, I don't really know what to tell you. When he's adamant, he's immovable. Worse, it sounds as if he was on the verge of a temper tantrum. Of course, it goes without saying that he leads two lives, one public and the other private. The public Harry never has temper tantrums. He's an extraordinary manager of people and problems, and I think those skills often spill out from the workplace into the personal life of the private Harry."

The waitress reappeared and asked for their order. Liz had the same contemplative look on her face as when they first sat down. She ordered a club sandwich and sipped her pina colada. Cody ordered a salad and a local specialty for an appetizer.

"In my opinion, it's the best and the worst thing about Harry. He wants to manage everything and everyone." Cody said.

"I know, it's ego. He has an enormous ego. And it's habitual that he wants to control everything. I've got one at home somewhat like him in that respect, as you've already been acquainted when he ordered that report. Although, I must say, mine has mellowed over the years."

"Sorry, I've put you in a difficult position, haven't I?" Liz asked.

"No, not really. I'm not telling tales when I tell you what is already public knowledge. You must know he has a reputation for being a womanizer. That didn't come from me. It's a known fact.

"The gifts? Money? That's a known fact. He's an overly generous person, not only with the woman he's seeing at the moment, even if it's short term, but generally, with everyone. So, forget the *bought woman.* That is definitely not him. Paying a woman is certainly not compatible with his ego."

Suddenly Cody's face lit up with an enormous smile as if an epiphany had struck her with lightening. "Yesss." The word lingered until the last hiss. "I think I get it now." Cody couldn't resist sharing her newly-found theory.

"What? What do you mean?"

"I think—not really sure."

Cody glanced at Liz, paused and squinted her eyes. She was pensive and serious. Her elbow on the table and the palm of her hand pressed at her chin.

"Bear with me for a moment. Consider this scenario." She waved her hand, pointing her fingers in the air as if conducting an orchestra. "A man has a reputation for being very charming, attractive and seductive. He likes to buy women expensive gifts. And when the seduction is done and the relationship has run its course to the boring stage, he extricates himself for no apparent reason. He retains his confirmed bachelorhood status and has effectively attended to his sexual needs with a clear conscience.

Sort of, *thank you miss, it was very nice, sometimes really good, but goodbye*. Very civilized, don't you think?"

"I don't really understand what you mean."

Cody turned and met Liz eye-to-eye and spoke emphatically: "Harry doesn't want you to know that you don't fit into that scenario. He doesn't want me to tell you about his past relationships. That's what he meant about *telling tales.* I think he feels threatened because he may be on the other side, that you're going to be the one to say, *thank you sir, it was very nice, but goodbye.* He's always the guy who says goodbye. Don't think he's ever been dumped by a woman, at least by someone he cared for."

"Cody, I hardly know the man. I don't have any expectations whatsoever. From what I gather so far, Harry doesn't have any expectations either. We're just enjoying ourselves."

"Ah, there's an uncertainty. I think he does have expectations and he's not admitting it, just feeling it. And, maybe, feeling more than he wants to. In any event, he definitely can't let himself be in the position of being dumped. As usual, his ego and pride must be intact."

The waitress placed their food on the table. They ate. Liz was still in a quandary. Cody had just given her something else to be irritated about besides Harry offering her money. But for the moment, she dismissed what Cody had speculated.

"It's not complicated. I'm just going to be as stubborn as he is and give him the money back. As far as expectations, we're having a great time lusting with each other, and he's been more than gracious and simply wonderful, but that's all it is, lust."

"You do like him, though?" Cody asked.

"Of course, what's not to like? He's a prince. He's always pampering me. Very attentive and affectionate. I don't need to mention, sexy, too. But I've never expected, not for a moment, that our relationship is anything but a short-term encounter, ships in the night and that sort of thing."

Then Liz had an epiphany. Wasn't Cody projecting what she anticipated all along, that at the end of the week—vacation over, fling over? She would, indeed, be the one saying, *thank you sir, it was very nice, but goodbye*, when they returned to New York, but only because that's what she expected realistically, for their fling to be over and appropriated as a happy memory.

The Beethoven chorus of *Ode to Joy* hummed from Cody's cell phone.

# CHAPTER EIGHTEEN

Cody pulled her phone from the bottom of her handbag. "Yes, luv. Well, then, get out of the sun. We're just finishing lunch. I know you've had a beer. Have you eaten? Don't know what we're up to. Thought we might browse some of the jewelry stores. You still want to buy me earrings, don't you? Okay, call me when you're finished. Love y'a, too. Bye."

"They're on the tenth hole. Andy wants to quit. Says it's too hot out there and he's sunburned. He's calling me when they're on their way back. Liz, are you okay?"

"Yes, fine. I know what I'm going to do. I'll give him the money back one more time. If he won't accept it, I'll just hide it somewhere in his bedroom, and tell him where it is when we get to New York. C'mon, let's go buy your earrings."

Cody paid the check and they strolled to the plethora of jewelry stores on Front Street. A delicate pair of diamond earrings in a window display caught Cody's eye. She and Liz went inside. Cody tried the earrings on. "Nope, too small for my lobes. I need something more pronounced, something more provocative."

They checked out the window display of another shop. Cody pointed to spiral-shaped earrings, the diamonds graduating within each curve.

"Stunning setting. Very unique. Still too small for me. That's something that would look good on your tiny ears. Liz, look, it has a matching necklace. Beautiful pieces, don't you think?"

"Yes, very. I'm not a diamond person. If I were, I probably would choose something similar. Very delicate and elegant. If I wear any jewelry, it's pearls. Too bad they're too small for you."

"Let's go inside, see if I can find something."

As Cody entered the shop, Beethoven pealed out again. She stepped outside the entrance door so she could talk on the phone. Liz went inside the shop.

• • •

"Hi, honey. We're on Front Street, a block from Reid."

Cody moved out to the sidewalk and leaned over to view the road. "I see you. Okay, I'll stay here."

No sooner had she snapped her phone shut than Andy and Harry exited from a taxi and approached the shop.

"Hi." Andy kissed her on the cheek.

"I can't seem to find anything," Cody said.

"Harry," Cody pointed over her shoulder to the display window, "in case you're interested, Liz likes those—the spiral ones."

Harry stepped around her and looked at the earrings and necklace. He nodded in approval. "Hmm. Very nice."

They went inside the shop. Harry found Liz in the middle of the store, admiring a menagerie of miniature crystals that were scattered in a display case, her focus on one piece.

"We're going back there." Andy pointed to a counter brimming with displays of diamond earrings. He and Cody walked to the back of the shop.

Harry kissed Liz on the cheek. "Hi. Doesn't look like you gals did much shopping." He eyed the one small bag draped on her arm and asked, "What did you buy?"

"Crystal glasses. Cody had them shipped. We've been looking for earrings for Cody. We've been to a few shops, but she can't find anything she likes. Oh, and I bought you a little thank-you present."

"You bought me a present?"

"Yes. You can't open it until we get back to the house."

Somewhat flustered and surprised, Harry smiled. A man who had everything, it was a foregone conclusion that no one was supposed to give him gifts.

"Does that mean I can buy you a present?"

"Only if you take this money back." Liz pulled the bills from her handbag and stashed them into his shirt pocket.

He accepted the money without a complaint. "Okay, that's a fair compromise. Now, I can buy you a present, right? So, have you seen anything you like?" Harry expected Liz to steer him outside and select the earrings Cody had suggested. Instead, she turned around and pointed, "See that little animal with the stone in the middle of its forehead?"

Harry looked in the display case. "The elephant?"

"Uh, huh. Isn't he beautiful?" Liz asked.

Harry shrugged. What was he supposed to say about a six-inch crystal elephant with a tiny diamond in its head? He humored her.

"Yes, I guess, as elephants go. Yeah, you could say he's beautiful. If that's what you want. Shouldn't it be put on a necklace, or a pin, or something?"

"I collect elephants. He will always remind me of five unforgettable days in Bermuda." She kissed him on the cheek. "Thank you."

Harry smiled. Her eyes sparkled. Liz had that same look in her eyes when they danced, when they watched The Chirp, when they made love. He was elated. Remind her? On second thought, he didn't want the elephant to be a *remembrance* as if it would be relegated to a memory bank of a dead past.

"Liz, see if you can help Cody. I'll take care of the elephant and join you when I'm finished."

Harry signaled to a salesperson. As the salesperson removed the crystal elephant from the display case, he spoke covertly to him: "What's your name?"

"Michael, sir."

"Michael, there's a pair of earrings and a matching necklace in a setting of spiral shaped, tapering diamonds. The jewelry is in the center of the display window. I want you to ship those pieces—earrings and necklace—to New York to the name and address on the back of this card. The paperwork gets mailed to me at the address on the front of the card. Have everything insured. I've signed a check from a local bank. You fill in the amount. You may have to call the bank. Feel free to do so. Can you do that when we leave?"

Michael nodded. "Yes, sir. I trust I can accommodate your wishes."

"Great. Now, Michael, do you see that woman in the back of the store, wearing a white blouse, blue and white pants? The one with the curly blond hair. I do not want her to see you remove the jewelry from the window. Okay?"

"Yes, sir."

"I would suggest waiting until we've left the store and then maybe a few minutes more."

Harry dug out a bill from the crushed money in his shirt pocket and slipped it to Michael, "For your help. If there are any problems, my cell number is on the front of the card. I'm the only one who answers my cell, but please, if you need to call, be discreet and make sure it's me, the printed name on the card. Okay?"

"Yes, sir." Michael read the card. "Thank you, thank you very much, Mr. Bergman. I understand perfectly. Shall I write up a separate transaction for the elephant?"

"Exactly! Thank you, Michael."

Liz stood alongside the counter where Cody posed in front of a mirror, a pair of earrings sparkling from her ears. Cody had given up a successful modeling career years ago, but when it came to fashion and jewelry, once again she assumed the demeanor of a professional. Cody spied Liz in the mirror and turned and asked, "What do you think, Liz? Provocative?"

"They're beautiful. And certainly not too small." Liz said. The diamonds, in a circular setting, almost covered Cody's whole ear lobe.

"Perfect." Harry smiled as he approached the mirror and said, "I applaud you, Cody. You're the only one who can get Andy to spend his money."

Liz thought there must have been a few thousand dollars hanging from Cody's ears, but no one discussed price. It was not a factor.

"Okay, sold?" Andy asked. "I need a beer."

# CHAPTER NINETEEN

Harry and Liz stood at the outside of the front door in their robes and exchanged hugs and goodbyes with Andy and Cody. Thomas loaded luggage into the trunk. Cody called her sweetie again.

Thomas opened the car door and Andy and Cody settled in the back seat. Harry leaned in the car window.

"Send my birthday greetings to your brother."

"Will do. Talk to you later." Andy said.

"Thanks for having us." Cody added.

"My pleasure."

Andy and Cody were leaving to celebrate her brother's fiftieth birthday. Harry hadn't mentioned their impending departure, and Liz only learned that morning that she and Harry would spend their last day in Bermuda alone.

Cody waved from the car and cried out, "Don't forget to tell Liz about tennis."

"Yeah, see you Wednesday. Safe trip."

Thomas drove off.

"Anything special you'd like to do today?" Harry asked as they returned to the breakfast room. He resumed drinking his coffee.

"Have you been to St. George's? I called an old friend in the charter business. He owns a yacht—the *Paradise Isle*. I'm waiting for him to get back to me. If he's available today, he'll take us for a tour around the island, stop wherever or whenever we want. Just the two of us. What do y'a think? Fancy a trip to the other end of the island?"

"Sounds great. I love being on the water."

The phone rang. "Lyle? Yeah, that's fine. Wonderful. Yes, we can be there by noon. Done. At Manny's Marina. See you then. Thanks, Lyle." Harry hung up the phone.

"Okay, we're booked. We've just enough time to pack a change of clothes. Bring something to wear for dinner. You know the rules around here, no flip flops, shorts in the dining rooms. I'll be upstairs in a minute."

Harry paused at the bottom of the staircase, pulled his cell phone from his robe pocket and tapped in a number as he climbed the stairs. Liz could hear him from the bedroom, talking to his mother.

"Yes, enjoying myself. No, Mom, I'll let you know tomorrow. I haven't asked her yet."

Liz removed a cotton pantsuit, shorts, a tee shirt and underwear from the drawers and piled them on the bed. She tossed a pair of sandals from the closet. I'll be packing everything in the morning. She was sorry this was their last day in Bermuda and wanted a few more days with him. She was sad and dismissed the negative thoughts that were rattling in her brain, reminding herself not to ruin today pining about tomorrow. Tomorrow could wait. So could reality.

She carried her clothes into Harry's bedroom and dropped everything on the bed. She wondered what it was he hadn't asked her yet. Maybe it was something Cody said, about tennis?

Harry fetched a small case from a shelf in the closet and placed it on chair.

"Would you like to join us for dinner tomorrow night? I think I mentioned I have dinner with my family Sunday nights. I plan to go to the house straight from the plane. We'd get in New York, actually Tenafly Airport, around five. It's about an hour's drive from there."

"Are you sure?" she asked. "Or is it just convenient, not to make another stop."

"Of course, I'm sure. If you don't want to, I'll arrange for a car to take you into Manhattan."

Liz fiddled with the clothes on the bed.

"You're being polite, asking me to dinner. I really don't want to go into Manhattan by myself. I don't think I would like such an abrupt ending, and it would be much nicer—"

Harry interrupted her, "Hey!" He stretched his arms out and fell across the bed and looked up at her. "If I didn't want to invite you, I wouldn't, especially with my family." He sat up and waited for a response. Liz turned away from his view.

"Are you thinking what I think you're thinking? What do you mean ending?"

He leaned forward and searched for contact with her eyes. "Look at me, Liz. We made a deal, remember? Nothing's ending. Who said anything about an ending, abrupt or otherwise? I thought we'd spend part of the evening together, and I'd see you home."

Liz turned and looked at him. "I'd like that." She pouted. A lone tear fell on her cheek. She got it all wrong again.

"Why are you crying?"

"You must know me by now. I overreact."

She assumed every day of the past few days that their fling ended on Sunday—the end of their vacation. Liz imagined the finality—an amicable parting once they arrived in Manhattan and he dropped her off at her apartment. Maybe at some future, very future time, he'd phone her to meet, perhaps to reinvent the sexual intimacy they had shared.

Harry embraced her. "I take it that's a *yes*."

She snuggled her head on his shoulder. "Uh, huh."

# CHAPTER TWENTY

Harry guided Liz down the ramp to the yacht, his arm folded under hers. Once again, Liz felt like a princess as they walked to the *Paradise Isle*, an impressively huge yacht that overshadowed the boats docked alongside it.

Two crewman wearing formal whites directed them on board and onto the bridge to greet the captain. "I'm Charlie. This is David. Feel free to ask for anything you need. Here, let me take that." David reached for the overnight case Harry held in his hand.

"Captain's waiting on the bridge." David said.

Harry nodded. "Thank you."

Harry knew the protocol. He had been aboard many times, customarily entertaining clients, although not recently, but it seemed nothing had changed in a few years.

Harry and Liz stepped onto the bridge. "How's it going, Lyle? This is Liz Brady. Liz, our captain Lyle Henshaw." Liz nodded.

"And Jones. I see, you're still the standing First Mate. Good to see you guys again." The men shook hands.

"What's the weather?" Harry asked.

Lyle was in a constant gaze, peering over the bridge at the ocean. Occasionally, he checked the dashboard instruments and glanced at Harry when he spoke. The engines revved. "No rain, no winds, a great day for a jaunt around the island. Want the slow route to St. George's? Very calm today."

"Sounds perfect."

"Charlie is serving lunch about two. And David's set you up in Donovan's cabin if you want to freshen up or nap. Remember, no alcohol on the bridge or in the cabins."

Harry and Liz walked to the stairs leading to the lower deck. "Lyle hasn't aged a bit," he said. "He still has a permanent sunburn, the Hemingway beard and that crazy captain's hat he's worn for years. I guess some things—some people—never change."

He explained to Liz, "Donovan's Reef and Key Largo are cabins, named after films, obviously. That's Lyle's sense of humor. The other two are named after beaches in Bermuda, John Smith's and Shelly's."

The mere mention of the cabin name and a memory flashed before him, one Harry didn't want to remember. He had been in the Shelly cabin when his wife walked in and caught him in the act with a client. His wife always hated entertaining, hosting a crowd of suits whose behavior eventually went awry with loose tongues and zippers, including her husband's. She had suspected him of adultery early in their marriage, and when she saw it with her own eyes, she was devastated. She slapped him in the face and never discussed the episode, but the regret and guilt, as it had many times in the past, resurfaced to sting Harry once again.

Lyle extended his head out of the window from the bridge and shouted, "Harry, were you planning to have dinner in St. George's?"

Harry turned and answered Lyle, "Maybe. Presents a problem getting back though, doesn't it?"

"Yeah, I don't want to risk cruising in the dark. Too much coral in these waters."

"We can get a taxi back to Hamilton. Don't think it'll be a problem. You can head out as soon as you've dropped us off."

"Okay, that'll work. Enjoy!"

• • •

High-gloss teak tables and enormous bucket chairs upholstered in bright red, purple and blue colors dominated the spacious lower deck. The bar curved around the lounge and a half a dozen stools hugged the counter. Easy-on-the-ears vocal music from the '60s and '70s permeated the room from overhead speakers. The air was climate-controlled and smelled of lavender mixed with the scent of the ocean.

"Wow, the dance floor is bigger than my living room." Liz said.

David approached them and asked, "Drinks?"

"Dry martini, up. Thanks."

"What can I get the lady?"

"You having a martini?" Harry asked Liz.

"Uh, huh. No olives."

Harry led Liz to a view of the shore and they immersed themselves in the plush cushions of a sofa. The *Paradise Isle* glided out of the marina.

"This is simply glorious." Liz said. She gazed out the window and consumed the view of mansions passing smoothly on the water, pastel-colored houses and contrasting green trees hanging onto the hills.

"We'll be out in the ocean soon." He paused, noticing her eyes aglow.

"Happy?"

"Very."

"Good. That's two of us. How 'bout some fresh air up top?"

"Sure."

"David, we're upstairs," Harry called out as they climbed to the deck.

They spread out on the chaise lounges at the back of the yacht in a canopy-shaded area and avoided the direct afternoon sun of a ninety-degree day. A refreshing breeze whirled about them as they sipped martinis.

"You can't know how much I'm enjoying this." Liz said.

Harry inhaled a deep breath of ocean air. Reminds me of fishing off of Jamaica Bay with my brother, except there isn't another boat on the water."

"Brother? What made me think you're an only child?"

"Well, I guess I am, now. My brother died in a car accident when he was sixteen. I was eleven. I'll always miss him in my life. He was my hero, but I'm I thankful all my memories of him are happy ones."

"I'm so sorry for you. I know what it is to lose someone close. I lost my sister. But at least her son was left to me."

Harry sat up, reacting to footsteps that creaked across the teak deck. "Oops, the crew is approaching."

"Sorry to disturb you. Lunch is ready down below," Charlie said.

The table rivaled the mores of culinary etiquette. Pastel pink and pale purple linens matched the décor of the room. A small vase of a variety of mixed fresh flowers graced the center of the table. Charlie served an arugula salad and baked red snapper and boasted about buying a fresh catch early that morning. The food was as delectable as the table arrangements were elegant.

Liz had experienced luxury before, but not as laidback as it was now. She had tolerated her husband's neurotic driven lifestyle—his need for the best seats in the theater, the best hotel accommodations, the best barber—the high-end of everything. She had understood his propensity for spending money flaunted his success as a trader, but it also engendered stress because he usually overplayed a situation and spent too much money.

Harry's lifestyle hadn't a hint of ostentation or frivolity. He didn't need to impress anyone with his wealth or success. There was no price or prestige suffused in his day-to-day living, only subdued and simple gratification.

Liz and Harry relocated to the sofa after lunch. Charlie served them coffee, and Liz leaned back and snuggled herself in the deep cushions next to Harry. He stroked her head and playfully twirled his fingers around her curls.

"I'm wondering about you."

"What about me?" She asked.

"You spent your whole career working for law firms?"

"For twenty-five years, give or take, not that I'd call it a career. I didn't choose it, it chose me. Lawyers pay well, and, generally, it's secure employment."

"You have a degree. You were never inspired to go to law school?"

"I grew up when girls were brainwashed into marriage and motherhood. I'm grateful I was an exception to the rule and managed to get a degree. Careers were not an objective, much less an option. I don't suppose you would know what I mean, being a man."

"Are you implying I'm a male chauvinist? I must confess I do have first-hand knowledge of female careerists. I'm inundated with them at my office. They're very capable, but too many of them are not very happy. However, I'm not biased against them."

Liz sat up straight, ready for a difference of opinion. "No? But almost all men are, without even knowing it. It's generally accepted, however unspoken in our society, that women are the weaker sex."

"Well, if I'm biased about women in the executive suite it's probably because of my mother. I think of a lifetime of contributions to her family—the love she showered upon my brother and me, and her husband. I view her life as mother and wife to be far loftier and more meaningful than those of any business woman I've ever met."

"But don't you want your daughters to pursue whatever they can be, something more than a wife—an addendum to a man?"

Harry sat up and unintentionally jostled her onto the cushion beside him. He was startled and sneered as he sat erect and faced her.

"Is that your definition of a wife? An addendum?"

"No. I didn't mean that so negatively. I meant—to use a cliché—realize their potential, have equal footing with men on the playing field and not be judged as the weaker, inferior sex."

"Your inferring there's an ongoing competition between men and women. I don't think of life as a competition, and I don't want my daughters to engage in a contest. More important than being a wife, an artist, a CEO, or whatever my daughters choose, I want them to be happy people. They need to learn what makes them happy without the pressures of having to mold themselves to what someone—a teacher, a father or whomever—thinks they should be."

"That's very idealistic." She said.

"Probably. Being happy with oneself is an accomplishment in itself and more difficult to achieve than fame and fortune. Who you are is far more important than what you do for a living."

Liz wouldn't relinquish her viewpoint. "However, there is the reality that women must deal with being treated as inferior human beings. You can't know what it feels like."

"True. Is that what kept you from law school? You have all the trappings of a career woman—intelligence, confidence and, of course, an additional asset, you're very attractive. I haven't detected that you've the ambition that usually goes hand-in-hand with those qualities."

"Is that a compliment or a criticism?"

"Neither. Just an observation." He said.

Liz said with an angst in her voice, "Lawyers do not have my undying admiration and respect, and I've never had the desire, much less the passion, to be one of them."

Harry paused and then bolted from the sofa. "You know what? I think this conversation is far too serious."

"Oh, really? Too confrontational for you? We could argue about something else."

He grabbed her hand and pulled her off the sofa, "No more talking. Up! We're dancing. Can't waste a perfectly beautiful dance floor and '70's love songs."

"You know, I've always thought I grew a thick skin having dealt with conceited and arrogant lawyers and not bothered by their criticisms, but you seem to get under my skin very easily."

"Ah, that's where I want to be—under your skin."

Her hand in his, they stepped to the dance floor a few feet from the sofa. Liz smiled and laughed softly, relieved that the feminism issue fell by the wayside.

Harry held her and swirled her around the floor. He released his embrace and guided her body away from him and back again. He continued to step in rhythm with the music and held her forcefully. She followed his lead and smiled. Her defensive mood mellowed. She loved dancing with him. He did have a way with her, to change her mood and to lead her wherever he was going.

"You're incredibly good at this."

"I sing, too." He joined the chorus of The Four Tops, fastened his body close to hers and in a lilting patter, sang at her ear, *Baby, I need your lovin', got to have all your lovin'.*

"Great fun, thanks." She hugged him. They stood breathless and panting as the last note ended the dance. "I'm done in."

"No, one more. A classic." Frank Sinatra crooned: *You must remember this, a kiss is still a kiss, a sigh is just a sigh.* He put her arms around his neck. "A slow number. I get to hold you very close," he said as he placed her head on his chest and they shuffled in tiny steps about the floor.

"I really don't care if you're a feminist. I confess, I just love to see the fire leap out of your eyes." He said.

*Moonlight and love songs, never out of date, heart full of passion,* Sinatra's voice pealed out across the dance floor.

"Playing with my feelings? Inciting me to react? That's very manipulative."

"No. Definitely not." He said. "I didn't know you felt so strongly about feminism. If I want to play with something, it's your body, not your feelings."

Jones crossed the dance floor. "The captain asked me to alert you, we're about forty minutes into St. George's in case you wanted to shower and change for dinner."

# CHAPTER TWENTY-ONE

Liz and Harry strolled the quaint streets of St. George's and blended with the tourists who teemed into the town on late Saturday afternoons. They leisurely window-shopped. Harry pointed to a pair of sunglasses in a display window. "Let's go inside."

A large woman in a multicolored, floral print dress and a head of flaming red hair approached him. "Aren't you the Mayor? In New York? We're from Buffalo. I saw your picture in the paper with the Governor."

"Well, no. Not right now. I'm on vacation this week. Have a good evening."

Harry shuffled Liz in the shop and looked over his shoulder, hoping to avoid his fan club from Buffalo.

Liz giggled. "You are quick."

"Prerequisite for the job."

*Job*? Liz hadn't given an iota of thought the past few days to her job or work, or for that matter any aspect of her life in New York. She hadn't a care in the world. She was ensconced in a far removed paradise and euphoric with her newly awakened passion and the attentions Harry lavished upon her.

"C'mon, I want to buy you sunglasses." He said.

"I don't want you to buy me anything."

"You want to deprive me of my pleasure?"

"No one could deprive you of anything."

"Really? What's that supposed to mean?"

"Oh, I guess, it means you usually get what you want."

"I'm not getting what I want. I want to buy you sunglasses and you're not cooperating."

"You've already given me more than you know. If you want to buy me something, I could do with a martini." She said.

"Okay. The lady wants a martini. A martini it is."

Harry led her out of the shop, across cobblestoned King's Square to a queue of taxis. He approached a driver who was idly leaning on his taxi, waiting for a fare.

"We need a taxi to the San Remo."

"Yes, sir. It's about twenty minutes up the old Surf Road. I know it well."

"Great." Harry and Liz entered the taxi. The driver drove up a rural, tree canopied road, replete with the pothole remnants of a Bermuda rainy season.

"I'm sorry, sir, for the bumpy ride, but this is the only road to the San Remo, and I'm afraid it needs repaving." The driver said.

"No problem. We're enjoying the air conditioning. And the carnival ride." He said. Each time the taxi engaged the considerable bumps and tossed their bodies at each other, they broke into laughter. The road wound circuitously around the steep hillside and after another treacherous turn, Liz collapsed on his body.

"You may as well stay on my lap, where I can hold you and keep you from hitting your head."

"Thank you. You're always taking care of me."

He broke into a broad smile. "Taking care of you seems to be my mission."

Finally, the taxi stopped at the top of a hill. Surrounded by trees and foliage so thick, the façade of the restaurant was completely obscured. Harry paid the driver and asked him if he had any interest in picking them up later and driving them to the Hamilton.

"Yes, sir. Sure. Here's my card. Just ring me when you're ready."

"Great! Talk to you later."

They entered the restaurant. The red checkered tablecloths, lit candles and the ubiquitous odor of garlic sent the message that the restaurant was an informal and cozy neighborhood establishment. A waiter approached them.

"We'd prefer to sit outside," Harry said.

The waiter directed them through the restaurant to the patio, sprinkled with only four tables and offering a panoramic view of the ocean. No one was eating outside, although the sun's heat had weakened and the temperature waned. The sun was slowly dropping and dusk promised a beautiful sunset.

"Oh, Harry, this is fantastic. The whole place to ourselves?"

"Giovanni doesn't kowtow to tourists, says they're more trouble than they're worth. He caters to local clientele who seem to want the air conditioning inside tonight instead of the great view out here."

"Giovanni?"

"The owner and chef, if he's still here."

The waiter interrupted, "Signore, something to drink?"

"Grey Goose vodka martinis, very dry. One with olives and one without." The waiter ceremoniously pulled a chair out that was lodged against the table, wiped the seat with a cloth from his arm and motioned for Liz to sit. He repeated the same ritual for Harry.

Is there any music tonight?" Harry asked as he sat.

"Si, signore. About twenty minutes, he comes to play."

"Giovanni still doing the cooking?"

"Si. You know him?"

"Yes."

The waiter handed them menus and left.

"Very romantic, Harry. Music, too?" Liz said.

"A guitar player, sometimes belting out an Italian song, at least the last time I was here."

A few minutes later, a large man in a typically white apron and chef's hat hurried to the table, the waiter following him with a tray of drinks. Harry stood up and grabbed Giovanni's extended hands.

"Buona sera, Harry. Come stai? So very, very nice to see you again. How you been? And des figili? Why so long you don't come to see me?"

"The girls are fine. Haven't been to Bermuda. Not like the old days. This is Liz, Giovanni."

"Hallo, very nice to meet you." Giovanni smiled, nodded his head and bowed to Liz.

"Lemme know what you wanna eat. I make ah some thing special for you tonight, eh?"

"Thank you, Giovanni. Good to see you again."

"You tell Tonio. I make it for you." Giovanni retreated to the kitchen.

"The old days? Did you come here with your wife? It's very romantic."

"No, with my daughters. Sometimes Cody and Andy came with us. The girls were a mess after my wife died, and we came to Bermuda often. I thought getting away would help. They loved the boat ride. Lyle's crew would entertain them, play cards, hide and seek and then we'd come up here for lunch and eat outdoors.

My daughters loved this place. Giovanni treated them like little princesses. They were very young, too young to lose their mother."

"Cancer?"

"Yeah, ovarian cancer. Three months watching their mother die. They were so grief-stricken they would break down in tears at the mere mention of her name or at the sight of her picture."

Harry looked across the patio, gazed at the ocean and the looming sunset. He eyed his martini and skimmed the glass with his finger, almost tipping it over. He sipped his drink. "They broke my heart every day. She was a wonderful mother who indulged them unconditionally, and they missed her terribly."

"They went to live with your mother?"

"My mother was a Godsend. She gave my daughters the semblance of family again, during Susan's illness and afterwards. But she did have issues, issues with me. She loved my wife and knew she was unhappy, and it was all my fault. They were very close—the daughter she never had. She blamed me. It took her a long time to forgive me."

"It's one thing to lose your wife, but cancer can't be your fault?"

"Not my fault that she had cancer or died, but that she was unhappy. My marriage wasn't—well, what one would call happy. Let's just say my mother had her reasons, valid reasons. I don't want to go there right now, if you don't mind. How about another martini? Food?"

"I don't understand. Why? She had a home, a husband, children."

"That's because you're biased. I take it Cody didn't fill you in about my marriage. I want to kiss you." He leaned over and placed his lips on hers in a long, amorous kiss.

"Are you in that sort of mood already?"

"I look at you, and I'm in the mood. I'm remembering this morning and the time before, and the time before that. It's our last night in Bermuda."

"You're changing the subject. You don't want to talk about your wife." Liz twirled the martini in her glass and looked out on the ocean. "I don't understand what you mean. But it's okay. You don't have to talk about it."

"Liz, it's called guilt."

"Huh?"

# CHAPTER TWENTY-TWO

Harry, once again, was filled with remorse about his failed marriage and steered the conversation to food. "Let's eat," he said, picking up the menus. "Pasta? If you like an authentic Italian sauce, unlike the sauce usually served in Bermuda, you're safe with Giovanni. He does the real thing, not to mention how long it takes. I think we'd better order an appetizer. Hungry?"

"Yes. You choose. You know the food here. Anything but fish."

Harry signaled for Tonio's attention, ordered more martinis and an antipasto.

"This time tomorrow, we'll be in New York." She said.

"Hmm, having dinner with my mother and Uncle Ted, and my daughters. Are you okay with that?"

"Uh, huh. I'm looking forward to meeting your daughters. You're mother sounds a bit scary."

Tonio returned with the drinks, recited the specials of the day and penciled their order on a pad. Guitar strings plinked in the background.

"Didn't mean to give you that impression. Believe me, my mom is not scary. Actually, she's a sweet, loving lady. Sometimes she can be outspoken, maybe too blunt at times."

"She does love you?"

"Of course. I don't fault her. And I do love her. She's my mother."

"What do mean by fault her?"

"For being angry with me. She missed Susan as much as my daughters did. There was nothing but grief when my wife died. I was a bastard in my marriage. Although I was discreet, I cheated on Susan all the time, and I was never there for her, but she was always there for me, for whatever I asked. My mother knew. She actually told Susan to divorce me. And when Susan wanted to leave, I wouldn't let her go."

"Why were you cheating?"

He looked away from her again. His eyes searched all over the patio, then up at the sky and over the patio railing at the ocean for some place to rest—any place, except her eyes.

"Not everybody gets married for the right reasons, Liz. My marriage was convenient. I was busy with me and my career. I had been seeing Susan on and off for years and she was always available to me. For sex especially."

He tapped his fingers on his glass. "I was well past thirty and bachelors were not promotable material in those days. I realized I needed to settle down. She was a looker. I thought of her as an uptick in my career, a wife who could entertain clients, impress company management—an asset."

"A trophy wife?"

"No, nothing like that. A beautiful woman who had substance. She was very intelligent and capable. Talented, too. I knew she loved me, and I thought that would be enough."

"You had two children together."

"That's the only happiness I gave her—two daughters. She wanted me, and I was never available. I never made the effort to meet her halfway."

Finally, he made eye contact with Liz. "It took a few years. She asked me for a divorce. We didn't grow apart. It wasn't like that, as if we had been together in the first place, if you know what I mean."

Harry stood up, his drink in his hand, turned and walked a few feet to the railing of the patio. He looked out at the ocean, pausing in what seemed an endless silence. He returned to the table and sat down again.

"I did love her though. She was my daughters' mother. When we didn't share a bedroom anymore, she had an affair with a younger guy who wanted to marry her. I told her I'd give her a divorce, but I wouldn't let her take my daughters, and I'd use the adultery to get custody of the girls. I knew she wouldn't leave me without her children."

Liz repositioned herself in her seat, shifting her body weight from one side to the other. Her eyes blinked excessively. She wanted to cry. She thought of her mother, suffering a life of bondage and subservience for the sake of her children. She knew her mother's marriage to her father was unhappy, but she never understood why her mother had tolerated his abuse until, on her deathbed, she confided to Liz, *You do know I wanted to leave him. I was only the handmaiden. His daughters were his reason for living. He loved you girls and wouldn't let me take you from him, and I couldn't give up my children.*

Liz, in absolute sympathy with Harry's wife, curled her mouth, her teeth bearing down and stinging her lip. Her body went rigid, exhaling generous sighs. Not that she was a diehard feminist, but what she thought were her past fears of being controlled by a husband suddenly resurfaced.

"What's wrong?" Harry asked. He noticed Liz's contorted face and rigid tense muscles around her neck.

"Men can be such tyrannical pigs." She said.

Harry leaned back in his chair and cringed, "I know, I'm loaded with the evidence, and, believe me, the guilt doesn't go away because you want it to." His voice trailed off in meaningless muttering.

Liz heard the repentance in his words. He didn't love his wife when he married her. Her mother had made the same mistake as Harry's wife, falling in love with a tyrant, loving him and empowering him to control her. At least, Harry learned to love his wife, but nonetheless he was still suffering from his past sins.

"Why does marriage cause such pain?" She asked.

"Hmm, I suppose, because we're all human and make mistakes, the wrong decisions and sometimes very selfish choices."

Giovanni appeared with an enormous tray of food, not only what Harry ordered, but plates of some of Giovanni's specialties.

"Just for you, I make a special spinaci. And a little taste of my gnocchi. Howa bout some vino?"

"Thank you, Giovanni. You know, we won't be able to eat all this food. No, no wine. Thank you."

The table was replete with platters of a taste of this and a taste of that.

"Ciao, Harry. I gotta go for the grandbaby party tonight." Harry got up and they shook hands. "Thanks again." Harry said.

"Doncha be so long to come see me. Eh?" Giovanni said. "Ciao, Miss. Nice to meet you." He bowed to Liz again and left them to their meal.

Tonio returned to the table, took their napkins from the table, placed them across their laps and dispensed minute portions of food to each of their plates. The guitarist wandered in playing *Al di la.*

"Signore, martinis?" Tonio asked.

"Not for me. I need food." Liz said. Harry nodded, "No, thank you."

In between placing morsels of chicken piccata in her mouth and forkfuls of gnocchi, Liz sporadically hummed along with the guitarist who strummed *Malafemmena.*

"This is a song about a very bad woman." She said. "She's sweet and has the face of an angel, but she's not an angel and betrays the man in her life. He can't forgive her. He loves and hates her at the same time. It's very sad."

As the result of two martinis, Liz lost her inhibitions as well as her editing skills. She babbled whatever thought occurred to her. "May I kiss you? Why do I always want to kiss you? Of course, you're very handsome—very sexy." She dallied and picked at her food, not eating any more.

Harry stopped eating. He kissed her on the cheek, pulled his phone from his pocket and left a message for the taxi driver.

"I'll bet women find you irresistible. Have you been with a lot of women?" She pointed her fork at him.

"My share, maybe more than my share. Why?"

"I'll bet you've a parade of women following you around." Her speech slowed and slurred somewhat. "Do you make love to them the same way? I mean—"

"What?"

Her words veered all over train tracks, going in diverse directions at the same time.

"That's why you're so expert in bed."

"Oh, am I? You finished eating?"

"Uh, huh." She dropped her fork on the plate.

"How about some coffee?" He asked.

"Yes. I would . . . love some cof . . . fee."

Harry signaled for Tonio. He ordered two large espressos. Tonio returned and cleared the table. Liz hummed again with the music and swayed in her seat.

"Y'a know, I've had my share as well."

"Oh?"

Her arms were in the air and her fingers dangled as she closed her hands together. "With you though, it's like, you plug in the outlet—" she paused, "and, bam, the lights go on!"

Tonio served coffee. It must have been the *bam*. Harry recalled her gestures and the unique description of his supposed expert lovemaking and her climaxes. He sipped his coffee, smiled and then released a soft laugh.

"Not funny. Haven't had an elec . . . tri . . . cal failure yet." She drank the last of her coffee.

Harry gestured to Tonio for the check. He anticipated Liz might be unsteady when she got up and stood up and moved next to her chair.

They waited in the front of the restaurant for the taxi. Her head rested on his shoulder.

"You do have the most beautiful blue eyes. Very sexy."

"And I'm an expert in bed." He added.

No sooner had they sat in the taxi, Liz placed her head in his lap. She pulled her legs up on the seat and fell asleep. Harry leaned his head back and dozed off. He was surprised and delighted she spoke of her pleasure when they made love and his beautiful blue eyes. He realized, of course, her words had been spoken under the influence of two martinis.

# CHAPTER TWENTY-THREE

Liz and Harry arrived back in Hamilton after ten o'clock, sated and sleepy. They went directly to the bedroom. Liz dropped her clothes on the floor beside the bed, too tired to bother about sleepwear. He kissed her goodnight on the cheek. She crawled under the sheets beside him and fell asleep.

Hours later, in the middle of the night, Harry felt a knee plunge into his ribs, awakening him. He sprang up to an erect position and found Liz squirming and struggling with some unknown demon while soundly asleep. He shook her gently and woke her. When she opened her eyes, she grabbed him with both arms and clutched his waist. She trembled, and he rocked her in his arms until the torment left her body.

"Bad dream? You okay?"

"Uh, huh. I was running and running, away from something—something—very ugly."

Harry helped her out of the bed. She leaned on his shoulder as they hobbled to the bathroom. He sat her down on a chair. "Don't move."

Liz sat limp, her head bent over. Harry dropped his pajamas on the floor, placed his hand under her arm and supported her into the shower. She wobbled as he held her in an embrace and positioned her back in the stream of water. After a few minutes of water beating on her body, she withdrew herself from his arms and stood gasping.

"Thanks," she murmured.

"Feel better?"

"Yeah, much better. But I don't get nightmares."

"Maybe too many martinis."

"I did overdo it. I seem to keep falling apart in your company. Sorry. Thanks for rescuing me again."

"No problem. I rather enjoy being your knight in shining armor."

She smiled and impulsively grabbed the body wash and lathered his back. She turned him around, rinsed the foam from his body and knelt down; the water splashed on her head as she licked and sucked him until he grew hard inside her mouth. He withdrew himself and reached to touch her, but she stepped backward and away from him each time his hands approached her and reached to kiss her nipples or to fondle her breasts.

"You've ruined me for other men. I want to ruin you for other women."

Liz stood dripping at the other end of the shower, out of the same stream of water he stood in. She sulked. He turned the water off.

"C'mere." Harry extended his hand, pulled her to his chest and held her around her waist. "It's never been like this for me either." They stood in the shower nude, dripping, shivering and abandoning foreplay.

"I'm freezing." Harry led her out of the shower and they wrapped themselves in robes.

"Better?"

"Uh, huh."

"Something warm to drink?"

"Tea?" she asked.

"Think we can arrange that."

• • •

They clung to each other as they stepped barefoot down the stairs to the kitchen. Harry prepared tea while she sat at the breakfast table and watched him opening and closing cabinet doors.

"Now, if you were Maddy, where would you hide the cookies?"

"In a cookie jar? Over there." She pointed to a large crockery tub in the corner of the counter.

They sat side by side in the breakfast room chomping on Cadbury biscuits and drinking tea. It was four o'clock in the morning.

"Sorry vacation is over?" he asked. He wondered if their last night in Bermuda precipitated the conflict she seemed to be experiencing. She said she *wanted to ruin him for other women.* She wanted to seduce him, but she didn't want him to participate.

"Yes. It has to be over sometime."

"Well, it's not as if we won't see each other in New York."

"Harry—" Before she could continue speaking, he kissed her amorously, savoring the residue of tea she had just gulped. He ran his tongue between her breasts and caught the falling drops from her wet hair as his erection escaped from beneath his robe. She leaned back and moaned. Her body writhed and burned with desire.

When they returned to New York, he would resume his lifestyle. If her desire for him waned, there would be other women who would indulge him, but it would never be her. No woman would ever respond to his touch and escalate his excitement the way she did. His pleasure and excitement had become intrinsically enmeshed in her desire for him.

He thought he knew what she was thinking when she spoke of women parading after him. She wouldn't compete with other women and needed to hear that he wanted her as much as she wanted him, that she was the only woman in his life.

Harry brought his head up, kissed her neck and whispered in her ear, "If you need to know, you've ruined me for other women, about four days ago."

It didn't matter if she believed what he said. He meant it. He needed to tell her and to assure her she wouldn't be a part of his past.

The last four days culminated in a last passionate session of lovemaking. Harry touched her inside, first with his finger then with his tongue. She stroked his erection with both her hands, and put him in her mouth. He moved away from her. He wanted to feel her vibrations that pulsed around his flesh.

In the throes of arousing each other, they indulged in horseplay of a kind—patting each other on the ass, vying as to who could give the loudest kisses, chasing each other and throwing pillows.

"No more," she said.

"Okay. Here." He positioned her on top of him and gently slipped his finger inside her, tantalizing her and arousing himself as well.

"Please, Harry."

Harry withdrew his finger and pushed himself inside her. Drenched with wetness, her slippery passage opened quickly as he pushed forward and backward, again and again in a state of ecstasy.

"I'm—" she stammered and erupted in dense beats against his erection and caused him to climax in rhythm with her vibrations. "Harry—," she cried out in an intense crescendo.

# CHAPTER TWENTY-FOUR

"Yes, coffee. Thanks, Maddy." Harry hung up. It was his eight o'clock wake-up call. Liz hadn't budged when the intercom buzzed. He watched her sleep, grinned and tossed the curls off her forehead. He leaned forward and softly placed his lips on her cheek. She opened her eyes.

"Morning," he said. "Dream again?" He continued to finger and play with her curls.

"Morning. A good one this time. The prince kissed the frog and she turned into a princess."

"Isn't the princess supposed to kiss the frog and he turns into a prince?"

"Apparently, my dream is very subjective. I'm the ugly duckling—the frog."

"Did they ride off to the castle and live happily ever after?"

"Didn't get to the *happily ever after* part. You woke me up."

Maddy knocked on the door and interrupted their fairy-tale chat. Harry brought the tray of coffee to the table and sat across from Liz.

"Sleepy?" He asked. "We didn't get much sleep last night, did we?" He poured coffee, sugar and milk, and stirred.

"I didn't need sleep. I needed you." She said.

"Me, too." Harry kissed her on the cheek, smiled and handed her a coffee.

Liz reflected on their last evening together and sipped her coffee. She remembered everything she said and everything he said. She would never forget what he said to her when she needed him to say it. *You've ruined* me for *other women, about four days ago.*" That might have been true at that moment. She didn't consider what might be in the offing.

"We have to leave for the airport by eleven. I want to be there about noon when the pilot does his pre-flight run-throughs. I told Maddy we'd be down for breakfast in half an hour or so. Do you want her to help you pack after breakfast?"

"No, nothing much to pack, almost everything's laundry." She stood up and took another sip of her coffee. "Better get hopping." She fled into the bathroom.

• • •

Harry looked forward to the evening, knowing the day would be spent packing, driving to and from airports and attending to the mundane aspects of traveling. At least they'd get to spend a part of the evening together, even if they wouldn't be alone.

He couldn't remember when he felt so good in someone else's company, on a high for four days. He marveled that in less than a week his manhood had been restored to him with a renewed vigor. Liz stirred emotions he hadn't felt with another human being. He wanted to be with her, to see her smile across the dinner table, to stroke her body, to hold her, especially when she needed him.

A moment later, he cautioned himself to slow down and try to inch back to reality. He recalled one of Andy's favorite quotes that was supposed to inspire him to slowly apply the brakes when he got smitten with a woman: *It's okay letting yourself go so long as you can get yourself back.* But what was he supposed to be going back to?

The day vanished in compulsory activities. They ate breakfast, packed their luggage and said their goodbyes to Maddy. Thomas drove them to the airport, and they boarded the plane at noon. Besides Harry and Liz, there were very few passengers. When he finally returned from conferring with the pilots, he sat down next to her.

"Where have you been all day?" Harry asked as he embraced her, inhaled her scent and kissed her on the cheek.

"The chair recedes into a lounge." He demonstrated. "Nod off, if you want. I'm getting a martini. Do you want one?" He signaled the flight attendant.

"Only one." If I'm meeting your family I don't want to be in the condition I was in last night at the restaurant."

"I thought you were very funny. One minute you were telling me the story of an Italian song, the next minute you were describing yourself in the depths of an orgasm. Remember?"

"You mean the *bam* thing? Yeah, but I'd like to forget it. I don't think your family would appreciate a command performance of last night."

The flight attendant came down the aisle, checking that passengers were buckled in their seats. The plane taxied to the runway. "Can I get you something before we take off?" she asked.

"No, thanks. We're fine." Harry said as he handed the glasses, still half full, to the attendant.

"Can you hold my hand?" Liz asked. "I've a bad case of nerves about take-offs and landings."

Harry held her hand and put his arm under hers, "Try to think of something else. Imagine we're in that back seat, over there. Of course, there's no attendant. We're all alone. And I'm undoing your blouse, button by button. I'm just about to kiss—"

"You're incorrigible."

"I'm trying to distract you."

"And get both of us into a state."

Harry leaned over, his blue eyes fixed on hers. "I rather fancy that state." He gave her a short kiss on the lips.

Liz leaned back in her seat. "I'll just close my eyes and take deep breaths. Nice, slow, controlled breathing." Her chest swelled as she inhaled deeply. "Suck in some nice, fresh cabin air. Exhale, one, two, three four. Inhale, one, two, three, four."

Liz concentrated, apparently not for the first time, seriously practicing an exercise and trying to fend off her anxiety of the plane taking off. Harry watched her, as she inhaled and exhaled and counted to four.

Liz closed her eyes and squeezed his hand. Her hands were clammy. Her face reddened and she pressed her head into his shoulder. Harry could feel her tense and rigid body against his chest. She was practically seated in his lap when the plane lifted off. He unbuckled his seat belt and struggled to put his arms around her.

"It's over, we're off the ground." He said.

Liz nodded, "Sorry." The red glow on her cheeks subsided to a pale pink. She unbuckled her seat belt. He held her for a moment and she sighed in relief. She unfolded her body from his arms and leaned back in her seat. "Thanks."

Reacting to her stress and comforting her had almost become a reflexive action for him. His anger vanished when she wept. After her bout with a nightmare, he held and hugged her until she recovered. He read her face the evening before and anticipated the forthcoming tears. Now, he felt her fear.

He never would have supposed the emotions of this confident and independent woman could be out of balance. Every time he sensed she was distressed, he wanted to hold her in his arms and tell her everything would be all right, or he'd make it all right. He didn't know if he could ever get back, or that he wanted to get back to the person he was before he met her. He much preferred the person she inspired in him—the person she needed.

# CHAPTER TWENTY-FIVE

Unknown to Liz, the plane had begun its descent. Harry persuaded her into a competition to distract her from the landing. He removed a pen and pad from his attaché and handed it to her.

"Beginning with the letter "A," then "B," etcetera, write down five film stars, last names only."

"You're kidding me, Harry, we're playing games?" Liz looked at him in disbelief.

"Humor me. Is your seat belt buckled?"

"Uh, huh."

Earnestly and in his ordering mode, he said, "We have five minutes. Whoever has more names, wins. Of course, I get to do the grading."

"Oh? What am I winning?" She looked at him askance.

"A martini, maybe a few hugs on the way to Westchester. Eventually, sex." He winked at her and set an alarm on his cell phone.

A pad on his knee, Harry turned his back to her. "Okay, start now."

"All right." Liz relented and began writing. *Patty Austin, James Arness*—don't know if he's considered a film star—*Ben Affleck, Alan Alda.* She rested her chin on her fist and tried to think of another name. "This isn't so easy." She went on to the next letter and wrote: *Harry Belafonte, Ingrid Bergman, and Humphrey Bogart.*

The wheels of the plane touched ground with a loud bump. Suddenly, she looked up, startled by the noise.

The alarm on Harry's cell phone peeled out. "Stop. You win." He said.

Liz leaned over and looked at the pad on his knee. It was blank. The pilot chimed from the overhead speakers: *The weather in the New York metropolitan area is clear and sunny, about seventy-five degrees. Thank you for your patronage with NetJets, serving all your private travel needs. I trust you've had a pleasant trip. Please remain in your seat while we taxi to the hangar. Have a wonderful day.*

Liz grinned. The palms of her hands were as dry as desert sand. "Thanks. You really know how to rescue me from myself."

"Just let me know when you plan your next trip. I'll be happy to accompany you."

Harry's driver, Tom, waited at the hangar, standing next to the car. "Hi, Boss. Good trip?" He gave Harry a soft hug.

"Yes, very good. How you doin'? How're the kids?"

"Good. Everything's good."

Tom extended his hand to Liz. "Hi, I'm Tom Bellamy."

"Liz Brady. Good to meet you." She shook his hand.

Tom was a well built, thirty-two year old, the remnant of a baseball career that never launched because of an accident that left him with a limp. Although he worked at sports writing and memorabilia shows, he relied on his steady job with Harry to support his family.

Tom loaded the luggage into the trunk of the car. His driving schedule wasn't supposed to include Sundays, but for the past few years, he accommodated Harry and made the same trip on Sunday in the late afternoon. Since there were so many hours Harry didn't use him, he reciprocated by being available for Harry on an informal, on-call basis. He didn't mind if Harry needed him at eight in the morning or eleven at night. He'd be there, and for whatever he could do besides driving. Harry appreciated having such an amenable and flexible guy working for him.

The car pulled up to a huge, colonial house, set behind the street by a hundred yards of scattered mature oaks and a rolling lawn. There were at least six bedrooms with green shuttered windows everywhere and an enormous backyard enclosed with flagstone. Liz could see water shimmering in the pool as they drove up the circular driveway. Harry rang the front door bell, announcing his arrival, and opened the door.

Rebecca rushed down the stairs to greet him. "Dad!" She threw her arms around him and turned and looked at Liz. "Hi, I'm Rebecca." She extended her hand.

"Liz. Good to meet you." They shook hands. Impressed with her natural beauty, Liz viewed Rebecca's high cheekbones above a wide chin and penciled lips. A blush of pink blended across her creamy and flawless complexion. She wore her brunette, auburn-streaked hair in a straight style that touched her shoulders. A band held her hair off her face.

"What the hell is that?" Harry pointed at her shorts that clung to Rebecca's body, emphasizing every curve of her thighs and buttocks.

"Dad, I don't wear these outside."

"Guess what? You're never wearing them again, inside or outside this house. Upstairs!"

Rebecca looked at Liz, and then shook her head back and forth as she fled up the stairs to her bedroom.

Harry took Liz by the hand and steered her down the hallway. "I don't know where she gets it from. Isn't there a fucking mirror in her room?"

Liz looked sideways at him. "Hey, I think she got your message."

"Sorry. I just don't understand why she can't see that she's walking around in her underwear. She's not a child. For chrissake, she's seventeen."

The family room was at the back of the house. It was an informal, large cozy room—the sort of very lived-in room that appealed to Liz. A floral sofa and burgundy chairs in a seating area included mahogany tables beside them. At the other side of the room, a recliner was situated in front of the television. Magazines and newspapers were scattered on the top of an oval mahogany table against the wall.

When they entered the room, Harry's mother got up from what appeared to be her exclusive chair. Harry kissed her on the cheek. "How you doin', Mom?"

"You know, same old, same old."

"Mom, this is Liz, Liz Brady."

"How nice to meet you. Come over here and sit near me."

"Good to meet you, too, Mrs. Bergman."

"Please call me Molly. I haven't been Mrs. Bergman for a very long time. Not since Harry's father passed."

Molly sat down and Liz sat on the sofa across from her. "Harry, help Elena to get us some drinks. What would you like, Liz? You drink martinis like him?"

"I do, but I think I'd like a dry sherry, or a wine."

"The usual for me, Harry."

"Mom, where's Sarah?" Harry asked.

"She went to the park to take some pictures. She only went for an hour."

"Oh." He turned toward Liz and explained, "My daughter has a passion for photography. She'd rather take pictures than eat or sleep." Harry left the room.

"So, you had a good time in Bermuda? Beautiful house?" Molly asked.

"Yes, very beautiful, unlike anything I've ever seen. I had a wonderful time. I think Harry did, too. I'm sure he'll fill you in."

"No, he won't. That's why I sent him out of the room, so we could talk."

Molly had a hint of makeup on her eyes, a bit of powder and lipstick, and snowy white hair wrapped in a bun at her neckline. Quite a handsome woman, Molly was pleasing to look at. Liz noticed Harry had inherited his eyes from Molly who had the same lively, midnight blue eyes.

"You've a lovely figure. You haven't been in menopause yet?" Molly asked.

"Supposedly, I'm finished with that. But lately I've been wondering. I've had a few mood swings."

"Some women are very lucky. They don't put on a pound. You look so fit."

"I work at it. I'm at the gym at least twice a week. Careful about what I eat."

"I know my son wouldn't tell you. So, I will. He's had the good judgment not to flaunt women in front of his children. He's never brought a woman here. That makes you very special to me. And to the girls. He doesn't tell much. But he may as well have when he said on the phone, *Please, Mom, don't ask me a lot questions.*"

Molly paused. "I don't embarrass you, do I?"

"No, I'm not embarrassed. But to be perfectly honest, we don't really know each other that well for me to be—well—special. We only met last week."

In only a few minutes seated across from Molly, Liz sensed her warm and simple personality. There were no airs or hidden meanings in her conversation. A cheerful and outspoken lady approaching eighty or so years, when she spoke, she gestured with her hands and expressed a liveliness for her age.

"Well, now you know you are, even if you only just met. It's important, you should know. He's my son, but he doesn't know about women at all. He's been with too many of the wrong kind. Not bad women, but the wrong kind, if you know what I mean."

Molly paused momentarily. "And he can't help being the boss. He gives orders all the time. And instructions. How to do this or that. Has he been bossing you around?"

Molly released her intense gaze at Liz when Elena and Harry entered the room. Elena carried a tray of drinks.

"Liz, this is our Elena." Molly introduced her as if she were a member of the family. "She's our irreplaceable blessing who keeps everybody in this house smiling." Molly touched her arm affectionately.

Elena, an efficient and down-to-earth, slim Polish immigrant, undertook most of the chores in the household. More importantly, she could put reins on Molly, make her take her medications and humor her when she became irritable with the pains of arthritis. She also pampered Molly's elderly brother, Ted.

"Elena, this is Liz Brady."

"Good to meet you, Miss." Uncharacteristic of Elena to voice an opinion, she added, "Welcome to the family. They've been waiting for you for a very long time."

"So true, Elena." Molly smiled.

# CHAPTER TWENTY-SIX

"Okay, Mom, you've had your fifteen minutes," Harry blurted as he sat down on the sofa next to Liz and handed her the sherry from the tray. Elena leaned forward and offered Molly and Harry their drinks.

"Apart from Rebecca walking around in her underwear, what have my daughters been up to?"

"Oh, you saw her *new* look, she calls it. She won't listen to me. She's got that streak of yours, that attitude—I'm going to do what I'm going to do. So?"

"I sent her upstairs to change. She's pissed." He sipped his martini. Uncle Ted on the porch, napping?"

Molly nodded and then leaned toward Liz and explained. "My brother. He's "eighty-five, likes his scotch and cigar out on the porch. Then naps like a baby."

Sarah burst into the room, flushed and sweaty. Her jeans bore brown residue at the knees, evidence of recent dirt that no longer clung. Unmistakably Rebecca's sister, she had the same creamy complexion and bright blue eyes. She was as much a natural beauty as her sister. The only apparent difference between them was Sarah's hair which was an ash blond color with curls that rambled all over her head. Her hair was coarse, curly and thick like Harry's.

Sarah plopped down next to Harry and kissed him on the cheek. "Hi, Daddy." She sat upright and lady-like, her hands in her lap, with an expectant look at Liz.

"Sarah, this is Liz." Harry said.

"Hello. Nice to meet you." Sarah spoke softly and directed her comment to Liz, "None of Daddy's girlfriends ever came here before." The naiveté of her remark crashed like a bomb on a pillow.

Liz smiled and looked at Harry for a reaction. "I'm happy to meet you, too." Liz steered the conversation. "So, did you take any pictures?"

"Oh, yes. There was this beautiful blue jay in a tree, making all sorts of noise. Would you like to see him?" Her face glowed with enthusiasm. "Daddy, can I show Liz the pictures?"

"Me, too?" Harry asked.

"Okay. I'll be right back." Sarah ran out of the room to fetch her camera.

When Sarah returned, Harry moved over on the sofa and motioned for Sarah to sit down between Liz and him. Rebecca followed Sarah into the room wearing a beige pantsuit and a powder-blue, low cut blouse, appearing demure and lovely. Harry didn't say anything but nodded his approval. Rebecca sat down across from Molly.

"You look very smart." Molly said.

"Thanks, Nana." Rebecca picked up a magazine and browsed, flipping the pages.

Sarah pushed buttons on her digital camera with rapid finger dexterity. "In this one he's eating a berry. Do you see it stuck in his beak? Here's another where he's jabbering away. I got a few of him flying off, and I had to use the zoom. Too bad, you can't hear him."

"They're great pictures, Sarah. Did you have a hard time getting these shots?" Liz thought Sarah must have climbed a tree, or sat in a pile of brush, from all the different angles in the photos.

"No, not really. Nana, do you want to see?"

"I'll see them later. Show your sister. I've got to see what's going on in the kitchen, if we're going to eat some time soon."

"Can I help?" Liz offered.

"Oh, yes! C'mon with me, help me push cook around. She makes a great goulash, but I've got to watch her with a roast."

Molly looked over her shoulder and addressed Harry: "Please try to wake Ted. He takes so long to get ready for dinner."

Liz followed Molly to the kitchen. It was obvious to her who ran this household. Molly moved along and everyone moved with her. Maybe that's where Harry got his propensity for managing.

Harry patted Rebecca on the head as he approached the porch. "Sorry, honey."

She looked up. "It's okay Dad. I know." She mimed her father and quoted from one of his many lectures: *You need to guard your virginity and be careful not to send the wrong message to hormone-infested boys.*" She paused and said, "Not that I see any boys around here."

"Drop the sarcasm, Rebecca. It's unbecoming."

As they entered the kitchen, Molly summoned Elena, "I think Liz would like another sherry, please."

"Yes, m'am."

Molly looked around at the dinner preparations, peeked in the wall oven and checked on the roast. Everything seemed to be in order.

"It'll be at least another twenty minutes." Molly said, motioning to Liz to sit at the breakfast table with her. Apparently, Molly had a lot more to talk about.

"Dear," she said, "if I ask my Harry if he's happy, he tells me, M*om, I have everything I need. I've been given so much. How could I be unhappy?* As if he knows what happy is, like he knows everything. He's content, but happy? No. Hmm."

Molly shrugged her shoulders. "He's been alone too many years. Truth is, he's lost too many people he loved—his brother, his father. And then Susan. Too much tragedy in this family."

There was a long pause. Molly continued. "He has feelings for you. I could tell, on the phone, in his voice. Sarah told me, too, *Nana, Daddy's got a real girlfriend. They're spending vacation together.* Sarah was so excited. I don't want him to mess up, if you know what I mean. How many chances do you get in this life?"

Liz wanted to cry. Her eyes watered and she could hardly form words. "You do love him very much." That's all Liz could say. She couldn't tell Molly she had no expectations of a future with her son. His mother had shared her heart and hopes and she wouldn't say anything that would disappoint her.

"I'll put my phone number in your purse before you leave. Promise me you'll call me if you need me, if you need to talk. Or if you need to know something. Maybe I could help. Promise? And you mustn't say anything to him."

"Promise." Liz said.

# CHAPTER TWENTY-SEVEN

Tom arrived promptly at eight-thirty to drive Harry and Liz into Manhattan. The car wasn't out of the driveway and Harry kissed her, "You don't want to go straight home, do you? Stop for a drink?"

"I've already had two sherries and a glass of wine. Another drink, and I'll pass out on you again. You'll be carrying me up to my apartment."

"I wouldn't mind you passing out on my bed."

"Is that a *your place or mine* offer?" she asked.

"Exactly. We'll stop at your apartment and Tom will help you bring your luggage upstairs. I'll wait in the car while you throw a few things in a bag. Come back to the house with me, spend the night."

Harry snuggled his head in her neck, slid his fingers down her cleavage and cupped her breasts. "I need you. Very badly. For the whole night and on my pillow in the morning."

"I need you, too." She kissed him.

"My place. Private and discreet. You can sleep in tomorrow. Mallory will make you breakfast, and if you like you can loll around all afternoon and be there when I get home. I have a meeting at four thirty, but I can reschedule and leave early."

"Just tonight. Don't cancel anything. You know, I do have a home to go to."

Liz put her head on his shoulder. Harry caressed her and stroked her hair. She loved when he played with her hair. Her hands gravitated to his chest. She looked forward to making love with him one more night.

"What did my mother have to tell you that was so important? Every time I turned around she sent me some place so she could talk to you."

"Nothing I can tell you about. It's a confidence."

"I should have known it would be a secret."

Liz sat up. "Harry, your mom isn't at all what I expected. She didn't mention anything about your marriage, or your wife."

"As I remember, I said she's a sweet, loving woman."

"True, you did. If you really need to know, she said there were too many women in your life. How your daughters had never met anyone you dated. That sort of thing. She was happy you brought someone home, that's all."

"The girls have met some of my friends on occasion. Nothing else? When you came out of the kitchen, your eyes were teary, as if you'd been crying. What did she say to you?"

"All I'll say is that she has your best interests at heart. Don't ask me. I'm not talking about it anymore."

The car pulled up in front of Liz's building. Tom followed her up the path to the doorman and rolled the luggage behind him. She led Tom to the concierge desk.

"Good evening, Ms. Brady."

"Hello, Andres."

"Good trip?" he asked. "We saved your mail. It's in a pile over there."

"Yes, very. Thanks. I'll get my mail tomorrow."

Andres, the concierge, buzzed her in and the glass door opened to the elevators. Tom and the luggage followed.

"Thanks, Tom." He dropped the luggage inside her apartment and left. She closed the door and sighed. It's good to be home. Returning home from vacation usually meant a shower, a cup of tea, a quick perusal of mail, inching back into her usual routine of the same old, same old.

Molly's words intruded on her thoughts, *Don't let him boss you around.* Why did she agree to go home with him? He didn't even need to persuade her. The promise of spending the night with him titillated her senses and her recent memory of thrilling sex. One more time. It couldn't hurt. She threw a change of clothes, sleepwear and cosmetics in an overnight bag.

Andres looked at her, his mouth open, as she fled past the desk and said, "Good night, Andres."

"Night, Ms. Brady."

The streetlight flooded the façade of a modern, three story brownstone surrounded by a ten foot wrought iron gate. A small driveway led to the slight ten steps in front of double doors. A single car garage was at the right of the building.

Tom opened the gate with his remote. Harry retrieved Liz's overnight bag.

"Tom," Harry called out, "Just drop my luggage inside and call it a night. Thanks."

"Okay. Night, Boss. Good night, Ms. Brady."

"Night." She looked up at the building. It was huge. How did one person use all that space? There must be a lot of unused rooms.

They entered a small anteroom which led to a wide hallway. She glanced to her left at an open living room, replete with antiques and lavish furnishings. Brocade drapes hung from elongated windows that soared to high ceilings.

Harry pushed some buttons on a panel mounted on the wall. He spoke into the intercom. "Mallory, I'm home."

They walked through the hallway to the kitchen. Liz stood at the entrance. She eyed the surrounding cherry wood cabinets that lined the walls and hovered over black granite countertops. The appliances were oversized and obviously high end equipment. A huge recessed niche comprised a windowed breakfast room with a glass table and six upholstered chairs. A small serving bar with a few stools and a settee were barely in view from the kitchen. It was a pristine picture realized from a decorator's illustration.

"Very beautiful home, Harry."

"Thank you. I don't really need all this space anymore. I used to entertain clients. Want a drink?"

"Sherry."

Mallory, Harry's housekeeper, a twenty-two year old skinny girl with a round shining face entered the kitchen. Her hair fell across her forehead which made her appear unkempt although she wore a neatly-pressed white cotton blouse and black pants.

"Mallory, this is Ms. Brady. She'll be staying tonight. I'd like a martini. A dry sherry for Ms. Brady."

"Yes, Mr. Bergman." She disappeared around the kitchen into the bar.

Harry spied slips of papers lodged under the wall phone in the breakfast room and shouted, "Mallory? Goddamnit, you've done it again! What the hell are these things? Messages?" He removed the scraps of papers from the phone.

Mallory entered the kitchen with the drinks and placed the tray on the kitchen island. Liz watched Harry's face flush. He paced back and forth in short steps and waved the papers in the air.

"There aren't supposed to be any messages. It's a very simple system. You do not need to speak to anyone."

Mallory stood at the kitchen island frozen for a moment. He continued to rant at her. His voice grew louder and louder. Mallory trembled like a statue in the throes of an earthquake.

"I'm sorry, Mr. Bergman, so sorry. The phone kept ringing and ringing."

"After one ring or two rings—or twenty rings—you simply disengage the phone and put it back on the receiver. The caller is relayed to a machine, remember? You don't need to speak with anyone. Clear?"

"Yes. I'm sorry." Mallory cowered. "It won't happen again." Tears loaded in her eyes with each blink of her eyelids.

"Let's go upstairs," he said. He took Liz by the arm and grabbed her overnight bag from the floor. His normal decibel level returned. "Mallory, please bring the drinks upstairs."

Mallory stood rigid at the kitchen island as they climbed a small stairway. Harry opened the door to a large sitting room comprised of a sofa, a centered coffee table, two easy chairs and a recliner, arranged around a television and a sound system. Two lamps lit up from the side tables as they entered the room. An adjoining bedroom, bathroom and an alley kitchen to the right completed the self-contained, separate apartment.

Harry picked up the remote to the sound system. Soft and mellowing Mozart background music filled the room.

"Come in." He said, responding to the knock at the door.

Mallory set the tray on the coffee table. "Can I get you anything else, Mr. Bergman?"

"Privacy! Good night." He didn't look at her and continued to read the slips of paper in his hands.

Liz sat down and helped herself to the sherry. "Have you recovered?" she said with a half-smile. She hadn't seen him in a temper with any of his help before. He treated Maddy and Thomas like family. He even hugged Elena when they left his Mother's house. Obviously, he frightened Mallory, yet, Liz noticed, he had continued to yell at her, trapped in his own bad temper and oblivious to the effect he provoked.

He removed his jacket, dropped it on a chair and paced around the room. “I went through a great deal of trouble installing this phone system, especially with the phone company. Very few people have the number and it works if I’m the only one answering the phone. It will only be the third time I’ve had to have the number changed because she can’t restrain herself from answering the phone. Now, I’ll have to use my cell.”

“Privacy issues?”

“Yeah.”

All of sudden Harry broke into laughter and stopped pacing. He threw the bits and pieces of paper, scattering them across the coffee table.

“I should be grateful she’s so dumb. If she didn’t write anything down, I wouldn’t have been the wiser. She doesn’t even know how to lie.”

He sat down next to Liz. “Sorry, my temper sometimes gets the best of me.”

She handed him his martini. “Chill.”

“So, what’s on the agenda? Television news? Tour of the house? Hot tub?”

“As if you didn’t know?”

Liz fell back onto the sofa. He sat beside her and kissed her. His tongue held her lips and then plowed into her mouth. He pulled her to his chest and unbuttoned her blouse.

“You’ve a mysterious power over me. I haven’t been with anyone in months. I thought I needed medication.” His hand grazed over her breasts and down her hip. He slipped his fingers down into her pants and found her wet and seeping inside.

Harry whispered, “I get near you, touch you, kiss you, and I lose control.” He glanced down at his erection.

Liz unbuckled his belt and unzipped his trousers. She inserted her hand inside and grasped his erection, “Bedroom?” she asked, as she stroked him.

“No. Here. Now.”

Harry pulled down her pants and slipped them off her body. Liz leaned back and stretched out on the sofa. Her blouse was opened and fell to her side, exposing her bra-filled breasts. He unclasped her bra and engulfed her nipples in his mouth. "Tell me when."

"Yes," she murmured and moaned with his first thrust.

He placed his hands under her backside, moved forward on his knees and pounced on her. She welcomed every lunge with rapturous sounds of relief and delight. She wrapped him in a web of throbbing pulses vibrating from her and traveling throughout his body as she climaxed and cried out his name, provoking him to finish at the same time.

# CHAPTER TWENTY-EIGHT

Liz awoke in a dark and somber bedroom. She stumbled from the bed and opened the drapes that apparently Harry had closed so the light wouldn't awaken her. The sunlight, like a spark of fire, burnt her eyes. The view of Manhattan granite buildings numbed her senses. She already missed the green, mellow Bermuda mornings and for the first time in five days, she faced the day alone. Harry hadn't awoken beside her and she wouldn't have coffee with him. They wouldn't spend the day together.

Liz viewed the bedroom in the light of day and admired the lush furnishings, aware, once again, of luxurious surroundings. She headed for the bathroom when her eyes caught little yellow post-its hanging from here and there—on the mirror, on the lamp and on the bureau. She picked off the post-it from the lamp and read:

*Miss waking up with you.*

The note on the mirror read:

*Thank you for a great evening.*

Another message on the bureau read:

*I don't want to be Mayor today. I love my job, but I'd rather be with you.*

Liz laughed aloud. If that's what he meant to do, make her laugh, she responded appropriately. She entered the bathroom and faced, yet another post-it on the bathroom mirror that read,

*I'll call you about eleven, on your cell.*

And in parenthesis,

*(Forgive me, I invaded your handbag for the number).*

Liz wrapped a robe over her pajamas, gathered the post-its and stuffed them in her handbag. She would read them again and they would make her laugh again. It was sensitive of him to realize it was the first time they hadn't woken up together and that he, too, perhaps, missed having coffee together.

She faced yet another post-it on the door when she started downstairs for coffee. It read: *Dinner tonight*? She plucked it from the door and slid it in her robe pocket.

Mallory must have heard her on the stairs and asked from the bottom of the staircase, "Can I get something for you, m'am?"

"Is there any coffee?"

"Yes, I'll bring you some upstairs. He left the newspaper for you. Do you want some breakfast?"

"No, thank you. I'll come down. Just some coffee, with milk and sugar."

Mallory brought a tray of coffee to the breakfast room table. "I've strict instructions to give this to you." Mallory held out the envelope in her hand.

Liz opened the envelope and read the handwritten message and cell number on the back of his business card: *If you need anything, feel free to call.*

Mallory stood before her and waited for instructions.

"Are you all right?" Liz asked. "Was he still angry with you this morning?"

"No, maybe a bit annoyed, I'd say. He's not easy to please, you know." Mallory appeared to be more at ease with a woman in the house and maybe because Liz had inquired about her well-being.

"Why do you stay?"

"Oh, I'm not staying. This is only temporary, 'til he finds someone. I have a new position beginning at the end of the month. We were never a good match anyway. I don't like being on my own in this big house. No one's ever here. I'm used to a houseful of kids, moms and dads coming and going, being busy all the time."

"Well, I wish you good luck."

"Thank you. Let me know when you want breakfast. He said you would want breakfast." Mallory slithered back to the kitchen.

Liz drank coffee from a mug. What did Mallory mean by *not easy to please?* Maddy loved him. Thomas and he shared a mutual respect. Martine had become a lifelong friend. Tom behaved like an old school buddy. Not that incompetence is an excuse to rage at an employee. Maybe she's not incompetent but just suffering from boredom.

Liz finished her coffee and the newspaper, went upstairs to shower, dress and gather her things in her overnight case. It was ten o'clock when she returned to the kitchen. She looked in the refrigerator for some bread to make toast. Mallory, a duster in her hand, entered the kitchen from the living room.

"Please, m'am, let me make you breakfast. What would you like? Waffles? Eggs? Some fruit?"

Liz floundered. She had no idea where the bread was kept, or the tableware, or anything, for that matter.

"You're on! Please call me Liz. How about one egg scrambled, some orange juice and a slice of toast? Maybe a slice of bacon?"

Liz peeked from the breakfast room while solving the crossword puzzle in the newspaper. She noticed Mallory's efficiency in her preparations—a tray with tableware and orange juice set to the side, the ingredients for cooking placed on the counter. She brewed a fresh pot of coffee, as well. Mallory brought the tray to the table and served her.

As Mallory walked back to the kitchen, Liz asked, "Mallory, Mr. Bergman is not easy to please?"

"Well, m'am," she held the tray under her arm, turned and glanced up at the ceiling. She curled her lips, "Seems I can't do anything right. I mean, I put too much vermouth in his martinis. I bought the wrong butter. By mistake, I put his shirts in the golf shirt drawer. Little things. Whining all the time. And then, the one thing I know I do very well is cook. But he won't let me cook him dinner. Sometimes he calls and gives me a list of food to order from the market, chases me out of the kitchen and cooks for himself. Doesn't make me feel very useful around here."

"Oh, I see. Well you did a great job with my breakfast. Perfect. Thank you." Liz smiled.

Liz's cell phone rang. The caller ID read *Unknown Caller.* She assumed it must be Harry. It was eleven o'clock.

"Hi, yes, fine. Mallory made me breakfast. I've just finished, about to go home. How's your day going?"

"As well as can be expected. Very busy."

"I loved your little notes. Thanks for cheering me up."

"My pleasure. You okay for dinner? About seven? I'll pick you up. Where do you want to eat?"

"Some place private. You choose. Harry, I can't spend the night."

"Oh? Why not?"

"Because I want to be in my own home, wake up in my own bed tomorrow. I do have a home."

"Well, then, invite me to your bed."

"No. I'm not inviting you. You know what I'm saying. Besides, I may have work waiting for me." Liz thought again of Molly's advice not to let him boss her around. She wanted to resume her routine and he encroached upon her intentions.

"I know what you're saying, but I don't have to like it, do I?" Harry didn't wait for a response.

"Okay, gotta go, a meeting in a few minutes. See you tonight. Bye."

"Bye."

• • •

On time, as usual, Tom pulled up in front of Liz's apartment building. He approached the concierge desk. "Will you please ring Ms. Brady." He waited while Andres buzzed her apartment. Liz answered, "I'll be right down."

She was glad Tom was in the lobby and not the Mayor. The town car double-parked in front of the building with the Mayor's license plates already gave the doormen something to gossip about.

They drove across the George Washington Bridge to New Jersey. Harry considered her aversion to publicity and chose an out-of-the-way, comfortable trattoria. They kissed a few times in the car. She grabbed his hands from her breasts and placed them on his knees.

"We're not going there. Just dinner."

"I'm being rejected?"

The maitre d' accommodated Harry with a special table, nestled away from the main dining room. They sipped martinis, engaged in conversation about what the day had been like. Liz listened intently to Harry, engrossed with details of his day at the office and exuding his passion for his work.

Didn't he want to know that the jewelry arrived safely? She tried to think of a comfortable segue to discussing the jewelry. He distracted her, and finally she addressed the conflict tugging at her mind all evening.

"Harry, please don't take this the wrong way." She gazed at her coffee and avoided looking at him. "I can't accept the jewelry. It's far too expensive."

"Expensive? That's an issue? Don't you like it? I wanted to buy you something special. There are no strings attached, no obligations. You're insulting me if you think for a moment that I'm treating you like—"

"I wasn't thinking that at all. The jewelry is beautiful and a wonderful surprise. But I can't accept it."

"Why? What is it you can't accept?" Harry looked at her in disbelief.

"I'm not used to that sort of a gift, even for a special occasion—like a birthday." An awkward silence fell between them. Harry waited for further explanation.

"I don't—I don't know how to accept it."

She felt self-conscious and unworthy of accepting what she thought should be a present to a wife for a twentieth anniversary, or to the loved one of a long-time, committed relationship. She was only a short-term sexual partner and not eligible to receive such an extravagant gift.

"Here's how you accept it. You just say, *I love the necklace. It's beautiful. And the earrings, very elegant. Thank you, Harry.*"

Liz wavered. Her lips quivered. Harry slid his chair next to hers. "Liz," he coupled her cheeks in the palms of his hand and kissed her, his eyes intent upon her and in an emphatic tone said, "I want you to have the jewelry. I'm not buying you and I'm not stroking my ego. Don't deprive me of my pleasure. Please."

For all its elegance and monetary value, Liz didn't want the jewelry. She had dated wealthy men who had proffered luxuries, and she had always managed to refuse tactfully beforehand because she knew there would be an unmentionable price to be paid and that it surely meant she had agreed to entrust herself to a man's control. But those demeaning and patronizing scenarios certainly didn't describe Harry's behavior. His motivation was the pure pleasure of giving and if she refused the jewelry, she'd be in the realm of hurting his feelings. He exposed his vulnerability, and she didn't want to hurt him.

"C'mon. No crying. A gift is supposed to make you happy." He wiped a few trickling tears from her cheek with his fingers and then kissed her again.

"Happy?"

"Uh, huh. You make everything all right."

Her resolve not to be with him that night faded with the kiss. Desire already tingled beneath her skin and collided with her brain. Her brain told her the so-called fling in Bermuda had evolved to an affair and now invaded her life in New York, but she had no resistance when she thought of his body, warm and writhing in rhythm with hers. She wanted him again.

# CHAPTER TWENTY-NINE

Liz snuggled beside Harry in the car. Her hand moved to his chest and she reached up and loosened his tie. His lips brushed across her forehead, gravitated to her mouth and ended the journey in a forceful, unrestrained kiss.

Tom double-parked in front of Liz's apartment building. Harry held her hand as he walked her to the doorman. They were halfway up the path when she asked, "Do you want a drink?"

He stopped and responded with questioning eyes, "If I go upstairs, it won't be for a drink."

She nodded. "I know."

He placed her arm under his. They continued walking toward the doorman who stood beside the opened door like a figure from a wax museum.

"Hi, Armando."

"Buono sera." The doorman closed the door behind them.

Andres greeted them. "Evening, Ms. Brady. Evening, Sir."

"Evening," Liz said.

Harry nodded to Andres who abruptly stood up in deference to the Mayor. Apparently, he recognized the man who held Liz on his arm. He stared at him from behind the marble desk and pushed the buzzer to the glass security door that opened to the elevators.

Harry pulled out his cell phone in the elevator and punched in a number. "Tom, call it a night. No. It's okay, I'll get a cab. Thanks. Night."

Liz fumbled with her keys and handed them to Harry.

"This one?" He asked.

She nodded and Harry opened the door.

"Can I hang your jacket?"

"Uh, huh." He removed his jacket and handed it to her.

"What about my trousers and shirt?" He playfully asked.

"You in a hurry?"

"With you? Never. Just a trifle needy."

Harry looked around the apartment, decorated in blues and yellows that coordinated nicely with the teak furniture, the blue carpeting and the water color landscape paintings on the walls.

"It's very cheerful. Very you. You're a neat freak. Everything's in its place."

He eyed the sofa and armchair below the wall-to-wall windows at the end of the room. "Very comfortable, too."

"So, where's George?" Harry spied the curio cabinet to the left of the alley kitchen. An array of elephant figurines of all sizes and materials crowded the shelves.

"George? Oh, from Bermuda. You named him George?" Liz asked and smiled. "There, on the top shelf, with Alonzo and Rafael. How did you know I named them?"

"I didn't. I decided he's a George from St. George's. He's in good company—they're all very unique. I'm impressed. Quite a collection," he said as he examined the shelves.

Liz retrieved two glasses, a bottle of Belvedere, vermouth and a shaker from the sideboard and passed in front of him into the kitchen.

"Harry, you make the drinks. I have it on the best authority that you're finicky about the vermouth in your martini. Olives are in a jar on the refrigerator door. I'll put on some music."

"I'm guessing the authority is Mallory since she always gets the vermouth wrong. Did you chat Mallory up, or did she chat you up?"

"Actually, we both *chatted* a little."

Liz chose a selection of orchestrated Bach from the disc player in the living room. Soft background music filled the room. She sat on the sofa.

Harry brought the drinks to the coffee table and sat beside her. "And what else did she tell you?"

"Nothing really. Something about being lonely in that big house with nothing to do. She said she's leaving at the end of the month. Do you have you a replacement?"

"Well, I wanted to hire this blond I met. Cute, very attractive and a somewhat sophisticated lady. Curly blonde hair, blue eyes, sexy athletic body, and I know I'd be in very good hands, but she's already employed."

He picked up his glass and sipped his martini.

"The agency suggested I hire a man and recommended a guy. His name is Fred. I have an appointment with him on Thursday.

"The blond wouldn't have worked out anyway. I'd want to try her out in every room in the house." He removed her jacket from her shoulders, unbuttoned her blouse, and slowly peeled clothing from her body as he jabbered. "I'd have to give up my job. Sit around having martinis. Strip her clothes off. And ravage her body."

She accommodated him and lifted her body as he slid her slacks from her hips down to the floor. A broad smile emerged on her face. She sat motionless on the sofa and restrained her urge to squeeze him. She watched his excitement grow as he removed each piece of clothing.

"Are you finished?" She sat erect, in her bra and panties and waited for his hands to touch her.

"Almost." He said.

He kissed her neck and both his hands swept down her arms as his eyes absorbed her body.

"Is it my turn yet?" She asked.

"I'm all yours. Be my guest."

She unbuttoned his shirt and unclasped his belt. He dropped his trousers to the floor and flung his shirt across a chair. They kissed in a long, tongue-probing event. They stumbled to the bedroom and continued indulging in foreplay, although they both were ready to incinerate. She stroked his erection and massaged his chest. Her hands traveled over his body to his stomach and groin. He placed his fingers against her mons and applied a slow pressure and wallowed in his hardened response to her muffled cries. They embraced and held each other as they fell on the bed.

"No more teasing," she said.

He entered her slowly and held his finger inside until he made his first surging thrust at her. Her hips rose to meet him again and again. Her pleasure accelerated in soft cries of relief until they both finished in the same heart-pounding, blood-surging climax.

Harry lay naked on his back for a few moments, then rolled over and caressed her neck and shoulders in small strokes. His arm rested at her waist. She watched him close his eyes, and they both drifted into a soothing sleep.

It was only a short while before the phone rang and startled her. She sat up, groggy and averse to engage in a telephone conversation. The ringing ceased and she listened to the message:

> *Liz, it's Josh. Please give me a call first thing. Need to file by three o'clock. Bye.*

Harry propped himself up, awakened by the message. He shook his head. "Another man in your life? Infringing on my time?"

"A client." She said.

"I know. Josh Starkey." Harry sat up and leaned his back against the headboard.

"Oh?"

"Listed as a client. In the report. They call you this late?"

"I think he's trying to psyche me for tomorrow. He probably wants to let me know he has an emergency. It's not late, not ten o'clock yet."

She put on a long shirt-like pajama top, unhooked a robe from behind the bathroom door and threw it to Harry.

"Shower?" She asked.

"No. I'll wash up. Could do with a coffee though. Do you have any decaf?"

"Yes. Coming up."

Harry draped the robe over his shoulders, gathered his clothes and entered the bathroom.

Liz went to the kitchen, prepared the coffee and returned to the living room.

Harry joined her on the sofa, half-dressed, his chest exposed and his feet bare. He rolled up his shirt sleeves and fastened buttons.

# CHAPTER THIRTY

Liz and Harry both still bore the afterglow of intimacy and he kissed her on the cheek. They hugged each other.

"I want to ask you something."

"What?"

"Wait until you get the coffee."

All day, Harry had been plagued with flashbacks of their time in Bermuda—*Chez Mere, the Paradise Isle*, and *the San Remo.* He'd never felt that someone else's happiness would make him happy. He wanted to know if she felt the same way, if she was happy to be with him. His mind tiptoed and cowered, not knowing exactly what question he wanted answered.

"You were with your husband for a lot of years. You were still in love with him, after all that time?"

"Yes, very much in love with him. That's the question?" She asked as she disappeared into the kitchen.

"No."

Liz brought a tray of coffee to the table and sat down.

"I think I'm asking if you felt the same about him after so many years."

"Yes, the same as when I met him. It was a love-at-first-sight and my feelings never changed. It wasn't moonlight and roses though, if that's what you're asking. We weren't made for each other."

"Whatta y'a mean?" He asked.

He cared about her. He simply wanted to know if she had feelings for him, but he didn't know how to ask her in a subtle way.

She sipped her coffee and volunteered more than he wanted to know. "It was a turbulent on again, off again, love affair. Oh, we shared a lot of the same things, music, baseball, restaurants, and a sense of humor. He liked to make people laugh and have a good time. We did an awful lot of laughing together. He drank too much and spent too much. And, of course, he was a married man with a child. Yet, he always made me feel like *the* woman, and not the *other* woman in his life. I didn't want marriage."

Harry drank his coffee and returned the cup to its saucer, and asked, "Why not? Didn't you want children? Where were you going with him?"

"My child-bearing years were over before I met him. Single motherhood was never my style. It's selfish. Cheating the child of a parent. I believe it takes two parents to raise a child and I never met the right man. Besides, I helped raise my nephew. He's the child I never had. We're very close."

Harry pulled a sock over his foot, sipped more coffee and listened as he donned the other sock. Liz babbled on with information nothing of what he wanted to hear nor what he needed to know.

"I did try to leave him. Many times. If we had a bitter argument the night before, there was always the phone call the next day asking me to meet him after work. If I didn't agree to see him, he'd be at my door at two in the morning, drunk and uncontrollable. We weren't always laughing."

"Doesn't sound as if you were very happy." He said.

"It did get better. He lived with me during the week and went home weekends to be with his son. Then, his wife divorced him and everything changed."

Harry realized what nagged at him. She threatened him when she told him she wouldn't go home with him. He thought about her during the day and missed the comfortable feeling he had in Bermuda of being close to her and knowing she'd be there in the morning. Not only did he ache for her sexually, but he wanted her beside him in his bed for the night and to see her smile when he awoke in the morning.

"You still in love with him? Miss him?"

"That would be delusional. How can you be in love with someone who's not here? Miss him? What I miss is the future we planned and never got to live out. We got married. He stopped drinking, not completely, but he wasn't drinking himself into oblivion, and the differences we had were put to rest."

"Any more coffee?"

She walked to the kitchen, talking over her shoulder, "I wouldn't trade the years I spent with him for anything. He was the love of my life. Not everybody gets that."

Liz refilled his cup and sat down again. She looked at him quizzically, as if the expression on his face would tell her why he was asking about her marriage.

"Harry, why are you asking me all this? Is there something on your mind—I mean—about us?"

"No, I just wanted to know where you've been, who you were with." He needed some words of assurance that she cared for him, and he didn't know how to ask the question he wanted answered without discovering that maybe she didn't have the same feelings that he did. He didn't want that answer.

He drank the remainder of his coffee.

"You mean the men in my life?"

"No, more about the one man in your life, the one you cared for. From what you've said, it was your husband. I've got to go. Have a seven-thirty meeting in the morning. Josh keeping you busy all day?"

"Probably. At least until three. Then, it could be later. It may be something more than a filing."

"I'm taking my daughters to see *Jersey Boys* tomorrow night. I thought we might have lunch, but it seems you'll be occupied."

"I think we need a little space anyway," she said.

"I'll call you tomorrow."

"I'll be here."

He threw his jacket over his shoulder. Liz walked to the door with him.

"We have a tennis date on Wednesday with Andy and Cody."

Obviously, he wouldn't see her tomorrow. Maybe a little space is a good thing. Liz hadn't answered the question he wanted answered, and he wasn't pleased with the answers to the questions he didn't ask. It occurred to him that she didn't have the same attachment that he felt for her. He felt somewhat empty and abandoned, as if he were a piece of half eaten chocolate, tasted and then tossed back in the box.

"Yes, I remember. Looking forward to it."

Harry kissed her on the forehead and hugged her.

"Harry, are you okay? Is something wrong?"

"A little tired, that's all. Good Night."

# CHAPTER THIRTY-ONE

Josh Starkey arrived at Liz's apartment at the break of dawn. He wore a navy blue suit and a gray tie with a touch of red, an appropriate uniform for a lawyer. His shirt reeked of a Chinese laundry odor and he needed a hairdresser who would style his hair aware that he was thirty-two years old, not twenty-two. But then, she thought, he probably wanted to look young and attract a bimbo just shy of jailbait age who would be in awe to date the son of a famous defense attorney.

Liz threw on a pair of jeans and a tee shirt when Andres announced Starkey. She printed out the document Josh had emailed the night before. He sprawled out on her sofa and drank coffee, reading and editing a few pages.

"I haven't really substantiated why we need to freeze this guy's assets. I need to get some more facts about the fraud."

Liz heard his voice, but she didn't hear what he said. Distracted, she tried to overcome the hurdle of morning coffee with Josh instead of Harry. She recalled that he looked agitated when he left the night before.

"Liz?" Josh stood up suddenly.

"Yeah?"

"I've gotta go to the office and get some documents I need. I'll be back in an hour or so."

She watched Josh walk toward the door and asked, "Why are you preparing the Order? I thought this was Peter's case?"

Liz hoped to have the opportunity to speak with Peter. She worked for Peter Handley, a Deputy Chief of the District Attorney's Office, not Josh Starkey. She wanted to let Peter know, at least marginally, about Harry. She didn't want to risk shocking him with a picture of her and Harry in the newspapers, had they been seen together and photographed.

"Peter's been at the hospital the last couple of days and I'm filling in for him. Marissa almost lost the baby. She's okay, but he wanted to be with her when she came home today. See you later."

"Oh." Well, that explains it. Poor Peter. Not good news. But he did say Marissa was okay and coming home today. Hopefully, it meant that whatever crisis occurred, it was over.

Her thoughts strayed to Harry again. His behavior last night preyed on her mind. He had acted annoyed, a bit abrupt. Why had he asked all those questions about her husband? Something she said had disturbed him? Impulsively, she decided to call him and hoped his meeting was over. She found the card he had written his cell number on in her handbag with the yellow post-its. She read them again, smiled and punched in his number.

"Hey, nice surprise to hear from you. Give me a sec. Need some privacy." Harry found a corner of the conference room and spoke, "Okay. How y'a doin'? What's up?"

"You still at your meeting?"

"Yes."

"Sorry, I'll call you later."

"No, it's all right. I've got a minute."

"Thought maybe I said something last night, or did something that offended you. You looked annoyed when you left."

"No. I'm fine. We had a good evening. Will you be home later? I'll call you when I can talk."

"Okay. Talk to you later. Bye."

Josh returned in the afternoon, much later than he said he would which meant they were behind schedule. He arrived with a finished edit and turned it over to Liz for revisions. He announced with his usual arrogance that he had to be in court in an hour. Now, the deadline became her responsibility because he probably stopped and had lunch while she sat idle and waited for him. She needed to work very quickly to meet his deadline. As usual, Josh created stress.

In the middle of an intricate process on the computer, she couldn't answer her phone when it rang. She knew it was Harry and called out across the room, "Let it ring, Josh." The caller ID would read *Unknown Caller*, but she anticipated Josh might recognize Harry's voice. She and Harry were not public knowledge and she needed to keep a rein on their privacy.

Josh picked up the receiver. "Hello. Yes, she's here, but she can't speak with you right now. Who's calling?" Josh placed the phone back in its cradle.

"You are a fuck-up," Liz shouted at him. She continued working at the computer. "I said to let it ring. It's none of your business who's calling."

"I thought it might be Peter."

Liz finished the edits and glared at Josh as the document spewed out of the printer.

"You are a nit. What part of *let it ring* don't you understand? Peter would call you on your cell, not my home number."

"Calm down, Liz." Josh approached the computer desk where Liz sat. He addressed her directly and picked up the document that had collected on the printer. "He said he'd call you back and hung up."

"Don't ever touch my phone again. Do you hear me? Hurry up and read that, and get out of here." She glared at him and repressed an impulse to reach up and slap him in the face.

"Chill, girl. Wow, you are in a mood."

Josh always got under her skin and when he left she felt relieved. She contracted to work for Peter Handley, not his condescending assistant who boasted his wealth and credentials, but hadn't an iota of couth. As soon as the opportunity presented itself, she vowed to tell Peter she would not work with Josh again.

• • •

Liz ate a sandwich and lounged on the sofa. She read the newspaper and waited for Harry to call.

Finally, the phone rang.

"Hi, are you alone?"

"Yes, sorry, I couldn't talk earlier."

"Who was that? Starkey?"

"Yes. I told him to let the phone ring. But, of course, he had his own agenda."

"Spent the whole day with him?"

"Uh, huh, and he makes me miserable."

"Liz, I'm surprised at you, letting him get to your cheerful disposition."

"Do you know him?

"His reputation precedes him. A conceited blue blood who got his job because his father plays golf with the governor. Don't quote me."

"What was your day like?" she asked.

"Somewhat boring, same old, trying to get people to agree. Meetings . . . catching up—."

"I miss you," Liz interrupted him.

"I know. It's the first day we haven't spent some time together." He missed her, too, but he couldn't tell her and kept his emotions in check.

She cut him off, "Well, enjoy your evening with your daughters. I'll see you tomorrow. Bye."

Was that all she wanted to say, that she missed him? He wanted her in his life and he wasn't sure she wanted him in her life, except sexually. He tried not to think about her. When she called him earlier, he was relieved that some of the negative thoughts that were swaying in and out of his mind all morning were dispelled. But what did she mean last night about needing a little space?

# CHAPTER THIRTY-TWO

Shadows crept across the club grounds and invaded the lush green landscape of the golf course. The sun still made its mark, but didn't burn as it did at noon. A moderate breeze kept the end-of-August heat at bay and perfect tennis weather prevailed. Tom parked in front of the clubhouse. Liz and Harry got out of the car and retrieved their tennis gear from the trunk. They strolled across the clubhouse lawn to the edge of the courts.

Cody and Liz brushed kissed each other on the cheek.

"Good to see you again, sweetie."

"You, too." Liz said.

"Hey, buddy, how's it going?" Andy addressed Harry.

"Good."

Andy placed his arm at Liz's shoulder. "Hope you're up for some stiff competition." They walked to the courts and politely hit balls to each other.

Cody and Harry chatted as they ambled to the courts. She kissed him on the cheek and asked, "Back in the swing of things?"

"Yeah, I guess. The birthday blast?"

"More like a wedding, but we actually enjoyed ourselves. Would have preferred to stay in Bermuda another day; however, family is family."

Harry arranged a visor on his forehead and removed his racquet from its cover.

"Andy tells me you and Liz had dinner with your mom and the girls. You're in a little thick, Harry. How'd it go?" Cody asked.

"Went well. My daughters like her. So does my mother."

"C'mon, guys," Andy yelled. "Let's get rolling. It's ten after already. We've only got the court for an hour and a half."

Harry and Cody walked to opposite sides of the court, hit a few warm-up strokes and they started the game.

Harry moved a step too late for almost every shot that came off his racquet, incurring more than an acceptable amount of unforced errors. Liz observed his lackluster attitude and halfway through the match, during a court changeover, she said, "We can quit if you're not up to playing." She thought he must have a cold or hadn't slept enough. His mind was someplace else and certainly not focused on tennis.

"Sorry, can't seem to get with it," Harry said.

Liz hadn't seen such dull behavior from him, and she likened it to his mood when he left her apartment on Monday night.

• • •

The men showered, dressed quickly and primed themselves at the clubhouse bar that was replete with pictures of golf celebrities hanging on mahogany panels. They ordered drinks and waited for Liz and Cody.

"So, what's bothering you?" Andy asked. "You were a disaster out there."

"Nothing."

"For God's sake, Harry, tell me another one. Something's on your mind. Why don't you just spill it, and get it over with before they get here."

"I don't know what the hell I'm doing."

"Doing?" Andy asked. "Doing, about what?"

Harry guzzled a full mouthful of his martini. He leaned on the bar. His hand was propped up at his cheek and supported his languishing head.

"I want to be with her all the time. I can't keep my hands off her. But I don't want to be attached like that. I can't."

"What are you saying?"

"I can't stop thinking about her, when I'm going to see her again, or if she wants to see me. What she means by a *little space*."

"Oh! What happened?"

"Nothing happened. She just pissed me off. She acts as if she wants to be with me—and I don't mean for sex—and then she tells me we could do with a *little space*. That's my line, when I want to quit seeing someone. And why the hell should I care if she had a miserable day yesterday?"

"You think she's dumping you?"

"No. It's not that." Harry shook his head and sat up straight. He picked up his glass and swallowed the last of his martini in a nanosecond.

"You sound pretty upset to me. Another martini?" Andy downed his beer and signaled the bartender. "Again, please."

"I'm totally confused. I can't figure her out. I asked her to dinner Monday night and she insisted—only dinner—nothing more. *I'm not going home with you.* So, I walk her to the doorman, about to kiss her goodnight, and all of a sudden everything changes. She invites me up for a drink, and whatever. One minute she's telling me we need some space and the next minute she calls me in the middle of a meeting because she thought she had hurt my feelings, or offended me."

"Harry, I think you're in love with her."

"No way. I don't even know what that means."

"Well, think about it. And I don't mean think about it as if you're deliberating whether or not to veto a finance bill. It's a simple yes or no issue. You are or you aren't in love with her. That's it."

"Andy, that's just not me. I don't get entangled."

"You're absolutely right. And, for sure, it's not you. It's not you to ask a woman to dinner with your family, and it's not you to buy her a gift, not until you've been seeing her for at least a few weeks. And then the gift doesn't usually cost in the neighborhood of five thou."

"How do you know what the jewelry cost? Cody couldn't know the price. What did she say to you?"

"Nothing, and I haven't said anything to Cody. I lost my pen. I thought I'd left it in your office. I spotted a fax coming out of the machine from the bank, confirming the payment to the jewelry shop.

"Now you tell me you think about her all the time, look forward to being with her. You get upset and threatened when she suggests not going home with you, or that she needs some space."

Andy turned and faced Harry and placed his hand on Harry's shoulder in a brotherly gesture. "I know all the symptoms. I've been there. You're very happy when you're with her, talking with her, sharing a meal. You feel free—liberated in a way, comfortable talking about anything. And let's not forget about the sex. Really good?"

"Yeah. I don't get it. I haven't been with anyone in months. The last time I had sex before Liz, I fell asleep because I couldn't perform. I thought maybe I needed some pills. Now, all of a sudden, I'm in overdrive every day."

"You're tied up in a knot, buddy. You're going to have to decide what you want." Andy's eyes riveted a laser stare at Harry. "Whatever you do, if you can't go with it, break it off now, before you both get hurt." He gently patted Harry on his shoulder.

Andy leaned back on the bar stool, tipped his beer bottle and gulped. A poignant silence fell.

Harry rhythmically tapped his fingers on his empty glass. "What the hell am I supposed to do?"

"Got me. I haven't got a clue. Wish I could help, because I know what it's like. Remember? I fell madly, outrageously in love with Cody. So whacked one time I left a client waiting three hours while I chased her to Connecticut to apologize, as if there were no phones or no tomorrow. I had to see her immediately, and face-to-face. Afraid I'd lose her."

Andy paused and swallowed another swig of beer. "Maybe there's a bright side, buddy."

"Huh?"

"Finding someone you want to be with all the time. You know, not everybody gets a second chance."

# CHAPTER THIRTY-THREE

Liz and Cody finished showering. They chose opposite sides of the locker room to dress, taking advantage of the spaciousness of the changing facility and dedicated mirrors for each of them. No other women present, they chatted freely from remote sides of the room.

"Obviously, Harry's mind was not on the game. He behaved like . . . , like—totally distracted." Cody said. "It's not like him." She continued and asked. "Didn't you have dinner with his mom and his daughters the other night?"

"Sunday."

Cody pulled her skirt over her hips and slipped her arms into a blouse and buttoned it. "So?"

"I really had a good time. They made me feel very at home. His daughters are beautiful. And smart. Sarah is so sweet."

"Don't you love Molly? She's a hoot."

"Yes. She's a very warm lady, easy to talk to and be around. Absolutely not what I expected."

"You know, he's never asked any of his female friends to dinner with the family. Did Molly ask you a lot of questions?"

"No. She talked a lot though. About Harry. Made me cry."

"Whatever could she say that would make you cry?"

"Well, not like . . . cry tears, not like that. You promise not to tell your husband."

"I can't promise that, but I can make him promise not to tell Harry."

Liz finished dressing. She faced the mirror, talking while she applied the scantiest amount of makeup to her eyes and lips. "She said Harry hasn't been happy because he's been alone too long. With the wrong kind of woman, and so forth, and that she doesn't want him to screw it up. She meant—."

Cody interrupted, "Oh, I think I know what she meant."

Focusing on the mirror in front of her, Cody brushed her cheeks with a powdery foundation. About to apply some mascara, a tube in one hand and the applicator in the other, she turned around and faced Liz from across the room. "Molly thinks her son's in love with you."

"No, she doesn't."

"Yes, she does. That's what she meant. She doesn't want him to mess up the relationship." Cody focused on the mirror again, slowly applying mascara to her lashes, as she spoke, "She and Susan used to talk all the time. Harry hated it. She actually told Susan to leave him. His mom's a wise, truthful lady."

"It's not like that."

"Like what?"

"We're having a fling, an affair. A very sexual affair. That's all. I couldn't tell her that."

"Fling? If you say so." Cody brushed her cheeks with blush powder.

Liz fingered her hair, fluffed it up and inspected it from several angles in the mirror. She gazed at her face, shook her head from side to side and sighed. She didn't want to believe Molly had long-term expectations for her son, and she recalled how she hadn't wanted to disappoint Molly and hadn't even hinted to her what she truly felt. She never thought, not for a moment, not for the whole week they had spent together in Bermuda that their mutual pleasure was anything but a sexual attraction. They indulged each other, nothing more. She had no reason to think Harry felt differently from what she thought.

"You think that, too, don't you?"

"Just an opinion, Liz. And it's not intuitive. It only just occurred to me. I mean—meeting his daughters and his mom is indicative of something, and it's not what I'd call a *fling*.

"By the by, don't mean to pry, but did he buy you the necklace and earrings?"

"Yes. That's a whole other story."

"Ready?"

"Yes. Just let me get my stuff together."

# CHAPTER THIRTY-FOUR

Liz spied Harry and Andy at the bar as she and Cody entered the restaurant and pointed to the right of the dining room. "They're over there, at the bar."

"No tables available?" Cody asked as she approached them.

"Having a cocktail while waiting on you," Andy said.

Cody looked at the empty martini glass and empty beer bottles on the bar. She waited with Andy as he signed the check.

Harry grabbed Liz's hand, kissed her on the cheek and they walked, hand in hand, to the dining room. She loved the touch of his flesh, sure and firm in hers, as if he were leading her somewhere she wanted to be, with him.

He leaned toward her ear and whispered, "I'd rather have you for dinner."

"How many martinis have you had?"

"Don't know. Are you monitoring? You know I have an unfathomable capacity for martinis. You're the one who gets tipsy on two."

"You're talking raunchy."

"Oops! A look of disapproval, Ms. Brady? Thought you liked raunchy?"

"Not in public. It's degrading."

"Okay, I promise not to be degrading. Until we're alone."

Cody and Andy caught up and stood behind Liz and Harry at the dining room entrance and waited for the hostess to seat them. Harry kissed Liz on the neck, and rolled his tongue over her ear. Liz was startled and withdrew abruptly. "Harry, please—don't."

"He's drunk." Cody whispered to her husband.

Liz, apparently annoyed by Harry's behavior, raised her eyebrows and shook her head as Cody scolded, "Harry, if you choose to medicate yourself with martinis, that's your affair, but spare us tasteless public displays."

"Cody, he's okay," Andy said.

"Sorry, Cody, if I offended you." Harry bowed.

"This way, please." The hostess motioned for them to follow her, pointed to seats and after everyone had sat down, handed out menus.

Andy swerved into a conversation as he read the menu. "The show any good last night? Is it the smash it's hyped to be?"

"Very entertaining. A real nostalgia trip for me. The girls loved it. They couldn't believe their dad knew the lyrics to the songs. As far as they're concerned, their dad was never twenty years old."

A waitress approached and stood in front of the table, pen and pad in hand, and wrote down their drink and dinner orders.

Harry offered his menu to the waitress and turned to Liz. "Do you drive? I know you have a license as an ID, but how come you don't have a regular driver's license?"

"Yes, I know how to drive. Haven't had a license in twenty years. No reason to drive in Manhattan."

"Do you color your hair? Have you ever had a pet? Do you prefer dogs or cats? When's your birthday?" Harry fired one question after another, obviously not pausing for answers.

Liz squirmed in her chair, but she was at a loss how to counteract or respond to his flippant mood.

Cody interrupted, "Have you spoken with your mom since Sunday?"

The waitress served their food and asked, "Anyone want a refill?"

"Water for me. I'm driving," Andy said. The waiter poured Cody and Liz some wine and left.

"Yeah, talked to my mom yesterday. She had a list of dos and don'ts as long as my arm. I was very good, Cody, I didn't say a thing, just listened and let her go on and on."

"Well, you've never been successful at escaping her wrath," Cody said, as a forkful of spinach made its way to her mouth.

"By the way, Liz, is that why she cornered you in the kitchen? To alert you to my errant ways. That's all she talked about on the phone, my errant ways, all of which should not be demonstrated to you. You never did tell me."

Liz glared at Harry. She disapproved of his sarcastic remarks directed at his mother. "She's concerned about you. And your happiness. You're an ungrateful son to talk about her that way as if she's an overbearing fool. She told me she loved you and that you were unhappy; that you've been alone too long, and she hoped you could be happy with—with me. Now, you've made me break a confidence. Are you pleased?"

"Sorry," Harry murmured.

Except for a few comments from Cody and Andy, who bantered about crisp versus fully cooked vegetables, a silence fell at the table.

"I don't like my broccoli overcooked," Andy said.

Cody scooped up some mashed potatoes on a fork. "Don't eat it then."

"Why can't they cook it like the carrots, nice and firm and crunchy?"

"The broccoli is not overcooked. It's you. You're picky."

The pervading tension subsided. Harry finished eating and placed his knife and fork on the plate.

"Hey." He grasped Liz's hand on the table and leaned over. "I said I'm sorry."

"You should be. Just don't tell your mother what I said."

"I promise."

The waiter served coffee. Andy signed the check.

Dusk fell as they strolled to the parking lot. They exchanged goodbyes and hugs. Tom was in the car, waiting for them and reading the sports page that was spread across the steering wheel.

"I've ruined our evening," Harry said as they entered the car. "Something's gnawing at me."

"What?"

"Let's go, Tom. Lex and thirty-sixth."

"I'll tell you later."

"Why not now?"

"Not the right time and place. Besides, all I want to do now is ravage your body." He picked up her hands and placed her palms at his lips. "I told Tom to take us to your place. You're asking me up for a drink." He kissed her on the cheek first, then her ear and then her neck.

"I'm not giving you another drink."

"I don't want a drink. I want you. You suggesting we make it in the car?"

"Of course, while Tom is in the front seat." She said.

"I'm very disappointed." He stopped touching her and removed his hand from under her blouse and placed her head on his shoulder. He leaned back and gazed out the car window.

"Is a car a fantasy place for you?" Liz asked.

"No, I simply have very pleasant memories of encounters in a car—my first meaningful sexual experiences. I was in college."

"C'mon, Harry, no bedrooms, motels?"

"Well, Mrs. Johnson—Lily—my political science professor, had pangs of conscience when we used her bedroom. She thought about her husband and kids. She got so distracted, she couldn't have an orgasm. The car was her idea. It was also her car."

"You went to bed with your professor?"

"Yeah. The loss of my virginity. Not exactly. I had some girls in college. Not for real though. Usually had to withdraw, or got close enough, but not inside. That sort of thing, somehow taking care of the urge. Satisfactory, but not complete."

"She had to be much older than you."

"Definitely not old. Thirty-five. I was about twenty-two. Beautiful woman. She seduced me while I struggled over a term paper. Taught me a lot more than political science."

"A Mrs. Robinson?"

"No. In fact, nothing close to that, rather a sincere, bright, lovely woman. We had feelings for each other. Her husband neglected her horribly. He spent more time in his lab than the mice. She needed to make love, and I don't mean sex."

"You actually had an affair?"

"I guess you'd call it that, however, short-lived. Eventually her conscience couldn't bear the cheating, the risks. She dumped me. So, after, about three or four months, it ended. I cried a lot, recovered and went on to grad school."

"Sounds very fly-by-night."

"On the contrary, I had genuine feelings for her. Used to try to bump into her on campus, ambush her for lunch, anything to be with her. I persuaded her to spend a weekend in Vermont, with real beds and not looking over our shoulders. I remember it as a weekend of pure bliss. She almost destroyed me and my last semester at school. I'll never forget her."

# CHAPTER THIRTY-FIVE

Tom pulled the car up to the apartment building. He opened the trunk and handed Liz's tennis bag to Harry. "Good night, Boss. Night, Ms. Brady."

"Night, Tom. Thanks." Harry said.

Andres greeted them as they approached the concierge desk, "Evening Ms. Brady, Mr. Mayor." He handed Liz a stack of mail.

"The name is Harry." Harry extended his hand.

"Good to meet you, Harry." Andres shook hands and buzzed open the glass door. At the elevator, Harry looked over his shoulder and saw a resident waiting for Andres to open the door. Andres engaged him in conversation until the elevator door closed.

"Savvy doorman, protecting you from your neighbors."

"He's also a gossip. They all are."

"You begrudge the help some on-the-job amusement?"

"It's probably all over the building already, from Monday, that you were here—The Mayor, twice in one week. I can hear the tongues wagging among the doormen. I know they're talking."

"Bother you?"

"No. I don't know many people in the building. I'm not active in the association and you're hardly grounds for eviction."

"That's good news."

Liz reached in her handbag for keys. He took the keys from her hand, opened the door and returned them to her.

When they were inside her apartment, he slid his hands inside her pants down to her backside and pressed her against his groin. She felt his erection.

"Sorry about my fit earlier. I'm angry with myself, and I took it out on you. Sarcasm seems to be my weapon sometimes. I think I've got it sorted out."

"Got what sorted out?" She asked as his hands made their way around her body. They kissed. His tongue was relentless on her lips and in her mouth, as they staggered into the bedroom.

"No playing. I need you." Liz said. She could feel wetness oozing inside her. When he touched her and placed his fingers gently at her cleft, her body unleashed in ravenous desire and flushed her skin with warmth. She flung her clothes off, wanting him inside and quickly.

He clutched her and softly gripped her neck. His tongue gently circled the nipples of her breasts. "Don't go without me," he whispered and entered her in one full thrust. He lingered for a moment and then rode her like a seesaw, faster and faster, until she called out his name, again and again, and finally cried out in a thunderous climax, digging her nails into his back. She felt Harry let go in a furor as she screamed. He fell beside her, breathless and in a state of euphoria.

"Liz, check my back, see if there's any blood." He said, as he gasped for breath.

She moved close to him and let her body fall on the top of his back and lightly kissed the tiny red swelts she had created on his back with her nails.

"Sorry, I didn't mean to hurt you."

"It doesn't hurt. I do like your remedy though." He rolled over and faced her. He stared into her eyes, "I'm in love with you."

"No, you're not." She rolled her head to the side to avoid his piercing blue eyes.

"Yes." He kissed her on the neck. "Don't want to hear it, huh? I've got to talk about it." He sat up.

"Okay, we're infatuated," she said. "It's not the same thing. It's sex. That's all."

"Didn't say it's the same thing and I know the difference. You've been there, both places at the same time. I haven't. I don't think Lily qualifies. I'm fifty-five, not twenty-two."

Harry went into the bathroom. Liz sat on the bed, naked and numb. She felt queasiness in her stomach and a twinge of gloom impaled her thoughts. She thought, obviously, he wanted to end this sexual obsession they both suffered from. She leaned over, picked up his clothes and carelessly folded them, placing them on a chair. She remained on the bed momentarily motionless.

Harry plopped down beside her, naked. He kissed her on the cheek and then her shoulder as she inhaled the faint scent of his cologne. She loved his habit of kissing her a half a dozen times, no matter where the kisses landed after they had made love.

"Could do with a nightcap," he said.

"Coming up."

She slipped into a robe and went to the kitchen to fix him a martini. Harry dressed.

Liz placed the martini on the coffee table and peeked into the bedroom. "Want to watch the news?"

"No." He put his socks on. "I'll be right out. We need to talk."

"All right."

Harry had only fastened the two bottom buttons of his shirt. She noticed his silky chest hair exposed and recalled the feeling of her hands traveling across his torso a short while ago. He carried his shoes to the sofa and slipped them under the coffee table. He picked up the martini and sipped it.

"Very tasty. Thank you."

• • •

"C'mere." She was standing and he wanted her beside him. Liz slid next to him on the sofa. "Harry, just say it. There doesn't need to be a long discussion. That'll make it worse."

"What are you talking about."

"I'm talking about what you want to talk about. Ending this thing."

"I'm not ending this *thing*! Whatever you call it. I'm not giving you up. I'm in love with you."

"No, you're not."

"Because you're not in the same place?"

"Harry, I do have feelings for you. It's not that—it's just that—it isn't anything more than it is."

The conflict that had overtaken Harry over the last two days had been resolved. He decided to swim with the current and let it take him, take him where it would. He thought he'd drown if he didn't tell her what he felt.

"You couldn't make love with me the way you do if you didn't have some feelings for me. You wouldn't be here. That's who you are. I know that much."

He held her tightly. “I need a time out. Do you understand what I’m trying to say? I’m in over my head, overwhelmed. If you want to get rid of me, tell me now. Tell me. I want you in my life, but I need to slow down.” He waited for her to respond and held her in an embrace.

“I don’t want to stop seeing you,” she said, “but I am confused. I don’t know what I want anymore.”

# CHAPTER THIRTY-SIX

Fred Walker met with Harry at his home the next day. They sat in the small sitting room off the foyer at the entrance to the house. Six feet tall and a lithe figure without an ounce of fat on his body, Fred's white shirt sagged somewhat at his slight shoulders. He had a blank, unwrinkled face for a forty-year old, and his eyes blinked excessively when he read the job description Harry handed to him.

Harry had already secured a report on Fred and had carefully analyzed every aspect of his background. He conducted the interview to interact personally to learn if he could employ a male housekeeper, rather than a female housekeeper.

He asked Fred, "Why did you leave the employ of Mrs. Rathbone? There's a remarkably complimentary reference letter included with your resume, so why would you leave?"

Fred looked up at the ceiling. He paused and sighed audibly. "I could never leave her. She left me. She died. A very kind and wonderful woman; she insisted on writing the reference letter when she was diagnosed. She had no family, just me, and she treated me like her son. I loved her. I do have the comfort of knowing I made her very comfortable her last days. I did my best and I know she appreciated it. She will always be in my heart."

Harry noticed Fred's eyes swelled with tears. "Sorry. Apparently, it was quite a loss to you."

Fred made no effort to hide his emotion.

"She awarded you a whopping severance package—in a trust fund? It's in the background check." He said. Harry wondered why Fred was seeking employment when he had a quarter of a million dollars at his disposal.

"Oh, that! It's mostly gone already. I paid my sister's mortgage, renovated my apartment, opened a retirement fund and made a contribution to the church's fund for battered women. That's all I needed to do. I want to keep my life simple. Oh, and I renewed my subscription to the ballet for the next two years. Bridey—I mean Mrs. Rathbone, and I were both big fans of the ballet. I used to escort her, and we both had such marvelous evenings at the ballet. We also attended mass together on Sundays."

"You know, of course, the job requires you to live here, at least during the week. It's a very comfortable living space, with all the amenities and privacy. Weekends are yours. However, I have restrictions about visitors. Are you attached to anyone—in a relationship?"

Tiny bubbles of perspiration surfaced on Fred's forehead. "Oh, my, that is a personal question."

"You don't need to answer if you don't want to."

"Oh, I don't mind. I really don't mind. I should think it is necessary for you to know something about me personally. Security and all that."

Fred groped in his trouser pocket for a handkerchief and wiped his forehead. "I lost my soul mate five years ago. We were together for twenty years. Since we were teenagers. AIDs. I almost died from overmedicating my grief.

"Now, I guess you could call me asexual. I'm not interested. I find the sexual practices of my peers quite abhorrent and dangerous, and I'm not involved with anyone, and won't be, ever again, except, maybe in a careful, very careful friendship, and friendship only, if that answers your question."

"Yes. It certainly does. I appreciate your straightforward disclosure, although it's more information than I need. I just want to be assured that whatever your social activities, hopefully they're discreet—not embarrassing to the Mayor's Office—and conducted outside my home."

"Absolutely understood."

Impressed with Fred's honesty and his confirmed personality, Harry decided to offer him the job. He liked Fred for knowing himself. Knowing oneself was an achievement in itself, and he felt grateful for Fred's transparency. He knew exactly who he was dealing with.

"You've read the job description? Do the services as outlined present any problems for you? If you have any questions in that regard, I'd like to hear them now."

"No. The duties are quite explicit, and I'm sure I'm capable of fulfilling them."

"Good, well then, I'm offering you the position, with the proviso of a two-month probationary period. We should know by then if the relationship is working satisfactorily. If you'd like a day or two to think it over, that's reasonable. If, indeed, you decide to accept, I hope you can start as soon as possible."

"I've already decided. I think I'd be a good fit here, and I accept your offer. If you like, I can start immediately."

"Great!"

Fred stood up and extended his hand. "Thank you. I promise I shall do my utmost to perform my duties to your satisfaction."

Harry dropped the papers he held from his hand onto the coffee table, and they shook hands. "Deal!" Harry said. "There's a contract to sign which will be available in a day or two."

"Yes, I understand."

Harry arrived home from his office that evening to find that Fred had rearranged the pantry and refrigerator by category—dairy, produce, meat, etcetera and so on and had discarded outdated packaged foods and bottled drinks. He had also reorganized the cupboards, separating cookware, utensils and small appliances. Everything in the kitchen was assigned a logical and convenient place.

"Mr. Harry, there's a martini at the bar, ready for pouring when you're inclined. Very dry, shaken, with two olives. I spoke with your assistant, Joe, as to what you usually eat for breakfast, your cocktail preference, what time you arrive and leave the office—a few things like that. I hope I didn't overstep or impose upon your privacy by calling him for information. He was very gracious and forthcoming."

"No, not at all." Harry grinned, happily surprised with Fred's initiative. His suspicions were confirmed that he had acquired something more than home management when he'd hired Fred. He not only performed the duties of a housekeeper, but many of the duties of a butler.

"You chose a good source. Joe's been putting up with my habits and peculiarities for a long time. He knows me like a wife knows her husband."

Harry walked to the bar, seeking the cocktail. Fred followed him.

"Let me do that, Mr. Harry." Fred poured the martini into a glass.

"Thanks."

Over the next few days, Fred managed to establish himself as an efficiency expert, attacking the wardrobe closets and drawers and wherever else he saw the need for reorganization and that which fostered his somewhat obsessive demand for order.

By Friday afternoon, despite the distraction of a new person in his home and the ongoing pampering Fred showered upon him, he was yearning for Liz. Finally, he set aside his pride and his resolve not to call her crumbled like stale bread. He phoned.

"Hi. How you doin?"

"Fine."

"What have you been up to?"

"Working and a girls' night out."

"Fun?" he asked.

"Good food. But the girls can get rowdy sometimes, flirting, getting loud and talking sex, if you know what I mean. I'm really not too comfortable in the company of lots of women."

"You and Cody got along great."

"Yes, we did. I really got on with Cody. I prefer a one-on-one contact. I have a best friend."

"I can appreciate that. I'm not good with a gang of guys either. What are you up to this weekend?"

"I'm visiting my nephew on Long Island. You?"

"Thought I'd play some golf tomorrow with Andy." He cautiously flushed an invitation to dinner from his gut. "Want to have dinner tonight?"

"I can't. I have a deadline, by Monday, and I promised to spend the weekend with my nephew."

"No problem. Maybe we can get together next week."

"Sounds good. Look forward to seeing you."

"Enjoy your weekend. Talk to you soon."

"You, too. Bye."

After Fred cooked him an excellent dinner in the evening, sated and mellow, Harry retreated to privacy upstairs, read a magazine and watched the seven o'clock news.

Fred rapped at the upstairs door. "Mr. Harry?"

"Come in. Thought you left already."

"Would you like a martini before I leave? Or something else?"

"No, thanks. Great dinner again. By-the-by, I'm advising you to stop spoiling me. I'm getting very used to it, loving it and before you know it, I'll be expecting it, like a spoiled brat."

Fred smiled. "All in a day's work, Mr. Harry."

After a slight hesitation, Harry said, "Say, Fred, do you think you could call me *Harry*?"

"I'll try, but I'd rather prefer the employee-employer relationship to prevail."

"Well, give it a go. *Mister Harry* is just a bit too formal for me."

"How about, *Boss*?"

"*Boss*? That may work. Good thinking, Fred. What are you doing here anyway? You're supposed to be out of here by seven."

"A few odds and ends to take care of."

"Well, be sure to keep a record of the extra time you spend here. I want you to get paid for it."

Harry appreciated foremost above all that Fred seemed to know instinctively what he favored: the newspaper at breakfast, a perfectly dry martini when he arrived home, adagios with dinner. Fred seemed to appear and disappear without being seen, but was always available. So far, Fred had read his mood perfectly.

"Well, enjoy your weekend."

"Thank you, Boss. You, too. See you Sunday."

# CHAPTER THIRTY-SEVEN

Harry phoned Andy, intent on making a golf date for some time on the weekend.

"Hi, Harry, want to do nine this weekend?" Andy asked.

"That's why I called. Tomorrow or Sunday?"

"I'm free tomorrow. Cody's going downtown, meeting your daughters for lunch and going shopping. Talk to the girls today?"

"No. Been busy."

"How's Liz?"

"Okay. She's spending the weekend with her nephew."

"I know. Cody rang her, asked her if she wanted to join them shopping. Said she had already committed to visiting her family. Tomorrow's good then? I'll call you in the morning, let you know tee time. Night. See you tomorrow, buddy."

Harry and Andy met at the golf clubhouse the next day and drank coffee to kill a half an hour before tee time.

"What's up with you and Liz?"

"Huh? Nothing. Just a little break from each other."

"You okay with that?"

"Yeah, so far." He lied. The time out wasn't working for him. He was grateful Andy could play golf. Hopefully, the game would take his mind off Liz.

Maybe he could persuade her to come back early Sunday, have dinner with his family and stay the night. He punched her home number and heard the same answering machine message that he had heard from his earlier attempt at eight o'clock from his home. Where the hell could she be at nine in the morning, unless she'd left for Long Island last night? He decided he'd try her on her cell later. He left a message and asked her to call him back on his cell.

When they walked to the sixth hole, Andy said, "So, give her a call. You'll feel better."

He didn't mention he had already phoned at the previous hole. His ego didn't want Andy to know he had already tried to reach her again, although he couldn't hide his agitated mood.

They finished playing golf at about two in the afternoon. The sun burned as hot as a summer's day in July. Sweaty and tired, Harry and Andy plodded to the clubhouse for lunch. Harry ordered his usual martini and gulped it down as if he were drinking a bottle of water after completing a five-mile jog. Andy ordered a beer and two club sandwiches.

"She must have turned her phone off. That's all I can think. I've just tried her cell again and there's no answer."

Harry's glass needed filling again.

"What's going on Harry? Lighten up. You're on your third martini, and we haven't had any food yet."

"Nothing. I can't get her on the fucking phone. That's all. I wanted to ask her to dinner tomorrow, with the girls. She's not answering her phone. Guess it's not going to happen."

The waiter brought the club sandwiches and placed them on the table. Harry had two bites, dropped the remainder of the sandwich on the plate and gestured to the waiter for another drink.

Andy waved his hand and shook his head at the waiter, motioning for him to ignore the order for another martini.

"The check, please," he said when the waiter approached the table. He signed the check, leaned across the table and quietly spoke to Harry, "You're coming home with me."

"Huh? No. I'm not. Gotta—got a headache."

"Headache? You mean heartache." Andy said.

Harry leaned back and closed his eyes.

"C'mon, get up."

Harry didn't move. He slouched forward and cradled his head in his arms on the table.

Andy followed the path to the parking lot and signaled to Tom to come to the clubhouse. "Will y'a give me a hand, Tom? Harry's about to pass out if he hasn't already."

The two men helped Harry out of his seat and supported him to the car. Tom strapped the seat belt around him.

"I'm taking him home. Fred's off weekends and I don't want him to be alone in this condition. Can you follow me? I'll need some help to get him upstairs."

"Sure." Tom followed Andy's car to his apartment building and parked next to him in the basement garage.

Harry had slept for the fifteen-minute drive. Tom and Andy lifted him from the car. They struggled to keep him propped up in the elevator and dragged him into the spare room of Andy's apartment. They dropped his body on the bed. Tom left the room and Andy lingered and looked down at the sprawled figure on the bed. He removed Harry's shoes.

Andy talked out loud, knowing Harry couldn't hear a word he said. "Yeah, I'm okay. No, nothing's wrong. You don't even know you're a goddamn lovesick puppy." He closed the bedroom door.

"Tom, I don't think he'll need you anymore today. We'll get a cab later."

"No problem. So long, Andy."

"Thanks, again."

An hour later, Cody arrived, two shopping bags in her hand. "Hello, honey. I'm home."

"Hi." Andy kissed her on the cheek, clicked the television off and eyed the shopping bags.

"Good shopping day? We have a guest. Harry's conked out in the spare room."

"Huh?

"Bought out Bergdof's?" Andy peeked at the items at the top of the bags. "How are the girls?"

"They're great. Rebecca can be a chore though. I had to keep her from buying a revealing black leather tutu. She thinks it's cute when half her ass is showing. Doesn't get it, that she looks like a teenage runaway who's looking to score with a John. And Sarah checks out all the price tags. She knows she doesn't have to do that. Where'd she get that from?"

"Her mother, probably. Susan's parents lived through the Depression. It's likely she was brainwashed never to pay full price for anything."

Cody brought the shopping bags to the bedroom, replaced her heels with slippers and went into the kitchen. Andy followed her. "What's for dinner?"

"You hungry already? It's only five o'clock. Didn't you have lunch?"

"Yeah, but I didn't get to finish my sandwich. Too busy watching Harry in his rush to over-indulge. He couldn't get Liz on the phone, so he downed a few martinis in sixty seconds and got soused so bad he passed out and couldn't walk. Had to get Tom to help me get him up here."

"What's the matter? I've known him to have a few too many, but never to pass out."

Cody turned the oven on and retrieved a casserole from the refrigerator.

"Liz?" she asked.

"Yeah. He doesn't know which end is up. You've heard that song about the guy who fooled around and fell in love. Well, at the moment, that's Harry.

"Give him another hour or so, let him sleep it off. I don't want him to be alone. Fred won't be back 'til tomorrow."

# CHAPTER THIRTY-EIGHT

Liz stepped off the train. Her nephew Robert and his wife Diana waited at the escalator for her to exit from the Long Island Railroad platform. Their two sons, Jonathan and Barry, aged nine and seven, stood beside them, animated and waving at Liz.

The boys, tall for their ages, resembled their parents in looks and behavior—blond and fair like their mother; healthy, athletic and energetic like their father. The male side of the gene pool hadn't deviated an iota. The boys had already acquired their father's confident bearing.

Robert embraced her. "You don't visit often enough. The boys waited all day and behaved as if they were on sugar highs."

"I missed you guys, too."

Liz hugged Diana.

"Hi, Aunt. Did you bring us a present from Bermuda?" Jonathan asked.

Liz grabbed the boys. They practically strangled her. Their grandmother, Liz's sister June, died from cancer before they were born, and they knew Liz as their dad's only family.

"Of course I brought you a present." Liz reached in her tote bag and flung a plastic bag to each of them.

The boys couldn't wait until they got in the car to open their presents. They walked to the parking lot, undoing the cellophane tape and inspecting the contents of the bags.

"Great!" Jonathan held the white sweatshirt up to his chest, imprinted with *Captain* in the upper left corner and *Nautilus* in large letters across the front. "I'm the captain of the Nautilus."

Barry's eyes squinted and his face contorted. "What's the Argo?"

"It's the ship Jason led on his quest for the golden fleece, dummy," Jonathan said. "Remember? You saw the movie with me." He described a scene from the movie to his brother as they jabbered on the way to the car.

"Got anything planned?" Liz asked Diana.

"We rented a movie for tonight. Robert chose an action film, adults only. Little League games at two tomorrow."

Both Robert's parents were dead. He lost his father at the age of thirteen. Aunt Liz, his rock and only surviving family, not only provided emotional but financial support when his father died, and even more so when his mother, her sister, died three years later. She became his legal guardian, and instead of moving Robert to Manhattan where she lived, she incurred a commuting chore and moved to Long Island because she wanted to minimize the adjustments Robert had to face in the aftermath of losing both his parents. Two years later, Robert left for college. Liz resumed her former life, fell in love and married her husband.

Liz missed his mother as much as Robert did and often saw her sister in his eyes. She and June had enjoyed a best-friend relationship that defied sibling rivalry, even though they had totally different personalities. Liz had referred to June as her sexy sister or the social butterfly and recalled her emotional adventure in pursuit of marriage and family. She flitted from man to man until she finally captured a handsome jock of a husband and a dream house with a white picket fence.

June was happy and fulfilled and wanted the same happiness for her sister. The conversations they had so many times came to her mind: "Don't you want a husband and children? You're so much prettier than I am, and you don't have to work at it, like I do. The guys just flock to you, and all you do is work, listen to high-brow music and read."

"I'm just not the marrying kind, not like you and Mom."

"Liz, it doesn't have to be the way Mom and Dad were. They fell out of love someplace. But that's not the way it's supposed to be. Well, look at me, I'm ecstatically happy. I have a great husband, a beautiful child and my own home."

Those conversations invariably ended with hugs.

"Well, whatever you want, I'm always here for you."

"I know. You're my best friend. I love you, too."

Liz felt how sorely she missed her sister and knew the ache would always be there. But then, as usual, she focused on the reality of the gift her sister had left her: Robert, and his family.

"Have you eaten?" Diana asked. "There's some leftover pot roast if you're hungry."

"Oh, that'd be great. I'm famished. I rushed to avoid the chaos at Penn Station and didn't have time to eat anything. Then I missed the express train anyway."

Robert carried Liz's overnight bag. "So, good vacation?"

"Yes. Different."

"Different is good."

She didn't want to present Harry as a problem, but she knew the conflicts she experienced would surface, however, subtly, once she told Robert about her vacation. They had shared confidences for many years and easily discussed their problems.

Robert certainly had more than his share of problems as a fatherless adolescent, and she recalled urging him to pursue his education. "Your mother is reasonably secure. You don't need to get a job to help support your mother. I'm doing that. Your job is to get good grades."

Nevertheless, she remembered Robert hadn't listened to her and assumed the responsibility of earning money for himself and his mother. He mowed lawns, shoveled snow and even babysat. When he was sixteen and his mother died, he took a part-time job as a busboy at the local Italian restaurant and when promoted to a full-fledged waiter, he had insisted upon helping Liz with the household expenses.

Robert's stamina and grit never ceased to amaze her, and in retrospect her efforts to pamper him seemed feeble. The gifts she gave him—tickets to opening day at Yankee Stadium, a trip to Bermuda at spring break, a suit from Barney's when he searched for his first job—never adequately expressed the love she felt for him. But they both knew he was as much a son as if she had borne him from her womb, and as the ever present person in his life, she would always be there for him, for whatever he needed. And he would be there for her.

• • •

"How do you do this every week?" Liz asked.

What a juggling act, she thought, watching two Little League games on the same day and at the same time. Simple luck had the games scheduled conveniently at the same ball field. She, Robert and Diana sprinted from one baseball game to another every other inning.

"C'mon, Aunt. You know better," Diana said. "We do what needs to get done."

After the game, the whole team celebrated their victory at McDonald's, and on the way home, Robert made a stop at Dairy Queen for milk and ice cream. The boys, in the back seats with their aunt, argued about who got the greatest hit and made the best plays at the game.

"A single is just as good, if not better, than a home run. A home run is just one run. I scored two guys on that single." Jonathan bragged to his brother about his recent triumph.

Robert interrupted and diffused the sibling competitiveness. "Jonny, don't forget, your brother's home run was the go-ahead run. Not so shabby."

However much she loved Robert's children, Liz could never wholly adjust to the incessant comings and goings and unending conversation in the company of the boys. They never stopped moving and they never stopped talking. She tried to calm them down as they fussed in the back seats, next to her.

"Hey, can you two lower your voices for your aunt, and sit still for a few minutes?"

"Take a breather, guys," Robert chimed in.

Finally, silence reigned. Liz watched idly from the car window as all manner of homes and sprawling green lawns rushed before her. Her mind wandered, not settling anywhere. Harry intruded upon her thoughts as an unwelcomed reality. They were getting the time out he had asked for. They hadn't seen each other in three days and didn't plan to see each other on the weekend. She had chosen to remove herself from the City and the temptation of living a short cab ride from him. Out of sight, out of mind. She needed some space and a time out as much as he did.

Liz feared this so-called fling was no longer a frivolous, short-term encounter. It was rather a full-blown affair that had slowed down, not to an abrupt halt, but idling in neutral and awaiting a recharging of batteries.

When they reached home, the boys immediately took over the family room and entertained themselves with video games. With an open view from the kitchen, Diana periodically glanced over to check on the boys as she and Liz prepared dinner. Robert set the dining room table.

"Thank God for video games." Liz said.

Diana chuckled. "I do. But we've got to impose restrictions. Those things are addictive."

"So, tell us about your vacation. What was different? What happened?" Robert asked from across the room.

Liz exhaled an audible sigh. "Oh, I met a man. Not sure anything happened."

"Aha! You met a man?" Robert looked up at her with a surprised look, but short of astonishment.

Diana pivoted from the sink where she stopped preparing a salad. "It's about time." She said in a lilting voice which matched her enthusiasm for the news. "Yeah, you need a guy in your life."

Liz loved Diana—a pretty woman, blond and petite. Her demeanor deceived everyone, for she could wrestle her boys into submission when needed. Diana was as strong in physique as well as in spirit—an intelligent, down-to-earth woman, possessed of common-sense. Liz often thought she couldn't have chosen a better wife for her nephew. As usual, she and Diana spoke as candidly with each other as she did with Robert.

"No. I don't. As a matter of fact, so far, this man has been wreaking havoc with my head. And my body."

Robert quickly grasped the body reference. "Been to his bedroom? You know, you're still a very attractive woman."

"We can't figure out why you don't date more. Give it a whirl and have some fun. No kids, no one to answer to, no responsibilities. Just exercise some care about safe sex. What could be better?" Diana echoed Robert's opinion.

"Well, rest assured, can't say I didn't enjoy a holiday in paradise and the thrill of a roller coaster ride in the bedroom." Liz smirked.

"He invited me to his home, and I spent the whole week with him instead of staying on the ship. We did have a great vacation together."

"Fantastic!" Robert dropped the napkins on the table, rushed over to Liz in the kitchen and hugged her.

"Don't get excited. It's not anything but an infatuation. We had a great vacation. That's all."

Robert drew a chair back from the kitchen table and sat, eagerly awaiting more information. He watched Liz skillfully peeling potatoes.

"You've got to be kidding, Aunt. You spent a week with this guy? And there's nothing going on." He leaned back in the chair, "You've come such a long way—I mean, after the depression. You deserve something more in life, not just that cheerful, happy loneliness."

Robert jarred her memory bank. He reminded her of his dogged persistence in urging her to see a doctor when widowhood attacked her. And when the symptoms of the depression subsided, he and Diana relentlessly suggested she socialize and seek male companionship. They arranged a blind date with Robert's widowed boss, and later with a divorced Little League coach, but to no avail. No one could entice her to seek even a fleeting association with the opposite sex.

"I don't want a man screwing up my life. I've been there and done that."

A pause in the conversation followed. The issue had already been discussed many times, and the differences of opinion would not be aired again. Silence prevailed.

Robert couldn't restrain his curiosity and a short time after, a broad smile broke on his face. "C'mon, tell us, what's he's like."

"Nothing much to tell." She looked up at Robert, "Except he has a lot of money and power, and we don't live in the same world. He says he's in love with me, but don't all men say that? I have no expectations that our little fling, however wonderful it was, is meant to go anywhere but the bedroom. So, don't go thinking it's something more than it is."

"What are you saying, you're not involved with him?"

"Robert, involved is *in love*. It's you and Diana, now, and when you were eighteen." Liz said.

"Yeah, so? But what about you and Phil? You weren't eighteen." He reminded her of her love affair with her husband and the gripping passion that had dominated her life at that time.

Liz alternated her attention between Robert and the potato peeling.

"That was different. I knew right away with Phil. Now, I'm totally—I'd say, maybe—ambivalent, almost like I can *take it or leave it*. I don't know."

Robert frowned. "Well, I'm still happy to know your body didn't die and go to heaven with your heart."

"What a thing to say." Diana commented in a reprimanding tone.

Robert grabbed Liz and hugged her. "Sorry, Aunt." Then he pecked her on the cheek. "You know me, always speaking my mind. We just want the best for you. And I'm the guy who thinks I know what that is."

"I know. I know you mean well. Love you, love you both."

Barry bounced into the kitchen. "Hey, Mom." He pulled on her dress and gestured he wanted to whisper in her ear, but his dad and aunt heard his question anyway. "What's safe sex?"

# CHAPTER THIRTY-NINE

Liz returned home late Sunday night. She dropped her bag in the middle of the apartment and turned on the television. The answering machine flashed a red light number five on the console. She turned the machine off, choosing to deal with the five messages in the morning. They probably were work-related.

Liz had forgotten her cell phone Friday night and left it next to the answering machine. Very few people had her cell number, but she checked the recent calls anyway and was surprised two messages were from Harry on Saturday, asking her to call him back. I can't call now, it's half past eleven already and Saturday's a long time passed. I'll phone him in the morning. Tired and sleepy, she wanted a cup of tea, a shower and a half-hour in front of the television, watching anything, and going to bed.

She sat on the sofa and mindlessly stared at the television. Although the time spent with her family kept her busy, she had thought of Harry throughout the weekend and wished he had made a clean break with her. She summoned up a host of reasons and flaws in Harry's personality to support her inclination to break it off herself. He could be very sarcastic, used to having his way all the time, controlling and domineering.

Worst of all, their lifestyles mixed like oil and water. Harry was the oil, rising to the top, leading the public life of a politician and billionaire. She was the water calmly moving on the bottom in the private, ordinary, self-respecting life she inhabited.

Nonetheless, she still ached for him, imagined him touching her, holding her and feeling the warmth and thrill of his body mingling with hers. She wanted the conflict between head and heart to end. The sooner it ended, the sooner she could get back to normalcy.

She slept well, and when the intercom buzzed in the morning, she awoke with a sense of clarity and vowed not to be readily available to Harry. In retrospect, it was a good thing that she wasn't accessible the past weekend. She would get on with her life as if he wasn't a part of it.

Liz answered the intercom. "Peter? Yes. It's okay."

She hadn't checked her home answering machine yet and assumed one of the messages was probably from Peter. That's why he's at my door at eight in the morning. She slipped into a robe and opened the door.

Peter Handley, fortyish and tall, was a good-looking man who grew handsome as he matured. He stood at her door.

"Hi. Aren't you answering your calls these days?"

"C'mon in."

Liz and Peter had worked together at her last law firm. As a novice associate, he profited from her experience and mentoring advice about the politics and personalities of the partnership. They struck up a close working relationship and casually kept in touch after they both left the firm.

After a few years, Peter had launched a successful career, handling some high profile cases in the Frauds Bureau of the D.A.'s Office. He rose to a position of authority, a Deputy Chief, and was well-known and respected. He recruited Liz when he learned she decided to freelance and work part-time. He still sought and relied on her expertise and judgment.

"Sorry, Peter, I got in so late last night, I was too tired to listen to messages."

"Coffee?"

"Thanks."

"What's up? How's Marisa?" She poured coffee into mugs, and they sat at the dining room table.

"I'll get right to the point. I'm in a bind. I've got thirty-two pages I need tomorrow by ten in the morning. The document's a mess. Three different assistants worked on it and lacking grade-school English and margin scratching, you can't tell what's in or out. I did the best I could last night with some revisions, but it's still the document from hell."

"I can imagine. You've really got to get rid of some of the incompetents in your office."

"Marisa's in the hospital for the third time. I spent almost the whole night there and I'm going back now. I thought if you could do a rewrite for me, editing for grammar, the whole thing, by tonight and email it to me, I could manage the final from home. I'd really appreciate it."

"How's she doing?"

"Not good, really. But she's improved this morning. More tests."

"Sorry to hear she's still having problems. Don't worry about the job. I'll get it to you tonight. But please promise me, you'll keep Josh away from me."

"You got it. No Josh. Gotta run. I jotted a few numbers on the cover if you have questions. Hang up if you get Josh. I'll probably be at the hospital the rest of the day, so try my cell when you're ready to send."

"Okay."

"Thanks again for saving my life. Love y'a."

The door no sooner slammed shut when the phone rang. The caller ID read *Unknown Caller.*

"Hi. Harry?"

"I've been trying to reach you. When did you get back?" he asked.

"Late last night."

"Missed you."

"Me, too. Sorry, I didn't phone. Forgot my cell at home. I got your messages, but it was too late to call you last night."

"Just wanted to say hello. Enjoy your weekend?"

"Yes. Very busy with family. Lots of activity."

"You?"

"Played golf with Andy. Did some office work. Watched the Yankee game in the afternoon. Of course, the usual dinner with my daughters. They were asking for you. So was my mom. Dinner tonight?"

"I'd love to, but I can't. I've just got cornered for a job. From what I can see, it's going to be a long day and maybe a long evening." Her vow to get on with her life without him faded like a hopeful dream, and like many dreams, quickly forgotten in the wakefulness and light of day. She wanted to have dinner with him.

"Later than eight or nine?" He asked.

"Could be. I can't. I want to, but I can't."

"I thought you worked part time."

"It's more of a favor than work."

"Okay, I tried. Talk to you tomorrow." Harry hung up.

She wanted to explain the urgency of the situation, but didn't get a chance to say anything more. She interpreted his abruptness as annoyance and wanted to call him back and tell him she really wanted to see him, but decided not to, knowing she would yield if he asked her one more time to meet after dinner. She wouldn't need persuasion.

Liz flipped through the document, hoping she could finish editing it by early evening and maybe call Harry. Peter had included his revised version and the original for her to cull whatever he had missed. It was twice the job she imagined, merging two sets of revisions into one document. It definitely would require her to work into the evening. She couldn't call Harry back knowing she might have to cancel if she agreed to see him after dinner. Canceling would be worse than refusing him now.

She spent the day feverishly immersed in the job, not taking a break and not stopping to eat. The day flew in and out like a tornado, leaving a refuse of stress and remorse. It was after eleven o'clock when she punched in Peter's cell number.

"It's me, Peter. Finally done. What a nightmare."

"I know. Sorry, Liz. I owe you."

"How's Marisa?"

"Much better, happy to say. The baby's okay. She's a hundred percent better."

"Good. That's good news. You home? I'm going to email in a minute. You shouldn't have to format, maybe do some editing in your language if you think it's necessary."

"Uh, huh. Will you be up if I have a problem?"

"Yes, feel free. I'll wait by the phone until the transmission is finished."

She waited for Peter's acknowledgement that he received the document and stared at the computer monitor, regretting she had committed her day and evening to Peter. What would he have done if she refused, or if she had plans and wasn't available? She didn't make the right decision. She should have refused Peter, not Harry.

"I've got it, Liz. Thanks again. Good night."

"Night. Good luck tomorrow."

# CHAPTER FORTY

"It's a favor." Harry uttered aloud as he paced around his office. He needed to see her. She didn't need to see him and was doing very well without him. Obviously, her priorities were not the same as his. She went away for the weekend, couldn't be reached and then refused dinner with him so that she could do someone a favor? She was supposed to want to be with him as badly as he wanted to be with her. He wanted to hit a few speed bumps to slow down the relationship with a time out, but he wasn't expecting a complete halt.

Harry struggled the next day as to whether or not to phone her. He knew if he called her, he would invite her to the fundraiser the following night. He had misgivings about inviting her to attend a political affair because she avoided publicity as if were a contagious disease, and undoubtedly, the occasion would be covered by the newspapers. In any event, he couldn't expect her to accept an invitation to a black tie dinner at such short notice, so it was just as well he didn't risk another rejection. Finally, he decided to attend the affair alone.

• • •

Liz worked out at the gym and felt physically restored and recovered from the exhausting work the day before. She tried not to think about Harry, but hoped he would call and invite her to dinner. She admitted to herself that she missed him. Thoughts of their lovemaking crept into her mind and tugged at her libido. He said he would call her today, so she checked her cell every hour, but there were no messages.

Finally resigned there would be no call from Harry, she phoned her best friend Lauren. "You free after work for a drink?" She wanted company, and it wouldn't come better than a tête-à-tête with her best friend.

"You're on. The Landings okay? Anything planned?" Lauren asked.

"Yeah. No, nothing on for the evening. Meet you at five-thirty."

Liz showered at the gym, hopped on the Second Avenue bus and got off at New York University Medical Center to keep her scheduled six-month follow up mammogram. Her last exam showed a mass, and after an ultrasound, nothing cancerous, and she hoped there wouldn't be a referral for another test and the accompanying anxiety of waiting for the result.

Liz undressed and waited for the technician. Tolerating the discomforting squeezing of her breasts and picture taking, she looked forward to relaxing with Lauren, exchanging the monotonies of the day. They always had some news and laughter to share, and she hoped to confide her conflicting feelings about Harry. Maybe an evening with Lauren would help her get back in balance, back to the no-problems, cheerful person who left for Bermuda two weeks ago.

She walked the few blocks from the Center to a local bar called the Landings. A low-key, conservative pub and unlike the neon beer-sign variety in the neighborhood, it suited Liz and Lauren to indulge in gossipy girl talk. They had bonded with the bartender a long time ago, and despite the usual crowd that resembled a youth movement, they blended in the atmosphere and felt comfortable as regular customers.

"Hey, how are you?" Lauren asked as Liz approached.

They hugged. Liz moved a stool next to Lauren and slid up on the seat. She greeted the bartender. "Hi, Mack. Chardonnay, please."

Lauren wore a dressed-for-success navy pantsuit with a white silk blouse. Her large green eyes, soulful and alert, compelled attention. Liz wondered how, after a hectic day's work, Lauren managed to look so primped and groomed, her hair perfectly in place and attractively streaked with blond highlights that Liz knew were a high maintenance item in her budget.

"You look great. Real spiffy!"

"Thanks. I called Sunday. Left a message." Lauren said.

"Just got my mammo. I didn't have a chance to phone you back. So, how was your weekend?"

"Boring, as usual. Worked Saturday. Thought you might want to see a movie on Sunday, if you got back early enough."

"Didn't get home 'til late. Had a good time with the kids. I worked yesterday, literally incarcerated with a dreadful job and didn't finish until eleven last night."

They small talked. They really hadn't had the opportunity to talk one-on-one when they met for the girls' night out on Thursday. Lauren updated Liz on events that occurred while she had been in Bermuda: last week's street fair, the pharmacist moving his business across the street, a new nail shop.

Suddenly, Lauren asked, "Liz, you've been back a whole week and I haven't heard a word about the cruise."

"I know."

"What's up? C'mon, give."

"Well, I got off the ship. I spent the week with a man, at his home in Bermuda. I met him playing tennis. We got back last Sunday. I can't tell you everything."

"Why not?"

"Anyway, it was a glorious vacation. I've never experienced such passionate sex before, not even with my husband. I thought, it's just a fling, an infatuation. Enjoy it while you can because the week will be over before you blink your eyes. Now, I'm confused, because it's not over. I miss him."

"So, what's he like? What does he do for a living?"

"Don't ask."

"Why? Is he Mafia? CIA, or something?"

Liz shook her head and turned her eyes from Lauren toward a couple sitting across from her at the bar, holding hands and obviously enamored of each other. She reminisced in fleeting thoughts of Harry, reliving the sureness of his arms around her and the renewed desire he stirred. "I'm fifty-two years old. I haven't been with a man since my husband. And God knows how long ago that was! Sex is not supposed to be a priority in my life."

"So, what happened?"

Liz looked closely at Lauren. "We had a great time together. He treated me like a princess. I had myself psyched a couple of times for what I thought was the inevitable, you know, vacation over, fling over. But it didn't happen. He said he would call me today, but he hasn't, and now I think that it's happening. I mean—that it's over."

Her eyes filled up and blinked rapidly as she halted the tears that were about to eke out.

"I haven't seen him in a week. And now, I can't stop thinking about him, the whole weekend, all day yesterday, trying to work, and today, waiting for a call."

Liz paused and reached for a tissue in her handbag, "I don't know what's come over me. I feel so juvenile, like a teenager who's got a crush on a rock star."

"Calm down. You're getting yourself upset." Lauren said.

"I know. I really don't want to talk about it anymore."

"Does he live here or in Bermuda?"

"Here. Yeah. That's the part I can't tell you about. It doesn't matter. It's over. Probably the best thing. We live totally different lives anyway."

"What do you mean?"

Liz's cell chimed. She retrieved it from her handbag and didn't recognize the caller ID. Harry's cell always read *Unknown Caller*. He could be calling from outside someplace, a restaurant, or using someone's phone.

"Hello?"

"Hi, Liz. It's Marisa, Peter's Marisa."

"Oh. Hi, how are you feeling?"

"Fine, I'm doing much better. They sent me home this morning, although I'm virtually bedridden for the next week, unless I go into labor again.

"Liz, Peter told me how you helped him out. He's very grateful. So am I. He doesn't know I'm calling you. He's in the garage. Thing is, why I'm calling. There's this party, a PBA fundraiser tomorrow night at the Essex House, black tie. Politically, he needs to attend. His whole staff will be there and because they've had so many problems with the recent indictments, he's got to show up.

"He doesn't want to go without me, and he won't go alone. You know him, he's a snob about appearances, people gossiping, is his wife really sick, and all that. We discussed who he could go with, and he said he'd be okay with you filling in for me, said the office knows you, and no one would think anything—strange—if an employee went with him. He doesn't have the nerve to ask you for another favor."

"Marisa, believe me, it wasn't only a favor. I'm being paid very well. He doesn't have to feel guilty about that. He's such a good guy. It's really hard not to help him, especially with the crew he has working for him. They're all self-centered careerists."

"Do you think you can go?"

"To the fundraiser? Yeah. Sure. I'm okay with that. Actually I could use a night out. But, please warn him though, he has to keep Josh away from me."

"Liz, I can't thank you enough."

"No problem. I'm looking forward to seeing some of those misfits from his office in black tie. I'm not home right now. Ask Peter to give me a call tomorrow morning with the time he wants to meet and anything else I should know."

"Thanks, again, Liz."

"Take care of yourself and the baby."

Liz hung up and turned to Lauren. "Sounds like it might be fun. I'm going to a black tie tomorrow night at the Essex House with a client."

# CHAPTER FORTY-ONE

Arm in arm, Liz and Peter strolled into the lavish banquet room of the hotel. "Our table is over there." Peter said. He pointed to the table number assigned to his office on the other side of the room and diverted her to the bar.

"Let's get a drink before we sit down. I'd like to avoid being bombarded with questions I'm anticipating from the friends of the friends regarding the indictments. I really can't offer them any explanations. I'll let my staff deal with it for the moment."

"Sure."

Liz had on the same red dress she had worn at Chez Mere and turned heads as she and Peter strolled across the empty dance floor to the bar.

"From the stares you're provoking, I think I'm going to have to protect you tonight. You do look very elegant, very fetching. Don't mind me if you want to—" He handed her a martini.

Liz interrupted him, "Thanks, Peter, but I'm leaving with the man I came in with. You, of all people, know there's a lot of razzle-dazzle pretense going on here. And you know me, it's not my style.

"So, your sister's flying in from California tomorrow to help. That's a blessing."

"Yeah, I can get back to a normal work schedule. Between you and me, I can't rely on Josh. As you well know, he doesn't interact well.

"Speaking of work, Ms. Brady, how many times are you going to refuse my offer of a permanent job? How can I entice you? You'd have carte blanche authority, a title that would look great on a resume in a few years, full city benefits, a thirty hour week, all the perks—"

Liz chomped on an hors d'oeuvre, "Stop, Peter, we've discussed this already, numerous times. Remember? I'm not interested in another career at this stage of my life, much less in your office. We get along famously now, and I like it just the way it is. Considering the fact that I can't tolerate much of your staff, but I do, for your sake. That's the best I can do."

"Exactly what I'd like to remedy. I need somebody in charge who'd wield a whip and at the same time demonstrate good judgment and dedication. You'd be perfect."

"Which reminds me, Peter, I've got to tell you something, but I can't tonight, at least not right now." Liz wanted to make him aware of her association with Harry and assure him that she had been discreet about the confidentiality of the District Attorney's Office. He should be aware, in case he might hear comments from someone. The possibility existed, however remote, that she and Harry had been seen together.

Peter ordered her another drink and handed it to her. "Excuse me for a sec, Liz." He turned and walked across the bar to chat with a police chief, who had summoned him with a wave of his hand.

Liz stood unobtrusively a few feet from the bar. She sipped her martini and idly surveyed the crowded room of the press corps, local talk-show hosts, columnists and the usual society crowd clustered at special tables. There must be at least three hundred people here, she thought.

Suddenly, she froze and almost dropped her glass. "Oh, my God!" She mumbled, "Why didn't it occur to me that he might be here?"

Harry strode directly toward her from across the room. She turned around, hoping he didn't see her, and scurried to join Peter at the bar. She intruded on his conversation and tried to move from Harry's sight. Her back to Harry and facing Peter, she finished her martini in one quick gulp.

"Good evening, Peter."

"Evening, Harry."

"Liz! How nice to see you here."

She turned around abruptly and with a half-smile, said, "Hello, Harry."

Harry's eyes slowly glided from the bottom of her figure to the top of her head. "Very seductive, as usual. Lots of players here tonight. You should give out tickets."

Harry shifted his eyes to Peter. "Peter, Liz needs another martini. Her glass is empty. She needs at least two to get in the mood. Maybe a dance. Depends on the sort of foreplay you prefer."

A signal from Harry's assistant across the room beckoned him to return to his table. He left Liz and Peter, stunned and facing each other at the bar.

"See you later. Save me a dance, huh, Liz?"

"What the hell was that all about? Do you know him?" Peter asked.

"Yes. I can't explain now."

Peter gaped, his eyes squinted and his brow tightened in a furrow. "Are you all right?"

"No, I'm not." Her voice squeaked in a high pitch. "Please get me another drink." Her body trembled and her lips quivered. How dare he announce in flaunting bravado that they knew each other, and sexually, which was outrightly embarrassing. If there had been anything left in her glass, she would have tossed it at his face. He meant to embarrass and insult her, and he had succeeded.

"C'mon. Let's sit down." Peter carried their drinks and led Liz to their table. She perfunctorily greeted the staff members she knew and sat down. Her body was trembling and still bearing the impact of Harry's offensive remarks.

The President of the PBA presided on the dais, microphone in hand, and urged everyone to sit down. A hush occurred in the room as the attendees scrambled to tables. Liz looked up and met Harry's eyes from across the room. He looked away.

Peter sat next to her. "How do you know him?"

Liz ignored his question and brought the martini to her lips, peering over the glass. Harry targeted his eyes on her again and didn't look away this time. He glared at her. For a moment, he turned and spoke with someone at his table, then resumed his former position and found her eyes again, unwilling to relinquish his focus.

She looked away. "I can't explain now, Peter."

The innuendos Harry spouted reeled in her head. Her head ached, and she felt the threat of a migraine developing. She reached in her purse for an Imitex and impulsively swallowed it with a swig of martini. He not only made it known she had been sexually intimate with him, but inferred that she was an available, marketable commodity. *Give out tickets.* "How could he be so cruel?" She whispered. And she thought she might be in love with him.

Liz shuddered, an acid stomach stinging her inside. She looked across the room again. Harry glared at her, his face void of expression.

"I can't do this." She sprung from her seat.

"What's wrong, Liz?" Peter asked.

She grabbed her purse. "Please forgive me. I'm probably ruining your evening, but I can't help it. I have to go."

"I'll take you home."

"No, you stay. Please. Both of us leaving will only make it worse. I'm perfectly all right. Good night. I'm sorry."

Liz rushed to the back of the room where she thought she wouldn't attract attention. She recklessly moved around tables like a mouse in a maze, desperate to find the exit. She hurried feverishly and her eyes quickly swelled as tears cascaded down her cheeks.

# CHAPTER FORTY-TWO

Andres was just about to push the buzzer to open the door to the elevators, and Harry interrupted him. "You'd better call her first. She's not expecting me."

"Ms. Brady? Harry's on his way up." Andres hit the buzzer that opened the glass door without waiting for a response from Liz.

Liz stood at the open door of her apartment waiting for the elevator to stop. Barefoot and still in her red dress, Liz's face was contorted and flooded with tears. "What are you doing here?"

"I followed you. I saw you crying." Harry slid passed her into the apartment, and she quickly closed the door. He turned around and faced her. Before he could speak a word, she yelled at him, "You bastard!" She beat at his chest with closed fists. Her arms thrashed aimlessly in the air, missing his face.

Harry tried to grab her wrists and restrain her. "Hey, stop it. Stop!"

"You despicable, chauvinistic pig. How could you say such things?" She shouted at him, her voice rising in a crescendo. "In front of everyone. In front of Peter."

Liz continued to pound away at his chest. "Calling me, calling me . . . a whore!" Harry finally caught her wrists and held them tightly. She stopped hitting him. Her adrenaline rush subsided and her head dropped on his shoulder.

"I'm sorry, Liz. I'm sorry."

She looked up at him, sobbing. Her knees wobbled.

"I hate you! You're a monster. How did I fall in love with a monster?" Her body went limp. She almost fell to the floor. He held her up and led her to the sofa. They sat down, and he placed his hands on her shoulders.

"Have you slept with him?"

"You have to ask that question?"

Infuriated, she tore his arms away and flailed at him once again. She attempted to strike him in the face, but lacked the energy to continue to attack him. Wet with tears, her face flushed to a crimson color and collided with his cheek. He embraced her and held her tightly.

"For chrissake, Harry, his wife is about to give birth. Do you really think he'd be flaunting adultery?"

"You walked in with him, on his arm, like . . . , like you'd just been together. What was I supposed to think? Liz, the younger guy who wanted to marry Susan? It was Peter. He had an affair with my wife. I lost control."

"No." She shook her head. "No, not Peter."

"Forgive me. I was so jealous—so angry. You had to wear that dress. It just reminded me of our first night together. You broke my heart."

Liz whimpered, childlike in his arms. She touched his face and glided her fingers down to his mouth. She brought her lips to his and kissed him with the desire she had been trying to void from her body and her consciousness.

"Harry, please make love to me." The tears trickled down her face.

They kissed each other savagely and she fell back on the sofa. He lay halfway beside her and unzipped his trousers and slipped them down from his waist. They yielded to unbridled passion, pulling and pushing their clothing aside to gain access to each other. She yelled his name out as she climaxed and his swelling succumbed to her tight, wet passage. They lay momentarily in the discomfort of rumpled clothing, but in a gratified stupor.

Harry fumbled with his shirt, which was half on his body and half off. He pulled his trousers up. She leaned on him as he supported her into the bedroom. As soon as she fell backward on a pillow, her eyes closed. She fell asleep immediately. He undressed her and drew the bedcovers over her naked body.

He grabbed a bottle of water from the refrigerator and dialed Fred on his cell as he gulped the water.

"Hi, Fred, I need a favor. Did I wake you?"

"No, it's only nine-thirty. What can I do for you, Boss?"

"I need to stay here tonight and look after a friend. I'm at Thirty-Sixth and Lexington." He blurted out the exact address.

"Can you pack me an overnight bag, pajamas, a toothbrush? A suit for tomorrow. Whatever you think I'll need. I'll be going to the office from here. Take a cab. The doorman will buzz you up. Apartment Twelve D."

"No problem. Be there in a jiffy. Do I need a name?"

"Brady. Thanks, Fred."

• • •

Harry returned to the bedroom to check on Liz. She was asleep, just as he'd left her, passed out. He watched her for a few moments and placed his hand on her forehead. She felt feverish. He wet a facecloth under cold water, positioned it on her forehead and tried to revive her by gently moving her head from side to side, "Liz? You all right? C'mon, wake up."

Finally, she moaned and opened her eyes, which narrowed to small slits. She was naked and tried to sit up, but could only manage slightly propping herself up.

"Can't keep my eyes open." She mumbled.

"Can I get you anything? Water?"

"No. I'm okay. Sleep, I need to sleep," she muttered as she fell back on the pillow and tossed the cloth from her forehead to the floor.

She didn't look well, but he felt confident she only needed sleep to recover. He showered and threw on a terry robe he found on a hook in the bathroom. He hung his tuxedo and her dress in a closet and gathered her underwear and placed it on a chair. He went into the living room, turned the television on to the ten o'clock news and waited for Fred.

The phone rang. Harry quickly picked up the phone, concerned that the ringing might disturb Liz.

"Hello." Harry said.

"Who's this? Is Liz there?"

Harry recognized Peter's voice.

"It's Harry."

"Can I speak with Liz? Is she all right"

"She's fine. Asleep. I'm staying with her. I'll tell her you called." Peter hung up.

Soon after, the intercom buzzed.

"You expecting Fred?" Andres asked.

"Yes, it's okay, Andres," Harry said.

Fred dropped the case and hung the garment bag in the nearest closest next to the door.

"If there's nothing else, I'll be on my way."

"Thanks again, Fred. Talk to you tomorrow. Night."

"Good night."

# CHAPTER FORTY-THREE

Two hours later, Liz stumbled into the kitchen and found Harry about to drop some scrambled eggs in an omelet pan. Her swollen eyes ached and her stomach churned. She leaned against the kitchen doorframe and watched him.

"Hungry?" he asked.

"No. My stomach's in an uproar. I just threw up. I shouldn't have taken that pill. I think I'd like some tea and toast. Maybe it'll settle my stomach. Want some toast with your omelet?"

"Yes. I couldn't find the bread. You're very organized though. Found everything else. Made some coffee, decaf."

"The bread is in the crisper, in the refrigerator. I know it's weird. Don't ask. Where'd the pajamas come from?"

"My new guy, Fred. Brought me a change of clothes. I didn't want to leave you. You didn't look well. You still look sick. What did you take?"

"A painkiller. I had a throbbing headache at the hotel. I thought I was getting a migraine."

"Not a good idea with a martini."

"More than one martini," she said.

Liz retrieved the bread from the refrigerator, placed two slices in the toaster and took some plates from the cabinet. She set some placemats on the table.

She watched Harry slide the omelet on a plate and cover it with another plate and waited for the toast to pop up, her back to Harry. He turned her around and kissed her on the lips.

"Forgive me?"

"Already have. I never thought you could be so hurtful. And vicious, as if I'd committed some unforgivable crime against you."

"I know. I felt so angry—at Peter—not you. Believe me, I'd give anything to take it all back. I didn't mean to hurt you. I love you. I'm truly sorry."

"Your anger is very scary. Eat your omelet before it gets cold."

Liz picked up the plate with the omelet and toast and brought it to the dining room table. Harry carried the coffee. He ate enough of the omelet to quiet his hunger pains, then pushed the plate forward and drank coffee.

"I don't feel well." She bit into the toast and dropped it on the plate. "Should I set an alarm?"

"Fred's going to call me on my cell. Headache? Any pain?"

"No. Just nauseous."

You need to sleep. C'mon, get in bed."

Liz lay down with her back to him. Harry sat on the side of the bed and gently rubbed her back. He kissed her on her neck. He had stripped her of her dignity. His ego in total disrepair and guilt menacing his thoughts, he leaned over to switch off the lamp and asked her again. "Please, Liz, tell me you forgive me."

She turned and directed her bloodshot eyes at him. "I forgive you, Harry. I understand, about Peter, though it doesn't help. I still feel violated." She swung her arms around his waist and clutched him. Her head lingered on his chest. "I do love you. I don't know what's going to happen to us, but I do love you."

"I love you, too. You must know, I do, especially from the jealous bastard you saw this evening. I'm so sorry, Liz. We'll be all right. I promise."

Harry watched her eyes close as her arms fell from him. He turned the lamp off, brought the covers to her shoulders and crawled in beside her. The lavender scent from her body comforted him, and for the first time in a week, he drifted off to sleep without tossing and turning like an insomniac.

• • •

Liz awoke with a headache, but not of migraine magnitude. Her eyes felt as if sand had settled in them. Weak from vomiting and not eating, she staggered into the kitchen, hoping Harry had made coffee. The carafe was half full.

She poured the coffee and placed the mug in the microwave, nuked it and noticed a sheet of computer paper hanging from the overhead cabinet door. She opened the door and the paper fell.

Harry had scrawled across the page in huge letters *Call Me* and signed *The Repentant One* with his phone number written below.

When she opened the refrigerator for milk, she found another sheet leaning against the milk carton. *Call Me. I didn't want to wake you* written on the paper. Yet another sheet was in the crisper. She took the bread out, put a slice in the toaster and laughed aloud. She felt better already.

She punched his number on her phone, "Hello? Harry?"

"Morning. How do you feel?"

"A little shaky. I'm sorry about last night."

"You have nothing to apologize for. It was all my fault. I was so jealous. Didn't know I could behave so badly. I promise you, I'll never hurt you like that again."

"I meant, sorry about passing out. Thanks for staying with me."

"Well, at least I was good for something. Anything planned for today?"

"Nothing."

"I'm leaving early. Pack a bag and Tom will pick you up. Fred will make us dinner. We'll have a quiet evening. We need to talk."

"Yes, I know."

Liz finally admitted she was in the throes of a full-fledged affair. She loved him. They needed an understanding of what they were doing. She didn't want to be in love with anyone, much less someone so removed from her lifestyle. What chance did she have of not losing herself again as she had with her husband, making adjustments and compromising, attending to a man's every wish and whim? Did she want to do that again? She was putty in Harry's hands. He would break her heart if she let him, and she probably would let him.

"Four o'clock good for you?" he asked.

"Fine. See you later."

She tidied the apartment and packed an overnight bag. She intended to stay the night and maybe Friday night, but certainly not the weekend. They were already both too needy to spend so much time together. Why did she fall in love with this guy at this stage of her life? She had been perfectly happy, almost perfectly happy before she met him.

The phone rang. She read the caller ID. It was Peter. She let it ring once more and braced herself for what she had to tell him. She picked up the receiver on the third ring.

"Hi, Peter. Yes, I'm fine. I'm terribly sorry about last night."

"It's okay. No problem."

"How's Marisa."

"Fine."

Peter came right to the point and wanted to know how she knew the Mayor.

"Liz, what's going on? Harry answered your phone last night. Are you seeing him?"

"Yes." She didn't offer any details. "I do want you to know that whatever work I've done for you has not been compromised in any way. And it's probably best if I didn't work for you anymore. I wanted to tell you last night. It just wasn't the right time or place. And, then—"

"Wait a minute. What are you telling me? Because you dated him a few times, you're quitting on me. No, that won't work."

"It's complicated, Peter."

"I know him, Liz. He's not a guy you want to get involved with."

"I'm already involved, and I don't want to jeopardize your name or your office."

"It won't last, whatever it is. It never does with him. He's a philanderer. Everybody knows that."

"I'm not expecting it to go on. But at the moment, it is what it is."

"You're not quitting me. Why don't you let me be the judge of the risks? I've gotta go. We're having lunch next week. You name the day. We've got to talk about this." He hung up.

Peter and Harry had a history, a very hurtful history. What made her think Peter would understand? She had to tell him, and she had to quit because his reputation might be at risk. Not only had she had a great working relationship with him, but she considered him a friend. There was no way to soften the blow of the news that she had to quit. It had to be said straight out.

The intercom buzzed.

"There's a delivery for you, Ms. Brady. Can you come down, or shall I send him up. You need to sign. He won't accept my signature." Andres said.

"I'll be right there."

Liz grabbed her keys and rode the elevator to the lobby. An enormous bouquet of roses filled the concierge desk. The FTD delivery man stood beside the roses and extended his clipboard to her.

"Please sign here." He ripped a receipt from the clipboard and handed it to her.

"Thank you," she said.

She placed the two dozen roses, already beautifully arranged in a vase, on the dining room table and opened the envelope attached to the flowers. She read the note aloud, *I love you, H.* And below in parenthesis *(I've never written that before).*

The man who sent her flowers was not the same man Peter was talking about a few minutes earlier. Her eyes filled up. When was the last time she received roses? Or for that matter, when was the last time someone wrote *I love you.* A lone tear escaped from her eye and she wiped it away with her fingertip and smiled.

She checked her email to see if any work was in the offing. Lauren emailed asking about the black tie night and she had replied in one word, *Disaster*, but then decided to change the downbeat response. She added an email: *Oops, no disaster, just received a bouquet of roses. Update you later.*

# CHAPTER FORTY-FOUR

Liz stretched out on the sofa and reflected on the upheaval of her emotions and relived the feeling of Harry's body next to hers in bed last night. There hadn't been a man beside her in that bed for a very long time, especially a man who was there to take care of her. She dozed into a peaceful nap, awakened by the buzz of the intercom. "Yes, okay." She answered.

"Hi, Liz, how's it going?" Tom asked as he stood in the hallway. "Beautiful roses."

"Fine, Tom. C'mon in. How are you? I'd like to take the flowers. Think I'm ready."

"I'm good, thanks. Boss said he left some stuff in the closet near the door." Tom pointed to the closet and removed the garment bag and case. "Probably didn't want to schlep all this stuff to the office."

When Tom stepped off the elevator, Andres gave him the once-over stare of scrutiny, from top to bottom.

Andres directed his questions to Liz. "Going on a trip? Shall we keep your mail aside?"

"No," she answered but didn't volunteer any more information. Tom, carrying an overnight case and a garment bag, the Mayor's car double-parked in front of the building, and Liz holding a vase of roses, was already too much activity for Andres to digest.

Harry met Liz and Tom at the door when they arrived.

"Hi, Boss." Tom dropped the luggage, took the flowers from Liz and placed them in the center of the dining room table.

"Evening, Tom. Thanks. That's it for today. I'll ring you tomorrow."

"Hi. Feel better?" He embraced her and pressed a lengthy kiss against her lips as if he hadn't seen her in weeks.

"I'm fine. Flowers have great healing powers. Thank you. Couldn't stand the thought of them wilting away in an empty apartment. You're beautiful to send them."

"A feeble attempt at apology. Fred's cooking up something special for dinner. Don't ask him though, it's supposed to be a surprise. C'mon, I'll introduce you."

They entered the kitchen.

"Fred, this is Liz, Liz Brady." Fred turned around and at the sight of Liz, his face blossomed into a broad smile like a photo of a bud fast-forwarded into bloom. His eyes twinkled.

"It's so good to meet you." Fred freed his hand from the spatula he held and shook hands. "Can I get the lady some refreshment, a drink?"

"Thanks, Fred. I'll take care of it," Harry said.

Liz and Harry walked to the bar. His hand in hers, he kissed her on the neck, a trigger area he knew would arouse her.

"What's your pleasure?"

"Hmm, as if you didn't know."

"Martini?"

"I've sworn off martinis temporarily. A dry sherry, please. So, did you say something to Fred about me? He acted a bit hyper, nervous or something."

"I phoned him and told him the lady I was in love with would be spending the night. I asked him to cook dinner for us. Said he'd loved to. It's not in his job description, but he's made me dinner a few times already. Very talented. He loves to cook. It's above and beyond everything else he does so well. I certainly hit the jackpot hiring him."

Harry, behind the bar, mixed a martini and poured it into a glass. "I forgot to tell you earlier. Peter called last night while you were asleep. I didn't want the ringing to wake you. He wanted to know how you were."

"I spoke with him this morning."

"Oh?"

"I told him he needn't worry about any work confidences being violated, and I tried to tell him I couldn't work for him anymore. I didn't tell him about us—in Bermuda—I mean, just that it was complicated."

He handed her a glass of sherry, took a sip of his martini and sat beside her at the bar.

"I don't have any problem with you working for him, although I prefer you didn't. He's not my favorite person."

"Well, you wouldn't have the problem, would you? It's his side that's at risk."

"That's not what I meant. I was referring to our past, Peter's and mine. As for confidences, I wouldn't expect you'd reveal anything to me about what went on in his office. If you did tell me something by chance that you shouldn't have, I wouldn't use it against him. I don't have a vengeance for Peter."

"That's really not the issue, it's not what actually transpires. It's what it looks like."

"I know. Are you changing your mind?"

"No. Even if it's not bad, it looks bad. He's not accepting it. He gave me the impression he doesn't care about the risks. He seemed more concerned that I was *involved* with you, as he called it."

"Oh?" Harry sipped his martini again.

"Called you a philanderer."

"Not unusual. What else?"

She turned sideways, faced him for a moment and expected to read his reaction.

"Isn't that enough? I think he hates you."

"Yeah, he probably does."

"Liz?"

She stared at the empty sherry glass, twirling her fingers around the rim, preoccupied in thoughts about Peter, his judgment of Harry, losing work and maybe a friend. If she had lunch with Peter, he would probably try to convince her to end the relationship. She turned and looked at Harry.

"What?" she asked.

"When I said you've ruined me for other women, I meant it."

# CHAPTER FORTY-FIVE

"It's such a joy to have a woman in the house," Fred said as he ushered Liz and Harry to the dining room. He drew a chair out for Liz and placed a napkin on her lap.

Fred had set the table with the fine china and crystal stemware from the dining room. Two red roses, each in a bud vase, were in the center of the table. Scented candles filled the dimly-lit room with jasmine and lavender. Chopin piano music lurked in the background. Fred placed a martini to the right of Harry's place setting.

Liz watched Harry's eyes wandering around the table and at the exquisite arrangement Fred had created. Harry sat down and his eyes followed Fred prancing around the room like a gazelle, gleefully lighting candles, pouring wine, repositioning a glass or a piece of silverware. Clearly, Harry was as surprised and in awe as Liz was.

"Coffee will be ready for you upstairs when you've finished dinner." Fred left them smiling at each other, gaping and speechless.

Liz sipped her wine. "I feel like I'm royalty, about to dine with the prince."

Harry leaned over and kissed her on the cheek.

"I didn't ask for VIP treatment. It was supposed to be just a simple, home-cooked dinner."

Fred had apportioned the meal on plates, placed them on silver warmers and covered them with lids. They had only to lift the lids and their knives and forks.

"You're the reason for all this pampering. You're going to have to move in."

Liz ignored his remark.

"Scrumptious," she said as she tasted the chicken. "You don't want to eat like this every evening. It's an invitation to overeat. You'd be a candidate for a diet in no time."

Harry poured more wine in their glasses.

"It seems you've hired another Martine." Liz said.

"I want you to come live here." Harry finished the last of his martini.

"You're not serious."

"Yes, I am serious, Liz. I want you to live with me."

"That's impossible. Don't talk like that."

She almost dripped wine on the table. He was being impulsive, moved by the ambiance Fred had created.

"You're the Mayor, a public figure, you can't openly cohabitate with someone."

"Who said I can't?"

"I said you can't. You're supposed to be an example of a high moral standard, a role model."

He finished eating, placed his knife and fork on the plate and leaned back. He brought his glass to his lips and drank the last bit of wine.

"Living together is a helluva lot better than being labeled a philanderer."

"The martini and wine are talking." She said.

"Are you finished?"

"Yes."

Harry turned the music off and blew the candles out. The dining room darkened. A night light in the anteroom guided them to the staircase.

Fred had made preparations upstairs as well. One lamp dimly lit the room. A tray arrangement with cups and saucers was placed on the coffee table. Adagios floated from the sound system. A candle burned and its lavender scent spread throughout the room. A post-it note stuck on the coffeemaker in the kitchen read: *Ready to Brew* and another post-it pointed the way to dessert: *Crème caramel in the refrigerator.*

Harry unbuttoned his shirt.

"I need some help."

Liz smiled, dropped her handbag on the sofa and pushed down on his shoulders, sitting him down. She sat beside him, slid her hands inside his shirt, across his chest and up to his shoulders, waiting for his lips to find hers. He kissed her neck. His lips moved down her cleavage to her breasts. She lifted her jersey over her head, exposing her bosom.

"We need a bed," he said.

"When I finish undressing you." She unbuckled his belt and unzipped his trousers. Her hands moved up and down his thighs.

"I'm on a tour. Want to see if I overlooked anything my first few trips."

"Can I tour with you?"

He stood up, letting his trousers fall to the floor. He unclasped her bra and kissed her breasts, his tongue licking and savoring her nipples. She peeled her pants from her waist and placed his hand on her thigh. They sat nude, kissing, touching and stroking each other.

"Enough exploring?" he asked.

"I never get enough of you."

They stepped quickly to the bedroom. At his first movement, he penetrated her. She screamed in delight. He didn't usually enter her so fully, but teased her until she begged him to go inside. She couldn't restrain her hips from meeting his thrusts and quickened the rhythm.

"More, Harry."

He pushed, faster and faster each time until she cried out in pleasure. He remained inside her and held the warmth and wetness of her long after he had finished emitting his fluid. He finally removed himself and clutched at her, his head embedded in her chest.

"Harry, are you all right?"

She stroked his hair and uncoiled her body to reach down to kiss him on the forehead. His blue eyes watered. He reached up to meet her with a kiss and held his lips on her cheek, breathing in short gasps. He held her tightly.

"I love you."

"I love you, too."

"I want you in my life, every minute. I need you," he whispered in her ear.

In spite of wallowing in the afterglow of their lovemaking and the romantic mood of their dinner, Liz could not withhold what she was thinking.

"Harry, you've already turned my life upside down. Please don't ask me to change everything in sixty seconds."

He rolled over to the other side of the bed.

"Not everything. Just move in with me."

"It's not fair. I do have a life."

Harry sat up. "What's not fair?"

"You, asking me to live with you. We don't know each other a month and you've got me so emotionally entangled, I can't think. I don't know who I'm supposed to be anymore—your lover or myself." Her head moved from side to side. "I don't know what I want anymore."

Harry leaned over and kissed her.

"Sounds like the same malady I have. Except I know what I want."

"You always know what you want."

"Do you want to marry me?"

"What? Marriage?"

Liz bounced up like a dolphin bursting out of water. She pulled pajamas from her overnight case and faced him, eye-to-eye.

"You're insane, really insane. Can you make it any more complicated than it already is? In case you haven't noticed, I'm a girl from Queens, and you're a billionaire and the Mayor of New York."

"And in case you haven't noticed, I'm still a boy from Brooklyn. Okay, enough! Glad we've got that settled." Harry sighed.

"Nothing is settled." She said.

She knew they were totally in love, but totally at odds with each other. They were arguing and for the first time, they verbalized and aired their differences, only this time the issue wasn't lust versus love, it was the underclass versus the upper class.

He got up and grabbed her by the arm.

"Kiss me."

They stood nude and faced each other. She lifted her head, her lips in proximity to his. He kissed her and she rested her head on his chest. He put his arms around her.

"Please, Liz, no more time outs. It doesn't work for me. I understand. I do. I know you're overwhelmed. So am I. The truth is I'll do anything you want, except give you up. Try me."

"Harry, I do love you. I never thought I'd ever love anyone again. I want to be with you, but I can't move in with you."

They showered together and tuned in to the ten o'clock news. Harry ate a crème caramel, stretched out on the sofa. Liz sat on a pillow on the floor beside him. He put his spoon to her lips. She opened her mouth and let the spoon lay on her tongue and swallowed the caramel.

"Do you think he made that from scratch?" she asked. She sipped her decaf.

"No clue. He's a man of many talents. And you're going to disappoint him. I really think he's expecting you to hang out here. You heard his comment about a woman being a joy in the house."

He stirred the caramel, readied it on the spoon, and brought it to her mouth.

"Yes, I heard. Look, Harry, I am hanging out here. Tonight and tomorrow night. You play golf on Saturday, and I'll come back Sunday and have dinner with you at your mom's and stay Sunday night. By then, you'll be sick of me and want me to go home."

Liz tossed and turned when they got to bed. He rubbed her back and tried to help her relax. He fell asleep with his arm on her back. She turned and stared at the ceiling, preoccupied with his offer to move in with him. He doesn't give up. If she didn't resist, he'd consume her in one gulp. Instead of the princess kissing the frog and turning him into a prince, the prince would kiss the frog and swallow the princess.

She crawled out of bed, closed the bedroom door and turned the television on, turned it off and decided to read. Reading made her feel sleepy, and, finally, she dozed off at two in the morning.

She awoke to the sound of running water from the bathroom, got up and stood at the open door. She stretched and watched him shave, half nude, in his pajama bottoms. She marveled at his body, the tight chest and the perfectly proportioned muscular arms wielding a razor from his hand to his face.

"I was up for a while, reading." She spoke to the mirror image of him.

"Go back to sleep. I woke up a few times and you weren't in bed. You didn't sleep well?

"You look pretty." She kissed him on the shoulder.

"Thought we'd have coffee together. I'll go back to bed later. I need the bathroom when you're finished."

Liz put on slippers and a cover-up over her pajamas.

"All yours," he said.

She returned to the bedroom as he drew his tie around in a final knot and adjusted his shirt collar. Standing in front of a full-length mirror, she spied him looking at her reflection in the mirror.

"C'mere, you lovely thing." He grabbed her, kissed her on the cheek and then opened the door to the stairway.

"I have a dilemma."

"Really?"

"I can't be in two places at the same time—here with you and at the office. Come downtown for lunch?"

"Absolutely not. I'm not announcing to the whole of New York City that we're seeing each other. Not a good idea."

"Sooner or later." He said.

"It'll have to be later, much later."

# CHAPTER FORTY-SIX

Harry left for his office and Liz slept another hour. She drank her second cup of coffee in the breakfast room and watched Fred moving around the kitchen, emptying the dishwasher, rearranging some items in the refrigerator and surveying the pantry with a pen and pad in his hand.

"Can I get you some breakfast, Ms. Liz?" Fred asked.

"No. Thank you. Have you had breakfast? Coffee?"

"Oh, yes, hours ago."

"Have a coffee with me. I've something I want to ask you."

"I couldn't, Ms. Liz. It's not appropriate."

"Fred, I'm not your employer, he is. Please?" she pleaded. "A coffee. And sit."

"No coffee, thanks." Fred obliged her and sat down across from her at the breakfast room table, his hands folded in his lap. "What can I do for you?"

"You put on quite an extravaganza for us last night. The dinner was delicious, to say nothing of the romantic mood you created. Everything was simply wonderful."

Fred's eyes blinked excessively, he smiled and his hands fidgeted. "Thank you. I'm glad you appreciated my efforts."

"I'm curious. Why so elaborate? We were really quite grateful, I mean, and surprised. But, why?"

"I thought that's what Mr. Harry wanted. I hope I have your word you won't repeat anything I say. I don't want to betray a trust. So far, Mr. Harry and I have been getting along very well."

"Absolutely, between you and me. I promise."

"Mr. Harry called me yesterday and asked if I would cook dinner for someone special, and that you'd be spending the night. He said he was in love with you, and how would I feel about you living here and taking care of the two of you instead of just him. Well, I told him that I thought that was just great. And I did think it was great."

She thought Harry had been impulsive when he asked her to live with him, but he had sought his housekeeper's input beforehand. He must have been serious, very serious.

"I was very happy to hear you'd be living here because, well, look around, there are no plants, no pictures, no pillows. It's a beautiful house, but it's bland and lonely. A woman in a home is more necessary than the furnishings. I know it was presumptuous of me, but I wanted to do my best to make you feel welcome."

"Oh. You did a wonderful job, making me feel welcome." Once again, she didn't think she fit the part, but she felt like the princess. She stood up, leaned over and kissed him on the cheek.

"Thanks, Fred. You are very special."

• • •

Harry arrived from work, dropped his attaché on the floor next to the stairs as he usually did. He expected Liz would be waiting for him. He didn't hear Fred puttering around. The house was silent.

"Hello? Liz?"

He walked to the bar at the back of the house and turned on some easy-listening music. As he passed the kitchen he saw Fred through the breakfast room window. Then he saw Liz on her knees, digging in what at one time had been a flowerbed, but long since neglected to weeds. He smiled, pleased to find the two of them together in some domestic endeavor. He walked outside.

"What are you guys up to?"

Fred jerked around and faced him. "Good Evening, Boss. We're about finished."

Liz stood up, tossed her gloves aside and wiped her brow with her hand.

"Hi."

"How y'a doin'? Gardening?"

"Planted some herbs that Fred uses. Basil, thyme, parsley. He'll have fresh growth from the garden in a few weeks. There haven't been any flowers there for some time, and it's going to waste."

"Are you going to be here to water them?"

She shook her head. "Harry, please, let's not go there."

"Just asking."

"Fred's doing most of the work. I'm helping out."

"I'll get your martini in a minute, Boss."

"When you're finished, Fred, we'll be upstairs."

She felt hot and sweaty when she took his arm. She reached up, kissed him on his cheek. He fixed his eyes on her as they walked up the stairs and talked. He loved when her eyes lit up as they did now.

"Looks like you were having some fun?"

The memory of his stressful day disappeared as quickly as a summer shower. He wanted it like tonight all the time, Liz waiting for him when he got home.

"What was your day like?" she asked.

"Few minor crises. The system was down for a few hours. Joe, my right hand guy, has a back problem, left to go home. Don't know if I'll see him next week. Could have been worse."

• • •

They slowly climbed upstairs to the comfortable, lived-in space.

"Missed you," he said.

"Me, too."

"Where would you like to go for dinner?"

"You choose. Some place not so public."

"I need a drink and a shower." Harry took off his jacket and tie and flopped in a chair. He turned the six o'clock news on the television. Liz stretched out across from him on the sofa.

Fred knocked on the door and served them martinis.

"Do you fancy some hors d'ouevres, a snack? Ms. Liz, Boss?"

"No, thank you. See you Sunday."

"Nothing for me. Thanks, Fred," Liz said. "Enjoy your weekend."

"You, too. Bye."

Harry drank his martini and eyed the television screen.

"Peter phoned me today."

"That's odd," she said.

"He tried to get you at home yesterday. And today. Doesn't he have your cell number? He thought I might know where you were. At least that's what he said. I think he wanted to talk to me."

"My phone's been in my handbag, up here. I haven't checked my messages."

"He's concerned. He didn't actually say that. He kept talking, saying nothing it seemed to me, to keep me on the phone. He talked all around the question he wanted to ask, about us. Never asked me straight out."

"Didn't think you two were exactly on speaking terms, if you know what I mean," Liz said.

"We don't talk at all. I don't have much contact with his office and when I do, I go through his staff, he goes through mine. It's been like that since I've been in office. I don't owe him any explanations.

"I wanted to get him off the phone, shut him up. I told him I was in love with you. I think he was rather stunned because of the *poignant pause* of silence that followed. He asked if you'd give him a call. You sure he doesn't have a thing for you?"

She stared at him and sighed. "No way!"

Not only did the animosity between them surface, but now she discerned a twinge of jealousy. It wasn't like Peter to condescend and call Harry. Even if she wouldn't be working for him anymore, she still wanted him as a friend. Suddenly her relationships seemed complicated and conflicted.

"He's a married man, remember. We're friends. It's platonic—a friendship. We've worked rather closely for the past two years. And before that."

"There's no such animal as platonic."

# CHAPTER FORTY-SEVEN

"You can't be serious, Harry. You're talking marriage? Yeah, I think Liz is a great gal, very classy lady, but you only met her a few weeks ago. What's the hurry? Andy asked. "Why aren't you seeing her tonight? It's Saturday night."

Harry, deep in concentration, eyed the distance from the golf ball to the hole and the curve of the green, seemingly oblivious to Andy's question.

"It's left to right, Harry."

"Yeah, I see. Relax, Andy, she turned me down. She won't live with me and she won't marry me. If she told me she loves me, isn't she supposed to say yes, when I ask her to marry me?"

Harry moved from side to side and viewed the prospective putt from different angles.

"She stayed at the house the last two days. Fred loves her being around. They really hit it off. They talk to each other as if they're bosom high school buddies. When I got home yesterday, I found the two of them planting herbs in the flowerbeds. You already know, my mom and daughters think she's manna from heaven.

"Okay, let me do this." He stood over the golf ball, lined his club up and took a few warm-up strokes, and then stepped up and hit it straight in the hole.

"Good shot. You're on today! What's that, your fifth par?"

"Uh, huh."

They plopped into the cart and headed for the last hole. The sun was blistering hot for an October afternoon and the greens played fast. Harry outplayed Andy by three strokes. Andy was really off his game.

"I can't beat you," Andy said. "Let's skip the hole and get some lunch."

"You mean a beer. Okay. You're not focused anyway. Got something on your mind?" Harry asked.

"As a matter of fact, I do."

"What?"

"You! What the hell do you think you're doing?"

Harry anticipated from Andy's tone that he disagreed with him about something. Maybe he shouldn't have told him about the fiasco at the fundraiser, that he asked Liz to marry him, or that he wanted to buy an apartment for Liz. Andy always spoke his mind, especially when he was upset.

"You mean about getting married or buying the apartment?"

"Both. You're goddamn lucky, you're hooked on a lady who has a head on her shoulders and won't run off to the altar with a guy she hardly knows because he has a few bucks and a great job. She's got some common sense."

"Then what's the problem?"

"You can't just buy an apartment in her building because she won't move in with you. What makes you think that's a solution?"

"Well, I thought, we could spend weekends there, maybe sometimes during the week. She'd keep her apartment and I'd keep my house, but we'd have a place together. What's wrong with that, no radical changes for either of us?"

"You've got to have your way, even if it costs a half a million dollars. Has it occurred to you that you might be smothering her to death?"

"I thought it would be a compromise—an alternative to moving in with me."

They sat at the bar and Andy ordered a beer.

"Make that two." Harry said.

"No martini?"

"Trying to curb my martini habit. I'll have one later, when I get home."

"Thought you're coming home with me, having dinner with us."

"Thanks, Andy, I'm sure you've had enough of me for one day. I'm good, really. Fred's left me some dinner in the freezer, and I brought some work home. Probably phone Liz and call it a night. She's having dinner with me and the girls at my mom's tomorrow, maybe staying the night."

"I hope you discuss it with her before you spend that amount of money."

"I intend to. It's not like it's happening tomorrow. I don't even know if there's anything available in her building. Does Cody know anyone in the real estate business? I need an agent."

"Probably. I'll ask her to call you. What's the hurry anyway, about living together? Why don't you slow down?"

"I feel good with her. We're good together."

"Do you know what I think? I think you're in love way over your head, buddy."

"Maybe so. But, so what? That's a bad thing? You know what we did last night? Had dinner at *Sei et Poivre*, went for a walk, stopped at Haagen Daaz for an ice cream, did some window-shopping on Madison Avenue. A lot of laughter and silliness, a little hugging and both of us went out like a light. I've never been so happy. And she was, too."

• • •

It was ten o'clock. The phone rang and Liz picked up the receiver on its first ring. She had waited for him to call since late afternoon.

"Hi, how are you'?" Harry asked.

"Had a good day. Brunch with Lauren at *Les Halles*, in the neighborhood. Too crowded and noisy. Couldn't hear myself think, but I had an excellent meal—filet of sole. You? What was your day like? Did you play golf?"

"Yeah. Beat Andy badly. Very hot today."

"Missed you."

"Your idea, Ms. Brady—a break—not mine."

"I know. Where'd you have dinner?"

"A Fred special. He wrote me three paragraphs about how to prepare dinner, from the freezer to the microwave, at what power setting and for how long it should cook. It was a chicken dish in a white wine sauce. He thinks I'm retarded in the kitchen. How'd I get so lucky? You in my life, and a housekeeper who loves to cook."

"You didn't have dinner with Andy and Cody?"

"Andy invited me, but I decided not to. Did you tell Lauren about us?"

"No, not really. Avoided all details, your name, your job, etcetera. I'd already told her I was seeing you—not you—someone. That's all she needs to know."

"We're not a secret."

Liz didn't want to confide any details to Lauren, knowing Lauren would urge her to marry him and make a new life for herself. Lauren was impulsive and would go with the flow. That's why she got mixed up with an abusive husband, falling for his charm, glib flattery and without thinking, ran off and got married in Las Vegas, much to her regret.

"Would you like me to cook you breakfast?"

"Are you inviting me now? Or tomorrow morning?"

"In the morning. I want to sleep in a little, so not too early."

"I want you now."

"Me, too. But I'm psyched for sleep, already hanging out in my pajamas, watching TV."

"Do I get to sleep in with you tomorrow?"

"You know the answer to that. We can lounge around in bed, have a bite to eat, go back to sleep, watch the ballgame, however the spirit moves us. Whatever we fancy."

"Sounds like I being lured to paradise." He said.

"About ten o'clock."

Liz felt the playing field had been leveled somewhat. They'd be in her home, on her turf, and she would be in control to create the scenario. She needed to feel she was in control of something in the relationship and not always dancing to his music.

"Okay, ten it is. Sleep well. Love you." He said.

"Love y'a."

# CHAPTER FORTY-EIGHT

Liz didn't sleep in as she said she would. Wanting everything to be perfect, she got up at eight and prepared for their rendezvous. She changed the bed linens, set the table and scented the apartment. She showered, sprayed on some perfume, applied some light makeup and changed into her best pajamas. She readied the clothes she would wear later—a blue pantsuit and a white blouse for dinner at his mom's.

Liz scurried around her apartment and the butterflies of expectation fluttered in her stomach. She hadn't experienced the heightened anticipation of waiting for a lover since the affair with her husband.

When she was in the supermarket the day before, she bought the yogurt flavor Harry liked, the same brand of strawberry jam in his refrigerator and the Snyder pretzels he sometimes snacked on with his martinis. His preferences were already enmeshed in her choices, and she thought it's happened too quickly. She fell so naturally into the cockeyed-optimist attitude she had suddenly acquired and wallowed in the last few days. She felt brand-new, like a forgotten CD whose music she rediscovered. For the first time in years, she shared herself with someone and felt like another person, revitalized and happy, not just content.

The intercom buzzed. "Thanks, Andres."

Harry stepped off the elevator with a shopping bag in his hand. He embraced and kissed her as she stood in the doorway in her pajamas.

The door across the hall creaked open. Her neighbor Irwin faced them, his garbage in his hand.

"Good morning, Liz." He left his door ajar, turned and walked down the corridor to the compactor.

"Morning, Irwin."

Harry entered the apartment and she closed the door quickly. "My bloody nosey neighbor. He's on the Board. He thinks it's his obligation to know who comes and goes and at what times. He probably heard the elevator and decided it was a good time to take a peek. Andres says he's always picking his brain, asking him what's going on in the building."

"Bother you?"

"He's a nuisance. He makes me feel as if I'm being spied on in my own home."

"How about a new home?"

"Harry, please. I'm not moving in with you. I'm just annoyed. Want some coffee?"

"Yes. That's not what I meant. I meant another apartment, a larger one on another floor."

Harry took the coffee from Liz, followed her to the sofa and sat beside her. She ignored his comment and the shopping bag he had dropped at the door. They embraced, kissing, fondling and touching each other in full-blown foreplay.

Their physical needs gratified, they fell asleep naked. She awoke to his finger sliding down and around her face. He lay next to her, his head propped up on his hand. His fingers dawdled about her face and hair, "Hey, sleepy, I'm hungry. Didn't you invite me for breakfast?"

"No. For sex."

She sat up and shook off the residue of sleep.

"I washed the pajamas you left. They're in the closet with your robe."

"Seducing me with comforts. Thank you."

Harry grabbed her at the waist and kissed her neck. They embraced.

"Why can't I get tired of you?" he asked.

"I'm addicted and getting worse. I want to inhale what you smell like and take the scent home with me and bathe my body in it."

Harry kissed her again and patted her on the ass as she left the bed on her way to the bathroom. He always flooded her with expressions of affection after making love—squeezing, hugging and kissing her.

When she returned to the bedroom, she asked, "What would you like?"

He pinched her cheek as he entered the bathroom.

"I'd like for you to come home with me."

"That's not what I meant."

"I know what you meant. Whatever the cook is cooking."

A few minutes later Harry joined her in the kitchen clad in pajamas and robe. He stood at the doorway and watched her breaking eggs in a bowl.

"Want some help?"

Liz looked at him sideways over her shoulder and laughed softly.

"No, I don't think so. Fred says you make a wicked omelet, but you make a mess. Oops, don't tell him I told you that. It was said in strict confidence. Harry, what's in that shopping bag? From Williams-Sonoma?"

"Almost forgot. A present." He brought the bag into the kitchen and pulled out a four-slice Cuisinart toaster.

"Had Tom pick this up for you the other day."

"It's beautiful. You didn't know we were having breakfast together until last night."

"The last time we ate here together, if you remember, you waited on toast while I ate an omelet. You needed an update."

"Thank you. You're very thoughtful."

"A little selfish, too. Don't want you waiting in here, while I'm eating out there."

"Haven't you spoiled me enough?"

"If you really want to get spoiled, you'd pack a bag and come home with me."

"Harry, please. Stop talking like that. You make me feel guilty. I can't move in with you."

"Frustrated, huh? Me, too. I'm not going to stop asking. I want you. I know you love me. Tell me where we're going, Liz."

Harry threw his arms around her waist. She wrapped her arms behind his neck, and they swayed and rocked in an embrace, their eyes fixed on each other.

"What are we doing? It's not as if we've got a lifetime ahead of us. My time is dwindling. Your time is ticking away on the same clock. What's the problem?"

Liz let her arms fall down from his neck. She turned away from him.

"I don't know, Harry. There's something inside me that just keeps saying I can't do that. We don't really know each other.

I'm not used to chauffeur-driven limos and expensive restaurants. Usually I feel very happy when I'm with you. Then sometimes I feel like I don't know who I am, and whoever it is, it's not me, and I don't fit in."

"Don't know each other? Don't fit in? Right! What I know is you're changing my life and I want my life changed. I want herbs growing in my backyard, flowers on the tables, window shopping on Madison Avenue and you—waiting for me in the evening and next to my pillow in the morning."

She shook her head in exasperation, feeling pressured again. He wanted something she couldn't give.

"Do you want to see a shrink?" Harry asked.

"Oh? You think I need one?"

Maybe he wanted his life changed, but she didn't want her life changed. It's likely a shrink would try to persuade her to make adjustments, compromises, and ultimately, to leave her life behind, lose her identity and live his life, not hers. Why couldn't they be just as they were now?

"No. I meant the both us, not just you. You keep pushing me away. You've got all these lines drawn, and you insist I don't step over them. We're a secret. No public places. Don't park the car in front of the building. I'm tiptoeing around you, wary of what's coming next and scared to death you'll disappear."

"There must be something wrong with me! Is that it? Because I don't want to move in with you? Snap your fingers and I'm supposed to drop my life, just like that. I'm not pushing you away. You're the one who keeps pushing me. We're here—together. Why isn't that enough?"

Harry turned her around. Her eyebrows arched and her face screwed up with an expression of worsening exasperation. A few tears trickled down her cheek. He put his arms around her and hugged her.

"Please, no crying, Liz. You break my heart when you do that. I just want to fix it, whatever's wrong between us."

# CHAPTER FORTY-NINE

The leaves had fallen reluctantly, covering the lawns of Westchester, evidence of summer ending. Liz inhaled the smell of newly cut grass and absorbed the aura of suburbia and family life where children grew up and seasons changed. A moderate breeze tempered the seventy-five degree weather, patting her cheeks and blowing through her hair. She looked forward to dinner with Harry's family.

Harry rang the bell and they entered the house. Molly must have heard the car and was waiting at the door. She hugged Liz. "Hello, you two."

"Hi, Mom."

"You're looking very smart," Molly said as she took Liz by the hand.

"Thank you. How're you feeling?" Liz asked. "You look well."

"You know, the same. Today's a good day."

Harry trailed behind them and greeted Rebecca who stood at the stairway. "How's it going, pumpkin?"

"Good, Dad. Hello, Liz." She kissed each of them on the cheek. "Sarah's in the kitchen concocting a special dessert for us."

They filed into the family room. Molly sat in her chair. Liz and Harry sat on the sofa and Rebecca curled up at their feet. Sarah came in the room, flopped on the sofa beside Harry and threw her arms around him. She said hello to Liz and leaned over and kissed her on the cheek.

"Is blue your favorite color?" Rebecca asked. "It really suits you."

"Thank you. Yes. Now that you mention it, I think it is. I seem to choose blue a lot."

"Sarah wanted to know if you streak your hair, or dye it. It looks great." Rebecca said.

"That's a bit personal, Rebecca, don't you think?" Harry asked.

"I don't mind Harry," Liz said. "Women want to know these things. I don't do anything to my hair, just shampoo and a conditioner. I do wish it wasn't so curly. There's always something about yourself that you would like to be different."

Molly chuckled and grinned at Harry. "Your daughter. Always the personal questions."

"And she has a big mouth." Sarah nudged Rebecca with a push to her shoulder, indicating to Liz that Sarah didn't approve of Rebecca revealing that they had been discussing Liz's hair.

"Good afternoon," Elena said as she entered the room with a full tray of drinks.

"Hi Elena, how's it goin'?" Harry got up. "Let me give you a hand." He removed the iced teas from the tray and handed them to his daughters. Harry smiled and winked at Elena, followed with a nod of appreciation of her ongoing efforts in taking care of the household.

Uncle Ted lumbered in from the porch. "Harry. Hello, Liz."

Uncle Ted looked and acted every bit of his eighty plus years. His words dealt with simple manners and only with what was essential. Slightly bent over, he moved slowly and talked slowly.

"Harry, their Uncle Aaron phoned me yesterday. Ben and Sheila gave birth. He wants us at his house for the holiday."

"I know about the baby. Ben called me. Seven pounds, six ounces and in excellent health. I told him I'd see you today, Mom, and give you the good news, except Uncle Ted has beaten me to the punch."

Ted paused and waited, not finished with the role of messenger.

Molly interrupted, "Harry, after Aaron spoke with Ted, Leah called me and told me. The family's beside themselves with joy, to say nothing of your daughters chanting all morning, *We have a baby cousin, Nana. They named him Harry, after our daddy.* You do know, they named the baby after you."

"Yeah, I know. I'm sure that didn't go over too well with Aaron."

"He wants you to call him." Ted said. "Complained that he never sees his nieces and you're obligated. They should know his grandson."

Molly interjected before Ted could finish his mission. "Harry, Leah told me they know everything, how you paid Ben's tuition and sent them money. She cried with happiness when we spoke."

Liz smiled and listened intently at what sounded like family drama unfolding. They must love Harry very much if they named the baby after him. She noticed a passing glance between mother and son. Molly's eyes sparkled when she said, "But you've got to call Aaron."

"Me? Call him? No, that's impossible."

"Harry, he begged," Ted said with empathy for Aaron. "For him to beg, you know, that's not like him."

"Sorry. I don't think so, Uncle Ted."

"You don't have to go," Molly said, "but you have to call, speak with him."

"Mom, I don't have to do anything where Aaron is concerned. If Aaron wants you, Ted and the girls for the holiday he should speak with you, Ted and the girls, not me."

Liz interjected, "Harry, there's blood between your daughters and their uncle. It didn't get buried with their mother."

Harry frowned, not only taken aback by her comment, but he looked sad, like his pet dog just died. It was obvious in her opinionated comment that she thought he was wrong. Liz noticed his face flushed to a crimson hue and a miserable expression emerged on his face. He shook his head. She knew she had offended his sensibilities and tried to undo the damage.

"Sorry, it's really none of my business."

"Dad, we won't go if you don't want us to," Rebecca said.

"Thanks, honey, but that's not the problem. We'll talk about it later."

"Are you going to call him?" Rebecca asked.

"I don't think I can do that."

"Harry, it's Rosh Hashanah," Molly said, "a time for forgiveness. Aaron's burden of hatred finally has come between him and his God, and he wants to put it in the past. Help him."

"Me, help him? Mom, he put Susan and me through hell. And he would have put Ben through hell, too, had he known about his problems. How do I forget that simply because now he wants to forget it?"

Elena announced dinner was ready. Harry asked for another martini.

• • •

Tom drove them home. Dusk had come and gone and artificial street lighting overcame the day that had begun in bright sunshine. Harry dozed on Liz's shoulder. He had three martinis and gave in to sleep when his eyes faltered and closed. He hadn't asked her to spend the night with him, and he hadn't told Tom where they were going.

"Harry?" Liz kissed him on the cheek. He shook his head, woke up groggy and asked, "Where are we?"

"In the Bronx, going over the bridge."

"Coming home with me?"

"Have you changed your mind?"

Harry took her hand and brought it to his lips and kissed it.

"Why would I change my mind?"

"You've been in a funk since before dinner."

"Have I? Must have been something you said. Or the family's dirty laundry. Not a great afternoon."

"I'm sorry Harry, I didn't mean to hurt your feelings."

"You didn't hurt my feelings, you pissed me off. You don't know anything about Aaron, what an overbearing and self-righteous asshole he is. He's had nothing but hate for me since I met him, because his sister wasn't a virgin when I married her as if she didn't make that choice. What he hates more is that his sister married a guy who was successful and earned a lot of money. Absolutely immoral as far as he's concerned."

Harry vented, gripped by anger accumulated for many years and that never lost its hold on him. He held Aaron responsible for many of the trials in his marriage.

"All he ever did was constantly criticize me. I didn't spend enough time with my family, I left Susan and the children alone too much, the house I bought was too big and not in the right neighborhood. He pontificated endlessly as to what Susan needed and how we should lead our lives."

Harry remembered the many heated arguments with Aaron and that eventually he stopped accompanying Susan and the girls when they visited her family to avoid him. He also made it clear that Aaron wasn't welcome in his home while he was there, but, for Susan's sake, he would arrange not to be home if a visit was scheduled. The rift caused a great deal of unhappiness for Susan, but Harry was at loss as to how to rectify the animosity between he and Aaron.

"And I should go to his home for the holiday with his family? The less my daughters see of him, the better off they are."

"Do you really mean that? I was thinking of your daughters. It's just not fair to deprive them of a relationship with their cousins because of their uncle." Liz said.

"He's not their uncle as far as I'm concerned. His wife, Leah, is my daughters' aunt and my sister-in-law and she's family. She's always treated me with kindness and respect, neither of which I received from Aaron, or for that matter, Susan's parents when they were alive. Leah always remembers the girls' birthdays and stays in touch with them. They know they're free to see her and their cousins anytime they want.

"I know you mean well, but stay out of it. I don't really want the girls around Aaron, if I can help it. He has nothing to offer them. I'm sorry for Leah. Her role in life is to make everyone happy. Unfortunately, she lives under the rule of that rigid patriarch. She's a fine person, and I love her. But he's done the damage, not me."

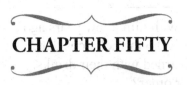

# CHAPTER FIFTY

"I'm happy for you, Peter. Please send my best wishes to Marisa." Liz said.

"Thanks. You can't know how happy we are. It's been very difficult but worth all the problems." Peter held the door to the café open for her.

"I kept thinking something's got to go wrong, but the baby's perfectly healthy. And Marisa's fine. I love to hear him cry."

"Peter, this isn't exactly an ideal place for me to have lunch with you."

"Don't worry, Liz, you don't have to look over your shoulder. Harry's having lunch with his daughters and besides he wouldn't take them here. And the City Hall that has lunch here has already gone. It's two o'clock."

"How do you know that?"

"I saw his car pull from my office window and Harry got in."

The waitress handed them menus as they sat down. "Would you like something to drink?"

"An iced tea." Liz said.

"Me, too." Peter said.

"I feel like I'm betraying him."

"Why?"

"I don't know. He isn't happy about my having lunch with you. Peter, I don't think you understand, he's so full of guilt about his marriage. He told me about your affair with Susan."

"I assumed he did. When he answered the phone that night, I knew for sure you were seeing him. He couldn't have told you everything though, because he doesn't know everything."

"What's that supposed to mean? Look, I don't care what's gone on between you two. If you guys want to hate each other, I can't control that. We're friends and I want it to stay that way."

"Liz, you don't want to carry on with this guy. He beds down whatever gives him an erection. I don't want to see you get hurt. I know him better than you do. One of the Assistant D.A.'s in the office had an affair with him a few years ago and found him in bed with her roommate. Who the hell does that?"

The waitress returned with their drinks.

"Can I take your order?"

Liz folded her menu and handed it to the waitress.

"The club sandwich, no mayo."

"The same, with mayo."

"Peter, please don't try to convince me not to see him. It's past that. We're too tight already. He wants me to live with him. Not that I intend to do that, but I'm in love with him."

"You can't be."

"Oh? Why can't I be?"

"Because it's not you. I know who you are."

"What's that supposed to mean?"

"It means, I know who you are."

"And who I am can't be in love with Harry? It doesn't fly, Peter."

Peter hesitated. He looked around the café. "The woman I carried a torch for couldn't be involved with the likes of Harry."

"What are you saying? I thought we were friends."

"We are. That's why I'm so concerned for you."

"What do mean *carried a torch*?"

"Nothing I want to tell you about. I'm over it."

"Well, I want you to tell me. If it's over, it's done and nothing to do with now."

Peter faltered and struggled for the right words to explain. "Well, all the time we worked together, I had feelings I never acted on because you were married, in love with your husband. I saw you grieving when he died, and I knew you were still in love with him and nothing could ever happen between us.

"I wanted a family and you were already past that. It's light years away. Don't misunderstand. I love Marisa. I have a newborn son. I'm very happy. I'm not hitting on you."

"I don't need to hear this, Peter."

"I never wanted to tell you. We've been a great team. I don't want you to stop working for me, and I can't sit by and watch that man trash your life. He manipulates people. Susan was madly in love with him and couldn't get out from under him. She self-destructed. I don't want to see the same thing happen to you."

"What do you mean she self-destructed? She didn't commit suicide, she had cancer."

"Yeah, I know. But she was hopeless, she gave up instead of getting treatment and extending her life. She chose to suffer with her illness. And die, as if she wanted to punish herself."

Liz had never seen Peter's eyes watering like a pool filling up and about to overflow. She took his hand and squeezed it.

"Hey, you're getting upset."

They had shared confidences before, especially when he met Marisa, and how he was so enchanted with her and the difficulties they experienced. When he finally decided to ask Marisa to marry him, Peter once again had turned to Liz to discuss his decision.

Peter's voice cracked. He pressed his hands over his face.

"I loved her. When Susan got pregnant, I wanted her to leave him and marry me, but he wouldn't give her a divorce unless she gave him custody of their daughters. She couldn't tell him she was carrying my child, and yet she couldn't bear the thought of having my child in his home, so she decided on abortion."

"You're saying he didn't know she was pregnant?"

"Yes. Then she couldn't bear the guilt of having taken a life. I didn't know about it until it was over. I was devastated. It was my child. There was no hope for us after that. I broke it off.

"Susan never told Harry. When I learned she was ill, I went to see her in the hospital. She told me Harry had suffered, that he had enough guilt to last a lifetime, that it was her fault. She lacked the courage to fight for her daughters and me and our child. That was Susan, blaming herself and forgiving everyone, including me, and even Harry. But it was his fault. That bastard wouldn't let her go."

# CHAPTER FIFTY-ONE

Drained of emotion and her head pounding, Liz wanted to sleep and maybe when she woke up, it all would have gone away. Peter said too much of what she didn't want to hear. She took an Advil and lay down on her bed.

As Harry had suspected, lunch wasn't about quitting her job. Everything had changed. She knew her friendship with Peter was over. He never should have told her he had feelings for her. What she regarded as a friendship had been something entirely different from his definition of friendship. The trust and sincerity of their relationship had been a deceit. She felt betrayed.

Liz knew she wouldn't work for him anymore. Why did Peter have to divulge the secret of Susan's pregnancy to her? She didn't need to know and didn't want to harbor a secret from Harry. Did Peter want her to tell Harry? Or did he just wish to apprise her of the ugly fact that he held Harry responsible for losing Susan and his child. She finally fell asleep, in a quandary.

The doorbell woke Liz. She answered the door, and let Harry in. He took abrupt second looks at her as he hung his jacket.

"Hi. You don't look well." He kissed her on the cheek. "What's the matter?"

"Nothing. A little under the weather. Not a good day."

"Did you ask Andres to just buzz me in and not to call you?"

"No, he probably took it upon himself. You are the Mayor."

"Don't think he should do that, unless, of course, you tell him it's all right." He unknotted his tie and opened the top button of his shirt.

"You had lunch with Peter? Did he change your mind about quitting?"

"No. That's done, at least as far as I'm concerned. But then so is our friendship. He wouldn't stop talking about you and how you're going to ruin my life. Not something you want to hear from a friend."

Liz went into the kitchen, the vodka and vermouth bottles in her arms. Harry followed her. She mixed a martini.

"Harry, I don't want to talk about it anymore. It's finished."

"Because of me?"

"Partly." Liz couldn't tell him the truth and she couldn't lie. "I can't listen to him going on about you like that."

"What do you mean *partly*? Tell me."

"No, not now." She offered him the martini.

He took the martini and placed it on the countertop. "Liz, now!"

She looked at the ceiling; her eyes moved quickly around the kitchen, resting momentarily on any place but his eyes. He pulled her toward his chest and placed his arms around her. "It's me, the man who loves you. I want you to tell me."

"Harry, it's a mess. He said he had feelings for me."

Her head dropped to his chest. The stress of her day culminated and erupted in tears.

"It's okay. C'mon, stop crying."

Liz took deep breaths, inhaling and exhaling slowly. "I'm all right. I've just been so, so tense."

"You said he just had a child. What the hell is he hitting on you for?"

"He wasn't hitting on me. It was years ago. I was married."

"He had feelings for you? What's that supposed to mean? That's platonic?"

Harry gulped his martini, placed the glass on the countertop and leaned against the sink, facing her. He bit his lip, shook his head and stared at the floor, in deep thought. The nightmares of the past loomed in the present. He relived the anger he felt when Susan had asked for a divorce and the jealousy of another man loving his wife. It was his fault. He drove her to another man. His failure as a husband and his selfishness in not letting Susan go reappeared and strangled him once again. She died but the past would never cease to exist and haunt him with guilt.

"I don't know why he had to tell me that now. Why would that convince me not to see you? That's what's got me so upset." Liz said.

"He really wants you to leave me. He hates me that much. For chrissake, he committed adultery with my wife. Was I supposed to be happy for them?"

Harry turned abruptly, rushed to the closet and pulled out his phone from his jacket pocket.

"Harry, who are you calling?"

"Peter. He's put you in the middle of a mess that's nothing to do with you. It's between him and me, not you."

"No, Harry, please don't call him. It's not just the affair. He's wants to get back at you. You may not have a vengeance, but he does. He won't give up until you know."

"Know what?"

"I can't tell you."

"What is it?"

"That's what he wants me to do. He wants me to tell you."

"Then tell me, whatever it is."

"I can't."

"Well then, I'll call Peter. If it's so important for me to know what's stuck in his craw and choking him to death, I'll give him my undivided attention. Anyway, if he has a problem with me, he should be talking to me, not to you."

Liz wrapped her hand around the phone Harry held. She snapped it closed.

"It's not a problem, Harry. It's his heartache. Susan had an abortion. It was his child and he holds you responsible."

"That's what he wants me to know?" Harry shook his head back and forth, sighing in frustration.

"I already knew."

# CHAPTER FIFTY-TWO

"Some friend, using you to get to me."

"How could you know?"

"I knew everything that was going on for the last eight months they were together. When Susan asked me for a divorce and told me she was in love with Peter, I had them watched, but I didn't learn about the abortion 'til after it was over. I never told Susan about the surveillance or that I knew about the abortion. What would be the purpose? All I cared about then was not losing my daughters."

He embraced her, putting his arms around her shoulders hugging and rocking her.

"It's my mess. Hate me for my past?"

"No, I hate Peter. I thought he was a friend. How could he use me like that?"

"Let it go. He's not in your life anymore. We both need to forget Peter. We need some music, a martini and a kiss."

"Uh, huh."

Harry walked to the living room, picked up a remote, programmed some 70's love songs from the disc player and slid his shoes off, pushing them under the coffee table with his feet.

"C'mere." He extended his arm and took her by the hand. "Dance with me. Dancing's a great remedy for what ails you."

They embraced. She stepped out of her shoes and placed her head on his chest, feeling the warmth of his body. She inhaled his body scent, reminiscent of when their bodies were entangled. She felt his touch on her skin as they moved slowly in rhythm with the music. It was a soft, romantic tune, and Harry spoke the lyrics as he led her in short steps:

"*In my life there's been heartache and pain, I don't know if I can face it again.*" He joined in the ensuing chorus in full voice, "*I want to know what love is, I want you to show me.*"

Liz grinned and looked up at him. "You're remarkable." A broad smile remained on her face as they stepped around the floor and

Harry continued to whisper the lyrics. She felt his breath on her neck, tickling her and stirring goose bumps on her arms.

"What was your solution again? Music, a kiss and a martini?" she asked.

"Dancing, too."

"Hmm, and the kiss?"

She stopped dancing, drew her arms around his neck and found his lips that willingly met with hers. The horror of her day disappeared.

"You make us some martinis," she said. "I'm taking a shower and I'll meet you in the bedroom for cocktails."

"Excellent plan!"

She scurried to the bathroom and he went to the kitchen.

"Hey," he cried out, "Don't I get to shower with you?"

She shouted back at him, "If you like vanilla scented body wash. You know, it's a small shower. It'll be a bit tight."

Harry left the martinis in the kitchen, unbuttoned his shirt and followed her to the bathroom. He threw his clothes on the bedroom chair and stepped into the shower, "You know, I love tight."

Harry lathered her body, touching and fondling strategic parts of her anatomy, from her buttocks to breasts, watching her cheeks flush to the pink glow of arousal.

"Don't you need your hair washed?"

"Nope, washed it this morning."

Harry pulled the shower cap from her head and flung it to the floor. "I like to see your hair get wet and the little curls dripping water on your forehead, down to your breasts."

Harry slid his fingers down her cleavage, caressing her breasts as he continued to lather her body. Water fell steadily on their bodies. Liz knelt down and put him inside her mouth, holding him with her lips, moving up and down and ravaging him. Water gushed on her face.

"Oh, God! You can't know what that feels like." His hands were on her head. "No more, Liz. Or I'll be gone."

Liz released her grip and Harry drew her up to his chest. He clinched her around her waist. His erection was hard on her belly. He pushed the palm of his hand against her cleft and massaged her.

They fell on the bed wrapped in one towel. He fell forward on top of her and entered her slowly, tantalizing her. She inhaled the scents of vanilla blending with the clean odor of his body and received him with noisy moans and pleas.

Writhing in an ecstatic finish as he completed his thrusting, she closed her eyes and fell into an abyss of rapture, calling out his name.

# CHAPTER FIFTY-THREE

Harry said he craved red meat. Liz suggested *Nicola Paone*, a local, well-appointed restaurant, known for good steaks, a quiet dining room and discreet seating arrangements.

"Excellent choice, Ms. Brady. Low-key atmosphere, conducive to eating and conversation at the same time. Been there often? The maitre d' seemed to know you."

"He's the same maitre d', but I don't think he remembered me. It's been quite some time since I've eaten there. Used to go there with my husband years ago."

Relaxed and sated, they waited for the light to change, about to cross Third Avenue.

A voice behind them called out, "Liz?" It was Lauren. "Hi. Out for an evening stroll?"

Harry turned away from the curb.

"Nice to meet you. I'm Lauren." She shook Harry's hand.

"The name's Harry. Pleasure."

Lauren stared at Harry and Liz saw her look of recognition. She turned and faced Liz. "I'm in a bit of a rush, expecting company. Give you a ring tomorrow. You home?"

"Yes. Tomorrow." Liz said. "Enjoy your evening."

Lauren met Harry's eyes again and said, "Good to meet you. Night."

The light changed. Harry and Liz crossed the avenue and climbed the sloping hill to Lexington Avenue.

"So, that's Lauren. Good-looking lady. How old is she?"

"Who wants to know?" Liz broke her strolling rhythm and stopped at his side, her head cocked to her shoulder.

"Don't look at me that way, I'm a one-woman man. Just curious. She looks younger than you."

"That's because she is, by seven years."

"Finally got to meet a friend of yours. Suppose we'll bump into Robert as well?"

"Lauren's my best friend. She recognized you." Liz ignored his sarcastic remark about meeting her family.

"Is that a problem?" Harry asked.

"Not really. Although now I'll be facing a lot of questions that I'd prefer not to answer."

They ambled up the tree-lined street, hand-in-hand. A pleasant evening breeze blew, noisily rustling the trees and disturbing the quiet and repose of the evening.

"Are you coming home with me?" Harry asked.

"I can't, I have a doctor's appointment at ten. When you're not there, I like to sleep in and loll around, and then hang out with Fred. I wouldn't be able to hang out."

"Fred enjoys you hanging around all right. I got an inkling the other evening of what you guys talk about. I found a note explaining the scents in the bathrooms. He especially wanted me to know that you chose the lavender scent for my bathroom and that he deferred to your judgment, even though he thought it too feminine. He's like a puppy dog around you. You pet him and tell him how wonderful he is, and he loves it, thrives on it. I'm not inclined to indulge him like that."

"You're very lucky to have found him."

"Yes. And lucky to have found you. You should be living with me. Liz—"

She interrupted, "Please Harry, let's not start that again."

"Just listen for a minute."

Liz spewed out heavy breaths. Every time they were together he brought the subject up. She thought they had tacitly agreed she would spend weekends with him and he would stay with her once or twice during the week. It was supposed to be a solution for him, but he kept badgering her anyway, for something more. He didn't give up.

"I'm listening."

"I'm looking at an apartment in your building, on the twentieth floor, two thousand plus square feet, lots of space. I have an appointment with a realtor on Sunday morning. I want you to look at it with me, see if you like it."

"You can't buy an apartment in my building."

"It's not for me. It's for us, for you."

"Huh?" She stopped walking, dropped his hand and turned and glared at him, "You can't be serious."

"Why not? We'd live there during the week and spend the weekends uptown. Or if you didn't want to go uptown, or if you get really pissed at me, you'd always have your apartment to go to."

"And Fred, what will you do with Fred?"

"We'd have the same arrangement as now. He's off weekends, so obviously he'd be there during the week. I've already discussed it with him and he's fine with moving. There's lots of space, and we can renovate it to accommodate whatever we want."

Harry wasn't impulsive. She assumed he had probably devised this plan with his usual thoroughness, and she wanted to know just how far he had gone.

"Harry, you're talking about half a million dollars."

"More, but the maintenance is inexpensive. So is the insurance. I've spent a lot more for a lot less."

"Oh, maintenance is a real factor to take into account compared to half a million dollars."

"It is. If something happens to me, you'll be able to handle the maintenance payments."

"What are you saying?"

"I'm saying if something happened to me, you would own it outright. You could even draw against the value, if you needed to. Or sell it, and keep the apartment you have now. You'd be somewhat secure."

His argument was perfectly logical to her. She knew he had the wherewithal to pay for it, but it infuriated her that he would spend more than half a million dollars to get what he wanted. She thought he was being wantonly self-indulgent.

"No, Harry. I am secure, at least, reasonably secure."

"You're not. You're comfortable, but, considering unforeseen circumstances, if you got sick . . ."

"Harry, stop it!"

Oblivious that they were walking on a quiet residential street in Murray Hill, her voice resounded from the pavement as she yelled at him: "You are not buying me anything." She turned and started to walk away, hastening her pace.

"You're going to stop me?"

Liz halted, turned and walked back to where he stood. Her voice continued to loudly spill over in the neighborhood like lava flowing from an erupting volcano.

"Is that a threat? You are an arrogant bastard to think you can have it all your own way, all the time. Spend a million dollars and she'll do exactly what she's told and what you want."

"And you're an independent bitch."

Liz swung her hand at him, meaning to slap him, but he caught her wrist on its way to his face. She felt her hand trembling in his.

"And your fucking temper is worse than mine." Harry held her arm out of reach of his body, seized with the instinct to protect himself.

"Let go of me." She squirmed and struggled, trying to jerk her hand from his wrist. "You're hurting me."

Harry released his hand and she stumbled up the two steps to the cement path leading to the doorman, panting in short breaths.

"Liz?" he called after her. "Do you want to leave me? C'mere and tell me that."

She turned around, tears streaming down her face. She stood in the middle of the path motionless for a moment, and then walked back to Harry, sighing through her tears. "No."

Harry placed her hand on his chest and threw his arms around her. He held her tightly. He pulled a handkerchief from his pocket, wiped the tears from her face and kissed her. "You have a wicked right." Liz sniffled as they walked arm in arm the few feet to the doorman and entered the building.

Expended of energy and suffering from regretful rage, Liz realized Harry could provoke her to a level of stress, the depths of which she had not experienced in her life. She behaved like an animal responding in a fight-or-flight for survival.

"Do you want a drink, a coffee?" she asked.

"No. Sit down." He motioned for her to sit next to him.

"I want to hold you. I love you. Don't fault me because I want to take care of you."

They settled in a calm and silent embrace, holding each other. Harry leaned back on the sofa. Liz lay across his chest. "I'm sorry. I do love you. But I can't help getting furious when I feel that you're wielding some kind of power over me, controlling and manipulating me with your money."

"You're the one with the power. I told you I'd do anything you want. Hopefully, it doesn't include any more brawls on the street because one day I'll probably hit you back. I think we need a referee."

"You mean a shrink?" She asked.

"Uh, huh."

"Right now, I feel like I need one." She said.

# CHAPTER FIFTY-FOUR

Cody referred Inez Finch to Harry. Cody and Inez had been college mates. Theirs wasn't a likely friendship because of their different personalities. Inez was the brainy, introvert and Cody the sociable, extrovert, but they shared a mutual respect and helped each other during their college years. Inez tutored Cody in math and science and Cody schooled Inez in fashion and cosmetics.

After college their career paths digressed. Inez went on to medical school and Cody pursued a modeling career, but they stayed in contact for an occasional lunch, aware of the limitations of their friendship.

When Susan became ill, Cody suggested that Harry seek counseling and she arranged a consultation with Inez, who had achieved a reputation as a skilled and compassionate therapist.

Inez had rescued Harry and his family from the throes of tragedy and guided them through their grieving. Harry especially remembered her compassion and the loving care she rendered to his daughters and his mother. He trusted her implicitly and without reservation. If anyone could help him and Liz, he believed it was Inez.

Harry called Inez's office to schedule appointments for Liz and himself. He floundered while on the phone, searching for words to articulate why he needed to see her again. "I think—no, I don't think. I know. I'm in love with a woman."

"And she feels the same?" Inez asked.

"Yes. But we seem to have issues. I don't know how to explain. There always seems to be something separating us, and I don't what it is. I'm afraid I'm going to lose her."

"Well, all I ask is that the two of you are sincere in making an effort to come to a meeting of the minds—motivated, so to speak—or else my work is for naught."

"Yes. I understand." Harry said.

"Okay, I think it best to arrange a few meetings separately at first, and, hopefully, we'll progress to some sessions together. Agreeable?"

"Yes. Very."

"Evenings?" Inez asked?

"Late afternoon or early evenings for me. Liz is available during the day."

"I have an opening on Tuesdays at 4:30 p.m. for you. And on Wednesday at 2:00 p.m. for the woman. Is that workable? What's her name?"

"Yes, that's fine. Liz Brady."

In the last two weeks, Liz and Harry each had a session with Inez twice a week, rather than once a week as originally scheduled. They both had a lot to talk about. They complied with Inez's advice not to discuss between them what had transpired at their separate sessions and to focus on understanding their differences and the conflicts they were dealing with.

Harry thought their relationship had improved since their sessions with Inez. He had stopped badgering her to live with him and they had fallen into the routine Liz had initially suggested, staying at his house the weekend, having dinner with his mother and daughters on Sunday and sleeping at her apartment once or twice during the week. Détente had become the prevailing status quo.

The sessions evolved to a weekly basis. After three weeks, Liz asked Harry, "You haven't been discussing our sex life with Inez, have you?"

"Discussing? No. Not in any detail, if that's what you mean. I remember she asked me once what I found sexually attractive about you."

"And?"

"I told her it was the dimples in your ass."

"You didn't. Be serious. What did you say?"

"You looking for a compliment?"

"No. I just found her recent questions about the depth of our sexual intimacy a bit intrusive. I mean, it's really very private, asking about the foreplay we indulged in, and did we shower together, and . . . whatever. So, what did you say?"

"If I remember correctly, I said *everything*, that I have an all-consuming urge to hug and kiss you, and when I do look at you and kiss you, I become very excited sexually. She didn't ask me anything more.

"Liz, maybe what she really was asking about is affection. If sex and affection is one and the same thing—integrated? We don't have any problems in bed. Or do we?"

Liz giggled. "That's the one place we seem to be in complete agreement. Is that all she wanted to know? Whether we're affectionate with each other?"

"I don't know, but feel free to ask her what she needs to know. She'll clarify what she meant."

"Okay."

Since their sessions with Inez, they laughed more, listened more and openly complained about each other's faults, unwilling to edit what they felt. He thought it was humorous when she called him a rich, spoiled brat who wanted his way all the time. But the thought struck him that Andy had many times accused him of the same trait of being selfishly unyielding.

He called her an independent bitch with an unbridled temper who wouldn't accept help or advice from anyone. "Don't you ever ask for anyone's advice?" he asked. "You know, it doesn't hurt to see another side of an issue."

After he impulsively criticized her, it occurred to him that they both suffered from the same malady. They were unwilling to relinquish their egos and give in to compromising with each other. He often saw the other side of an issue, but it didn't move him to change his mind or behavior. She was on the same page.

"I usually know what's good for me. I know better than anyone else who I am. Why would I ask for an opinion about what I want or need?" Liz said.

"Well, you seem to listen to what Inez has to say."

"She doesn't tell me what to do, or what to think. She prefaces almost everything she advises with, *It could be,* or *it might be,* and then, in so many words, tells me to consider this or that and figure it out for myself. Usually, she's so unimposing and easy to talk to."

Fred arrived as he usually did at nine o'clock, Sunday evening and dropped his overnight bag in the dining room. He spied Liz about to brew some decaf.

"Hi, Ms. Liz. Let me get that for you."

"Hey, Fred. How was your weekend?"

"Absolutely splendid. Visited with my sister and nephews. She's an outrageous cook, made my favorite pot roast. How 'bout you? Good weekend?"

"Yes, very."

Harry entered the kitchen with a letter from the pile of mail he was attending to and offered it to Liz to read.

"Fred, how y'a doin'?"

"Good, Boss."

Liz read the letter. The Metropolitan Opera Guild invited the Mayor and guests to attend their annual cocktail party and a performance of *Turandot*. The Guild would be honored if the Mayor would RSVP his acceptance and the number of guests attending.

"Would you like to go? It's a week from tomorrow."

"Mondays are black tie," she said.

"Yes, I know. It's actually quite an intimate reception, no more than a hundred people. I haven't attended the last two years. I know you enjoy opera."

"Yes, I'd love to see *Turandot*. It's a new production this year."

"Before you say yes, be aware that there's likely to be press coverage and the possibility of your picture in the paper the next day."

Liz smiled. "I'm all right with that."

"Sure? Because we don't have to attend the reception. We could just go to the performance."

"I don't have a problem with publicity. I'm not working for the D.A.'s Office anymore."

Inez cautioned Harry that Liz was a private person. She wasn't accustomed to and didn't enjoy the spotlight that came with the Mayor's Office. He thought she'd probably feel more comfortable among a crowd of people she didn't know if she had a friend to talk to.

"Liz, should I ask Andy and Cody?"

"Yes, that's a wonderful idea. Cody loves the opera as much as I do. I think she'd love to go. I don't know about Andy."

"We'll talk golf, you girls can talk opera."

It would be the first time she would be on his arm in public. Harry was surprised and pleased. Liz had an aversion to his celebrity, preferring to dine in out-of-the-way restaurants and avoid encounters with the public. She behaved like a fugitive sometimes, almost paranoid when they walked on a street if someone looked at them. And she still complained when Tom double-parked in front of her building as if the tenants in her building monitored Harry's visits. He had Inez to credit if Liz had even a small change in her attitude.

Harry phoned Andy. Andy answered enthusiastically, "*Turandot*. A cocktail reception? We'd love to. You know Cody's an avid fan, especially the Italian repertoire. I don't take her often enough."

Cody grabbed the phone from her husband. She had surmised what the conversation was about.

"Yes, we'd love to. You're buying Liz a new dress, right, Harry?" Cody waited for his approval. "It's a coming-out party. Oops, don't tell Liz I said that."

"No problem." Harry said.

"Can you put her on the phone?" Cody asked.

Harry handed Liz the phone, "Cody wants to speak with you."

"Hi, sweetie. What a great idea. Thanks for thinking of us. It's an occasion, and we should have a new dress. Are you free tomorrow for shopping? Harry's buying."

"I have a doctor's appointment at eleven, but I can meet you after. I'm so glad you're coming. I'll phone you in the morning, and we'll make definite plans. Okay? Bye." Liz hung up.

"Again? Didn't you go to the doctor last week?" Harry asked.

"More check-up stuff."

# CHAPTER FIFTY-FIVE

Liz's primary doctor had made the appointment for a consultation with a surgeon, a Dr. Charles Rodman, from Sloan-Kettering. The doctor told her what to expect. The radiologist reported a suspicious mass and recommended a biopsy.

Dr. Rodman informed her in detail about the biopsy he would perform. It would be a simple procedure and done on an outpatient basis. The pathology report would take a few days and disclose whether or not there were cancer cells present. The doctor scheduled the procedure for the following week, on a Tuesday. "The sooner the better." He said.

Liz hated the thought of her breasts and the biopsy becoming a conversational subject of opinion and speculation. She didn't need discussion of her problem, so she decided not to share the news with anyone except Lauren.

Liz welcomed walking the few blocks to meet Cody. A walk on a sunny, crisp fall day cleared her head and changed her mood. She focused on shopping for a dress. Harry had given her his credit card and told her to spend what she needed, and she accepted because she wanted to look the part of the Mayor's companion, a role Inez suggested she might make an effort to fulfill, instead of *perceiving yourself as his subservient mistress*. Inez's words rang in her ears. Inez likened an altered perspective of oneself like acquiring a new wardrobe.

"A new style can be invigorating. I speak from experience, having had numerous makeovers. See if it suits you. If it doesn't, there's always an alternative. You needn't see yourself as someone who needs to *fit in.* You have an obligation to yourself to be exactly who you are: an intelligent, confident, classy woman. Remember, that's who Harry loves, that woman who owns her own mind."

Cody waited and passed the time admiring shoes in a shop window. "Hey, Liz." They cheek kissed each other. "Have you had lunch?" Liz shook her head, and said, "No."

"We can grab something when we're finished." They walked along Madison Avenue.

"Let me clue you in about Maude. Don't be fooled by her dress or her manner. She's worn what looks like the same black dress for fifteen years, since I've known her. And she won't cater to you, you know, redo the shoulder or take the bow off because you ask her to. I think she's got a thing about people with money. I think she hates people who have money, that's why she's never gone mainstream with her talents. She's a pro and charges like one. She knows she's good."

Cody rang the bell to the shop and opened the door at the sound of the buzzer.

"Hello, Ms. McClure. You haven't put on any weight. That's good. What's the event?" Maude came right to the point and paid attention to only the minimum of courtesies, avoiding small talk and comments about the weather.

Liz had never been in a shop like Maude's: two open, spacious rooms that looked like a staged set from a European period film. An antique desk dominated the front room. Lavish burgundy brocade drapes hung at the two windows and matched the upholstered chairs and settee set to the side of a huge, ornate mirror. An overhead fan propelled a soft breeze throughout the space, although the air conditioning hummed in full force.

Liz spied what she surmised was Maude's workplace in the back room, sequestered by a partition at the rear of the shop. Only partially visible to her, it appeared fully-equipped with the accouterments of fashion design and dressmaking. Obviously, Maude's business was a one-woman operation, and Maude wore all the hats.

"This is Liz Brady," Cody said. "We're attending an Opera Guild cocktail party, a week from today. We each need a dress. Not much time I'm afraid, but I hope you can accommodate us."

"How do you do, Ms. Brady." Maude extended her hand, absorbing Liz's figure with numerous facial expressions and eye movements that stopped and rested on one and then another part of her anatomy.

Liz recoiled. Maude's eyes were undressing her. At least the motivation wasn't sexual like that which she had experienced from men, but, nonetheless, she still felt like a carcass in a meat factory and the look-over wasn't any less demeaning.

She directed Liz, "Please turn around. Okay, very nice. Yes."

Maude spoke with a slight accent, a product of somewhere in Europe. Clearly, she was over fifty years old but appeared ageless, owning a flawless complexion that required very little makeup and spirited green eyes. High cheekbones and a broad chin highlighted her large but proportioned nose and mouth that was in harmony with an overall attractive face.

"Give me a few minutes. Help yourself to refreshments." Maude walked to the back of the shop and drew back a floral curtain, walked behind it and left it open.

"Want something, Liz? Sherry, coffee?" Cody stood at a table laid out with coffee, chocolate, sherry—a variety of refreshments.

"Sherry, thanks. What's she doing back there?"

Cody poured the sherry.

"Selecting, scrutinizing, from an inventory of hundreds of dresses, all shapes and sizes, designed and sewn by her. You'll see." She handed Liz a pony glass half-filled with sherry.

Maude returned and pulled a rack of dresses from behind the open curtain. "Please, Ms. Brady, step over here. She took a pink satin strapless dress from the rack and drew it up to Liz's chin. They both assessed the image in the mirror.

"No, wrong color." Maude said.

"It's lovely, I think I'd like to try it on."

"No, it's not for you." Maude rehung the dress at the end of the rack and pulled off another garment, a midnight blue, sleeveless dress with tuckered straps plunging down from the neckline to a bodice that suspended in a moderate flair off a dropped waist.

"Try this one." Maude said. "The dressing room is over there."

Liz looked at Cody for a reaction. Cody shrugged her shoulders.

"Okay." Liz said.

Liz came out of the dressing room, holding a strap of the dress on her shoulder so it wouldn't fall down. Maude motioned for her to move in front of the mirror, prepared to alter the dress. Maude picked straight pins from an elastic pincushion on her wrist and skillfully pinned some fabric at the back of the dress and then sat on the floor, altering the hem and lifting it to Liz's knee.

"Wow! That's it, Liz." Cody stood up and admired the reflection in the mirror. "That's perfect. Maude. You'd better do the same for me. We're going together."

"The man," Maude queried Liz, "does he fancy elegant sexy or whorish sexy?"

"Cody, elegant?" Liz asked.

"Elegant, definitely. Like that red dress you wore at Chez Mere."

"Does it look like the red dress?"

Liz looked in the mirror and smiled at the result of Maude's temporary pins.

"Yes, it's stunning. It looks great," Cody said.

"It's one of my original designs, a bit expensive and it requires a lot of adjustment."

"Doesn't matter. It may be the last—" Liz caught herself before she blurted out remnants of the conversation from her doctor's visit that had drifted in and out of her thoughts all morning. It had occurred to her that she could possibly be sick, very sick. Liz turned and looked at Maude.

"Whatever it costs."

For years, Maude had been dressing Cody for ten more or less pounds and readily selected two dresses off the rack for her.

"Try both." Maude said.

Cody chose a pink dress and handed Maude the other one, "I'm not feeling at all yellow."

• • •

They stopped at a corner bistro, near Cody's apartment, and ordered lunch. "We got lucky," Liz said.

"I always get lucky at Maude's. She never fails me. Thing is, she gets more and more expensive. Andy doesn't understand. He thinks anything over two thousand dollars for a dress is sacrilegious, a disrespect for money. He hasn't heard about inflation. I'm not telling him how much I paid 'til I have to. Don't say anything, even to Harry, you just don't know. Okay?"

"Okay. I did spend a lot of Harry's money today. Well, he's always asking me if I need anything. The latest offer was for a fur coat since the weather's gone cool. He should be very happy. He bought me big time today. Oops."

Liz realized what she said and smiled at Cody, waiting for a response.

Cody laughed. "Freudian slip, uh?"

"I'm getting over it, at least trying."

Liz rambled, not so much in conversation with Cody but thinking out loud, assessing some of the highlights of how her life had changed since she met Harry.

"He transferred ten thousand dollars to my bank account last week. He said it's his fault I'm not working for Peter anymore, and I need the income, which isn't the case. Why would I need income anyway? His assistant has arranged accounts for me all over the neighborhood: at the dry cleaner, the pharmacist, the supermarket. Not that I've charged anything on them. And it's useless to argue with him. He's so unmovable."

Liz's eyes welled up in tears.

"I never thought I'd love anyone again. I mean, like this. I love him so much."

How much she loved Harry had nothing to do with the differences she had with his lifestyle or his celebrity. For the moment, she surrendered, and love conquered all.

"Sweetie, you okay?"

She was out of control and without reason. The emotionalism of menopause seized her, and suddenly, her anxiety about her possible health problems overwhelmed her. She just felt like crying and broke out in muffled sobs.

# CHAPTER FIFTY-SIX

Liz recovered from her crying jag as quickly as it had occurred. She hadn't revealed to Cody what transpired at her doctor's visit, although the words almost spilled out involuntarily with the tears. If she told her about the biopsy, Cody wouldn't consider it a confidence she should keep to herself, but would tell her husband, and maybe even Harry, firmly believing it was in Liz's best interest for Harry to know.

The phone rang, "Hi, how y'a doin'?" Harry said. "Didn't get a chance to phone you. I've been very busy with a few emergencies downtown."

"Hi, Harry."

"How'd you do shopping?"

"Great. I spent too much of your money."

Harry laughed. "If you spent any of my money, I'm happy. And whatever is too much, it's not enough. You're worth so much more."

"In the thousands."

"Good! Must be some dress."

"Shoes and a purse, too."

"Hmm. Do I get a rehearsal with the necklace and earrings?"

"Absolutely not. I want to surprise you."

"Actually, I like surprises. Liz, do you have any plans for Wednesday? It's Rosh Hashanah."

"No, nothing all week. What's up?"

"I'm taking the family to Aaron's for the holiday. I'd like you come with us."

"Huh? How did that happen?"

"I still feel bitter."

"Why are you going then?"

"I can't stop thinking about him—about Aaron. He was so pitiful. I've never seen him like that. He sat at my desk this morning, weeping, telling me how sorry he is. He's always been so stoic and unemotional. He reminded me of myself, crying like that, begging Susan to forgive me and promising her I'd take care of our daughters."

Harry's voice cracked. "And I thought a lot about what you said that Sunday. And you're right—Susan is a part of my daughters and that part didn't die with her. And right or wrong, I've denied them knowledge of their mother, things Leah can tell them. And Aaron's her brother—the brother she grew up with, and they were very close."

Liz held the phone firmly against her ear, frozen and speechless. She could feel him trampling on the hatred and bitterness she heard when he had spoken of Aaron in the car. He could forgive Aaron for the sake of his daughters. She wanted to cry for him.

"Will you come? I need all the support I can get to do this."

"Of course, I'll go. I want to. You know, you're going to make your daughters very happy."

"That's the idea. At least they'll know I tried."

"You'll have to educate me about what to expect. It'll be my first Jewish New Year."

"My nephew is presiding, so it'll be in English, except maybe a few prayers in Hebrew."

"I'm so happy for you, very happy. Have you had dinner?" Liz asked.

"Fred's whipping me something up in the kitchen. Want to join me?"

"No, I'm tired. Had an exhausting day spending your money. Ready for bed already."

Liz thought it was a positive turn of events and she was eager to hear more details. "So, what made Aaron come to your office?"

"I guess he knew I wouldn't call him back. And then, I think he had to let me know Ben told him everything."

"Told him what?"

"Long story. Ben and Sheila had some problems when they were very young, a real mess. I gave them some money. They were just kids. They got pregnant. Sheila was only sixteen."

"Oh, Harry, how awful."

"Ben couldn't tell his father that he dropped out of school and gave up his scholarship to get a job. They each still lived at home.

Sheila got sick and had a miscarriage. There were doctor bills, no income and lots of lies. He came to me, asked me for a loan."

"Just kids." Liz said.

"Yeah. Doing what kids do, breaking your heart."

Liz wondered if Harry thought his daughters might be faced with a similar predicament at some future time. She knew he would be their life-support whatever problems they faced.

"I took care of the doctor bills, paid his tuition and arranged to have some money sent to them every month, 'til he finished school, so they could get married and live together.

"I did it as much for Leah as Ben. I couldn't bear the thought of Aaron disowning his son and Leah losing her only child which is what would have happened had he known. I am very fond of Leah."

"So, they got married?"

"Uh, huh. I asked Ben not to tell his father or anyone else. It wouldn't serve any purpose for anyone to know. My mother would only be stressed, but she did know something was going on because Ben and I were on the phone a lot. In a Jewish family the son goes to his father for help and certainly not to the uncle who's estranged from his father.

"I set up an account in Sheila's name and they told their parents they had saved enough money to get married, so Aaron reluctantly consented. Sheila's parents weren't keen on the marriage either, but they relented eventually. They had a very private wedding, only their parents attended."

"So, how did Aaron find out?"

"I can only think Sheila insisted Ben tell his father why they named the baby Harry. It's the New Year and she wants a clean slate. She wants her husband to be relieved of the deceit they've harbored for too many years. Ben would have to tell his father the truth. They told Sheila's family years ago, but not Aaron and Leah."

"You're making me cry, Harry."

"I didn't know what to say to Aaron. He asked me to forgive him. He said he owed me, for his only son's happiness and would I share the joy of his first grandson and come to his home on the holiday."

"Have you spoken with Ben?"

"Yeah, he called this afternoon and asked me to please come for his father's sake. I called Leah and told her we were coming.

"Can you stay Wednesday?"

"Yes, I already thought I would. Should I meet you at the house?"

"No. We'll pick you up, then go to my Mom's and pick them up."

"Ask Tom to be sure to put my bag in the trunk."

"C'mon, Liz. My daughters know you stay with me at the house."

"I don't like to flaunt it. You know, send messages."

"Okay, I'll tell him. Anyway, that's the only place there'll be room for a bag. What happened at the doctor?"

"Nothing. Everything's fine. Follow-up visit."

# CHAPTER FIFTY-SEVEN

Aaron and Ben greeted everyone "*Shana Tova*, meaning *A good year*. Perfunctory hugging ensued. Aaron embraced Harry and thanked him for coming. Harry held on to Leah a little longer than a customary hug.

"It's so good to see you, Leah, and looking so well."

"I'm so happy to see you Harry. You can't know how long I prayed to be a family again."

Harry introduced Liz to his in-laws. He used the word fiancé. Liz glanced at him with a look of disapproval.

Sheila carried her newborn from his bassinet and placed him in Sarah's waiting arms. He was wide awake and alert for family introductions. Sarah rocked Little Harry and held him close to her breasts, as if he were a treasure she would never relinquish. She had never seen, much less held, a newborn infant before.

"What beautiful little fingers, they're perfect. Daddy, he's so awesome."

"My turn, Sarah," Harry said. He sat down with the baby on his lap and spoke softly: "Hello, Little Harry—Ben's heir and Sheila's joy, we welcome you." The baby gurgled as if in response.

"Yes, it's a pleasure to meet you, too. Uh, huh." Harry's voice faded to a whisper as he continued babbling with the baby's finger wrapped around his index finger.

Liz watched Harry in his display of unconditional affection as he kissed the baby's hands and forehead several times. Suddenly, Little Harry cried out in a startling scream. Everyone smiled and Sheila retrieved the baby for nursing.

Sarah asked Sheila unending questions about the baby. "When will he be able to see us? Does it hurt when you nurse him? Is it all right if I watch you nurse him? Can I hold him again?"

Harry was reminded of Susan, when she held her first born. He was surprised to see his daughter so seized by her maternal instincts and wondered why he had never noticed how much she resembled her mother.

Everyone in the room was unanimous in affection and love for the baby and well-disposed for an auspicious beginning of the holiday. In a very few minutes, a tiny spark of life had dispelled many years of a dark past.

"Come everyone, it's time to light the candles." Leah directed them to the dining room.

Leah set an exquisite table, demonstrating an artistry acquired from preparing many Rosh Hashanahs. Two loaves of challah bread covered with white lace linen sat at both ends of the table with the appropriate sliced apples and bowls of honey placed at the sides of the bread. Leah's silver and fine china adorned a linen tablecloth and the *kiddish* cup, was appropriately placed at the setting for the head of the family. The glasses at each of the placemats were already filled with kosher wine.

"The table is beautiful, Leah," Molly said. "I'm so very happy to be here."

"Thank you. It's been too long."

"Yes. It's been some time since I've seen such a holiday table so well done," Harry said. He guided Liz to a chair next to him, sat down holding her hand and winked at her.

"A few prayers first, then we eat."

Aaron recited in Hebrew the blessing of the candles. Ben paraphrased a translation: "Blessed are you, Lord, our God, ruler of the world, who has kept us alive, sustained us and enabled us to celebrate this season," and then Ben paused and stammered when he came to translating what Aaron had added to the prayer, *and especially grateful for the presence of my sister's family*." Harry gasped and took Liz's hand and squeezed it.

The prayers and blessings continued over the wine and the challah, and then over the apples and honey, spoken in Hebrew by Aaron and echoed in English by Ben.

Harry observed father and son had already resumed the close rapport they had once known. Ben had confided to Harry it had become an onerous obligation the past few years to be with his family for the New Year. Now, he noticed Ben and Aaron broadly smiling at each other, both sharing the happiest of events, free of deceit and bound by forgiveness.

Leah cautioned her nieces, "Don't eat too much of one thing, you must have a little of everything." The meal ensued amidst recitations, blessings and the partaking of symbolic foods for which Ben explained the meanings. Leah had prepared a feast of myriad delectable dishes and everyone ate heartily.

"The honey cake is the prize of the feast, to usher in a new, sweet year," Ben said.

Aaron offered a closing prayer in English: "May Elijah's spirit enter this home and renew our hope. May we be released from the bondage of confusion, prejudice, regret and hate. May we be forgiven for our sins. May war come to an end and people live in peace."

Ben ended the meal with the customary grace after meals and everyone retired to the living room, seeking Little Harry again.

Sarah had seen a picture in the living room of her mother with her Uncle Aaron when they were teenagers and commented to her dad, "I didn't know my mother was so beautiful when she was my age."

"And you girls inherited the better side of the gene pool. You've both got her good looks." He noticed Sarah's admiration as she viewed her mother's picture, and that it didn't stir the usual sadness of loss but engendered a broad grin from Sarah. Apparently, she had made a connection—a very happy one, with her mother.

Harry thought his daughters would never know the burden their mother had endured in the family rift and they would only know love and affection from Susan's relations. The many years of hostility had melted like snow from a mountain and softly crushed the angst of a long, horrible winter. A momentous change had occurred in Harry's life, and he embraced every moment with relief and enthusiasm.

# CHAPTER FIFTY-EIGHT

Tom arrived at 9:00 p.m., prompt as usual. He waited at the curbside of Aaron's house.

The evening ended with a plethora of heartfelt goodbyes.

"Thanks for coming," Leah said. Aaron hugged Harry again and stood grinning next to his son. Harry kissed Leah on the cheek.

"Thanks again, for a wonderful evening." Liz hugged Leah.

"Good night. Thanks for having me."

While the girls lingered and chatted with Sheila, Tom ushered Molly and Ted into the car.

"See you on Saturday. Don't forget, four o'clock." Sheila had invited them to an informal ladies get-together her mother had arranged for her girlfriends to visit the baby. Liz politely declined saying she had a prior commitment. She didn't feel it appropriate to accept a family invitation that Harry wouldn't be attending. They treated her like part of the family, but she didn't feel quite like family.

Finally, everyone settled comfortably in the car. Ted chose to sit in the front with Tom. It wasn't often that the seats in the car were all occupied. Tom asked the group, "We all ready to go?"

"Dad, it was just wonderful. I had a great time. Thanks for taking us." Rebecca said. "The baby is so sweet. My cousin is really a smart guy, isn't he? He's so handsome."

"Uh, huh." Harry leaned back and dozed, his head on Liz's shoulder and his hand folded in hers.

"Nana, look." Rebecca couldn't resist pointing out to her grandmother that her dad was holding Liz's hand while fast asleep.

"Ssh." Molly whispered.

Liz grinned. No one spoke. Only the noise of the car's motor could be heard.

Finally, the car stopped and jolted Harry awake.

"Good night, pumpkins. Talk to you tomorrow."

Liz said her good nights and kissed Rebecca and Sarah on their cheeks.

Tom helped Ted from the front seat and then offered his hand to Molly in the back seat.

"Thank you, son, for making such a wonderful holiday," Molly said.

"We've Aaron to thank. I guess, it's been the day it's supposed to be, a day of forgiveness. Love you, Mom. Night."

Liz and Harry were in good spirits, the residue of a happy evening. The car sped toward Manhattan.

"It was a great evening, Harry. I can see it in your eyes. You're very happy. So are your daughters." Liz said.

"I'd be happier, if you married me."

"We don't need to get married."

"I do. Kiss me."

Liz embraced him. She ran her fingers through his hair and down his face and met his lips. Harry fondled and kissed her. She fell lower in the seat, then sat up abruptly and tucked her blouse in her pants.

Tom pulled the car up through the gate and in front of the garage.

"Thanks, Tom. Good night."

They entered the house and climbed the stairs to the apartment. He stopped her and unbuttoned her blouse, stroking her breasts.

"Harry, Fred may still be up. Wait!"

"I want you right here, on the steps. Touch me."

She reached down to his erection and held him in her hands.

"One more minute." His eyes closed as he expelled a deep sigh. He grabbed her hand and led her up the final steps.

They entered the upstairs living space. "Aren't we supposed to get bored with each other, or something?" He said.

Liz tore off her clothes, dripping in her own arousal. She had been distracted all evening, visualizing making love with him. She rushed to the bed and fell down, nude and impatiently watched him remove his socks. It had been four days since they had been together.

Harry lay down beside her. He held himself and bit his lip. "You'd better do this, slowly, because I can't . . ." He placed her hands on his erection. She enveloped him in her hands and rubbed him against her pubic lips. She couldn't wait and lunged forward on him.

Liz and Harry gazed at each other engrossed in greedy pleasure. At first, they moved slowly forward and backward, moaning and breathing in rhythm with each stroke and hastened to a sudden burst of vibrations and cries of satisfaction.

They lay there for a while, expunged of desire and energy. Liz sat up beside his naked body and Harry indulged his habit of placing little kisses at her neck, her forehead and her face after making love.

She fluffed his hair through her fingers. "You need a haircut. I'm not going to the opera with a guy who needs a haircut."

# CHAPTER FIFTY-NINE

Liz spent the better part of Friday researching the internet for information regarding the biopsy that she would undergo on Tuesday. The procedure, a stereotactic biopsy, used a computer and needle to extract tissue from the questionable mass. There would be a wound mark at her breast, maybe bruising. She would need a few days to heal and wouldn't be able to see Harry unless she chose to invent a lie to explain the bruise.

Unable to shake her curiosity, she browsed through the general breast surgery files Google presented, but cautioned herself not to delve deeply into researching when she had no clear definition of her condition. She hadn't been diagnosed yet, and she clung to the hope that the tiny protrusion in her right breast had nothing to do with cancer.

Liz looked forward to the weekend with Harry, hoping it would distract her from what was on her mind—the lump in her breast. Fred treated them to a home-cooked masterpiece and left. After dinner, they watched a movie.

"Where are you going now?" Harry asked. Liz made her third trip to the kitchen and gulped the latest glass of water with a Xanax.

"Just getting some water," she said. "I feel jittery."

"I see that. Something on you mind? Do you want to talk?"

"No. I'm fine."

She cuddled up next to Harry, her head in his lap and within minutes fell asleep.

After a half an hour, he nudged her awake. "C'mon, in the bed." She leaned on him as he guided her into bed and tucked her in.

• • •

The next day Harry and Liz had a tennis date with Andy and Cody at their club. They decided to play a sexist match—the men against the women. Liz wanted to be any place but on the tennis court. She struggled to project some enthusiasm and made excuses for her lack of vitality.

At the court changeover, Liz sat motionless and stared at the ground. She and Cody hadn't won not even one of five games so far and probably because of Liz's errors.

"Are you okay?" Cody asked.

"Not focused."

"You can say that again."

"I'm sorry, Cody. I'm feeling a little tired. I took a Xanax last night and sometimes that makes me groggy the next day."

Liz's mind was in limbo. Various scenarios galloped in her thoughts as though she were riding an unrestrained horse without reins. If she needed a mastectomy, chemotherapy would be necessary, before and maybe after, or radiation. She'd lose her hair, suffer from nausea and her body would shrink in emaciation. Would both breasts be removed, or just one? What if the cancer had metastasized? Would she be told if she were terminal?

At dinner, Cody caught Liz staring out the window and poked her at her elbow.

"So, have you tried the dress on, with the shoes and jewelry?"

"Yeah. Looks great. I hid it in a closet. I want to surprise Harry." Liz mustered a short smile.

"How was the holiday?" Andy asked.

"Really good. I reconciled with Aaron. They named the baby after me. Of course, the baby was a total delight, just a beautiful little boy. As expected, Leah outdid herself with the food. I hope everyone doesn't continue to call him *little* Harry."

Harry continued to expound details of the holiday evening with Aaron's family. Liz listened and didn't offer any comments. She stared out the window again and fiddled with the food on her plate.

The next day Liz consented to look at the available apartment in her building without murmuring an objection. She went with the flow knowing that if the diagnosis was cancer, she wouldn't be seeing him anymore. She wouldn't burden him with her illness. He wouldn't be buying the apartment, and as unhappy as she felt when she thought about it, she wouldn't be in his life anymore.

Harry conferred with the realtor who volunteered a lengthy history of the evolution of the apartment and its previous owner in her sales pitch. Liz didn't listen and ambled through the apartment, totally uninterested.

Harry only dealt with preliminary questions to satisfy the realtor of his interest and thanked her for her time as they exchanged cards. He told her he'd be in touch, but he'd appreciate if she didn't call him.

They boarded the elevator and stopped at Liz's apartment on the twelfth floor. She brewed some coffee and they settled on the sofa, relaxing before the trip to his mom's for dinner.

"So, what do you think, Ms. Brady?"

"You know what I think. Are you mad or simply crazy?"

"When are you seeing Inez again?" Harry's eyes squinted as he frowned.

"Wednesday. Why?"

"Because you drive me crazy when you do that."

"Do what?"

Harry's face flushed. "You know what I'm asking, yet you ever-so-nicely change the subject. Or ask me a question as if it's an answer. You avoid telling me what you think, or what you want. Would you do me the favor of asking Inez why you do that? Or maybe I should ask her. Maybe it's me. Maybe I'm the one who shouldn't get frustrated."

"I'm sorry, Harry. I didn't even realize what you were asking." She didn't have the emotional stamina to argue with him and thought, anyway, he really doesn't want to know what I want if it's not the same thing as he wants.

"I'm sorry." Harry said. "I didn't mean to go off on you like that. There's something else nagging at me."

Harry kissed her on the lips and put his arm around her.

"I feel so frustrated because I don't know what you want. I'm trying very hard to meet you someplace, and I don't seem to be getting there. I know we're better than we've been, but I'm impatient."

He placed his other arm around her and hugged her.

"Harry, I'm not feeling up to talking about the apartment right now."

She felt immersed in a pool of water and drowning in the uncertainties of whether or not she had cancer. Was it life-threatening, when would the pathology report be available and if she did have cancer, was it an aggressive cancer? What treatment would she need?

When they arrived at Molly's house, Liz felt relieved and happy when Rebecca and Sarah rescued her. The girls distracted her with their cheerfulness. Absorbed in their lives, she thought of them as two younger sisters who confided in her and shared their hopes and secrets with her. She loved his daughters.

The girls tore Liz away from the family room before dinner to spend some private time with her. They girl-talked and gravitated from one bedroom to the other, giggling and chatting endlessly. Harry's daughters both had a pervading enthusiasm, and Liz felt infused with their élan when in their company. Something new was always happening, or changing, and whatever it was, it was exciting.

Rebecca described her latest crush, "He's very smart and a hunk. He wants to be an actor. We get to choose some electives this year. Maybe I should take a drama class next semester. What do you think, Liz?"

"You should explore whatever you fancy. It's a time for you to experiment, find out what inspires you, what you have a flare for, like your sister and her photography."

"My guidance counselor says I should be getting better grades, that I'm not working up to my potential. I think a three point average is totally fine."

"Yeah, but she's right. Working for good grades is a discipline that will open doors to whatever you decide to study."

Rebecca asked Liz her personal opinion about everything female. Outspoken as usual, the latest advice she sought concerned the hygienic value of tampons versus pads. The question took Liz completely off-balance. "That's a strictly personal preference, so far as I know. I have no idea whether one is better than the other."

"Liz, there's this cute guy at school who follows Sarah around like a lost puppy. Will you tell her, she's at least got to talk to him? He's really cute, blond curly hair and blue eyes. But he's so shy."

Rebecca shared Sarah's secrets with Liz, and Liz often served as a buffer between the two distinct and separate personalities. Sarah no longer chose silence when she disagreed with her sister's criticisms, but asserted her opinion with confidence and relied on

Liz to support her. Sarah interrupted, "Not everyone is looking for a boyfriend, like you."

Rebecca continued her commentary, "This guy's in her photography class, and he told me he thinks Sarah doesn't like him because she brushes him off all the time. But she does like him. She's gotta get with the program. You should get with the program, too."

Rebecca immediately looked away from Liz.

Liz was startled at her comment and looked askance at Rebecca. She knew Rebecca habitually didn't think before she spoke and probably never would acquire any editing skills. She recognized Rebecca made a slip, and that she preferred to withhold what she meant, but Liz prodded her, "What do you mean, I should get with the program?"

Rebecca cowered momentarily and then reluctantly offered a response, "Why don't you want to marry my father? You love him, don't you?"

Liz dropped her hands in her lap. "Yes, I love him. More than anything." She paused and drew in a long breath and exhaled.

For the past few weeks, Liz had lived with Harry's lifestyle, his celebrity and his wealth, but those issues no longer intruded negatively as they once did. Inez had reinforced her identity and she no longer feared losing herself in a relationship. She realized Harry never asked her to change anything about herself to accommodate him. She had grown confident that she could walk with him in his life and retain her autonomy, except now, the thought that she might have a disease loomed before her and plagued her heart. She could not entertain a future with Harry.

"I can't answer you. I don't know why." A few tears trickled down her cheeks. Liz lied. She knew why. Harry had endured watching his wife die, and she would never forget the last few months of watching her husband fade day by day. She wouldn't subject Harry to the anguish of a loved one's illness and possible death.

"I'm sorry, Liz. I didn't mean to make you cry." Rebecca said. She and Sarah moved to her chair and hugged Liz.

Harry knocked on the door and walked in. He looked at the three of them hugging each other, "We're—" He glanced at Rebecca, then Sarah, "at the table. What's going on?"

"Nothin' Dad." Rebecca said.

"Hmm, yeah. Looks like nothing."

Liz wiped a few tears from her cheek with her fingers.

"Liz? You okay?"

"Yes, fine. Just talking. C'mon girls, let's go eat."

# CHAPTER SIXTY

After the Sunday family dinner, Liz didn't go home with Harry as she usually did. She explained to him that she didn't want to travel from uptown the next day to the morning appointments she had scheduled in her neighborhood for a hairstyling, a facial and a manicure at the same salon. The afternoon was reserved for leisurely plucking her eyebrows, immersing in a scented bubble bath and maybe dozing on the sofa. She had decided to devote the day to indulging her body to create a relaxed and alluring person by five-thirty. She wanted to be at her best, looking forward to her first public evening with the Mayor and determined not to let her apprehensions about the biopsy overshadow the occasion.

Liz phoned Lauren. "Hi, how're you? Is it a bad time?" Liz asked.

"No, actually. Not busy at all today."

Lauren wanted to accompany her to the out-patient facility on Tuesday, but Liz insisted it wasn't necessary. She was appreciative of Lauren's offer, but didn't want Lauren to take any time off. She could manage the procedure alone.

"Did you tell him?"

"No, and I'm not telling him. There really isn't anything to tell. It may be nothing, a cyst, a benign tumor."

It occurred to Liz that, however unlikely, Lauren might call Harry. "Lauren, please promise me you won't say anything to Harry."

"I wouldn't do that, Liz. I know you don't want him to know. I don't understand why, but I won't tell him. You sure you don't want me to go with you?"

"Yes, I'm sure. Thanks again for offering. I don't want you to worry. I'm okay and I'll be fine. I'll give you a call when I get home."

"Big night tonight?"

"Yeah, I feel like a teenager going to her first prom," Liz said.

"Try not to think about the other stuff."

"I'm not. Gotta get crackin'. Have an appointment at ten. Talk to you tomorrow."

"Knock 'em dead tonight. Enjoy! Bye."

"Thanks, again."

• • •

The intercom buzzed. "Harry's on his way up." Andres said.

"Thanks, Andres."

Liz waited at the open door of her apartment for the elevator to arrive. Harry stepped off the elevator and stood frozen in the hallway. He stared at her, absorbing every fold of the supple blue dress that enhanced her body and bright blue eyes.

"You look fantastic. Unbelievably gorgeous. Tell me it's all for me." He moved across the hallway, embraced her and lightly pressed his lips against hers.

They entered the apartment and Harry closed the door.

"The jewelry is perfect. Have my work cut out for me tonight, keeping the competition away from you."

"What competition? No one could compete with you in black tie, so handsome and de rigueur." She ran her fingers through his hair. "Great haircut. You sexy thing."

She visualized the body that lurked beneath the black tie costume and imagined her hands beneath his white shirt, touching his chest, undoing the bow tie and removing the studs.

"I'm ready. Just need to get my jacket and purse."

Harry's cell rang. "We'll be right down." Harry laughed. "That was Andy. Cody told him to phone, said she didn't trust me not to lure you into the bedroom because she's seen you in that dress. Very funny, isn't she?"

Cody had made reservations at the Grand Tier Restaurant at the opera house for six o'clock, instructing the maître d' that they would be attending the Guild reception, and it would be appreciated if their schedule could be observed. Dinner went like clockwork, and they were at the Belmont Room a little after seven.

As soon as they stepped into the room, a waiter, dressed in a formal black bolero jacket and red bow tie approached Harry. "Mr.

Mayor, we've arranged a special table for you and your guests. Please follow me."

"We're getting the deference treatment," Andy said. "Okay with me. Rather sit than stand." The waiter took their orders for drinks.

"Harry, Roger's on his way over here." Andy said.

"Hey Harry, where the hell have you been?" Roger nodded hello to Andy and Cody, who ignored him. He turned and gazed at Liz while speaking to Harry, "Where have you been hiding her? No wonder I haven't seen you around. I'm Roger," he said as he extended his hand to Liz.

"I know who you are." Liz smiled. She recognized him as a sportscaster from ESPN. His face dominated the station.

"Nice to meet you," she said. Roger held onto her hand and placed his other hand on top of hers.

"She's taken, Roger. Go away, and if you want to play golf, give me a call on my cell tomorrow."

"Harry, can't you share sometimes?"

"Do you want a tail on your car tonight?"

"Nice to meet you, Liz." Roger winked at Liz and released her hands. "See you folks."

They sat down and the waiter served their drinks.

"Thanks for getting rid of him, Harry." Andy turned to Liz and said, "He's a real piece of trash. We were all having cocktails at the club one night after playing golf, and he hits on Cody while I'm sitting right next to her."

"Andy, he's harmless bravado." Harry said.

"If you ask me, he's always had a crush on himself, the epitome of vanity." Cody said.

Liz gazed around the room. Except for the expensive jewelry on display, she thought the event could be a funeral for all the tuxes and little black dresses. Wearing a blue dress that enhanced her eyes, she was glad not to have to resort to wearing her go-everywhere, black cocktail dress, thanks to Harry.

She wore the necklace and earrings Harry bought her in Bermuda and was certain her jewelry was far more unique and elegant than the razzle-dazzle she observed. Although the theme for women's jewelry throughout the room was generally conservative, some of the women ran the gamut from overpowering to ostentatious, and the profusion of mascara and lipstick use made some of the women stand out like madams in bordellos.

The opera echelon of present and past board members clustered at two tables at the end of the room, obviously reserved especially for them. Groups of chatting attendees spread across the room, glasses in hands and in evening dress regalia, portraying a lively social gathering of patrons of the arts. Liz felt comfortable but distanced from the crowd, not being a member of the so-called important people of New York.

"I should make an appearance with the Board," Harry said as he took her hand. "Come with me, Liz?" Harry knew many of the board members on a first-name basis. He had donated to the Met long before he became Mayor, and the members didn't change much from year to year.

The CEO rose from his seat to greet Harry. "Thanks for coming, Harry. We can always use some public relations. Good to meet you, Ms. Brady," he said when Harry introduced Liz.

The board members gathered in an informal circle before the reserved tables. Liz felt confident, deftly chatting and intermingling with the board members. She had been a Guild member and Met subscriber for over twenty years and was well-informed about the current opera productions and fund raising campaigns.

Liz commented to the president. "I think you're in need of a resurgence of youth. Maybe you should sponsor another competition for a new opera, bring some new blood into the house?"

"That may very well be an excellent suggestion. It proved daring and challenging ten years ago. We should probably try it again."

The public relations director approached Harry. "Mr. Bergman, can we get a few shots for *Opera News*?"

Harry turned to Liz. "Are you all right with that?"

"Uh, huh." She nodded her approval although she would have preferred Harry go solo with the publicity.

In a matter of seconds, three photographers emerged from the crowd, positioning Harry, Liz and some of the board members. Liz spied a badge on the jacket of one of the photographers. After a few minutes of bright lights and requests for smiles and gestures, Harry said, "Okay, guys, that's it." Harry uttered some pleasantries to the board members, shook hands again and ushered Liz away from the tables.

"Guess we made the papers," Liz whispered to Harry. "The *Post*, if I read his badge correctly."

"Sorry, didn't notice that the newspapers were here. He did say *Opera News*."

"He did. But it's okay."

"Really?" They walked across the room.

"What happened to that lady who was so against having her picture taken with me?"

"Oh, well, she's no longer a fugitive from public scrutiny. And I heard she became overwhelmingly attracted to the Mayor, something about him being so enticing and sexy in black tie that she couldn't resist and threw Harry over for him."

"Well, as you know, it's already a matter of record that the Mayor is totally enchanted with the lady.

"What's with Ashley, the old timer, the guy you were in the corner chatting tête-à-tête? Did he make a pass at you?"

"Are you jealous?" Liz giggled. "He simply wanted to recruit me for some fundraising efforts. Quite a gentlemen, as a matter of fact, and he knows how to flatter a woman. Said the board needs some style and substance, and he believes I could make a valuable contribution, etcetera, etcetera. Very charming."

"Well, what did you say?"

"I told him my dance card was full."

"Huh?"

"He suggested the three of us have lunch. I said he should speak with you, that you're the one with the busy schedule."

Harry grinned. "We could do that, if you think you'd like to get involved."

They strolled across the room and returned to their table. Andy and Cody stood nearby, chatting with a couple. Liz and Harry sat down. Harry didn't care whether or not he was in the public's reference. He leaned over and kissed Liz softly on the lips and whispered, "I love you."

# CHAPTER SIXTY-ONE

Liz turned the disc player on and chose some soothing adagios to help her relax. She lounged on the sofa and read a packet of instructions mailed from the outpatient surgery facility detailing the procedure to remove the cancer. The surgery was mandatory. There were no options. Pre-surgery tests and another appointment with the surgeon had already been scheduled.

The phone rang, "Hi, Liz. It's Rebecca." Liz heard her sobbing in the phone.

"What's wrong, Rebecca?"

"I don't know what to do."

"What's wrong? Where are you?"

"I'm at school."

"Why are you crying?"

"I can't talk. I'm on a public phone. My cell phone is in my locker."

"Okay, calm down and get in a cab and come here." Liz wanted to hold her and tell her whatever the problem, it'd be all right.

"Where?"

"My apartment, Twelve D. Get a cab to Thirty-Sixth and Lexington. It should only take ten minutes from downtown. There's only one apartment building on the corner."

"Okay."

Liz put the teakettle on the stove and prepared a tray. She paced around the apartment, stress mounting with every passing minute. She checked the bathroom medicine cabinet for relaxants, anti-depressants, painkillers. Why was Rebecca crying like that? Her boyfriend dumped her? She failed a course?

Rebecca would call her dad and confide in him if it were a problem with a boyfriend or school, and she wouldn't be weeping uncontrollably, in either case. Whatever was wrong, Liz surmised it had to be something she couldn't share with her dad and something she couldn't dismiss with a shrug of her shoulder. Should she call Harry?

The intercom buzzed. "Rebecca here to see you."

"Thanks, Andres." Liz opened the door and waited for the elevator. Rebecca stepped off the elevator, her eyes red and swollen. Liz held her arms out. "Honey, what's happened?"

"Oh, Liz, I don't know what to do. You've got to help me."

"Come inside. Calm down. We'll have some tea and talk."

Liz hugged her. She held onto to her and squeezed her. "It'll be all right. Sit down. I'll get the tea." She had never seen Rebecca out of control, crying and whimpering like an abused animal. At the moment Rebecca wasn't the confident, precocious young lady she knew.

Liz fetched the tea and Rebecca sat down on the sofa and blurted out, "I'm pregnant."

Liz stopped short on her way across the living room. She paused for a moment. "Oh!" she said. Cups and saucers clashed and tumbled on the tray she carried. She set the tray on the table in front of Rebecca.

"I didn't get my period. It's been six weeks. My breasts are sore. What am I going to do?"

Rebecca brought her hands up and covered her face. She burst into sobs. "I can't tell my dad. I just can't." Liz took Rebecca's hands from her face and embraced her as she continued to sob. Liz felt like crying with Rebecca. She was facing cancer surgery and now Rebecca was pregnant.

"Hey, your father loves you more than anything in the world. He might have a fit of temper, but you can tell him anything. He'll always be there for you. No matter what."

"Did you try a pregnancy test?"

"No. I've gained five pounds in the last month and I'm nauseous in the morning. I'm afraid to take one of those tests in case it's positive."

"Have you been seeing someone? I mean—who is the father?"

"No. It only happened once. I had too much to drink. We were kissing and I fell asleep, or I passed out. I opened my eyes and he was inside me. I don't know if he took my pants off or if I did. I . . . I can't remember. We shouldn't have even been in the bedroom. It was a party."

"Did you tell him *not to*?"

Rebecca's words poured out between sobs and intermittent sniffling. "I didn't have a chance. After, he said that I wanted to, that I said okay. I got drunk and it was too late. When I woke up, he was fucking me. I don't even know him, where he lives."

"Did he use a condom?"

"No." Rebecca gasped and tried to suppress her tears, but nonetheless the tears continued streaming down her face. She leaned over and held her head in her hands.

"Go into the bathroom and wash your face. Stop crying."

Rebecca came out of the bathroom, somewhat calmed. She had mustered some composure. So had Liz.

"Put your jacket on. We're going to see a doctor around the corner, at a drop-in clinic. Don't worry, no one will know. I'll fill out the paper work for you. You have to see a doctor, see how far gone you are before you can decide what you're going to do."

"Okay."

Liz and Rebecca walked in silence the short distance from the apartment to the clinic. The room was crowded, but there appeared to be adequate staff, moving and rushing around the premises. Liz filled out some forms and presented it to the nurse.

"I'm her aunt. She's missed her period."

A stone-faced nurse took the papers from Liz and led them to an examination room. They waited patiently for the doctor. When the nurse appeared in the room, she instructed Rebecca to place her feet in the stirrups and told them the doctor would be with them momentarily. Liz noticed Rebecca's hands shook and her body trembled, revealing her apprehension. Liz empathized with Rebecca. It was her first internal examination and not conducted under relaxed circumstances.

Luckily, the doctor was very caring, He worked slowly and calmed Rebecca throughout the exam. Afterward the nurse ushered them into the doctor's office. Liz held Rebecca's hand while they waited for the results.

Finally, the doctor appeared and sat down behind his desk, a half-smile on his face.

"I expect you'll be happy to know you're not pregnant. You missed a period probably because of a hormone imbalance, a thyroid problem or a cyst. We don't know the cause yet. You'll need additional tests to determine why you're not menstruating. Meanwhile, take these pills," he said as he wrote on a prescription pad, "for three days. You should get your period by Sunday or Monday. I'm also writing an order for a scan and a test for S.T.D.'s."

Rebecca's lips quivered and a few tears trickled down her cheek. She wiped them away with her hand. Liz hugged her and said. "It's okay, honey."

"Aunt?"

"Yes?"

"I'd like to talk to Rebecca alone for a few minutes. If you would wait outside."

"Yes, of course."

Liz left the doctor's office, sat in the waiting room and wondered why the doctor wanted to talk to Rebecca privately. Twenty minutes later Rebecca appeared in the waiting room. They left the clinic and walked to a nearby pharmacy. Rebecca was still sniffling.

"God, what a mistake. I swear, I'm never having sex again."

"What did he say to you?"

"Everything. Diseases. Pre-marital sex. Pregnancy. Told me never to believe a man who wants to make love to me and doesn't have a condom. My partner should be protecting me from pregnancy. He wanted to know if it was consensual, if you are my guardian and was there someone at home I could talk to.

"He said if I chose to have sex, I had a responsibility also to take care of myself and not to rely only on my partner who might be exposing me to herpes or diseases. He did get a little angry and told me to stop crying and behaving like a child. You won't tell my dad?"

"Of course not. He shouldn't hear that from anyone except you. You'll find a time to tell him."

"I'll never tell him."

"You'll have sex again, too. If you want to swear off something, swear off drinking. You're obviously not able to handle liquor. You've got to learn to protect yourself, which may be the only good thing that comes out of this. I'm sure it won't ever happen again. Not like that anyway."

Traffic got heavy as the day neared the rush hour. Liz hurried, knowing Molly would be worried if Rebecca wasn't home yet. "Where are you supposed to be right now?"

"On my way home. I skipped my last class. It'll be all right if I call. Can I use your computer to check if there are any homework assignments for tomorrow?"

"Sure. We'll put some ice on your eyes, try to get some of the swelling down. Rebecca, you're going to have to see your regular doctor and arrange for those tests. Give him that doctor's card and the orders for the tests. Does Nana go to the doctor with you? You'll have to tell her you missed your period, but you don't have to tell her about the sex, unless you want to. She's a very understanding woman if you choose to tell her."

"I can't tell her anything. She'll tell my dad. I have to call her when I get upstairs. She'll worry if I'm more than a half-hour late."

Rebecca stopped in the middle of the street and threw her arms around Liz.

"What a relief. It's over. Thank you, Liz. Thanks. I love you. I don't know what I would've done."

"I love you, too, honey."

"Rebecca, you may not feel like it now, but if you can't talk to Nana, or your dad, you may want to talk to Inez. You've seen her before. I could call her for you, and you needn't tell your dad. Anything you talk about with Inez is private because she's bound by an oath not to discuss clients with anyone, including your dad."

"I'm all right now. I just want to forget the whole thing."

"You know, it doesn't all just go away because you want to forget it."

When they arrived at the apartment, Liz went in the kitchen to prepare an ice pack for Rebecca's eyes. Rebecca sat down at the computer and waited for the school website to connect. She spied the top page on top of the packet that Liz had placed next to the computer. She didn't make the connection that the *Pre-Surgery Instructions for* Surgery had anything to do with Liz. She skimmed the instructions and dismissed the information as if it had something to do with her work.

"Finished?" Liz asked as she emerged from the kitchen with the ice pack.

"Yeah, nothing due tomorrow."

Liz thought Rebecca was too confused about what happened to her, and the full impact of her experience had not yet taken effect. Harry would have the police and a private investigator out looking for this boy if she told him, whether what happened was rape or wasn't rape. And he would probably want to bring charges against the parents who served liquor at that party. Only Rebecca could make the decision to tell Harry. In any event, Liz thought it definitely was not over.

# CHAPTER SIXTY-TWO

Liz met with Inez for their usual Wednesday session. She had canceled her previous weekly appointment, mistakenly disclosing to Inez that she had a biopsy the day before and wasn't emotionally equipped for a session. She hadn't meant to tell Inez about the biopsy, and when the words slipped out, she knew Inez was obligated to keep the matter confidential.

"I can see you're anxious, Liz. What did the pathology report disclose? I'm here to help you, remember?"

Liz neither wanted to discuss the procedure, nor the results. After Inez pleaded with her, she finally succumbed and revealed she needed surgery, her tears gushing like water from a broken faucet. Inez hugged her while she cried.

Inez suggested ways to cope with her disease. "It's important your family and friends know about your illness. Their support will sustain you through the trials you face. I'm sure Harry will want you to stay with him while you go through this. I can recommend a support group as well. When is the surgery scheduled?"

"I don't know yet. I saw the surgeon for all of ten minutes and he told me to write down all my questions for a further appointment. He's arranged pre-surgery testing. So, I don't know what I'm dealing with yet. For all I know, I may need a mastectomy. I'm not telling Harry anything. I have a friend who'll help me."

"Why? You need all the support you can get right now, and he's the person closest to you."

"Inez, I can't burden him with this. He fell in love with a healthy woman. That's not me anymore. Right now, I'm a patient. I won't be his patient. I know what it's like to be the caretaker. It almost destroyed me, and I won't be responsible for Harry assuming that role."

Inez countered her reasoning. "This is not the same situation as your husband's terminal illness. Harry loves you, and you can't just shut him out. Your cancer has been found at an early stage and is probably treatable."

"I wish I knew that to be true. I don't know the extent of the cancer yet. I can't offer him what I've been to him, and I'm not the person he fell in love with anymore."

Liz imagined the worst case scenarios, losing a breast or both of them, enduring chemotherapy or radiation treatments, taking medications that would cause side effects, undergoing endless tests and the anxiety of waiting for results. Her whole life suddenly was reduced to one colossal problem, cancer. What could she possibly offer Harry in her condition? It was a total horror story, and she wouldn't make him part of it.

"He doesn't need me, and he doesn't need my problem."

"Have you asked yourself what does Harry need? His need may be to love and take care of you."

Liz smirked. "I'm already his dependent and now, I'm not only the dependent, but the sick dependent."

"Liz, you are not your submissive mother who depended on your father. And however controlling Harry is, he is not your domineering and abusive father. You're comparing apples and oranges. You've got to adjust your thinking to the facts, and whatever you're thinking, not telling Harry what's happening is not a positive course of action."

Inez could not dissuade her. Liz, stubborn and unwavering, had already decided what she wanted to do. She was going to leave Harry. She listened to Inez, but what Inez advised did not penetrate her biased judgment.

Liz walked to the door. Inez was beside her. "Inez," Liz hesitated.

"Yes?"

"Would it be out of order for you to call Rebecca? I can't tell you, but something's happened and I can't be there for her, not if . . ."

Liz was convinced that Rebecca wouldn't handle the loss of her virginity as if nothing happened. She recognized Rebecca was a precocious and opinionated young woman, and from her outward behavior, appeared to have everything under control. But Rebecca was also emotional and sensitive, desperate for approval and in need of self-esteem. In addition to the fact that she planned to leave Harry and wouldn't be in contact with Rebecca, she thought Inez was a professional, equipped to help Rebecca through a painful experience.

"Because you're ill? What's happened?"

"Yes. I can't tell you. It's a confidence issue. Rebecca needs to talk to someone and not her father. I suggested she call you, but I don't think she will. She needs to be persuaded. Can you call her?"

"All right, if you feel that strongly. Shall I tell her you suggested I call because you're concerned about her well-being, and you think she should have a visit with me?"

"Yes, exactly."

"Promise me you won't stop coming to see me. You know, I'm already paid. Try to stay positive. You will survive this, you do know that?"

"Yes. Thanks, Inez. I'll make an appointment after the surgery. Goodbye."

"Bye, Liz. God bless. Please keep me posted."

• • •

Liz flopped on the sofa, emotionally drained and fell asleep. The buzz of the intercom awoke her. "Lauren's on her way up." Andres said.

"Okay."

Lauren greeted Liz with a hug, "Hi. See the doctor?"

"Yeah. They did some pre-surgery tests. The doctor went over the pathology report with me. It's a Stage I cancer. The tissue around the biopsy has to be removed—a lumpectomy—and nodes from under my arm. Then another pathology report to determine the extent of the cancer cells, whether it's aggressive and if it's in my nodes. Then, who knows? The surgery's absolutely necessary. I don't have a choice."

"I've taken Monday and Tuesday off." Lauren said.

"The doctor said the prognosis is good. I'll be fine on Tuesday. A wound, soreness. That's all. The worst part is the waiting, not knowing how bad it is."

They sat on the sofa. Lauren leaned over and hugged her.

"You don't need to take two days off. I appreciate you're going with me as it is."

"You know I'm here for you, for whatever you need. Just ask."

"Want a coffee?"

"No, I can't stay. Just stopped by for an update. I'll go with you Monday, stay over. You may not need nursing after the surgery, but you're going to need moral support, someone to talk to. Stop being such a self-sufficient ninny. You'll want company. I've got plenty of time coming to me. We'll watch TV. I'll make you dinner."

"Yeah, and you've got some guy in your office who's dying to take over when you're not there. You don't need to jeopardize your job right now."

"Stop it, Liz. Let me do what I need to do to help you. I'm your friend. Remember? You're still not telling Harry?"

"Not discussable."

"Okay. And the weekend? Are you going to stay with him? Or have you changed your mind?"

"No, I'm breaking it off Friday. I can't hang around knowing I'm planning to tell him I don't want to see him anymore. It's bad enough. I don't want to drag it out."

Lauren walked to the door and Liz followed her.

"Okay, maybe we can get together Saturday night. I'm working in the morning."

"Sounds good. Thanks again." Liz hugged her, "See you Saturday."

# CHAPTER SIXTY-THREE

"What are you doing?" Harry stood in the doorway to the bedroom.

"Packing my things."

Liz wouldn't look at him. She knew if she did, they'd be on the bed in a matter of minutes.

"You going somewhere?" Harry asked. He walked into the room and stood beside her.

"I'm leaving. It's not working."

"Whatta y'a mean? What's not working?" Harry froze. Liz bowed her head and stared at the bag she packed and fidgeted with some garments.

"I can't see you anymore."

"What's the matter? Let's sit down and talk."

"No, that'll only make it worse."

"What's going on? Whatta mean *leaving*? Why?"

"You're not happy and I'm not happy. You want me to live here or marry you. I don't want to live here, and I don't want to marry you. We're torturing ourselves. It's always in the way."

"In the way? I thought Inez was helping us."

"Helping us get somewhere I don't want to be, but someplace you want to be. That's what it's all about. It doesn't work for me."

She lied. It had been better—a détente that had been working for her. However dependent she had felt, she no longer was threatened by his controlling personality and she no longer feared losing her identity in his lifestyle. The cancer was the problem, nothing more.

"I don't want to talk about it anymore," she said.

Harry threw his arms around her, "Look at me, tell me you don't love me."

Liz wouldn't look at him. "Don't Harry. You know I love you. You're making it worse."

She broke away from him, tore out of the bedroom and scurried down the steps to the bar. She poured some sherry and sat, anxious and unwilling to indulge in a heated confrontation.

"Liz?" Harry passed quickly through the kitchen and sat next to her at the bar. He placed his hand under her chin.

"What am I supposed to do?"

"Let me go and let me be." Liz pulled his hand away from her face and avoided looking in his eyes.

"You really want to do this? It's over? Just like that?"

His face reddened and his arms flailed in the air.

At all costs, she had to avoid his anger, which she felt he was on the brink of expressing. He would argue and scream and she would weaken and cry. She couldn't let that happen.

She slipped away from him, hurried up the steps to the bedroom, grabbed her bag and jacket and walked cautiously down the steps. She saw him seated at the bar, his head leaning forward and staring at his hands. He turned and looked at her. She wanted to say she was sorry. Instead, she hurried out the door without a parting glimpse or a parting word.

• • •

Crying and unable to sleep, Liz replayed the scene in her mind again and again, reliving the look of disbelief and pain on Harry's face. He loved her. In return she inflicted pain.

She took a Xanax, lay on the sofa and tried to nap. Her thoughts strayed to the wonderful evening at the opera a week ago. He allowed her to be herself and made no criticisms or demands of her. He never asked her to change anything in any way about herself or to be anyone except herself.

The phone rang. Liz viewed the caller ID and let the machine take over. Lauren had called again. She punched in her number even though it was late, eleven o'clock.

"Hi."

"Tried you earlier this evening. There was no answer. I thought maybe you changed your mind."

"No."

"You've been crying?"

"Yeah, but I'll get over it. Don't have much choice."

"I don't know why you think that, you know, you do have a choice. You don't have to break up with him. You're not even giving him a chance."

"Lauren, I can't be the disabled lover. Right now, I can't be anything but a sick person. It's one thing to be dependent, to feel inferior, but a liability as well? I'm not the woman he met in Bermuda. Besides, it's done. It's over."

"Okay. I hear you. I'm working in the morning. Are we on for tomorrow night? See a movie?"

"Yeah, I guess."

"Liz, take a sleeping pill. Get some sleep. See you tomorrow."

"Bye."

Liz couldn't sleep. Plagued with self-hate, Lauren's words echoed in her mind. She hadn't given Harry a chance. She missed him already and felt empty and numb. Nothing mattered anymore.

What did she do to deserve this hell? Was it her fault? She recalled the many discussions she had with Inez about her mother's dependency, telling her how she vowed when she was a child never to become her mother—the submissive woman who was bound emotionally and economically to her husband. She would take care of herself.

Not only had she always taken care of herself, but everyone in her family: her sister, her nephew and her husband. She pampered Phil, exceeding his needs. He so enjoyed the role of the beloved and she was the partner who did most of the loving. And although she felt that he loved her, he never took care of her when she was ill with the flu, or had a painful wisdom tooth pulled. He just wasn't empathetic, and she never expected his sympathy, much less his help with the everyday tasks of living. She never depended on him or anyone else.

Liz believed the fears of domination in her past had died and were buried long ago, but the conflicts she thought had been resolved still plagued her mind. She didn't need a man in her life to take care of her. She swallowed a sleeping pill as her demons preyed upon her like a predator, threatening to consume her. Maybe she had made the wrong decision. Maybe she did need someone to take care of her. Maybe she needed Harry. She finally dozed off to the welcome peace of sleep.

# CHAPTER SIXTY-FOUR

The doorbell awoke him. Harry checked the outdoor surveillance camera. Andy stood at the gate waiting to be buzzed in. Harry pushed the switch that opened the gate and tied his robe around his waist.

What the hell was Andy doing here at eight o'clock on a Saturday morning? They didn't have a golf date. Harry walked down the hallway and opened the door. Andy flew passed him.

"Any coffee?"

"No, you got me out of bed."

Harry followed Andy to the kitchen. Disheveled and sleepy, Harry stumbled, opening and closing kitchen cabinets, searching for coffee.

"You look like hell. Where's Liz?"

"Not here."

"I had a message on my machine last night. You can't make it tonight?"

"She's gone. She packed a bag and walked out last night."

"What are you saying?"

"She left."

"You had an argument?"

"No. Left, as in not coming back, as in doesn't want to see me anymore. Finished!"

"You're kidding?"

Harry found the coffee and the filters. He poured water into the coffee maker.

"Don't ask. I don't know why. I don't know what the hell came over her. She wouldn't say anything, except I should let her go."

"Well, call her."

"I can't."

"Whatta y'a mean, you can't?"

"You had to be here. I know her. She made up her mind. It's no use." Harry's voice cracked. "I called last night to cancel, so you could make other plans."

"Screw the plans. What're you gonna do?"

"Do? There's nothing I can do. She's a woman who means what she says. She wasn't in a temper or a mood, just fucking adamant. *I'm leaving*, is all she said. Wouldn't even look at me."

He had tossed and turned the night before. He tried to sleep, got out of bed several times and paced around his bedroom. Now, the opportunity to vent presented itself and Harry succumbed. The thoughts that had flooded his mind throughout the night spewed out like water from a street hydrant.

"Thing is, I thought everything had gotten so much better. I stopped nagging her to move in with me. She was the happiest I've ever seen her at the opera. She didn't flinch at the photographer taking pictures and told me she loved the photo in the *Post* of me kissing her on the cheek."

Droplets of tears fell from his eyes.

"She had the goddamn board members charmed and enjoyed every minute of them falling all over her. We had a great evening."

Harry poured the coffee, milk and sugar in mugs and handed one to Andy. Harry sipped the coffee.

"I know we'd gotten better. Inez helped us. Liz never even hinted that she wasn't happy. What the hell happened?"

"Harry, get dressed. We'll play some golf."

"Andy, it's raining."

Harry grabbed a paper towel from the counter, ran it under the water faucet, applied it to his eyes and wiped the tears from his face.

"I'm all right."

"No, you're not all right. You need company. You're coming home with me. Cody will make us some breakfast. We'll play cards, watch the ballgame, do something."

Harry mumbled, talking to himself, as if Andy wasn't there. "I'll get over this. Like I have a choice. It'll take time, but I'll get over it."

# CHAPTER SIXTY-FIVE

Liz took the prescribed post-surgery medications and slept. Her right breast was sore when she moved, but not painful. When she awoke at nine o'clock in the evening, she crept out of bed, stepped slowly into the living room and found Lauren asleep on the sofa. She tossed a throw blanket across her body, picked up the remote from the coffee table and turned the television off. Still tired, she dragged herself to the kitchen and placed the teakettle on the stove.

The long, stressful day ended. She and Lauren had been at the hospital at seven in the morning. The surgery went smoothly and they were back in the apartment by early afternoon. Liz assured Lauren she could fend for herself, but Lauren wouldn't leave her friend alone. She kept a vigil while Liz slept through the afternoon and then dozed off herself.

The phone rang and woke Lauren. She picked up the receiver from the end table. "Yes?"

"Hi, is Liz there?

"Who's calling?"

"Marisa."

"Hold on, please." Lauren spied Liz in the kitchen and called out from across the room. "It's Marisa?"

Liz stood at the kitchen doorway, shook her head and waved her hands, indicating she did not want to speak with her, and then impulsively changed her mind.

"I'm making tea," she said to Lauren. She moved slowly across the room and reached for the phone.

"Hi. How are you?" Liz asked.

"Great! Overjoyed with our new baby Matthew."

"Congratulations. I'm happy for you."

"How are you?"

"I've been better."

"I just wanted to let you know that Peter has no problem about you bringing Harry to the christening. You know—that they don't get along. He said that's your choice, and he'd like him to come with you."

It was obvious to Liz that Peter had not told Marisa what transpired at their lunch a few weeks ago. As far as Marisa knew, the lunch was simply to persuade her to continue working for him. She wondered just how much Marisa knew, probably only that Peter didn't approve of the relationship, and probably nothing about his affair with Susan. But something must have changed his mind about Harry.

"You did get the invitation?"

"Yes, I did. Last week. I didn't reply because I thought I might be able to make it, but I can't."

"Because of Harry? You don't want to go without him?"

"No, Harry's not an issue. I'm not seeing him anymore."

"Oh?"

"I've just had surgery today, and I don't think I'll be up to a party by Saturday. I'm all right. Everything went well. I'm just feeling weak and sore."

"Oh, my God, surgery? What happened?"

Liz was glad to have a legitimate excuse not to attend the christening. She did not want to see Peter again, and definitely did not want to hear any more of his criticisms about Harry.

"Breast cancer. I'm very lucky it was caught early. The doctor said he removed all the suspicious cancerous tissue. It'll take a week or two for the breast and underarm wounds to heal."

"I'm so sorry. Do you have someone to help you?"

"Yes, thanks. My friend Lauren has been with me. I'm okay. I don't mean to be rude, Marisa, but I don't feel like talking. I'm very tired. I'm going back to sleep."

"I'm sorry I woke you up. Take care of yourself. If I can help, please give me a call."

"Thanks. Goodbye."

Lauren brought in a tray with tea and tuna sandwiches and placed it on the coffee table. "Didn't know you didn't want to speak with her."

"It's okay. I've been avoiding replying to the christening invitation. I thought she would call if I answered that I wasn't coming. She called anyway. Just as well I talked to her tonight and got it over with."

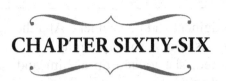

# CHAPTER SIXTY-SIX

The next day Lauren awoke before Liz and drank her first cup of coffee in the kitchen. The intercom buzzed and she responded to the doorman, "Who?"

"Peter Handley," Andres repeated.

"Okay." Lauren placed the mug on the kitchen counter, grabbed her robe from the sofa and threw it over her shoulders. She rushed into the bedroom and shook Liz gently. "Liz, wake up. It's Peter Handley?"

Liz sat up, blinking excessively and forcing her eyes to stay open. "What? What time is it?"

"Peter Handley?" Lauren repeated.

"Huh?"

"On his way up."

"For goodness sakes, what's he doing here?" Liz slid out from under the bedcovers. She found her robe at the end of the bed and wrapped it around her body, covering her pajamas.

"I don't want to see him."

The doorbell rang.

"Should I tell him you're sleeping?" Lauren asked.

Liz clenched her teeth on her bottom lip. She expelled a deep breath, paused and nodded. "Never mind, I'll get it."

Liz opened the door.

"Liz, Sorry to burst in on you. I know you're not well, but I couldn't phone."

"Come in, Peter." Liz scowled.

"Marisa told me—"

Liz went in the kitchen, poured a coffee and asked, "Coffee?"

"Yeah, thanks."

He stepped into the kitchen and stood beside her, his eyes fixed on her hands.

"I'm sorry, Liz. Very, very sorry. Friends don't do what I did. Forgive me. I don't know what the hell I was thinking, that—that I should render judgment and punishment. And then throw you in the mire with me. I was wrong, so very wrong."

Her head tilted, she looked up at him and searched for eye contact. "I'm still angry."

Peter caught a glimpse of her eyes and then veered his focus to the coffee.

"I wanted you to hate him the way I did. I had a good cry that afternoon when I got back to the office and realized what I asked of you. I should be grateful. I've been blessed. I married a wonderful woman, I have a beautiful, healthy baby son. What drove me to such hate? And insisting you to hate him, as well.

"I can't tell you how many times I tried to call and apologize. I hoped to have the opportunity at the christening, but, well, when Marisa told me, I had to tell you face to face. Are you all right?"

Liz believed him. She recognized his sincerity and the former rapport they had shared for many years. He had humbled himself. Apologetic and humble was not the proud persona he usually strutted in and enjoyed. Over the years, his apologies had been limited to minor mistakes with a work product, or being late for an appointment, nothing of any impact upon his conscience. Apparently, he now felt truly regretful.

"C'mon, sit down."

Lauren tossed pillows on the sofa. She had tidied the sofa bed when Liz and Peter were in the kitchen.

"Lauren, this is Peter Handley. Peter, my best friend Lauren Benson. She's been with me through this horror story."

"Hi, good to meet you."

Peter nodded.

"If you'll excuse me, I'm going to shower." Coffee cup in hand, Lauren retreated to the bedroom.

Peter sat next to Liz in the living room. He fiddled with his hands, at first, resting them on his knees, then settling them in his lap, and finally gesticulating as he spoke.

"You should know, I let it all go. I don't blame him anymore. I realized I wasn't innocent and probably as guilty as Harry in a way. I never used a condom. The signs were there. Susan was nauseous all the time and her breasts hurt. I should have known what happened and taken responsibility. Instead I put my head in the sand and let her handle everything alone."

"You used me to get back at him. I can't say I'll forget it. Wish I could," Liz said. She reached for his hand and squeezed it.

"I do forgive you, though. Sometimes I think we're all cowards and don't have the courage to face our demons. I'm certainly not exempt."

Peter threw his arms around her and hugged her. His chest made contact with her wound and she flinched backwards.

"Sore there," pointing at her breast.

"Sorry."

For a moment she felt the intimacy of a man's arms enveloping her and her body reacting. She ached for Harry.

Peter's eyes watered. "I'm so sorry Liz. Please believe me, I'd give anything to take back what I said—all the hatred I vented."

Liz decided there was no point in telling Peter his plan of revenge had failed and that Harry already had been aware of Susan's pregnancy. He was in the depths of repentance, and she knew it would only exacerbate his remorse. He had enough regret to deal with.

"Truth be told, you and Harry are none of my business, even if he does have a reputation. I should have relied on the fact that you're the best judge of character I know."

"Peter, I don't want to go there. It's over."

"Yeah, Marisa told me."

"It's not discussable. Okay?"

Peter stood up. "Gotta get to the office. Hope you can still call me friend."

"I'm glad you came."

"If I can help in any way while you're in the way of this illness, just call. You know, if you need a shoulder to cry on, or someone to talk to, I'm around. Please, give me a call."

"Thanks. I will."

Liz drew her robe around her hips, stood up and walked to the door with him. He took her hand and kissed her on the cheek.

"Get well. And call me. Let me know if you want to work, or if I can help in any way."

Liz thought she would never call him. Although relieved Peter had released her from the burden of hating him, she knew it would never be the same friendship they had enjoyed for so many years.

"Thanks. Enjoy your son."

# CHAPTER SIXTY-SEVEN

Any normal, adult male would consider Helena Goodwin an attractive woman. She was good-looking, intelligent, and decidedly livelier than her serious demeanor on the local news station. She was covering a story when she accidentally bumped into Harry on the steps of City Hall, except maybe it wasn't an accident. They chatted a few times on the phone, and he invited her for dinner, relieving himself of the loneliness and the doldrums that invaded his psyche in the evenings. Although he wasn't sexually attracted to her, he thought he was at least passing time in pleasant company.

When he learned Helena had made reservations for tonight at Daniel's, a romantic, up-scale East Side French restaurant known for its lavish décor and excellent cuisine, he realized something had changed from their previous dates.

Harry lolled on a plush sofa in the lounge, sipped a martini and waited for Helena. He was aware the restaurant unfortunately reeked of the *see and be seen* aura, and he expected he and Helena would be in the public forefront, providing food for the hungry gossip columns again.

He stood up when Helena entered the lounge.

"Hi, sorry I'm so late. Traffic. No cabs. Had to use the company's car service." She spoke quickly, her hands gesturing in hyperactivity—the New York City reckless rushing mode and stress encompassing her behavior.

"Relax, you're worth waiting for."

She inhaled a deep breath and composed herself. "Am I registering my complaint with the appropriate city agency?"

"Hardly. More like complaining about the weather to the weather bureau. Drink?" Harry sat down again.

"I ordered one with the maitre d' on the way in. So, do you approve of my choice?" She sat next to him.

"Yes. Excellent."

"I've even a better suggestion for after-dinner drinks."

"Oh?"

Helena didn't make eye contact with him and instead fussed with her suit jacket, brushing the lint from the sleeve.

"My place. The kids are with my mother for the next two days. Lots of privacy for a change."

"Just drinks?" he asked.

"And however the spirit moves us."

It was obvious what she had in mind, and she confirmed his suspicions that the invitation was for sex. Evidently, she had no qualms about suggesting what her expectations were for the evening.

"Sounds exciting." Harry lied politely. After all, he might be receptive to what was in the offing.

The maitre d' entered the lounge, placed their cocktails on a tray and escorted them to a table. A waiter set their drinks at the place settings. They sat down and he handed them menus.

Harry, accustomed to being the pursuer, disliked Helena's aggressiveness. If her straightforward approach was supposed to excite him, it had the opposite effect and launched him into thoughts of Liz and how they effortlessly fell into foreplay without a verbal consent for sex, except maybe expressing a few lustful comments.

When Liz initiated making love with him, she stroked him, fingered his hair or slid her hand beneath his shirt. There were no preliminary conversations, only her touch on his body. He already made a comparison.

Harry felt uneasy with the conversation. Helena was not only overly attentive much to his embarrassment, but also engaged him in numerous questions regarding the hiring practices of his office, which could hardly be of interest to her. She had a weird way of hitting on a guy.

"Do you prefer to hire accountants over lawyers, or vice versa?"

"No, I don't care what degree they've earned, just so long as they're qualified for the position they've applied for."

"And the credentials presented to you?"

"Well, the resumes detail the experience I would examine and evaluate."

Harry was rescued from Helena's interrogation when the waiter appeared and served their food. He tried to make a connection between sex on the agenda and her journalism degree springing into action. Maybe she was apprehensive. He successfully diverted the conversation to the theater she had seen recently and her last vacation, hoping she would seize the opportunity to talk about herself. Unexpectedly, conversation with Helena suddenly had become a chore.

"I really don't enjoy the islands. Too much poverty. Where do you go to get away?" she asked.

"Bermuda usually. Spent a week there not too long ago. Love the weather and the ambiance. Very laid back and provincial." Remembering Bermuda ushered in thoughts of Liz, appearing again like a door-to-door salesman. He changed the subject. "Are we finished?"

"For dinner. I hope not for the evening. Excellent meal. Thank you."

• • •

"Please, make yourself at home." Helena said. She hung their coats in a hall closet. Harry followed her down a wide corridor, decked out like an art gallery, replete with paintings on both walls. The apartment was huge, as was the gourmet kitchen they passed before entering the living room. Reminisces of the Fifth Avenue building remained in the towering ceilings and windows. Obviously, no expense had been spared in gutting and modernizing the entire apartment.

"How long have you lived here? It's enormous space for the City."

"About twelve years. Yes, I know. Three boys require a lot of room." She turned the sound system on. Debussy's *La Mer* filled the room. "When I married John Jay, we renovated. The apartment has been in his family since it went co-op in the early fifties. What would you like to drink?"

"A cognac, if you have."

He sat on a floral chintz sofa in the center of the room, surrounded by all manner of antique furniture.

"Take your shoes off if you like. Get comfortable."

Helena was running in a marathon and continued to move forward, far ahead of him. Harry was uncomfortable because he was not in control of initiating intimacy. He might have enjoyed seducing her, but she didn't allow him the opportunity as she blithely directed every moment.

She placed a cognac in his hand and sat beside him, the fragrance of her perfume passing faintly before him. She raised her glass to his and offered a toast, "Cheers."

Harry nodded, "Cheers" he said, sipped the cognac and then eyed the liquid as he swirled it around the glass.

"I'd appreciate if you could slow down a bit."

"Oh?" She jerked her head back and turned to look at him.

"Sure." She stared at her glass and the cognac. "Of course, if you're not inclined, it's not a problem."

"Do you have a plane to catch?"

She laughed loudly. "Sorry."

Silence settled in the room except for the tinkling piano of Debussy permeating the room. Finally, her pace quieted, and she leaned back on the sofa.

"Find it difficult raising three boys by yourself?"

"I'm not really raising them by myself. My mom's always available. And I've got plenty of help, a full-time nanny and a housekeeper. And, of course, a cleaning crew."

"Don't have much time to yourself. I expect the job is very demanding. Do you get away, play golf, tennis?"

"I don't mind. Actually, the job's been a lifesaver since I lost John Jay. I had something other than grief to immerse myself into."

Harry uncrossed his legs and placed his cognac on the coffee table. He leaned forward, sliding his mouth along her cheek. She turned toward him to receive his kiss. He reached beneath her blouse for her breast. His heart raced. He recalled Liz's round, plump breast in his hand as he caressed Helena's slight protrusions and remembered the flowery, lemony scent of Liz's body.

Helena began frantically to pull off her clothes.

He whispered, "Slow down, or I'm worthless."

Harry found her lips again and kissed her softly. She met his lips and locked her mouth forcefully on his. When she released him, they were gasping for breath.

"I'm ready, if you are," she said as she rose from the sofa, her blouse unbuttoned and her skirt zipper undone.

Harry discarded his jacket on a nearby chair and unknotted his tie as he followed her to the bedroom. He dropped his trousers on the floor, his erection escaping his briefs. She had already crawled in bed, her bra and panties pasted to her body. He slipped under the covers next to her and removed her underwear. He placed his hand on her thighs and moved to touch her wetness. She pushed his hand away.

"No. Go inside." He complied and entered her. He missed the slowly, graduating arousal he enjoyed with Liz, touching and stroking her until he felt the initial thrill of entering her, tight on his erection.

Helena lay there, moving slightly as she adjusted her body to his thrusts. His rhythmic strokes led him to ejaculate and without any indication to her, he let the emissions flow as immediately as the urge occurred. He fell off her, more relieved than satisfied.

"Thank you," she whispered.

Harry stared at the ceiling. The rumpled bedcovers covered his torso.

"You didn't climax," he said, not that he cared.

"I know. The shrink says I'm withholding until I really get to know someone, you know, before I can let go, but I still enjoy it."

# CHAPTER SIXTY-EIGHT

"You're all over the goddamn papers again. Andy said in between gasps for breath.

Up until now, Harry and Andy had talked about the market, the economy on a downswing and probable baseball trades. Harry anticipated that sooner or later Andy would ask questions about the recent quips or pictures of him in the gossip sections of the newspapers.

"Is that what you want?"

The treadmill was on the last three minutes of the workout he programmed. Andy faltered. He turned the machine off.

"I can't control the press. They print what sells. Besides, so far, it's harmless, not hurting me or anyone else." Harry bench-pressed his last two reps. "I'm done."

"Me, too. I've had it for today," Andy said.

Harry climbed the steps from the basement gym to the back of the house and drenched with sweat, he wiped the perspiration from his forehead.

"Hey, Fred?" He called out as he entered the lounge, "Need two beers."

Andy followed him. They sat and leaned their spent bodies against the bar.

"No glass, Fred. Thanks." Andy said.

"Your daughters see the papers?"

Andy wiped the beads of moisture from his face and neck with a towel and wrapped it around his neck.

"Yeah. I told them it's just a date, not to pay attention. Nana was pissed, though. She's still upset about Liz, which, of course, is all my fault. She said I'm a going through male menopause, dating a younger woman. Harry mimicked his mother's words: *She has three young boys and you're too old for her.*

"Your mom's right," She's thirty-five. There's twenty years between you two. When she hits fifty, you'll be seventy. She'll be going through the changes, still sexually active, and you're prostrate will be failing. Nice scenario to look forward to. Where you going for dinner?"

"Don't know. She's making the reservation."

"Second time this week? As they say, from the frying pan into the fire."

The *Post* had published a picture of Harry and Helena at *Babbo Restorante*, smiling and toasting one another. The caption read *Serious Campaign*? The week before it was a picture of Harry waiting in the lobby of Helena's Fifth Avenue apartment building with the caption, *More Than News?*

"Are you involved?" Andy asked.

"No. Just having dinner."

Then Andy asked the question that was foremost on his mind, "Been to bed with her?"

"Not for public consumption."

"Goddamnit, I'm not public consumption. I take it that's a yes."

"Cody wants to know, doesn't she? We've been to dinner a few times. That's all." He lied. From the expression on Andy's face, Harry knew Andy didn't believe him.

"What's the problem?"

"The problem is you're still in love with Liz. And although your taste in women is improving, Helena Goodwin, widow of entrepreneur, John Jay Goodwin, and mother of three very young boys, is not your type of gal. She catches the World Series home run, but she won't give the ball back to the guy who hit it—very clutching and needy. And possessive.

"She's looking for a father for her children, not a friend, or a lover. She said as much in her interview in *People Magazine*. You ready for fatherhood to three young boys?"

"Nothing to worry about, Andy. She doesn't exactly excite me. I'm so not inclined."

Harry, disgruntled, recalled his disappointment of their last meeting and how empty he felt afterwards. He had already decided to break their date for that evening.

"Not inclined? Well, what the hell are you seeing her for? And no sex? I don't believe you. It's just not who you are. C'mon! You don't fool me. Liz is still on your mind."

"Andy, do me a favor. Keep Liz out of the conversation. That's finished."

"You wish. It's not finished and it's not over. It ain't over 'til the fat lady sings, and she's patiently waiting on stage to sing her aria. It's been a month and you're still complaining about not sleeping well. You're on edge all the time, you snap at everyone for nothing. Rebecca cuts a biology class and you collapse into a tirade. You have two martinis by six o'clock, and you're popping a Xanax when there's the mere hint of a crisis in the office."

Harry's temper was about to burst like July Fourth fireworks. His arms flailed in the air.

"What the fuck do you think I'm supposed to do?"

"You've got a heartache and you won't try to fix it. You won't see Inez. Try to get some balance, some closure. And God forbid you should call Liz."

Didn't he have enough pain? He tried desperately to stop thinking about Liz. They had been together a very short time, and it seemed there were memories for a lifetime that would rush in when least expected, when he ate an ice cream, when he watched Fred storing his flourishing herbs, when he saw a woman wearing a red dress.

Andy didn't need to remind him about Liz. She intruded in his thoughts like a telemarketer, calling incessantly at inopportune moments and harassing him. Now Andy badgered him as well.

"You're supposed to call her, ask her for a drink. Something. Talk to her, find out why."

"She told me why. Many times. We're too different. We're not a fit. She's a woman who knows her own mind and she's perfectly happy without a man in her life. Doesn't want to live with me or marry me."

"Meanwhile, you're dating a woman who's probably planning your wedding, and it's splashed all over the papers. Are you sending a message to Liz? Or to yourself? Convincing yourself and the rest of the world that Liz was just a fling, an infatuation? That's bullshit."

"Andy, get off my back. The monkey's screaming at me all day long as it is." Harry's voice cracked and dwindled almost into inaudibility. "I don't need you yelling at me, too."

"Sorry. Somebody's got to say something."

"You've said enough," Harry murmured.

As usual, Andy didn't restrain voicing what was on his mind, telling-it-like-it-is and being honest to a fault, especially with his best friend. Harry got the message. Obviously, Andy was disturbed with his behavior and thought he was depressed and not doing anything about it.

"I'm taking a shower," Andy said. He left Harry at the bar.

Harry's hands lurched forward and covered his face as the tears rolled from his eyes. It was over. She didn't want him. She left him. There wasn't anything he could do to change that. She took his heart with her, and the loss left a pain and a torment he faced every day. He would never again feel the edgy excitement and emotional freedom while in her company. He missed her easy smiles, her eyes shining at him, her touch on his body and the feeling of her arms around him. He'd never known the happiness he felt with her, and he would never love anyone again.

# CHAPTER SIXTY-NINE

Nearly a month had passed since Liz's surgery. Her wound had no sooner healed and the radiation treatments were scheduled. She completed the first ten days' of treatments and felt fatigued, an anticipated side effect. No one had cautioned her that the listless feeling she experienced could possibly be a side effect, although she knew that reactions, or the so-called side effects of the treatments, were different for everyone.

She felt too weak to play tennis or work out at the gym, but wanted to do something physical. Her body urged her to lie down and indulge in an afternoon nap. Instead, she paced about the apartment, considered doing this or that, and did nothing.

The phone rang.

"Liz?"

"Rebecca?"

"Uh, huh."

"Hi, Honey. How are you?"

"Okay. Miss you something awful. So does Sarah."

"Sorry. Things happen."

"I know."

"I don't think it's a good idea for you to call me. I don't think your dad would approve."

"He's already told me I'm not to call you. I don't care what he says. Whatever it is, it's between you two, not us. I don't have to tell him."

"I hurt him. I can understand him not wanting you to talk to me. I miss you, too. I hope, after some time passes, we'll be able to talk to each other, have lunch, and keep in touch."

Liz did not want to strand Rebecca out in the cold, in the aftermath of a storm's devastation. She could leave Harry, but not his daughters. She hoped Rebecca would understand she wasn't discarding her, but that their relationship was on hold.

"Liz, are you sick?"

"No, what makes you ask that?"

"Well, I phoned last week. You weren't home. But there was this message on the machine, something about being indisposed and not available for work. It sounded like you were sick."

"No, just taking a break. I'm fine."

"And then, I remembered I saw that paper when I used your computer to check my homework assignments. It said something about surgery instructions."

"Oh, that. It was nothing. I had a mole removed from my arm. Nothing serious. Is that why you're calling?" Liz lied, biting her lip. "It's all done a long time ago. No problems.

"Did you go to the doctor? Have you told your dad?" Liz asked.

"No. No one knows except you and me. Not even Sarah. I'm so ashamed. I did go to the doctor with Nana. I told her I missed my period. I got to see the doctor alone, so I was able to tell him everything. He prescribed birth control pills and a scan. I have an underactive thyroid—hypothyroidism. I'm taking medication, but I have to go for another blood test and a follow-up visit in a few weeks."

Then the real reason Rebecca called surfaced.

"Liz, he keeps phoning me."

"Who keeps phoning you?"

"The boy I was with that night."

"Oh. Did you speak with him?"

"Yeah. He tracked me down through a friend at school who gave him my telephone number. He apologized, said he was sorry. I told him I never wanted to see him again and hung up. But he keeps phoning me and leaves messages that he wants to see me. I asked Nana if we could have our number changed, but I couldn't tell her why. Just that some boy keeps phoning me. Now she wants my dad to talk to him."

"Maybe you should speak with him and tell him why you don't want to see him, that he took advantage of you when you had too much to drink. You'll have to convince him that you don't want to see him. If he starts to chat with you, hang up. Does he know where you live?"

"No, I don't think so. He wouldn't come to the house, would he?"

"I hope not. Rebecca. Maybe you should discuss this situation with Inez. I asked her to call you. I think it's important for you to talk to her."

"So does Nana. I don't want to. Inez has already phoned me. I didn't call her back. I want to be left alone. I just want the calls to stop, so I can forget the whole thing."

"It would be nice if you could forget it and it went away, but that's not what's happening."

"Nana told me not to tell my dad about missing my period because he'd only get upset if the doctor prescribed birth control pills for a few months, even though they're to regulate my period. She's mad at him anyway, about him and that woman in the newspaper. Did you see the pictures?"

"Yes. I did. Rebecca, I want you to promise me something you may not understand right now. If your father asks you if you've been in touch with me, tell him the truth. You've always been honest with him. Don't start lying to him now."

"He won't know."

She urged Rebecca not to lie to her father for fear it would destroy the trust father and daughter enjoyed. If she lied, Liz would feel responsible. She wanted to encourage her to see Inez and offer to go with her, but there was the conflict of asking Rebecca to lie to her father.

"And I don't want you to call me. If you have an emergency, like the last time, that's an emergency. But we can't be talking behind his back. I know you don't understand. Right now, it's the way it's got to be. I've got to go. Send my love to Sarah and Nana. Please tell them I'm sorry for the mess I've made. We'll be in touch. Promise. Bye, honey. I love you."

"I love you, too."

# CHAPTER SEVENTY

Inez phoned Liz to ask her about the results of the surgery. Liz hadn't made an appointment as she said she would.

"I'm fine," Liz said. "No cancer."

"Sounds like an excellent result."

"Well, yes. Except the radiation treatments are wearing me down. I don't have any energy for anything, and I can't fall asleep without pills."

"It's perfectly normal to feel weak and unhappy when you're going through treatment. However, relying on sleeping pills can be addictive. Have you spoken with the oncologist? Contacted a support group?"

"No. Support groups are not my style, Inez, you know that."

After a long pause on the phone, Inez said, "Liz, can you come in now? I have nothing scheduled until late in the afternoon. We should talk."

"Yeah, I guess."

When Liz arrived, Inez smiled, signaling to Liz that she was pleased. "You look great. You haven't lost a pound and you have some color in your face. Want a drink, water, soda?" Inez asked. Liz sat on the patient's sofa.

"No, thanks. Wish I felt great. I'm not sure what I'm doing here."

"Trying to feel better, I hope. What were the details of the pathology report?"

Liz sunk into the leather sofa beside Inez. Inez leaned forward, her eyes fixated on Liz.

"According to the report, no cancer cells were found in the tissue surrounding the biopsy site. The doctor said the surgery was successful. No cancer was found in the lymph nodes. If that's the case, why the hell they want me to have all these radiation treatments is beyond me. Something about the incidence of hormone receptors and the likelihood of the cancer recurring."

"Uh, huh." Inez nodded. "It's standard treatment. I'm sure the doctor told you the radiation is to insure that no cancer cells remain, if they weren't detected."

"It doesn't matter. I'm doing what they recommended, not that I agree with it. Had a bit of a row with the doctor. He won and convinced me to be safe not sorry. I just want it to be over and it's not. Another twenty days. I've only had ten treatments, and I feel like hell. When is it going to end, so I can get my life back?"

"You're denying your illness. You have cancer and it still requires treatment. That's a fact."

"That's the problem. There's only one fact in my life since I don't know when, and it's cancer. There's nothing else. I have no life. I can't sleep and I'm too tired to work. I cook and then I don't feel like eating. All I do is take walks and lie down. I don't want to do anything." Liz let her head droop, clasping her hands in her lap.

"You've got to focus on how lucky you've been to survive this disease. One or two months of your life is a small loss compared to the alternative."

Liz stared at her hands and blurted out, "I've lost Harry, too." Tears flowed across her cheeks. Inez held her in her arms while she cried.

"Lost? No, not lost."

Inez leaned sideways and found Liz's eyes.

"You left him, rejected him, remember?"

Liz stopped crying and sat straight up. She exhaled deeply and scanned the ceiling.

"Yeah. I know. I did it. I hurt him. I miss him so much. I didn't want him to see me sick, or feel obligated to take care of me. I thought—I don't know what the hell I was thinking. I brought this on myself and there's nothing I can do about it."

The consequences of Harry not being in her life, and the guilt that she hurt him was hers alone. She wallowed in regret.

"Why do you say there's nothing you can do? Have you considered calling him?"

"Impossible. He's not feeling any pain. He's already found a replacement, Mizz, what's-her-name, from CBS. They're in the gossip columns every other day. Photos, too. I take it you don't read that stuff."

Liz sighed. "It's too late. Maybe I should have just done nothing and let this goddamn disease run its course, then leaving him wouldn't be such a monumental mistake. Why did I tell him I didn't want him in my life?"

"Liz, you're allowed to make mistakes."

The phone rang. Inez picked up the receiver. Liz surmised it was her next appointment and stood up.

"Yes, two minutes." Inez said.

"Before I forget, have you been in touch with Rebecca?" Liz asked.

"No. I left another message, but she hasn't phoned me back. However, Molly called me and said Rebecca's been sad and withdrawn lately. She's cut a few classes and her grades are suffering. Molly said she's trying to convince Rebecca to make an appointment with me. Can you tell me something I should know?"

"I can't tell you. She has to."

Liz sniffled and wiped her nose as they walked to the door.

Inez handed Liz a card. "Please, write down the name of your oncologist. I want to speak with him before I write you a prescription for an anti-depressant. I think it may help you with the doldrums you're experiencing. Can you come next week?"

"Yeah, I guess. I do feel a bit better. Thanks."

"By-the-by, Liz, I saw the pictures. It may be a cliché, but don't believe everything you read in the papers."

# CHAPTER SEVENTY-ONE

No matter what occurred in his personal life, Harry's love of his job never faltered, although, at the moment, his enthusiasm for work was at stage right awaiting an entrance. It had been commonplace for Harry to come to the office Monday morning full of energy and hop-to-it orders, intent upon implementing ideas accumulated from the weekend. Today was not one of those past, robust Mondays.

Engrossed in a pile of paperwork, he looked up for a moment and felt Joe's eyes scrutinizing him. Joe, his assistant, had worked for him for fifteen years and could read his every gesture and grimace, as well as his mood.

"How was your weekend?" Joe asked.

"Okay."

Harry thought a moment about their relationship and how they didn't indulge in small talk about the weekend or the weather. They liked it that way. If something personal interfered in the affairs of the office, they spoke about it. Otherwise it was all business between them. It had been that way since Harry rescued Joe from the stress of an options trading desk, recognizing Joe's genius with numbers, and Harry knew that Joe's gratitude and loyalty knew no bounds. Why was he asking him about his personal life, his weekend?

"Something wrong?" Harry asked.

"No. You don't look so good, Boss. You feel okay?"

"No, I'm fine. Probably didn't get enough sleep last night, that's all."

Harry's cell phone rang. "Hey, Andy. What's up?"

"Did you change the code for Manning reports?"

"Oh, yeah, months ago. The Liz thing, remember? Want the new one?"

"Not if you don't want me to have it."

"You can use it anytime you want. Who're you looking at?"

"Probably should tell you. Let you do it."

"Do what?"

"Let you make the call."

"Whatta y'a mean Andy?"

"Cody was having lunch at Whitney's, a midtown pub. She's sitting at the bar with her friend, waiting for a table and looking out the window. She spies Liz crossing the street and decides to ask her to join them for lunch. So she chases down the street after her.

"You pretty much asked Cody not to let you know if they were in touch. I understand, you don't want to know, and I'm not supposed to tell you. She and Liz have chatted on the phone a few times, but Cody says that you're off limits in the conversations.

"Anyway, Cody's waiting for the light to change when she sees Liz go into Sloan-Kettering on Third Avenue. She gets to the lobby of the building, the elevator is going up, and Liz is gone."

"What are you telling me? Cody saw Liz go in the cancer center. So, what? She was probably visiting someone."

"Don't think so, buddy. It's a treatment center, not a hospital where you visit patients. You go there for consultation and treatment."

"C'mon, Andy. What are you saying? Liz has cancer?"

Harry couldn't digest what Andy suggested, that Liz was receiving treatment for cancer. It wasn't as if it were an impossibility. He hadn't seen Liz in a month. He remembered she did have too many doctor appointments, but she said they were follow-ups and nothing was wrong. He dismissed Andy's speculations.

"Okay, don't listen. But do me a favor, get an updated report from Manning."

"You're reaching."

"I know, you think I'm crazy, but do it for Cody. She's hysterical. She thinks Liz is sick. I'm not supposed to tell you, just get the info. Cody thinks if it's bad news, you won't be able to handle it."

"If they're talking, why doesn't Cody just call her and ask her?"

"Sure, like Liz will tell her. C'mon Harry, get real! If Liz didn't volunteer any information when they chatted on the phone, she's not going to now."

Harry leaned back in his chair. "For Cody's peace of mind? Her intuition again?"

"Yep. Whatever."

Harry was silent for a moment, then let out a sigh of resignation. He did not like the idea of spying on Liz, especially remembering the circumstances of the first report. And he definitely would not call her.

"Okay. You tell your wife, she owes me."

"Call me later. Let me know what you find out." Andy hung up.

"Joe?" Harry called out across the room. "Can you get the Manning agency on the phone? Need an updated report on Elizabeth Brady. They have a bio on her from August. Do you have the code?"

"Yeah, I have it."

Harry did not want to believe Liz would not have told him if she were sick. Yet, she could have gotten sick after she left. That was a distinct possibility. That would explain her not telling him, because she wouldn't call him and ask for his help. She was too stubborn. But it was more likely Cody was flying off on one of her intuition sprees.

"Boss, your daughter's on the phone. On two."

"Hi, Rebecca. Where are you?"

"School. Just checking, making sure we're having dinner tonight."

"Yeah, where do you want to eat?"

"I don't care. Sarah wants Italian."

"How about Little Italy? Angelo's?"

Harry waited for a response and was confronted with silence. What's the matter? Down in the dumps?"

"No. Nothing's wrong." She said.

"Rebecca, c'mon, tell me. Maybe I can help. Boyfriend problem?"

"No, nothing like that."

"What? You going to make me worry all day?"

"Just wondering, Dad, why don't you want me to talk to Liz? Why did you have to split up anyway?"

"I thought I explained. Do we have to go over it again? Did you call her?"

"Yes, yesterday. I wanted to know if she was all right. You aren't talking to each other, and I wanted to ask her about her surgery."

"What surgery?"

"She had a mole on her arm. I just wanted to know if she was all right. Don't worry, I'm not going to call her again. She told me not to call her."

"Back up Rebecca. What surgery?"

"She had a mole on her arm and had it removed. She said it was nothing serious."

"Yeah, but how did you know about it?"

"I saw a paper in her apartment, a few weeks ago."

"In her apartment? Why were you in her apartment?"

"I was in the neighborhood and I just stopped by. We had tea. It was before you split up."

"You never mentioned you'd been to her apartment. Why not? Did she tell you then that she was sick?"

"No."

Harry's head reeled. He had too many questions and no answers that satisfied him. Why would Rebecca be in Liz's neighborhood? Why didn't she tell him she had been to Liz's apartment? Neither Liz nor Rebecca had mentioned it. Did they share a confidence about Liz being sick? He speculated they shared a confidence about something, something neither one of them revealed to him.

"How did you know she was having surgery?"

"I didn't know. I was checking my homework assignments on her computer, and I saw this paper with instructions for patients having surgery, like the one Nana got when she had her gall bladder operation. *Don't wear jewelry the day of surgery. Don't eat or drink after midnight.* I didn't read the whole thing, I had to get home."

"Rebecca, you're not telling me everything. What else?"

"Dad, please, I've got to get to class. I've told you everything. Liz is okay. She sounded fine yesterday."

"Okay. See you later, pumpkin."

"Bye, Dad."

Anxiety loomed upon Harry's consciousness. There was a definite possibility Liz had cancer. Cody wasn't being an alarmist. A mole could be cancerous. It could mean melanoma. He wanted to call Liz and simply ask her. But if she hid it from him a month ago, she wouldn't tell him the truth now.

"Joe? Please get Manning on the phone again. I want to speak to someone in charge."

"Done, Boss."

After several minutes, Joe went to Harry's desk and said, "Got a vp in customer service. His name is Anderson. He's on line one."

"Thanks."

Harry swiveled his chair around and picked up the receiver.

"Mr. Anderson? Mayor Bergman here. I called in an order about an hour ago for a report on Elizabeth Brady. When may I expect a response?"

"Hasn't been assigned yet. We're behind with a few emergencies. It was processed on a personal account, not from the Mayor's Office. The police department and medical requests are prioritized first. Say the word and I'll change it."

"No. It's personal. How bad is the backup?"

"Thirty-six hours, maybe thirty."

"Conservatively, a day and a half? Harry asked.

"About that. Could be sooner though."

"Well, whatever you can do to expedite it would be appreciated. Thanks for your help."

# CHAPTER SEVENTY-TWO

The roads were wet and reflected a black, high-gloss shine in the rain. Traffic hurled puddles indiscriminately in the air, splashing over medians and curbs. The temperature was fifty-five degrees, evidencing that winter was making an end-of-October early entrance on a New York gray, rainy morning. On his way downtown to his office, Harry peered out the car window, feeling like the weather—dreary and in need of sunlight.

Dinner with his daughters the night before was supposed to cheer him and lift his spirits. Instead, sadness overtook his every thought, and the same aura still lingered in the morning. He was entrenched in sympathy for Rebecca and upbraided himself for his failure as a father. The only help and comfort Rebecca received came from Liz, and he forbade Rebecca from calling her. His daughter had conveyed her suffering of not only the loss of her virginity but her self-esteem, and he had nothing to offer her to relieve her pain. He didn't know what to say or how to advise her.

Rebecca clung to Liz. She wanted Liz to talk to, to possibly help her. He thought that's probably the real reason she called Liz the day before, not necessarily to find out about Liz's surgery.

"Tom, can you swing over to Ariston? I want to send some flowers."

"Okay."

Rebecca had supplied some of the missing answers at dinner, but they were not the answers he sought. He asked her about Liz, if she was sick and he persisted in badgering her throughout the meal.

"What brought you to Liz's neighborhood? Why didn't either one of you tell me."

Harry speculated again about a confidence he suspected they shared, and he wanted to know if Rebecca knew Liz was ill. Rebecca could not escape. He didn't give up and kept asking the same questions over and over.

When Sarah went to the restroom, Rebecca relented in tears, not sparing Harry any of the details of her traumatic episode of drunken sex and the mistaken pregnancy, and ultimately the reason she went to Liz's apartment. Sarah returned to the table to find her father holding her sobbing sister.

He brought his daughters to his home. Fred made tea. Sarah watched television in the lounge. Harry and Rebecca talked privately in the living room.

"It's statutory rape, Rebecca. You're underage. You sure you said it was okay?"

"Please, Daddy, stop asking me that. He didn't rape me. It was my fault. I mean, why was I in the bedroom with him?"

Harry didn't know how to comfort her, except to tell her he would always love her, no matter happened.

"You've got to forgive yourself. We all make mistakes, and we learn from them."

"Dad, you don't understand. I've ruined my life. It's probably all over the school. No decent boy will want to date me unless he wants sex. I'm a whore. I'm on the list of the girls who do, and I won't ever be able to change that."

"Stop talking like that. One mistake does not make you a whore. What makes you think everybody knows? You said he's in college. He doesn't go to your school."

"He has a younger brother and friends in my classes who go to my school. They'll know. It's news that travels fast." Tears sprinkled her face.

"If he knows you're underage, I shouldn't think he'd be boasting. He'd be subject to arrest."

"Dad, I lied about my age. He thinks I'm eighteen."

"Oh."

He didn't know how to deal with Rebecca's guilt and self-abasement and he wanted his feisty, confident daughter returned to him. Rebecca kept repeating how she shamed him, getting drunk, and that she behaved like a fast and loose stupid little girl who didn't deserve anyone's love.

It hadn't been the usual dinner outing with his daughters. For one reason or another since Liz was gone, everyone in his life was mad, sad or unhappy. His mother hardly talked to him, except to tell him Rebecca had been walking around the house in a fog, detached from everyone, and Sarah had buried herself in her photography projects and was unavailable for conversation.

Even Avery asked for a few days off, not mentioning any particular reason why, and Harry thought it was probably to escape the gloominess that pervaded his home. Avery didn't function well around unhappy people, and Harry was unhappy.

Tom parked the car, and Harry entered the florist shop.

"Good Morning, Mr. Mayor. How are you?"

"I'm good, John. Nice to see you again. Two dozen roses. I guess, the pink and peach. I need a card."

Harry wrote:

> *Thank you for helping Rebecca. I'm very grateful. It was wrong of me to forbid her from talking to you. She's free to call you anytime. She needs you. Sincerely, H.*

He sealed the envelope and handed it to John to include with the flowers. Harry humbled himself. He didn't care if his ego was at stake. He would beg if it was necessary in the cause of his daughter's well-being. Besides he knew Liz loved his daughters, and she would render her help unselfishly to Rebecca. Harry filled in the address on the order form. "Can you deliver sometime today?"

"Of course. It'll be done this morning."

"Thanks."

He left the shop and focused on the tasks of the Mayor's Office and hoped the pleasure he derived from his job would change his disposition.

# CHAPTER SEVENTY-THREE

Harry arrived at the office a half hour later than his usual seven thirty. Few employed in municipal government could boast as he could that his staff arrived early. He inspired and respected them. In return they benefited him with achievements. His love affair with his work was a sustaining constant in his life and today it was serving an additional purpose—overriding his depressing thoughts.

Joe yelled out from the other side of the room. "Morning, Boss. Andy's on two. Do you want to call back?"

"No, I'll take it." Harry picked up the receiver. "Yeah, don't tell me you're canceling dinner. I need a home-cooked meal, and Fred's taken a few days off."

"No, we're still on. Dinner's at seven. Be early for cocktails. Had any word from Manning?"

"Sorry, I meant to call you, but I had a problem with Rebecca. I totally forgot about getting back."

"What's wrong?"

"Nothing I can tell you about. It's private. My daughter needs help, and I'm useless. I think she needs to see Inez."

"Sounds serious. What happened?"

"Young woman's dilemma."

"Oh, a woman's issue? Is she all right, nothing serious, like pregnant, or anything like that?"

"Thank God, no. Thanks for reminding me. It could be a lot worse. I'll check with Manning again. They were backed up yesterday and said it might take some time. Talk to you tonight."

"Okay, buddy. See you later."

Harry pulled up Anderson's number from his computer and dialed the Manning agency.

Mr. Anderson was apologetic and matter-of-fact: "Yeah, sorry, did the best we could. It's on my desk as we speak. I'll fax it right away."

"Thanks." Harry hung up.

"Joe, can you get the incoming fax?"

"Sure, Boss."

Joe brought the first few pages to Harry's desk and said, "It's still coming in."

Harry leaned back in his chair and turned past the first two pages, bypassing the same information in the report from months ago. He walked to the machine and stood beside Joe as he pulled another page from the fax tray and handed it to him. Harry fixed himself next to the machine and read:

> *"Dr. Charles Rodman performed a lumpectomy from eight a.m. to ten a.m. on October 5 on an outpatient basis. Diagnosis: mucinous carcinoma in the right breast. Successful removal of marginal tissue. Pathology analysis is forthcoming. No complications.*
>
> *Patient examined in recovery room at twelve-thirty p.m. and released to Ms. Lauren Benson.*
>
> *Referred to oncologist, Dr. Robert Franz at Sloan-Kettering for consultation and radiation treatment."*

The next page detailed the results of the initial biopsy, pre-surgery tests, the anesthesiologist, attending hospital personnel throughout the surgery and an admittance form.

Liz had lied to Rebecca. Harry drew in a few deep breaths. Beads of moisture collected on his forehead. Acid attacked his stomach and he felt queasy. Why did she lie? He anticipated the worst. It was serious. Women die from breast cancer. God, don't let her die. He panicked, jumped to conclusions and then realized, it couldn't be major surgery on an outpatient basis, nonetheless, it was still life-threatening.

Somewhat relieved, Harry wiped his forehead and walked back to his desk. He dropped in his chair and phoned Inez. She was in a session and he left a message.

Joe appeared at his desk with two more pages.

"One more to go," he said.

The next page reviewed the post-surgery pathology report. There was no evidence of cancer cells and a list of the radiologist's findings concerning cell contents in medical terms unknown to Harry. The last page reported the results of an oncology consultation with a Dr. Franz at Sloan-Kettering, a post-surgery visit with Dr. Rodman, an order for a mammography at N.Y.U. Medical Center and a follow-up visit with Dr. Franz after one week of radiation treatment.

"Joe, can you get a Dr. Robert Franz at Sloan-Kettering on the phone? Leave a message. My cell number, if you don't get him."

Harry phoned Tom, who wasn't supposed to be available to him until three in the afternoon.

"Tom, are you busy?"

"Just dropped my kids off at school. Whatta y'a need?"

"Can you pick me up downtown? As soon as you can."

Harry didn't wait for an answer, as if Tom didn't have the option to refuse.

"Half an hour good?" Tom asked.

"Fine."

Harry accessed Liz's home number on his cell. He didn't intend to speak with her and just wanted to know if she was home. He was hell bent on facing her and didn't want to give her the opportunity to refuse to see him. There was no answer. He sat back, suffering from a bundle of mixed emotions, anger because she didn't tell him about her illness, sympathy that she was dealing with cancer and regret that he hadn't called her.

He phoned the doorman. Andres would know if she had gone out. "Andres, it's Harry Bergman. Is Ms. Brady home?"

"Hi. No. She's at the hospital. She's usually back by half-past. Do you want me to tell her something when she comes in?"

"No. And please, don't mention I phoned."

Harry's cell rang as soon as he hung up. "I'm downstairs, Boss. Whenever you're ready."

"Be right down, Tom."

"Joe, I'm leaving for the day. Reschedule me, huh? I'll call you in the morning."

# CHAPTER SEVENTY-FOUR

"Liz's place, Tom."

Harry settled in the back seat of the car. His cell phone rang and he bolted to an upright position. "Hello, Harry. It's Inez, returning your call. How are you?"

"I'm okay. It's Liz. She has cancer."

"I know."

"You know?" Adrenaline flushed his system. His temper flared, his voice raising a few decibels. "Why didn't you tell me?"

"As much as I would have liked to have told you, I can't divulge a patient's confidences."

"Why wouldn't she tell me? Do you know why? There's got to be a reason."

"Harry, calm down. It's complicated and I cannot discuss my sessions with Liz. I can tell you she's in good health. I saw her last week, and she has some issues she's addressing. She's coming to see me again this week. I can tell you she's been very responsive.

"I just spoke with Liz to let her know your mother made an appointment for Rebecca. Liz wants to accompany her because Rebecca's reluctant to see me. At the moment, she seems to be more worried about Rebecca than herself. I intended to call you since Liz said she would like your approval."

"Yes. It's absolutely okay with me. Rebecca needs to see you. She's had a terrible experience, and Liz has been her only support."

"I trust I can help her. Molly is worried, as well. As far as letting you know about the cancer, I tried to persuade Liz to tell you. It was in her best interest for you to know, but she was adamant that you shouldn't share her problem. Are you all right, Harry?"

"I'm upset, confused. I don't understand why Liz couldn't tell me the truth, and I'm lost as to how to deal with what's happened to my daughter. Can you keep me posted about Rebecca? I'm glad Liz wants to go with her to see you. At least that's a plus."

"Have you spoken with Liz?" Inez asked.

"No. I'm going to see her now."

"Good. Call me if you need to talk."

"Will do. Thanks for getting back."

Harry leaned back in the car, wrestling with his anger. He was in that battle in his mind again, facing the reality that she did not want him, yet she supposedly loved him. It didn't make sense to him.

He prepared himself mentally as to how he should approach her. He had no emotional reserve when it came to Liz. He cautioned himself not to be confrontational because she would either react in a temper or break down in tears, and he had no defense to her temper nor to her tears. He needed to maintain some objectivity if he was going to find out why she lied to him, and if he could do something to help her.

His cell rang again. "Dr. Franz here. I'm returning a call from the Mayor. With whom am I speaking?"

"I'm Mayor Bergman."

"You're really the Mayor? How can I help you?"

"I need some information about a patient of yours, Elizabeth Brady."

"Are you related? You must know I'm not at liberty to divulge information to non-authorized persons. I'd be at risk legally."

There was a pause and silence.

"Doctor," Harry urged him, "I promise, she won't sue you."

"I'm glad you're so confident. Yes. Ms. Brady is a patient of mine. What is it you want to know?

"About the cancer."

"Does she know you're calling me? Have you spoken with her?"

"No, obviously, she doesn't want me to know. And I don't have the answer as to why."

The doctor expounded to Harry about the specific cancer Liz had. "It's a slow-growing, rare type of cancer. A lumpectomy was performed successfully and the patient is undergoing radiation treatments.

"I just had a follow-up visit with her. I'm not at the office and I don't have her records in front of me. If I remember correctly, the latest pathology report indicated an excellent prognosis. However, she requires radiation treatments and possibly medication to prevent recurring cancer."

Harry went over the scene in his mind of their last meeting, when she bolted out the door without saying goodbye. It was the weekend after the opera. He only saw her once that week and nothing in her behavior indicated that she was sick. Maybe the cancer had something to do with her leaving him.

Dr. Franz explained many patients experience some side effects as the radiation treatments progress.

"Generally, it's fatigue. She may suffer skin abrasions for which there are remedies. I received a call from her therapist last week. She wanted my approval to prescribe an anti-depressant, which I okayed. I am concerned about the depression because, as I remember, she has a history of depression. It's beneficial that she's conferring with a therapist."

"Thanks, doctor."

"Glad I could help."

He phoned Andres again. "It's Harry. Ms. Brady come in yet?"

"Hi, Harry. Yes, about fifteen minutes ago."

"Thanks."

# CHAPTER SEVENTY-FIVE

The doorbell rang and startled her. Liz looked through the peephole. She only had a view of Harry's head bent downward and couldn't see his face. Andres must have let him pass the desk without announcing him as he usually did for all visitors. Why was he here? Had Inez already spoken with him about Rebecca's appointment?

She opened the door. "Hello, Harry. Come in."

Her head sloped toward the roses on the dining room table. "Thank you for the flowers. They're very beautiful. And the note."

Liz stepped backward, five feet away from him. She felt uneasy and a distance between them made her feel somewhat comfortable.

"My feeble attempt at thanking you for helping Rebecca."

"I suppose she told you what happened."

"Yes. Certainly wasn't anything I wanted to hear."

He stared at her. She avoided his eyes and turned away, and clasped her hands.

"When I got your note, I called Inez to let her know I would like to go with Rebecca for her appointment, if that's all right with you. I asked her to get your approval. Rebecca's not herself."

"I know. I've spoken with Inez. It's okay. Actually, I'm grateful. I really don't know how to help her and she confides in you."

"I want to be there for her, for whatever I can do, even if she only wants to talk." Liz stood silent. She clasped her upper arm and nervously rubbed it repeatedly. There was nothing more to say. Their business was finished.

"It's nothing to do with us," she said.

"I know."

She couldn't imagine what he was thinking. He was almost sneering at her. She was desperate to tell him the truth, that she made a mistake, that she missed him and wanted to be in his life, but she thought he might react in a temper if she confessed she lied to him. Her voice faltered as she asked, "Can I get you something to drink? A coffee?"

"No. Thanks. Can we sit down?"

She bit her lip and restrained the tears welling in her eyes. "Uh, huh."

Liz sat on the sofa and Harry took the armchair across from her. He leaned forward and asked, "Why couldn't you tell me?"

"I couldn't, it was something—something, only Rebecca could tell you."

"I'm not talking about Rebecca. I didn't expect either of you would have confided that incident to me." Harry stared at his hands, fingering his thumbs back and forth as he intermittently glanced at Liz.

He paused and waited. She knew what he meant now, but couldn't answer him. She was numb.

Finally, he spoke. "I mean, about the cancer, that you were sick."

Liz cowered and heard the torment in his voice. The anguish of the lie she told him emerged before her as it had again and again. At last the truth was known, and suddenly she felt relieved that he knew, but she was at a loss for words to assuage what she thought was his anger.

"Harry, I'm . . ." Her throat tightened, gripping and holding her speech, "So sorry, so very sorry." She gasped for breath. Her hands covered her face, and she wiped away the tears rolling down her cheeks. Her words tangled in her mouth.

"I should have told you."

Harry released a forced, long sigh, closed his eyes for a moment and shook his head back and forth. His resolve to maintain some objectivity disappeared as quickly as a black cloud disappears after a heavy shower. He regained his composure, although his face was contorted in tense muscles and a wrinkled brow.

"You hate me. I know that's what I deserve. I lied to you. I didn't mean to hurt you. Please, Harry, stop looking at me like that."

Liz got up suddenly and bolted to the bedroom.

Harry paused for a moment, inhaled a deep breath and then followed her. The bathroom door slammed as he entered the bedroom, and he could hear her sobs passing through the bathroom door and filling the bedroom. He turned the door knob, but it was locked. He knocked on the door and pleaded with her.

"Liz, I'm not angry with you. I'm angry at myself for not calling you, for letting you go so easily."

"Please, go, Harry. Please."

"Liz, I can't. I can't leave. I need you in my life. I love you. I'll always love you. Please, Liz, open the door. Talk to me."

The sobbing subsided. A deadening silence filled the bedroom.

Harry retreated to the living room and sat on the sofa. Lingering doubt overcame his thoughts. If she didn't love him, he had to hear her tell him. His hands groped his face and massaged his forehead and he looked up when he heard the latch unlock. Liz opened the door and stood in the bedroom doorway.

"I'm not leaving." He said. "Not until you look me in the eye and tell me you don't love me and never want to see me again."

Her face wet with tears, she stammered, "I do love you. I never stopped loving you."

Harry leapt from the sofa and grabbed her and held her tightly to his chest. His eyes closed. He couldn't speak and wallowed in the closeness of her body, soothing his heartache and relieving his pains of emptiness.

Finally, he whispered, "Why?" Her head lingered on his shoulder as he spoke in the air.

"I didn't want you to see me get sick, and sicker, and feel obligated to take care of me." Liz whimpered and began crying again.

"You stupid, stupid woman." He separated from her, placed his hands on her shoulders and found her eyes, still filled with tears.

"Don't you know, you're all I want in my life, to take care of you. I want to spoil you, pamper you and make you happy. Why couldn't you tell me the truth?"

Liz hesitated and fixed her eyes on his, "I have these demons—about my father. I'm scared of being controlled, winding up like my mother, being dependent and not good enough."

"Not good enough? You're everything to me—the light of my life, the smile on my face. For the first time in my life, I feel whole and happy with everything when I'm with you."

Her river of tears ebbed into a stream of trickling droplets. They embraced. He didn't let go for a moment for fear they would separate again. He could feel her heart pounding and his body trembling in response to her touch. She clutched at him, crying again. His arms enveloped her.

"Tell me you love me. Tell me you'll never leave me again."

"Harry, I love you more than anything. I haven't had a moment's peace or happiness since I left you. I've been so miserable without you. I feel so guilty about how I hurt you. I made a horrible mistake."

They sat on the bed. He held her and rubbed her back, comforting and calming her.

"Forgive me?" she asked.

"I'd forgive you anything."

"I wanted to call you, after the surgery, to say I was sorry, even if you didn't want me anymore. But then, I saw those pictures in the paper. You, at a restaurant, with that television woman. And then, I couldn't."

Harry unlocked himself from her arms and held her hands, searching for her eyes.

"I was desperate to get you out of my heart. All I thought about when I was with her was you. She was a mistake. I make mistakes, too."

Harry pushed her hair off her face, remembering what she felt like inside and how the rushes of arousal seized his body when she stroked him. He leaned over and gently touched her lips with his fingertips. Her face was ashen. He drew her near and kissed her softly on the lips.

"You know, you don't look well. Lie down for a while. I'll be right here beside you. We'll get a bite to eat later and talk some more."

"I'm a little sore, from the radiation. I get tired quickly. But I'm fine. It's been a month since the surgery."

She unbuttoned the center of his shirt and slid her hand on his chest and broke into a grin.

"Harry, I ache for you. Please. Touch me."

She glided her hand on his shoulders and then down to his stomach and groin.

"Not a good idea, you're not well."

"Please, Harry. I need you."

# CHAPTER SEVENTY-SIX

She pulled his shirttail from his trousers and found his erection inside his underwear and at his belt. She stroked him gently while he massaged her thighs, his fingers slowly approached what she wanted touched. They lay on the bed. She pulled his trousers down his legs. She had no bra on, only a mini tee shirt underneath her blouse. "Leave it on."

He caressed and kissed her legs as he removed her panties. She sat up and drew his shirt down his back and off his arms. Her lips nipped at his chest.

Harry entered her and held himself there for a moment without moving, savoring the thrill of her flesh enveloping him. He could feel her tiny eruption on his erection. She was flooded with desire as he came down her again and again. She kept peaking and not letting go.

"Liz," he murmured. She screamed and clutched at him as they vibrated together in his loins. He turned on his side, gasping for breath.

"You okay?"

"Yes, very okay."

Harry kissed her hand and lay his head on her stomach. He heard her heart beating, inhaled her scent and watched her eyes close as she peacefully dozed in the afterglow.

When she opened her eyes, his lips were on her cheek. He whispered, "You're going home with me tonight. Wherever we decide to live, uptown or China, you're going to marry me." His fingers combed her eyebrows and played with the curls on her forehead.

"I know."

"You're in my life forever. Promise me."

"I promise. There is no happiness for me without you. I'm going wherever you take me."

Harry knew he had changed, and he would never go back to who he was before he met her, that he would always feel the depth of fulfillment and wholeness he felt with her. He would willingly relinquish his soul and his self to her.

"C'mon. Take a shower with me."

"No. You go first," she said.

"Alone? No way." She had kept her tee shirt on while they made love, hiding the wounds on her breast and under her arm.

"You don't want me to see?" He wanted to see. He wanted to participate, to share whatever she felt about her scars.

"It's ugly."

"Tough. I'm going to look."

"No, Harry." She scurried into the bathroom. He raced in after her and pushed the door aside. She didn't have the energy to struggle with him.

"C'mere." Harry pulled her shirt over her head.

"What's so terrible? It's healed. Red from the radiation. That's all. What's so bad? Get over it. Time will come when you'll hardly see a scar."

"How do you know?" Liz turned from him and stepped into the shower. He followed her.

"Because I spoke with Dr. Franz earlier. He discussed your treatment, what to expect, the probability of the cancer returning. He said you had an excellent prognosis."

"You called my oncologist?"

"Yes."

Harry soaped her shoulders, her back and buttocks with body wash. He handed her the lotion bottle and took another one from the ledge and lathered himself. He cuddled her and positioned her under the streaming water as the foam flowed off their bodies.

"How did you find out?" She asked as they exited the shower. She grabbed two towels and handed one to Harry.

Harry wiped water from his eyes.

"If I tell you, you can't throw anything at me and you can't cry. Okay?"

She giggled. "Oh, another report?"

"Yes. Cody saw you go into Sloan-Kettering and pleaded with Andy to phone me and get an update from the agency. And then, Rebecca read some papers in your apartment about surgery instructions. I thought she knew something I didn't know, and I kept pestering her at dinner the other night. That's when she told me what happened to her and why she was in your apartment. You have no idea how much she misses you, how much she needs to talk to you."

"I love your daughters, you know that. I can't wait to see them again." Liz sniffled.

"Hey, no more crying. We're going to be fine." He grabbed her and hugged her, the towels lodged between their bodies. He released her and she finished drying her body and slipped into a terry robe. He wrapped his towel around his waist and tilted his head as he peered in the mirror and discerned a shadow of a beard.

"My shaver still around?"

Liz went into the bedroom, retrieved his robe from the closet and flung it onto his head.

"Your shaver's in the drawer."

"Thanks. Hmm, nice. I wasn't entirely discarded.

"Are you up to having dinner with Cody and Andy tonight? They're expecting me, and I know they'll be very happy to see you and to know that you're all right. But I'll cancel if you want to be alone, eat someplace in the neighborhood."

"Oh, I'd love to see Cody. Besides, you know, I'm not crazy about eating out."

"Have a lie down for an hour. We've plenty of time 'til six-thirty. When you get up, we'll have a coffee and call my mom and the girls."

Liz shook her head and giggled. Harry was himself, in control again. He mapped out the agenda. She left him in bathroom, shaving. She went in the bedroom to dress.

The buzz of the razor didn't inhibit his speaking.

"The doctor said you may have some side effects, fatigue from the radiation. We'll get you through this. You'll have people around who love you and want to help you. Me and Lauren, Cody and Andy. We'll keep you out of the doldrums. If I know my mom, she'll be on the phone with you every day. My daughters, as well. And you know how Fred worships you. He won't be able to do enough for you."

Harry finished shaving. Had she heard what he said?

"Liz?"

She didn't answer and, alarmed by the silence, he hurried to the bedroom. Liz sat on the bed, tears spilling down her cheeks. He plopped down beside her and embraced her.

"Hey, what's the matter? No crying."

"Nothing." She slipped out of his embrace and looked up at him with tearful eyes and smiled.

"I'm so happy I could burst."

# CHAPTER SEVENTY-SEVEN

"Good Morning, Fred.

"Good Morning, Ms. Liz. Sleep well?"

"Oh, yes. And no pills. Thanks again for the marvelous dinner last night. Besides the delicious food, you create a fantastic, oh-so-romantic atmosphere."

"You're very welcome. Truly, it was my pleasure. I'm so very happy your home."

"Ms. Liz?" Fred leaned toward her ear as she approached the breakfast room and whispered, "He was singing in the shower this morning."

Liz smiled. "I heard him." She winked at Fred.

"Morning, Boss."

"Morning, Fred. Thanks again for dinner. It was superb."

Harry dressed in a navy blue suit, white shirt and Liz's paisley tie; he looked like a primped and polished model, ready for a photo shoot. He kissed Liz on the forehead.

"You should be sleeping."

He sat down at the breakfast table and drank coffee from the mug Fred placed in front of him.

"I wanted to have coffee with you. I'm going back to bed when you leave. Fred's going to help me do some more unpacking later this afternoon."

"Don't get yourself tired. Have a nap when you get back from treatment. Remember, Tom's driving you and waiting until you're finished. Do you want company? Cody volunteered to go with you anytime."

"No, I'm okay. I'm used to the routine. It goes pretty quickly when you're in good spirits."

"Let Fred do the unpacking. You know, he's a master at ordering things. Move my things around, if you need more space. Have you made any plans for next week, Thanksgiving?"

"No. My nephew is spending the holiday with his in-laws. He's invited me, but I said no. I thought we'd spend the holiday with your mom and the girls."

"That's what I thought, too. I need to persuade my mom to eat out, but now that you're coming, she's going to want dinner at home. It's too much work for her even with the cook and bringing in help. She has to have her hands in everything. Elena isn't available on Thanksgiving. She's always had that holiday off to spend with her family.

"I'm sure you could persuade her not to cook. What do you think? Can you call her and give her a nudge, suggest you'd like to eat out? Make up some cockamamie reason."

"I'll try. Your mom's not easily persuaded, or duped for that matter. I'd rather tell the truth. I was going to call her today anyway."

"Whatever you think. She's so ecstatic that you've moved in with me, I'm sure she'll go for anything you ask."

Harry finished his coffee, fetched a refill in the kitchen and sat at the breakfast table again.

"I spoke with Maddy and Thomas last night while you were sleeping. I was thinking when the treatments are finished, we should take a vacation, go to Bermuda for a week."

"Oh, Harry, what a great idea! Can we, really?"

"We could leave the Friday after Thanksgiving. I'll take the week off. We'll celebrate the end of radiation treatments. Leave from LaGuardia. Get in about one in the afternoon. Maybe go back to the San Remo. And definitely visit Martine's, have a dance, relive our first night together?"

"You're such a romantic. Just you and me for a whole week. And my favorite time of year in Bermuda, when the hot summer's over."

"Whatta y'a think?"

He got up and leaned over and kissed her on the cheek.

"I think, I can't wait. It's too fantastic. I love you. You do make me very, very happy."

• • •

Cody opened the door. "C'mon in. What are you doing here?"

"Liz kicked me out of the house and sent me here to have a martini with you guys. Said I was getting in the way, and she couldn't cook because I was stalking her. I'm supposed to bring you back at six-thirty, seven."

Andy laughed. "Stalking her? Groping her is probably more like it. Why is she cooking us dinner? She can't be up to that."

"Fred's helping her. He won't let her exert herself. For a woman who didn't want a man in her life, now she has two guys falling all over her. She and Fred are like sticky glue together.

"Oh, better put your foot down now, Harry. That's a real problem," Andy said.

Cody smiled. She mixed a martini and handed it to him.

They settled in the living room.

"Are you getting used to taking a few orders instead of giving them? A problem for you?"

"Problem? Cody, she could ask me to perform cartwheels and I'd be happy to oblige. I'll do anything she asks if it'll make her happy. Thing is, she doesn't ask me for anything, only my presence and a few hugs. We've only been together two weeks, and I have to keep pinching myself to prove I'm not in a dream.

"Got something important to talk to you about. We're going to Bermuda, the day after Thanksgiving."

Andy lifted his beer to his mouth. "Yeah? That's a great idea, getting away."

"Well, not exactly getting away. More like, getting married. That Sunday. Hope you don't have any plans next weekend, because you'll have to cancel them. Stay at the house, of course."

"What?" Andy was shocked. His eyes blinked rapidly and he asked, "Married? That's only a week and a half from now. No more martinis for you. The booze has gone right to your head."

"Harry, how wonderful!"

Cody grabbed him and hugged him.

"I'm going to cry. I'm so happy for you. We should be celebrating. Going out to dinner, instead of Liz cooking."

"Cody, Liz doesn't know yet."

"Huh?"

Cody gaped, her mouth wide open. She was speechless.

What do you mean, she doesn't know?"

"I'm not telling her. 'Til that Sunday. It's a surprise. I'll have to tell her an hour or two before the ceremony, before the rabbi and pastor arrive. Give her the ring. Probably break the news after breakfast, so she'll have a little time to let it sink in."

"A surprise?" Andy looked at him incredulously.

"Maybe you should ask her if she wants to get married? Has it occurred to you that maybe she doesn't want to be surprised."

"Andy, I wouldn't plan this unless I was sure. And I have it on the best authority, my daughter, that she's waiting for me to ask her to marry me. They've been hanging out together a lot. Liz meets her at school after her treatment, they have a Starbucks, or lunch, whatever. Liz goes with her for sessions with Inez. They have this mutual morale-boosting thing going on. Done a world of good for Rebecca. And Liz.

"Everything in my life has changed. The girls stayed overnight at the house a few times. Sarah loves to stay over. Fred's been a prince, accommodating all of us. He's had his hands full, but he told me he loves the house being alive with two teenagers. That's his thing. He wants so to be part of a home.

"Anyway, Liz told Rebecca, *If your dad doesn't ask me to marry him in the very near future, I'm going to ask him.* Of course, Rebecca didn't mean to tell me, it just slipped out." Harry winked at Andy.

"Besides, it's all arranged, except for a few women things I need Cody's help with. I phoned from the office yesterday, but you guys weren't home. And then I couldn't speak freely from my place last night." He sipped his martini and walked over to the window, eyeing the panoramic view of Manhattan.

"Harry, you are crazy!" Cody said. "You still need a license don't you? How are you going to manage that?"

"It's very easy to get married in Bermuda. You file a Notice of Intended Marriage, fourteen days beforehand. It gets published in two local newspapers and that's that. That's already done. As far as signatures, Joe's idea. I played the con man and I must say I was outstanding. I simply asked her to sign an insurance form. Joe prepared the *notice* and slipped it under a small pile of papers that supposedly contained the form. He had all the information he needed from the Manning report. All that was needed was a signature.

"You wonderful sneak," Cody said.

"Joe's arranged the plane and hotel reservations for everyone, Lauren, her nephew Robert and his wife, Tom and his wife, Fred, Aaron's family. Had to get Rabbi Grabauer to fly down. No rabbis in Bermuda. My mom, Uncle Ted and my daughters are staying at the Fairmont Saturday night and then at the house on Sunday. I don't need to keep you two a secret. She wouldn't question you coming for the weekend."

"How many people have you invited?"

"I don't know. Joe has the list. Just family, a few friends. I hired a wedding planner, a Mrs. Fairlee. We had lunch together yesterday and covered everything pretty carefully. I've spoken with Thomas and Maddy several times. Also Martine. Mrs. Fairlee's going to Bermuda this weekend. She'll stay 'til the wedding and coordinate with Martine, and meet with Thomas and Maddy. Martine is closing the restaurant that Sunday. I can't wait to see her face."

"Wow, Harry, it sounds absolutely marvelous. I'm getting excited. What do you need me to do?"

"I could buy her a ring, but I think she should choose her own wedding ring. I'm stymied as to how to pull that off?"

"I'll take care of it. We have a date to go shopping on Monday. I'll steer her into Harry Winston, and under the guise of Andy buying me a ring for our twenty-fifth anniversary, we'll look. Just looking, if you know what I mean.

"Liz is anticipating marriage sometime anyway, so it's really not premature to be looking at rings. I'll phone ahead and let Archie know what we're really doing there. He's a pro at handling secrets. He'll goad her 'til he's sure what she wants and then put it aside. Can you get me a ring of hers so it can be sized correctly?"

"Yeah, I can do that."

Harry was glad of Cody's enthusiasm. She was already scheming how to play the scene out.

"As far as a dress? That's a cinch. She's already been to Maude's. Maude will come up with something smashing. She always does. And I know where Liz bought her shoes."

"Great. Love you, darlin'. Knew I could depend on you. Harry dug in his pocket for his wallet and extended his credit card. Whatever else you think she'll need."

"Done. I'll take care of it. This is going be a blast!"

# CHAPTER SEVENTY-EIGHT

Liz jumped out of bed when she heard a car pull up in the driveway. She ran to the window and looked out. "Harry," she called out, "I've just seen Cody and Andy get out of a taxi. What are they doing here?" She looked down and saw Thomas carrying four pieces of luggage into the house.

Harry stepped out of the bathroom. "Surprise, I asked them for the weekend. Thought we might like some company, at least for a few days. We'll have next week to ourselves."

"Great idea. Awful lot of luggage for a weekend. They going someplace afterward?"

"Not that I know of."

"C'mon, let's go down and have coffee." She said.

Harry walked over to the window, placed his arms around her shoulders and directed her back in the bedroom. He knew Andy and Cody would be carrying a lot more luggage than anyone would need for a weekend: Liz's wedding dress, his tuxedo, as well as their own dress clothes. He diverted her from the window.

"Finish your coffee. Let them get settled, and we'll all have breakfast together."

"Can we have dinner at Chez Mere tonight? Will you dance with me?"

"I've already booked the *Paradise Isle* for this afternoon. Thought you might like to go back to the San Remo this evening with Cody and Andy."

Harry thought it imperative that he keep Liz away from the house and away from the Hamilton town center altogether. If he knew his daughters, they would be doing some last-minute shopping in town. And he expected Mrs. Fairlee to be around the house in the afternoon. She was working out of Maddy's cottage and meeting with Martine in the late afternoon. The *Paradise Isle* was the solution. He had already conferred with Andy and Cody, and they thought it a good idea to direct Liz away from the preparations.

"How about Chez Mere tomorrow night?" Harry asked.

"Okay, tomorrow's good. What time are we supposed to be at the marina?"

"Noonish. We have extra time if we need it. Lyle's waiting on us."

Liz walked to the bedroom door, about to go downstairs. Harry rushed in front of her. He didn't want to risk her seeing Cody unpacking in the guest bedroom or Thomas carrying more luggage upstairs. He and Cody had planned it that way. It was his job to keep her in the bedroom 'til they met for breakfast at ten.

"Where you going? C'mon, have a shower with me."

"Just saying hello," she said.

"Later. I need my back scrubbed."

"You don't need your back scrubbed. You want to be stroked. Be careful of my scar, the skin's coming off." Liz kissed him on the lips and clutched him around the waist.

• • •

All the plans for the wedding were in place and everything proceeded as arranged, except Liz noticed some unusual occurrences the day before and was somewhat suspicious that something irregular already happened or was about to happen. She asked questions that put Harry on edge.

"Harry, why is Maddy sleeping in an upstairs bedroom and not in her cottage?"

"We're redoing her bedroom. She needs new furniture, painting, whatever." He lied.

"It's not very private for her. And she has to climb all those stairs." Liz said.

The phone rang twice after ten o'clock the evening before. Liz was within earshot when Harry took the calls from Joe and he couldn't lie about who was on the phone.

"What's so important that Joe's calling you on the weekend, and in Bermuda?" Joe had run into some snags scheduling flights with NetJets and needed Harry's input.

"Nothing critical, just keeping me informed."

And today, when Harry ordered a taxi to drive them to the marina, she asked, "Why do we need a taxi? Where's Thomas?"

"He's got some errands to attend to." Harry said. Unknown to Liz, Thomas had been transporting family and friends from the airport to their hotels.

Harry had already informed Giovanni about the surprise wedding when he invited him to the affair a week ago. When they arrived at the restaurant, Giovanni winked at him in recognition of the secretive arrangements. Harry was relieved. The day had passed in a pleasurable diversion of a trip to St. George's on the *Paradise Isle*, and Giovanni outdid his culinary expertise and prepared a splendid dinner for the group.

Before she went to bed, Cody dropped a clue, commenting, "Big day tomorrow." Andy and Harry looked at each other. Andy grinned, rolled his eyes, and they both ignored the remark as if nothing had been said.

The little lies had answered Liz's questions and if she had any suspicions, they were quashed.

• • •

Harry woke Liz up with a kiss on her cheek.

"Good morning. How is the love of my life this morning?"

Liz sat up, threw her arms up in the air and stretched.

"I feel wonderful, like The Chirp.

"Good dream? Did the prince kiss the frog and turn her into a princess?"

"As a matter of fact, yes. There must be something about you, this house and Bermuda that causes me to dream that dream again and again."

"Harry, I meant to ask you last night, what did Cody mean by *big day tomorrow*? Do you have something planned? Another surprise? At Chez Mere tonight?"

"I have no idea what she meant." He lied again. The time was fast approaching when he'd have to tell her. He walked across the room, opened a bureau drawer and covertly slid a ring box into his robe pocket. "You ready for breakfast?" he asked.

"Uh, huh."

They went downstairs. Cody and Andy were still in their robes, drinking coffee and reading the newspaper in the breakfast room.

"Good morning. What a beautiful Bermuda day," Cody said.

Maddy couldn't stop smiling at everyone, humming and singing as she cooked breakfast. She overflowed with cheer and verve, dancing around the kitchen. Harry made two trips to the kitchen, supposedly to refill his coffee cup. His actual mission was to silence Maddy. He put his fingers to his lips when he entered the kitchen in an attempt to remind her that the wedding was a secret.

Summer had left Bermuda. The summer weather had not. It was a balmy seventy degrees in the morning, promising another five degrees in the afternoon. Perfect weather for a wedding. Sunshine beamed from every window in the house and a breeze of the perfumed air of scented flowers flowed from the living room out through to the patio.

"Oops." Mrs. Fairlee said, knowing she was supposed to be a secret from Liz. She popped into the room and quickly passed into the kitchen. "Just getting some coffee."

"Liz, this is Mrs. Fairlee, Maddy's decorator." Harry introduced everyone. "Our guests for the weekend, Cody and Andy. Harry smiled. Cody and Andy grinned.

"Nice to meet you," Liz said as she sat down.

Mrs. Fairlee smiled and scurried out of the kitchen.

"You really are generous, Harry. A decorator to do Maddy's bedroom?"

Maddy served breakfast. There was silence at the table and an air of expectancy. There wasn't anything to talk about except a wedding, which was a secret, so no one spoke, except Liz.

"What are we up to today? Liz asked. "Tennis? Or are you guys playing golf? Are we booked for Chez Mare tonight, Harry?"

"Uh, huh."

Cody, Andy and Harry glanced at each other and Andy said, "Harry, I think it's time. Anyway, I, for one, can't stand the suspense anymore."

"Suspense?" Liz said. "What's going on?"

"Liz, come with me. I want to show you something."

He took her by the hand, led her into the lounge and they sat down on the sofa.

Liz gaped, surprised to see flowers everywhere. Mrs. Fairlee had received the last of the flower deliveries while they ate breakfast.

Liz looked around the lounge and noticed the bar was replete with glasses, scattered from one end to the other and yet to be arranged. A table of favors had been set up in the rear end of the room under the window. Mrs. Fairlee still had some work to do.

"Are we throwing a party?" She asked.

"Yeah, guess you could call it a party." He took the ring from its box and slipped it on her finger.

"Actually, a wedding. This afternoon. Three o'clock. Think you can you make it?"

Liz stared at her finger, unable to utter a word, swallowing and gulping, and her eyes lingering on a dazzling set of diamonds that glittered from her finger.

"Oh, Harry!"

"Of course, you know, I go with the ring."

She folded her arms around him and squeezed him with the intensity of her emotion. Tears sprung from her eyes.

He hugged her and wanted to cry with her. He was the happiest he'd ever been in his life.

"We're getting married?"

She kissed him all over his face, his forehead, his chin and his lips, and cried on his shoulders. "I'm going to marry you? This afternoon?"

"Uh, huh. You've got to calm down."

He didn't want her to calm down. She was excited and ecstatically happy. He would remember forever what she looked like at that moment, her eyes shining and lit up like the diamonds on her finger.

"In a few hours, a lot of people will be here. Rabbi Grabauer and a pastor from Bermuda, my mom, Uncle Ted, and my daughters, Aaron's family. I spoke with Robert. He and Diana are coming with your nephews. By the way. he's a bit miffed at you for not telling him that you were ill. Fred, Joe, and Tom and his wife, Thomas and Maddy. Also, Giovanni and his wife. Lyle and Jon. Peter and Marisa, if her mother can babysit. And Inez and her husband."

"Peter and Marisa? How did that happen?"

Liz was dumbfounded.

"Peter called me last week. Apologized. Said he couldn't reach you at your home number or your cell. Wanted to know you were all right and recovering. I told him you were living with me, we were getting married, and he and his wife were welcome to come to the wedding. All right with you?"

Liz smiled. "Of course, it's all right. It's wonderful."

"Cody bought your dress from Maude's and got your clothes ready. Lauren will be here in about an hour. She and Cody are going to help you dress. My daughters and my mom will probably pop in on you, as well."

"I don't believe you. You're too good to be true. Oh, I do love you, so very, very much."

"The musicians will be arriving an hour before the ceremony. After the pastor and the rabbi have their way with us, we'll have some cocktails here. Martine's closed the restaurant to the public, and we're all going to Chez Mere for dinner."

"Happy?"

"Oh, God, I've never been so happy."

She was breathless. She paused and gazed at her finger again.

"Harry," she looked up at him, wiping the tears from her cheek. "You didn't ask me this morning."

"Ask you? Was I supposed to ask you to marry me?" He joked. "You said *no* the last time. I didn't want to take any chances."

Liz giggled. "No, about the ending. My dream. It had an ending this morning. When the prince kissed the frog?"

"And? How did it end?"

"The frog turned into a princess, they rode off to the castle and lived happily ever after."

"Oh, I knew it was a happy ending, and, of course, they lived happily ever after."